A Spark in the Shadows

Light & Shadows
Book One

G. L Preston

A Spark in the Shadows – Gem L Preston

A Spark in the Shadows
Copyright © 2024 by Gem. L. Preston/Gemma Seabourne
All rights reserved.
First edition, June 2024.

Cover art copyright © 2024 by Gem. L. Preston
www.glpreston.com

This book is a work of pure fiction created from the author's imagination.

A Spark in the Shadows – Gem L Preston

To the women who have been silenced, underestimated, or cast aside—
This is for you.
May you reclaim your power, your voice, and your story.
And may I give you Altair, Iolas, and Casius.
May you find strength in their darkness, and light in your own.

CHAPTER ONE

Olwyn

"P-please, I swear I don't know of any rebellion—"

The man's voice trembles, the words breaking as he drops to his knees, hands clasped together in desperation. His ragged brown britches and dirt-marked shirt hang loosely on his frame, streaks of grime and sweat smudging his face.

The large man before him moves in a blur. The man's cries are abruptly silenced when his mouth descends onto the merchant's neck. The vampire lifts him effortlessly, gripping him like a ragdoll, and I must swallow my gasp as I hide behind a stall.

A vampire.

He finishes draining the man and drops him to the ground. Blood gushes out, a crimson torrent against the pale, windswept sand. The ground drinks it greedily, and a dark stain spreads outward, inching towards the cracked cobblestones that border the narrow city streets.

What in Corph's name has happened? Why is there a vampire here?

I cover my mouth to muffle my breath, which feels like hot gusts of wind against my palm, and creep behind the canvas of two run-down tents, the fabric frayed and stained with smoke and years of neglect. I avoid nipping past the vampire as he dumps the man's body on the ground, knowing I'll likely be next if he catches me.

Vampires haven't darkened our streets in months, not since the last chill of winter faded and the rains came, and—judging from the screams that pierce the silence around me, the smell of copper in the air—some shit is happening right now. They've never before resorted to killing the civilians.

The vampire turns as I peek through a hole in the fabric seeing inside the tent a small stretch of street beyond and revealing the armour the vampire wears—emblazoned with a white flame . My blood runs cold, a chill creeping up my spine as if death's hand had brushed against me. Only King Draven's elite warriors bear that mark—the white flame against the black leather—the warriors he sends into war. These are his men.

If this is the end—if King Draven's vampires are here to wipe us out—I have to get away from the market, now. My mind races. Vampires don't need to feed on humans, but I've been told that never stops them from killing just for sport.

The human palace—it looms in the distance like a granite sentinel, its towering walls promising sanctuary or perhaps a tomb if the vampires have already made it there. It's a long shot, but the only place that might hold against these creatures. I take a shaky breath and steel myself. Staying here is certain death. I just need to move fast, stay low, and pray I'm not seen.

Dying in the market is a sobering thought. I wonder what my mother will think if she finds out her only child has perished in such a place, after stealing food, of all things. I might never see her again, never hear her scold me for risking my life like this. If only I'd stayed in my chambers.

But the vampires control all the imports of food into Avantra, and don't they just love to keep their cattle underfed? Try to diminish our strength as much as possible, to keep us weak.

It all stems from a history written in blood—centuries-old conflicts where human rebellions nearly toppled entire vampire strongholds. Long before the vampiric lords carved out their kingdoms, humans had discovered ways to fight back, using witchsilver and ancient magics capable of turning the tide.

To prevent future uprisings, the vampires learned that control over resources was control overpower itself. Keep the humans hungry, and they'll be too preoccupied with survival to dream of revolution. Starve them just enough, and they won't have the strength to rally against their immortal overlords. That doesn't stop the vampires fighting amongst themselves of course.

I freeze as the vampire sniffs the air, his dark eyes snapping to the tent, and to my exact position crouching behind the material.

With a quick lunge, I hurl myself sideways, rolling just in time as the vampire's sword slices through the tent like paper. The blade misses my neck by inches, and I scramble to my feet, heart pounding.

"Come here!" the vampire snarls, lunging for me.

Without a second thought, I snatch a small iron pot from the ground and hurl it with all the strength I can muster. It sails through the air and smashes into the vampire's face, the force jerking his head to the side with a sickening thud. He snarls in surprise, eyes narrowing as the impact slows him only momentarily.

I don't wait to see the full effect. I'm already sprinting, throwing myself over a low wall and plunging deeper into the maze of city streets as fast as my legs can carry me, my heart hammering in my chest.

Vampires are quick, much too quick. But I know every alley and twist of this city, and I'm not going to let some bloodsucking animal catch me tonight. I hear him crashing behind me, and I sprint faster, the narrow streets working to my advantage. The streets are so close-knit, but when I reach the palace courtyard, I need to be smart.

I can hear him growling not too far behind. But I run and skip between buildings, glad I had chosen to wear my ragged brown breeches, and not one of the flowy dresses my mother often forces upon me.

"Stop!" The vampire's voice rips through the streets behind me, and I dodge carts, barrels, citizens running for their own lives. They see me and their eyes widen, scrambling out of my way as they flee from the vampire.

"Shit, shit, shit." I curse when I round the corner. People scream and run in every direction, but the gates are closed, no doubt to stop them from entering the palace. Panic twists in my chest as I skid to a halt, eyes scanning the chaotic scene. Are the king and queen keeping their own people out? The question gnaws at me, a momentary spike of doubt that feels like a dagger to the gut. Or is the situation outside the palace walls so dire that even civilians are being denied sanctuary?

I send a silent prayer up to the gods as I make a sharp right, desperation surging through my veins. A sharp cry leaves my mouth as I smack my shoulder hard against the corner of a brick wall, pain flaring through the joint. But there's no time to pause, no time to think. I grit my teeth and keep moving, weaving through the crowd and searching for any way to break through the chaos.

The adrenaline running through me won't allow me to stop, not while the vampire is so close. I vault onto a trader's cart abandoned by the courtyard wall, its wheels creaking under my weight, splinters tearing at my palms as I climb the stacked boxes to climb onto the wall edge.

The vampire comes skidding around the corner, his leather boots leaving faint marks on the wet cobblestone path.

"There you are, you little rat!" he growls, baring his sharp fangs.

I try to scramble away, rolling over the wall's edge. My body twists awkwardly in midair, and I slam into the courtyard below with a jarring thud. Pain explodes through my side as the breath is knocked out of me, and for a moment, the world spins. I struggle to pull in air, my vision swimming.

Can't breathe.

I struggle to catch my breath as I push myself up, my hand warming against the cool stone. I dart towards the grand palace doors.

But the doors are already open… and all I can smell is blood in the air.

Pain sings from my shoulders, spreading like wildfire down my spine, making my feet stall stupidly as if rooted to the ground. A yank of my hair has my eyes watering as the vampire's other hand clamps around my throat, cutting off my air supply.

The night air is thick, suffused with the sickly-sweet scent of blood, clinging to my nostrils like a second skin, mingling with the acrid tang of sweat and the stale, musty odour of the city streets—streets that reek of rotting wood, wet earth, and the faint, lingering traces of spice from the market stalls now overturned in chaos. It's suffocating, almost as much as the vampire's grip on my throat. My senses blur and swim, my vision edges with darkness, but I latch onto the pain like a lifeline—a cruel, jagged thread that keeps me conscious, keeps me tethered to the here and now. Each throb of agony is a reminder that I'm still alive, still fighting, even as my breaths grow ragged and desperate.

"Got you, ya little bitch," he growls triumphantly.

"T-took you… long enough," I choke out as I try to grin, despite losing my bloody air.

He releases me with a sneer, but my legs betray me, wobbling like jelly, muscles quivering as if they've forgotten how to hold my weight, and he backhands me across the face. My neck hurts as my head snaps to the side, and all I see is white-hot stars as I try to clear my vision. I taste blood in my mouth and feel a stinging sensation on my cheek where he struck me.

Raising a trembling hand, I wipe away the drop of crimson that has formed on my lip.

He chuckles at the withering glare I send his way, his pupils dilating as it fixates on the blood on my hand. His grip on my arm tightens as he pulls me forcefully against his chest. The musky scent of his breath, thick with the metallic tang of blood, makes me cringe and turn away in disgust. I can feel his heart beating through his chest, a rapid thumping that matches the wildness in his eyes.

"You smell delicious," he sneers, his lips curling as he twirls a lock of my silver hair through his free hand. "Perhaps I should take a bite now?"

I lock eyes with him, determined to stand my ground despite the terror creeping up my spine. My throat tightens as I bite back a scream for help, refusing to let him see my fear.

"Do it," I challenge him with false bravado. "I'm sure your king will be elated when he finds out you have drained the princess of Avantra."

For a split second, I see doubt flicker in his eyes, his grip on my arm loosening just a fraction. But then his lips curl into a sly smile, and a shiver of unease runs down my spine. "There is no princess of Avantra."

I smile and feel the sting of my split lip as it pulls. But there is a glint of fear in his eyes as he leans in closer.

"You lie," he hisses, leaning forward so his bloody teeth grit in my face.

I laugh in his.

"Try it," I mock him. "Only one way to find out." As I speak, I feel the adrenaline coursing through my veins, readying myself.

This is it. This is where I die. The thought sends a shiver of cold terror through me, but I force myself to stay focused. I can't let him see my fear. I can't let him win.

I brace myself for uncertainty and fear to flicker across his face if he does believe me, but what I see instead chills me to the bone. A sly smile creeps onto his lips as his eyes dart towards the palace doors behind me.

"Luckily for you, we can prove it right now. His Majesty is waiting inside."

Panic rises, a hot, churning wave in my chest, threatening to break free and drag me under, but I force it down, forcing myself to stay in control.

I have to think.

I have to survive.

I swallow the bile rising in my throat, but I casually shrug my shoulders, trying to hide the unease building inside me. "Well then, let's not keep the king waiting."

He laughs, pulling me forward. I stumble trying to keep up with his large strides, but he drags me along, uncaring if I fall. The palace is a shambles, its former grandeur reduced to a broken shell. Torn fabric hangs like ghostly shrouds from the smashed windows, fluttering in the breeze like the wings of trapped birds, and guards lay slain upon the floor, their throats ripped out…

But only guards. Where are the servants?

I can hear commotion coming from the throne room, where my parents must be. My throat thickens with fear at what I'm about to see… if they're still alive.

When we enter, I see them, kneeling and broken, a mix of relief and despair floods through me. They're alive, but at what cost? The sight of King Petr, my father, trembling like a leaf, and my mother, Queen Alexis, eyes wide with terror, makes my stomach twist. I have to stay strong for them.

But their figures are shrouded by a murky, all-encompassing shadow that seems to be closing in on them. The dim light from the flickering torches barely cuts through the darkness, making it seem like they are trapped in a never-ending night. There are a few vampires standing behind them, each looking bloody and triumphant.

And before them all… before them, standing tall and imposing, is the man that has haunted me in my nightmares for most of my life. The vampire who betrayed his own king to claim the throne for himself.

The vampire King Altair Draven, who can wield darkness.

He turns and…

Oh.

I was expecting a formidable, death god-like creature, with monstrous features. Instead, death is… beautiful. But the beauty does nothing to ease the terror crawling up my spine. My heart races, a wild drumbeat against my ribs, but I force myself to stand straight, to meet his gaze without flinching.

His dark hair cascades in loose waves, hiding his pointed ears—a trait he cannot hide that marks him as a vampire, closely related to the dark fae. A black earring hangs from one lobe as his inky strands curl gently at the ends, grazing just past a strong, rugged jawline. Muscled arms and shoulders hidden underneath finely tailored leathers. The air around him crackles with an unseen energy, tendrils of shadow curling at his feet, reaching, yearning like lost souls trying to find their way back to the light.

He looks young. He can't be that much older than me, at twenty-six cycles.

But those eyes.

Eyes—which I swear widen slightly as he sees me for the first time—one of the blackest nights, and one as blue as the pictures of the sea I have seen… and both are pinned on me, his chest expanding as he inhales deeply.

His expression is intense and not at all welcoming. And it's heightened by the only imperfection marring his face, a scar—long since healed—trailing from his hairline and through his eyebrow, past his blue eye and ending on his cheek. Whatever it was would have almost blinded him, but it really doesn't take away from how gorgeous he is, even if it makes him look more dangerous.

But I know beautiful things can still be weapons, like a polished blade hidden in velvet. My heart pounds in my chest like a war drum, my breath shallow, yet I force myself to meet his gaze, to stare into the black abyss of his eye.

A tall guard on the dais coughs, and the king blinks a few times.

I hear my mother's voice, low and trembling, from her kneeling position in front of her throne. Her black hair is dishevelled, and her face is smudged with kohl from crying. My father kneels next to her in silence, visibly shaking and looking like he may piss himself at any moment. The tall guard standing behind her, in the king's armour, stares at me, and it makes me fidget where I stand. He stares at me like he has never seen a woman before.

The brute holding me lets go and takes a step back, a smug grin spreading across his face as he surveys the situation. "I have a gift for you, Your Majesty. Caught this one scurrying around the marketplace. Claims she's the princess."

I force myself to ignore my mother's pleading, the desperation in her voice clawing at my resolve. "She's no one!" she cries out, and my father's grip tightens on her arm as she scrambles forward. "She's mad! Just the city craz—"

I glance over my shoulder at the guard. "I am not making a claim, I am stating a fact. Or are you as unintelligent as your appearance suggests?" My jaw clenches as I turn and lock eyes with the king, and my pulse races, but I don't bow, don't lower my gaze. I refuse to give him the satisfaction of seeing me cower like my parents. But it is unsettling to insult someone holding me prisoner, not knowing how they will react.

The king's gaze remains fixed on me, and for a heartbeat, I catch a flicker of surprise in his expression.

Behind me, the guard shifts restlessly.

"Why you little—" the guard's voice starts to rise in anger.

"What happened to your face?" The king's words are like shards of ice, cutting through the tense atmosphere.

"What happened to yours?" I ask with a smile, hearing my mother suck in a gasp.

I feel every eye on me, the judgment, the shock, and the anticipation. The guards' shifting stops, leaving only the low crackle of the torch flames to fill the oppressive quiet.

But the king's lips curve into a thin, unsettling smile. He tilts his head, eyes glinting with a dark, almost playful amusement.

"I'll ask one more time. What happened?" His voice is deep and smooth, too calm, too composed—a tone that makes my breath hitch, as if he's already decided my fate, and I'm merely awaiting judgement.

But that's not the only thing that takes my breath away. It's the flash of his two sharp canines as he speaks.

My stomach rolls.

And why has the temperature in the room plummeted all of a sudden?

I look up and his gaze startles me.

The *viciousness* in it.

No. This is it. I can feel the inevitability of it like a vice tightening around my lungs—he'll kill me, and there will be nothing left but a stain on the cold stone floor. His gaze pins me like an insect under glass, and I fight the urge to shrink away, to hide from the rage radiating from his dark, fathomless eyes.

His guard takes two steps in front of me. "She was—"

"I was asking *her.*"

My throat tightens as I struggle to speak under his scrutiny, my eyes darting nervously between the two men.

Well, if I'm going to die, I might as well do it being myself.

"Your guard is slow on his feet," I say boldly. "But luckily for him, he's quicker with his hands." I tilt my chin up, wearing my injuries like a badge of honour. I refuse to let them embarrass or intimidate me.

"Olwyn," my mother hisses, and the tall guard's lips part.

I can feel her disapproving gaze on me, but I will not back down. I won't cower like them before this creature. If he is going to kill me, he can do it whilst I stand.

But the brute behind me laughs, as if proud of himself. As if he hasn't realised I just insulted him, not praised him.

The tallest guard standing behind my mother, frowns, a glare aimed at his comrade. He runs a hand through his honey brown hair, shaking his head.

The king's head tilts, reminiscent of a feline's movement—sharp and intimidating.

In the blink of an eye, crimson splashes across my vision. The guard who had marked my face is now a ruin of flesh and bone, his limbs severed and flung apart like a child's broken toys, his head rolling to a stop near my feet. His mouth hangs open in a silent scream, eyes wide and glassy with the shock of death. I want to scream, to wail at the senseless brutality of it, but my throat seizes up, trapping my voice like a bird in a cage. A metallic scent fills my nostrils as droplets of his blood cling to my skin.

I'm going to be sick, but I bite down on the inside of my cheek to keep from retching.

My mother's cry echoes through the room, while my father doubles over in disgust and horror at the gruesome sight. The sound of retching mixes with the overwhelming stench of death and decay that now permeates the air.

The king's face is a mask of indifference, carved from cold marble, devoid of any trace of remorse or humanity. His eyes are now black pools, empty of mercy, reflecting only the cold, hard glint of power and control. Shadows ripple around him like living things, retreating from the bloodied corpse with an almost sentient reluctance, as if they crave to finish what they've begun.

"I told you not to harm any civilians," the king says.

As if the guard can hear him now.

"Nikolas," he directs at one of the guards. "Go and check on my men. Punish anyone ignoring my orders." One of the guard nods and leaves.

There is no trace of remorse or humanity in King Draven's expression. As a vampire, he is not a creature of emotions, but of power and control.

But his shadows curl back, away from the body they have just torn apart, and slither back into place around him. One shadow drifts close to me, a thin, dark tendril that snakes forward, reaching out like a curious finger to brush my skin. I jerk away, my heart pounding in my chest, the chill of its presence lingering on my arm like a bruise, and I swear I hear a low, whispering hiss of disappointment.

I glance back at my parents, their faces twisted in terror and disbelief. My mother's hands are clasped tightly to her chest, her blue eyes wide with fear. My father's face is pale and drawn, his grip on my mother's hand shaking. I am not surprised by his silence—he always prefers a drink to confrontation, leaving my mother to bear the weight of ruling. When faced with larger men, he becomes a coward, retreating into the shadows of his own cowardice rather than standing firm. So I don't expect any heroic acts or words from him.

The sound of the king's steps draws my attention, as his black boots walk through the blood, to stand directly in front of me.

I inhale sharply, my breath catching in my throat, bracing myself for the stench of rot and decay I expect to cling to him like a shroud. But instead, there is a faint scent—patchouli on a soft breeze, delicate and unexpected, tinged with something darker, like a whisper of midnight air. It twists around my senses, masking the danger beneath.

My body freezes, every muscle locking in place as his hand reaches out. His fingers are cool as they grip my chin, surprisingly gentle, the touch of a predator toying with its prey. He tilts my face towards his.

His black eye flashes the faintest shade of blue—a flicker so quick, so subtle, that I almost convince myself I imagined it. But no… it isn't fully black. I see it now, within its depths—shadows, swirling like smoke trapped in glass, moving with a life of their own. My breath catches, a sharp intake that chills my lungs.

"You're the princess?' His whisper cuts through the thick silence, a blade of sound that slices through my thoughts. The disbelief in his voice is faint, almost masked by a darker, more dangerous undertone, as if he's tasting the words, savouring them. "This is the one the prophecy speaks about?"

My heart falls into my stomach.

He knows.

He has found out.

My mother throws herself to the floor.

"I swear Your Majesty, she is no one. She has no powers—"

"Silence!" he snaps, the king's gaze fixed on me, his expression unreadable.

My eyes narrow as his own travel over my face, my hair, my eyes. I can feel his piercing stare burning into my skin and I can't help but shrink back a little.

"I finally found you," he says so quietly.

His hands move in a blur, too fast for my eyes to track, and then—*crack!*—a blinding, white-hot agony shoots through my arm. I scream, the sound raw and desperate, as my shoulder is wrenched back into place with a brutality that steals my breath. Pain flares, burning through the fog of shock, and I clutch at my shoulder, feeling the jagged edges of torn muscles beneath my skin. But his voice cuts through the agony.

"Hiding her from me is enough to warrant your deaths, but planning a rebellion on top?" The king tuts, releasing me and turning gracefully.

A rebellion? My mind races with confusion, remembering the man's words in the marketplace. The two vampire kings have held control over the human lands for decades, often fighting over stretches of land when they have a disagreement. Have my parents been plotting against them? Sick of the poor state in which we must live in? If they have, this is the first I have heard about it.

"Did you really think I wouldn't find out?" he mocks them and his guards chuckle. Their laughter echoes through the throne room, making it feel more like a dungeon than a place of royalty.

My mother mutters. "P-please, Your Majesty—"

"What are we going to do to rectify this situation?" He asks.

There is nothing I can do but helplessly watch my parents plead for their lives. The shadows peel themselves away from the walls, rippling and fluttering like dark moths drawn irresistibly to his side. They move with a strange, almost sentient grace, curling around his feet, twining up his legs, as if they're alive, as if they hunger for his command. Another ribbon of darkness slithers toward me, cautious, like a wary beast, and I cringe away again, my skin crawling.

But when I see him take a step towards my parents my heart pounds in my chest and I take a step of my own, not even registering the blood staining my boots as I try to steady myself.

The king's head turns slightly, hearing the movement, his eyes fixed on me with amusement. The large guard with curly honey-brown hair watches me with curious eyes, his head tilting slightly as if trying to figure me out.

"I don't know what rebellion you speak of," I say, "But they only kept my magic a secret to protect me. I-I can't even use it."

Magic, I scoff internally. The very thing that sets me apart and makes me valuable to the king and his court. It's ironic that I can't even tap into the power supposedly running through my veins.

But it doesn't matter.

The king's eyes narrow, his gaze boring into me as if he's searching for something—fear, perhaps, or weakness. When he speaks again, his voice is deceptively soft, like silk brushing over a blade. "Is that what you think?" His gaze doesn't waver, and I feel as though he's peeling back my skin with his eyes, searching for something hidden deep inside me.

For a brief moment the king catches the eye of the large guard who looks between us with a suspicious look on his face.

"I believe," he says slowly, each word a carefully measured note of menace, "I have found a way for you to repay me." His eyes, cold and calculating, flick over me like a hawk sizing up its prey before turning back to my parents, who tremble like leaves in a storm.

"Anything, Your Majesty." My mother's soft whimper echoes through the throne room as she speaks.

The king's deep voice rumbles with satisfaction. "Good. Then I will leave you and your city in peace. No more blood will be shed at my command. And there will be no further talk of rebellion."

My father is a slow man, but he seems to realise something far quicker than I. His face turns ashen, his eyes wide with horror as the king's words sink in. I feel the room closing in on me, the air becoming so thick I feel I might choke on it. The king's smile is slow, deliberate, as he turns to face me fully, his voice as smooth and dangerous as a coiled serpent.

"Because I'll be taking her."

CHAPTER TWO
Altair

Two thoughts keep swirling around my mind.

One, I have found her.

Two, I want to rip apart those who had kept her from me.

The Gods themselves must have *finally* conspired in my favour. There was an instinctual certainty that it was her. I also knew from the way my most loyal friend and guard, Iolas, watched her, as I realised, he saw too.

Her silver hair, her bright green eyes—they were the markers I had been searching for, the signs that had haunted my dreams. But it wasn't just her appearance; it was the way the air seemed to hum with energy around her, the way my own power had reacted, flaring for a split second in her presence.

A whisper. That was all I had needed to make my decision to invade Avantra. A scholar who had sworn on the Gods he had met the princess of Avantra before he escaped the city—a princess that no one knew existed.

I had told my guards that no civilians were to be harmed. The guards in the palace had unfortunately lost their lives once they attacked us upon entry. But they wouldn't have been the last to die if anyone else had tried to stop me from finding her.

A princess described in a prophecy. Set to end the war that had waged between the two vampire clans for almost a decade.

With silver hair and green eyes.

Silver hair that looked like a cascade of moonlight, shimmering subtly in the flickering torchlight. And how bright those eyes are, even when they burned right through me like a forest set ablaze.

The prophecy had been a shadow over my reign, as short as it's been, and a constant whisper in the dark that promised an end to the bloodshed and the war between the vampires. A prophecy that many have taken to mean that Olwyn will wipe out our entire existence. The fear of witches magic still runs deep within the vampires.

I took my crown at eighteen, and it had been years since I first heard it—spoken in hushed tones by seers and scholars alike—foretelling a silver-haired human princess, with magic of the great sorceress in her veins, who would bring about the cessation of the vampire's destruction. I had heard it when I had served the old king, had laughed and dismissed it then as mere myth, a story to give hope to those humans who had none. Because there was no way she was alive. That I would find her.

Until now.

Olwyn's fear had been obvious, despite the way she tried to suppress the way she shivered.

She was so lean and malnourished she was practically scrawny, and something compelled me to shield her from further cruelties. I would have torn the entire palace down. Ended their lives right then and there if Iolas hadn't cleared his throat to bring my attention back to the room.

That pathetic excuse of a queen whimpered as her pathetic husband cowered beside her, doing nothing to try and protect his wife and his *daughter*.

But I also saw that fire in her eyes, that defiance. Heard it in the way she insulted my guard, with a wit almost as quick as Iolas's. I struggled not to allow my lips to turn up at that, especially when she wasn't facing Mikael, the guard who delivered her to me.

I'd been a split second away from ripping out the queen's tongue when she lied, but then I noticed Mikael approach Olwyn again.

My reaction had been rash but justified. Seeing her filthy clothes splattered with Mikael's blood only intensified my anger. He had *touched* her, and that was unforgivable. The idea that anyone else could lay a hand on her, that anyone else could even think to harm her, was intolerable.

No one would touch her.

Not whilst she was mine.

But it wasn't just Mikael and the prophecy that ignited my fury; it was something deeper, something primal that surged within me the moment our eyes met and almost took my breath.

I noted her chest heave once I spoke, the sharp, quick scent of adrenaline once she saw my teeth.

Interesting.

She was repulsed by us. She had been taught all the ways in which my kind were *horrific*. How we were all killers and bloodthirsty, despite us not needing blood to survive. She had been taught that we would use her up for the magic that allegedly ran through her veins.

The magic I *knew* ran through her veins.

And yet, even with her fear, she stepped forward and tried to save the king and queen from my wrath. Her defiance was a stark contrast to the craven submission of those around her. While the queen and king cowered, Olwyn stood tall, her spirit a flickering flame against the encroaching darkness. This boldness was not only unexpected but electrifying. It stirred something deep within me and plagued me with guilt.

To her, it was a dangerous game she was playing, standing up to me in a way that no one had dared in years. But it was that very courage, that reckless bravery, that drew me to her. It was as if she didn't fully comprehend the danger she was in—or perhaps she did, and simply didn't care. Either way, it both angered and excited me in equal measure. It was what caused my shadows to reach out in curiosity.

The king had been foolish. Boasting drunkenly in a tavern with some of his guards that he had been planning to fight back against my kind. It had been the perfect excuse to raid them, and now I had been gifted the perfect way to free her from them. To remove her from their palace, even if she believed it to be in revenge for them keeping her from me.

I couldn't help the smile spreading across my face as I told them I'd be taking her. As I told them everyone would believe it was pre-arranged, that she joined me willingly, or I would return to Avantra and slay them all. It was a lie of course but would hopefully prevent anyone from entering Noctura to try and 'rescue' her.

But I left smiling, because she'd never be kept from me again.

I can't wait to go home. I can't wait to see her.

CHAPTER THREE
Olwyn

Eight moons later

If Lord Dazeem dares to interrupt me again, I swear I'll try and cut his fucking tongue from his wretched head.

My gaze remains fixed on the vampire seated across from me.

His oily, sallow visage, framed by a perpetual sneer, embodies everything repugnant about his kind—an embodiment of the very rot I would love to eradicate.

The irony hangs heavily in the air, as the vampire lords gathered to discuss the very issues plaguing *humans,* when the plague is *them.* The escalating border skirmishes to the south between humans and vampires, fuelled by misunderstandings and territorial disputes, seem almost trivial in the shadow of their greed and arrogance. Though even in their chatter I can tell they're holding back their words. I can't help but roll my eyes at Lord Dazeem's simplistic and moronic assumption that humans were intentionally provoking the vampires—or instigating the issues in the first place.

Like *that* would happen.

Mortals with no powers of their own, poking *vampires*—creatures that were stronger, older, and some that magic.

He clings to the notion that these incursions are deliberate acts of antagonism, failing to understand the growing frustration among the humans. From what I've heard, they're fed up with their crops being taken, fed up with their lands being ravaged every time the two vampire kings quarrel over territory. It's a constant strain, and they've had enough. But the more I think about it, the more I realise that these pockets of fighting are mostly isolated to the south. The further north, the less it affects them, but in the south, where the tension is greatest, the human resistance is brewing. It's creatures like him—those who refuse to see the bigger picture—that have only driven our two peoples further apart.

"And do tell, Lord Dazeem, what do *you* think we should do?" I ask with a scathing tone, dismissing his ideas with a nonchalant wave of my hand.

As I speak, I notice Iolas leave the room suddenly, his exit abrupt and unannounced. My brow furrows in confusion, a quiet unease settling over me. It's unlike him to slip away without a word.

But I push the thought aside, focusing on Lord Dazeem, still standing before me, eager to hear more of his pointless ramblings. I can't afford to let distractions pull me from the task at hand. Yet, in the back of my mind, a part of me wonders if Iolas's departure means something more. Perhaps I should be concerned.

"Dole out adequate punishments," Dazeem responds, earning approving nods from several of the vampire lords and ladies. Adequate punishments, according to Dazeem, will be killings. Leaving the humans to hang on the borders as a warning.

"So, you think they should be slaughtered?" I ask, my voice laced with silk and steel.

"You are too soft-hearted." Lord Damien grins.

"And My Lord is *too* bold." I glare at him, and his grin falls.

My frustration wells up inside, wondering why I am even obligated to attend these tedious gatherings. I know why, of course. Iolas has told me. Altair has decreed that I must learn more about the kingdom I now live in, understand the politics, the power structures. But even as I sit through these meetings, I can tell the lords are keeping things from me. They avoid talking about anything of real importance, always skirting around the deeper issues.

I assume it's under Altair's orders—they don't want me to know too much, to have too much power. It's a constant reminder that I am an outsider here. They are no doubt questioning why Altair has allowed a human on the council, of course, a captive no less, but no one will outright ask him. Only Altair knows his true motives.

But while the king remains absent in another idiotic fight with the vampire king of the east, I am left to navigate this treacherous web alone, with only the echoes of scheming whispers for company. The isolation I feel is a constant reminder of my precarious position—a reluctant figurehead in a realm that resents me. My parents' surrender to the king's demands have left me stranded in a political purgatory.

Because I am a part of a kingdom I never asked for, taken by a man I hate, and surrounded by enemies on all sides. But, as my auntie once told me, the only way out of a storm is through it.

It had taken me a good few months to build up the courage to talk back to these lords, too terrified initially that they would rip my throat out. But the tall guard—Iolas—who had stood behind my mother on the night before I was taken had become my personal guard, and he ensured that they knew the king would make them suffer if that ever happened.

I haven't laid eyes on the King in what feels like an eternity—eight moons, to be exact. If anything, I consider myself blessed for the respite from his presence.

The vampire king of the Daeva clan has torn me away from my parents, the reigning king and queen of Avantra, when they dared to hide me and allegedly started a rebellion against the vampires.

I harbour an enduring resentment toward my parents for their acquiescence, for letting him waltz right out of the palace, his fingers wrapped around my wrist, without putting up more of a fight.

Naturally, I resisted him vehemently at every juncture of that arduous journey back to his kingdom. Yet, he remained ominously silent, not uttering a single word *directly* to me that accursed night, and I hadn't heard a word from him ever since.

"Not to mention my cousin, Celeste is having issues in her court," Dazeem says, talking about vampires that live in the faerie realm.

"Yes, Dazeem." Lord Nilo interrupts. "But her issue is with the new *High Queen*. We have enough problems in our own realm to go worrying about anyone else's right now. It's a political nightmare if we involve ourselves."

Their voices drone on. I sit here, my patience waning, as the other lords chatter on with their tiresome updates about the Faerie realm and distant cousins. Their words seem to blend into an indistinguishable hum, and I stifle a yawn behind my hand as my free hand scribbles across a piece of parchment.

Finally, I've had enough. "No more for today," I declare, pushing my chair back from the ornate table. "You may go."

They grumble but do as I say. After they shuffle out of the chamber, the soft footfall barely registers, but my senses flare in alarm. A cold draft sweeps through the chamber, prickling my skin, and my pulse races as I spin around, half-expecting an attack. The scent of old wood and the faint, coppery tang of blood lingers in the air, heightening my sense of unease.

"My apologies for startling you," Lord Dazeem's voice drips with insincerity, his lips curling into a mockery of a smile as he performs an exaggerated bow. His thin, pale fingers twitch slightly, and his hooded eyes gleam with a predatory light as they drink in my discomfort, revelling in it. "But I couldn't help but notice your distress in the meeting. I just wanted to extend some advice, as one of the Lords. It is... *unbecoming* of a woman in your position to show such weakness."

Excuse me?

"Your concern is noted, Dazeem," I say, my tone like ice. "But what I do or do not show is none of *your* concern."

The vampire's lips twist in a secretive smile that makes me uncomfortable. "I think you've played this game for far too long, don't you?"

"Game?" I stammer, taking an involuntary step back as he advances, my heart fluttering like a hummingbird. Panic claws at my insides as I glance around the room—a gilded cage with no exit behind me. My only escape is blocked by Dazeem, whose figure looms larger with every step.

Where is Iolas?

In a blink, Dazeem is upon me, moving with a speed that blurs in the centre of my vision. His deep blue eyes blaze with hunger, and a mix of desire and malice. A chill radiates from his body, seeping into my bones as his fingers clamp down on my chin, his grip like iron. I gasp, my retreat halted as my back collides with the unyielding wall behind me. His sharp fingers dig painfully into my skin as he holds my chin, keeping my face still.

"The king will have you killed if you do not release me," I tell him without hesitation, my voice trembling, my eyes locked defiantly onto his.

Try not to show fear.

That had been one of my first lessons from Iolas. Early on, when he had seen how the lords treated me with verbal contempt, he had taken it upon himself to train me—how to hold my head high, how to mask the tremors in my voice, how to appear unshaken, even when everything within me screamed otherwise.

I have no idea if it's true what I had said about the king, but decide to play that card nonetheless. My hand slips down, heading towards my thigh.

He scoffs, his grip on my face uncomfortably tight.

I hiss as he squeezes my cheeks. "The king is heartless. He left you here all alone," he hisses, his voice dripping with disdain. "He doesn't want you. He doesn't care who has their way with you. And besides…" His words trail off as a sinister smile curls at the corners of his lips. "Who will believe you?"

His weight is suddenly lifted from me, and I gasp for breath, pressing myself even harder against the wall. My eyes widen as Dazeem is brutally slammed against the table, the wood cracking along its middle.

My gaze moves beyond Dazeem's terrified eyes and the large hand that holds him by the throat, tracing over the hard, muscular form beneath a finely tailored set of black leather armour. My eyes snag on the face I have been praying never to see again.

The king.

His shades are like a dark tide washing into the room. His gaze is a cold mask, and he speaks with a chilling calmness, "*I believe what I see with my own eyes.*" His voice is a low rumble that seems to vibrate through the very walls.

Amidst Dazeem's futile struggles and apologies, I spot the king's second in command, Ailith, leaning casually against the door frame. A sly smirk plays on her dark full lips, and her curved blades remain sheathed at her sides. Her hands are crossed over her chest, clearly relishing the spectacle before her.

Ailith is almost as terrifying as Altair, general to his *Ombresang*—an elite group of female warriors in his army. Legendary and fierce.

"Do you have anything else to say?" Altair asks.

Dazeem's eyes widen impossibly further, his head shaking in sheer terror as his fingernails scratch futilely at the king's hand. The king, without a word, extends his free hand toward Ailith, who steps forward with a casual flick of her wrist, offering one of her gleaming blades.

Dazeem's fangs snap down.

Shit.

The atmosphere in the room chills, the shadows flickering from around the room. The king, who has been relatively calm up until this point, lets a dangerous silence fill the space as a flicker of darkness surrounds him, his cold, steely gaze enough to freeze the blood of anyone who dares to meet it.

"You dare. To *me*?"

Fear slithers along my veins. My legs wobble and it takes all my energy not to slide down the wall.

"No, please! Your Majesty—" The pitch of Dazeem's voice raises, hurting my ears.

The sound of Dazeem's scream echoes in my ears, mingling with the sickening crunch of flesh and bone as the king brings the blade down on Dazeem's wrist. I instinctively cover my ears, my first movement since they entered the chamber. But I can't tear my eyes away from the blood splattering across the table, staining the wood a deep crimson. My breath catches in my throat as I realise, seeing him in the flesh again, just how easily the king could turn that same violence on me.

"Touch her again, touch my *wife* again, and I shall remove your head. Do I make myself clear?" The king's voice is sharp like a knife, cutting through the chaos of Dazeem's cries even as goosebumps erupt all over me at him acknowledging our linking. I feel a flush of anger and fear at the possessive claim, but also an unwelcome hint of security in his words. In vampire culture, such a declaration isn't just a warning—it's a binding vow.

Dazeem, his tears still flowing, nods fervently in response. The king releases his grip on the trembling vampire lord, and Dazeem falls from the table and collapses to his knees as the king steps back, his sobs now muted.

The king turns his attention to Ailith. "Get rid of that for me, will you?" he asks with a nod towards the lord, as if he were a speck of dirt on the floor.

Ailith's lips press together in what looks like an attempt to suppress a smile, taking her sword back and sheathing it before helping Lord Dazeem to his feet. She escorts him out of the room and closes the door behind them, leaving behind a chilling silence in the wake of their departure.

I struggle to remove my gaze from the blood that now drips off the edge of the table, and my heart thunders within my chest as the king finally turns his attention toward me.

"Altair," I murmur, my voice barely above a whisper.

Every muscle in my body tenses as he storms in my direction, his imposing presence casting a long shadow over me. As the king's warm bronzed fingers brush against my skin, I fight the urge to flinch. My heart pounds in my chest, not just from the fear that has taken root during Dazeem's attack, but from the disorienting mix of emotions swirling within me—relief, anger…

Altair's eyes are cold, but they travel over my chin before snapping back to meet mine.

When I first met him, I had expected a monster. And while he certainly was one, his beauty had caught me off guard. Now, as his fingers trace the line of my jaw, I am reminded of the dangerous allure he possesses—a charm that could just as easily be a weapon.

His sharp eyes are pools of darkness, so deep they seemed to border on black. The one time I had dared to look closer at them it looked as if smoke wisped around his iris. But I quickly looked away once he caught me staring. But the shadows disperse, flickering out of his blue eye, leaving it shining.

To most humans, his appearance would be mesmerizing—his angular features and piercing eyes framed by hair the colour of midnight. But as my gaze drifts to the sharp, glistening fangs peeking from his lips, my stomach churns. I can't shake the image of how many innocent throats those fangs have torn open, how much blood they have spilled. It's maddening that something so outwardly beautiful can embody such cruelty and darkness. His tongue brushes over a fang before he retracts them.

"Is that the first time anyone has dared lay a hand on you within these walls?" His voice is deceptively calm, but there's an undercurrent of something darker—possessiveness, perhaps. I hesitate, caught between fear and defiance, sensing a trap in his words. What does it matter to him, this pretence of concern?

I stutter in response, his warm scent overwhelming me, "Wh-what?"

"Is that the first time he, or *anyone*, has touched you?"

With a trembling nod, I admit, "Yes."

He lets out a low, guttural growl, a sound that makes the air around him vibrate with his rage. "I am sorry you were treated with disrespect," he mutters, more to himself than to me. His eyes narrow, the fury in them unmistakable, and I wonder if he's angrier at the defiance of his court or at the mere fact that he now must address it.

"And I apologise for my court," he utters with what sounds like regret in his voice. "It seems that my warning before I left was not taken seriously enough. It won't happen again."

A warning?

He seems genuinely annoyed.

But then, I am his *property*.

And if he is to remain king, he has to keep control over his playthings. Gods forbid news of any weaknesses would get back to Altair's biggest threat: the vampire king of the Damu clan.

Besides my parents, apparently.

At the time of the King's violent intrusion into our palace in the middle of the night, I had no idea of their treachery—only that *I* had to pay the price for it.

After a moment, I find my voice and ask, "How long are you back for?"

His head tilts, but the lack of expression on his face unnerves me. "Already eager to get rid of me?" he asks, his tone calm but dangerous.

My fist clenches at my side. "Well, I've been attending most of the council meetings without you, so I might as well continue it," I snap, my tone laced with a hint of annoyed sarcasm.

His eyes slightly widen, clearly taken aback by my bold response. It shouldn't surprise me; after all, our last meeting was the night he tore me from my family's grasp, dragging me to this cursed place. That night is a blur of fear and rage, a makeshift wedding under a full moon with a vampire priestess who recited vows in a language I didn't understand. It is a union forced upon me, not one born of choice, but one that has bound our kingdoms together, effectively extinguishing my parents' rebellion almost as quickly as it had begun.

I haven't heard from my parents since Altair took me, and there is no way he'd allow me to visit them. According to Iolas, he believes they're too unpredictable, and he's convinced that seeing them would only put me in danger, or at risk of running away.

I have no idea if there have been any repercussions from the Damu clan. If there has been, I haven't heard about it.

Our union had been a strategic move, a chess piece in the grand game of politics and power. The king gains control over me because of my place in the prophecy—the woman foretold to play a pivotal role in the balance of power.

By holding me, he secures leverage over King Sovran. I have no illusions about where I stand in Altair's heart, and he definitely knows I feel similarly. We are bound by circumstance, not by choice, and that fact hangs between us like an unspoken truth.

And he knows that if I have the opportunity to bury a dagger in his back, I will—not that it would do much. You can kill a normal vampire by cutting off their head or staking their heart with a silver dagger. But those vampires stand out. Instead of two sharp canines, they have a full mouth of sharp fangs.

But only a witch-made silver blade can kill a *pureblood* vampire. And Altair has ensured all the ones here have been hidden from me. That doesn't stop me from carrying a plain dagger now though.

But Dazeem is also a pureblood, so the blade wouldn't have killed him. And I had been frozen, caught off guard by being manhandled for the first time since I arrived in the vampire kingdom, the shock of it leaving me momentarily paralyzed.

The king finally breaks the silence. "I'm staying for a while," he states matter-of-factly.

I blink, startled by his words. "Staying?" The single word slips from my lips, heavy with a mix of apprehension and curiosity. His prolonged stay could mean anything—a new plot, a deeper scheme, or perhaps something worse. A chill runs down my spine as I wonder what new role I will be forced to play in whatever drama is about to unfold.

He nods, his expression serious. "Yes, I have matters to attend to, and it seems there's much to be done here as well."

I can't help but feel a mixture of emotions at this announcement—relief that he will hopefully now take over the council meetings, and a lingering apprehension about the implications of his extended stay.

A torrent of questions and concerns swirl within me, threatening to escape my lips. Have my parents told the people of my existence? Are my people, my family, fighting to reclaim their kidnapped princess? Are the vampires waging war against my kind? But I hold my tongue firmly behind my teeth, my doubts about the truth of his words rendering me reticent. My mind whirls with the possibilities, each more sinister than the last. But could I trust any a word that falls from his lips? Doing so would likely be dancing on the edge of a blade. For every truth he tells, there could be ten more lies hidden beneath.

"Very well," I murmur, dipping my head slightly, a gesture meant to be neutral. I avert my gaze, not in submission, but to mask the storm brewing behind my eyes.

"I have to leave, but I shall see you in the dining room this evening," he says, his tone deceptively light.

My head snaps up. "Why?" The word escapes my lips before I can stop myself.

"For dinner," he replies, as if it were the most ordinary thing in the world, as if we had ever sat down to a meal as husband and wife. His smile is thin, almost mocking. "You are my wife. It's only natural we for us to dine together." His voice is calm, but the command is unmistakable. There's no denying this isn't a request. Yet, there's a flicker in his eyes, something almost… curious, as if he's waiting to see if I will dare to defy him.

I feel the protest rising in my throat, but I bite it back, my teeth clenching painfully. I know better than to give him the satisfaction of my resistance, especially when he seems so amused by it, a glimmer of dark delight dancing in his eyes. I've fought against him before, tried to resist when he took me from Avantra, but it was futile. He picked me up like I weighed nothing, throwing me effortlessly over his shoulder as if I were a mere burden. The memory stings, the helplessness still raw, but I don't let it show. I won't give him the power of seeing me struggle, not again.

And every time I push back, it feels like he's taking notes, learning, waiting for the perfect moment to strike. I need to be smarter than that, more careful. So, I swallow my defiance, forcing a smile.

Taking a deep breath, I lower myself into a shallow bow, my gaze fixed on the floor. "May I retire to my suite, *Your Majesty*?" The words are formal, measured, but beneath them, my defiance simmers, as I look up at him. His lips press into a thin line, his gaze lingering on my chin as if considering whether to let me go or not. My heart drums against my ribs as I wait for his response.

His lips thin slightly, but he simply nods, his eyes lingering on my chin before darkening. I walk past him, maintaining a safe distance as I traverse the sprawling palace. In the early days, when I had first arrived many months ago, it had been all too easy to become lost within the labyrinthine hallways and the multitude of rooms branching off in every conceivable direction. But, with time, I have grown familiar with the palace's intricate layout, perhaps even more so than my own home.

I've spent countless days wandering these halls, followed closely by the ever-watchful eyes of my personal guard, never questioning me or stopping me as I entered each, looking for something—anything—that might give me an edge, a piece of information, a hidden door, a weapon. I've found little more than lavish tapestries and gilded corridors, yet these quiet explorations are my only semblance of control, my only way to carve out a space in this place that belongs to him.

The only place that has offered solace beyond my chambers has been the water gardens and grand library, where I seek refuge among the ancient tomes and the hallowed silence, escaping the relentless pressures of my newfound role as queen of the Daeva clan.

It's not just living around the vampires who weigh on me. My heart aches for the humans—those who suffer under the tyranny of the vampires, their lands ravaged, and their lives controlled by creatures who only see them as pawns. I want to protect them, to find a way to stop this endless cycle of bloodshed and oppression.

But here, in this court, I am surrounded by nothing but the cold, indifferent faces of the vampires, many of whom I couldn't care less about. The lords and ladies who are nothing but bloodthirsty manipulators, eager to see the balance of power shift in their favour—they are the ones I would gladly watch fall. The others, the ones who simply want to survive in this world of cruelty, they are the ones I want to fight for. But in this place, I feel more and more like a prisoner than a queen.

The vampire palace defied every grim tale I'd ever heard as a child. Instead of a dark, foreboding fortress, it stands bright and magnificent, like a jewel set against the mountains. I had gasped when I first saw it, struck by the brilliance of the grey stone that seemed to glow under the sun's rays, the slender towers reaching heavenward, their spires adorned with intricate filigree. But even then, beneath my awe, a chill had settled in my bones. For all its beauty, I believed I knew the truth—this place was a gilded cage, a façade hiding the horrors within.

Horrors I haven't actually witnessed yet. I wonder if the violence is real, if it's happening behind closed doors, in places I can't go, or if it even happens here, in the heart of the Daeva clan. Are the humans truly safe, or is their suffering merely concealed by the beauty and opulence of this world? The more I learn, the more I realise how little I know of these creatures—of their true nature. And though my growing distrust of them grows with each passing day, part of me is still compelled to seek the truth. What are they really capable of? Where are they hiding the horrors I have been told of?

When I had entered the palace, I was greeted by an expansive courtyard, bathed in the warm embrace of sunlight. Exotic flora I had never seen cascaded from marble urns, their vivid blooms releasing a delicious mix of scents into the air. The palace's interior was no less enchanting, with sweeping, arched windows that framed picturesque vistas of lush gardens and serene water features.

The palace's splendour is a cruel mockery of the hardships my people have endured since the vampires seized control. While we scrape and struggle to survive, this place gleams with luxury. Every polished stone and silken drape are a reminder of what has been taken from us—of the homes we've lost, the freedoms stripped away. I cannot help but wonder if the king understands this, or if he cares at all. But I doubt it; to him, we are nothing more than tools, commodities, and perhaps that is why this place, in all its beauty, feels so unbearably cold.

There had once been peace, fragile and fleeting, but it held for a time—fractured only by small disagreements, petty rivalries, the sort of squabbles that never should have escalated. But that peace ended when Altair murdered his king and took control of the Daeva kingdom. The air still tastes of blood from that day. No one knew what he had against King Sovran, but the animosity was fierce and personal. Whatever history there was between them, Altair's betrayal shattered the delicate balance, starting a war that would drag on for years. And that war… it changed everything.

I find myself thinking back to a time when vampires and humans walked side by side, long before war and treachery shattered that fragile peace. As a child, I attended a learning academy where we shared our classrooms with vampire children, learning, playing, and growing together under the same roof. I recall a boy with inky hair and eyes as blue as summer skies, a girl with dark skin and a laugh that could light up a room, another boy whose infectious grin made him friends with everyone. Those days seem like a lifetime ago, memories blurred like a dream I can barely grasp. Now, all that remains is the bitter aftertaste of betrayal and loss.

I shake my head to dispel the memories, my focus sharpening on the sound of soft footsteps trailing behind me. My heart leaps, a mix of surprise and recognition coursing through me. Iolas Thorne, my ever-watchful shadow, is there, his presence like a gust of fresh air in the otherwise stifling palace. I glance up at his tall frame, his curls catching the dim light, and find him grinning down at me.

"I heard there was a commotion. The *one* day I'm not there with you, and you go and get yourself into trouble."

"You can shut up," I grumble under my breath, my footsteps hastening as I move toward the spiralling staircase that will lead me to my suite.

Iolas's curly honey-brown hair, neatly cropped on the sides but left just unruly enough on top, gives him a look of effortless charm. His face is all sharp angles, softened only by the rugged handsomeness that seems at odds with the disciplined grace in his movements. Where the king is all brooding intensity, Iolas is the light-hearted counterpart—a playful presence that brings a rare ease to my life in this palace. Yet, beneath the easy smiles and teasing words, I wonder how he's earned the king's trust despite their stark differences.

Iolas is… fun.

He makes me laugh, something I hadn't realised I needed so badly until he came along. But I also can't ignore the way he watches me, his playful banter a cover for the deeper concern in his eyes.

For I am just a little human in a palace full of vampires who probably want to drain me.

Not that any of the members of staff have ever expressed an interest it that. I think they know they would suffer at the hands of the king if they did.

No. Most of them have been… pleasant. Even granting me small acts of kindness. Extra morning rolls for breakfast. A small smile. A vase of flowers for my room.

I can't deny it—sometimes, I wonder if all the rumours I've heard about vampires, the stories of their cruelty, their bloodlust, are true. Or perhaps they've been twisted, exaggerated over the years to make them seem like monsters when, in truth, they might be more like us than I ever imagined. These little acts of kindness... could it be that there's more to them than I thought? Perhaps the vampires aren't all bloodthirsty tyrants, or maybe their violent nature is a product of the war, of the manipulation that twists everything. If they were allowed peace, could they coexist with us?

But then again, who am I to question the way things are? The vampire kings wage war, and we, the humans, are caught in the middle— pawns in their battle for power. Is this all part of their grand scheme to manipulate us, to make us see them as monsters so we'll be too afraid to rise against them? Or are we the ones who have been manipulated, our perceptions shaped by years of suffering and hatred?

I wish I knew the answers. Part of me feels the tension in the air, the way the war has divided us, made everything so strained. There could be peace, if only someone had the courage to seek it. But every time I think about it, I wonder if I could ever trust any of them enough to build something new. Can there be peace between vampires and humans? Or have we already reached a point where the divide is too wide to cross?

But whilst here, Iolas is a presence I don't mind spending time with. It is a comfort to have someone who felt more human than vampire by my side.

But…

"Why did you leave?" The irritation in my voice is undeniable, though I try to keep it light. "I could have used your sword there."

Iolas's grin only widens, clearly unfazed. "I heard the carriage arrive outside and wondered who was approaching. We weren't expecting Al's return today. And my sword? During a meeting? I didn't know you were into that sort of thing."

"Shut up," I grumble, rolling my eyes. "Lord Dazeem was being his usual charming self."

His smile fades, eyes narrowing. "What did he do?"

"The king dealt with it," I say quickly. "It's fine."

"Fine? You look like you're ready to kill someone." His voice drops, losing its playful edge as he steps closer. Suddenly, he's so near that I have to tilt my head back to meet his gaze. There is no need for me to respond; his eyes carefully scan my face, focusing on my chin before flaring. "What did he do, Olwyn?"

I pause, then let a small, grim smile cross my lips. "Grabbed me. Altair removed his hand."

Iolas blinks, then lets out a low whistle. "Good. I'm sorry. I should have been there."

"It's fine," I repeat, softer this time. "You had to greet the king."

He shakes his head. "It's not fine. I'm *your* guard, Olwyn. And it's a job I take seriously, I shouldn't have left you unguarded. Even though nothing's happened before today, I shouldn't have trusted the men around you. I did send a replacement, but Al got there first. I'll apologise to the king."

I open my mouth to protest, not wanting him to get into trouble for something beyond his control, but he raises a hand again.

"Don't worry, little witch. The king's had me around so long, he wouldn't know what to do without me. I'm too valuable for him to get rid of. And not just because I keep you in line with my stunning looks and sharp wit. Now." He leans down, head tilting. "Want me to kiss it better?" He avoids my slap, and then the bastard winks, before turning and continuing down the corridor.

I let out a huff, trying to cling to my irritation, but it's hard when he's looking at me like that, all mischievous and confident. He has a way of turning everything into a joke, but I know he means what he says.

I think over his words and wonder exactly how long he has been around. He realises I'm not walking and turns back around.

"How old *are* you?" The question slips out before I can think it through.

His eyes widen in mock horror. "Bit rude to be asking a vampire's age, don't you think?"

My cheeks flame instantly. Shit. I've offended him. But before I can stammer out an apology, he bursts into laughter, the sound rich and warm.

"It's all right, Olwyn," he says with a teasing grin. "I turned twenty-seven, ten moons ago. One moon after the king."

Huh.

So, Altair *is* young.

They're the same age as me.

"Twenty-seven?" I echo, blinking. "That's it?"

He catches the perplexed expression on my face and raises an eyebrow. "What is it?"

"I just… thought you were both older," I blurt out, realising too late how that sounds.

He scoffs, feigning offence. "Well, *thanks*. Didn't think I looked that rough."

I shake my head quickly, my blush deepening. "You don't! You look… good. Really good."

He leans in with a wicked grin. "Good enough for you to ask me how old I am, huh? Careful, Olwyn. A few more compliments, and I might start thinking you're interested."

I roll my eyes, trying to suppress a smile as I start walking again. "You wish."

"Oh, I know," he replies with a playful wink, falling into step beside me. "But don't worry, your secret's safe with me."

"Secret?" I scoff, side-eyeing him. "You're delusional if you think I'm harbouring any secrets."

He chuckles, the sound light and teasing. "Maybe, but you can't blame a vamp for hoping. I mean, you did just call me 'good'—'really good,' in fact. That's practically a declaration of love in some places."

I snort, shaking my head as we continue down the dimly lit corridor. "You've got quite the imagination, Iolas."

"Got to keep things interesting around here somehow," he says, giving me a mock-serious look. "After all, when you've been alive for as *long* as I have, you've got to find ways to entertain yourself."

I raise an eyebrow at him, still amused. "All twenty-seven years of your eternal existence?"

"Hey, don't knock it," he replies with a grin. "Some of us age like fine wine. Not that you'd know anything about that—being the innocent little thing you are."

"Innocent?" I arch an eyebrow. "You really are delusional."

We reach the corridor leading to my chambers, the air between us crackling with the easy banter.

"So, Olwyn," he leans against the wall with that familiar smirk. "Do I get a goodbye kiss, or are you just going to leave me hanging after all this flirting?"

I roll my eyes, but the smile pulling at my lips is genuine. "I think you'll survive the night without one, you rake."

He sighs dramatically, hand over his heart. "Ah, the cruelty of a queen, leaving a poor vampire wanting."

I shake my head, pushing open my door, but the warmth in my chest lingers as I glance back at him. "Bye, Iolas."

"Bye, Olwyn," he replies, his voice softer, carrying a note of something almost tender. "Take a nap, and dream of all the things you're too shy to do while you're awake."

I step into my chambers, shutting the door in his wicked face, the wood clicking shut, but the playful energy he's left in his wake lingers, wrapping around me like a warm cloak. For a moment, I wonder if that was his intention all along—to pull me from the dark thoughts clouding my mind. If so, it worked. I find myself smiling, despite everything.

My room is nicer than my own back in my parent's palace, a sanctuary of light and luxury, but the opulence feels like a mockery of my captivity. The light from the windows filters through sheer drapes, casting a gentle radiance across the space, but I can't help but feel suffocated by the very walls that trap me. The intricate carvings on the four-poster bed are beautiful, but each night I lie awake, wishing the carved wood could splinter under my fists and give me a way out.

A richly textured rug covers the polished wooden floor, its muted hues complementing the soft, pastel colour scheme of the room. A delicate chandelier hangs gracefully from the ceiling, its crystal beads chiming softly whenever a breeze sneaks through the barely open windows. The scent of fresh flowers from the gardens below mingles with the lingering aroma of burning candles, a mix of sweet and smoky that clings to the air.

Against the wall opposite the bed, there's a door, solid and unyielding, its presence a constant taunt. It has been locked ever since I moved in, and I've spent countless hours trying to pick the lock. But the door remains steadfast, a barrier between me and whatever lies beyond.

To one side, a door leads to my ensuite bathroom. The bathroom is as luxurious as the room itself, with marble countertops, a deep soaking tub, and gold-finished fixtures that gleam.

It's an incredibly pleasant prison for a little witch.

Little witch.

The term echoes in my mind, a reminder of one of the reasons the vampire king has chosen to claim me. When I was young, one of the remaining magic-wielding witches from Aesteria had told my parents of a prophecy.

The prophecy spoke of a witch born with extraordinary powers, one who would bring about great change in the realm. My parents feared this change more than anything—they knew that great power could be both a blessing and a curse. To them, the prophecy was a death sentence, a target painted on my back from the moment I was born.

When I was young, I lived with my aunt while attending the academy. I remember the sound of distant bells, the crisp parchment under my fingertips, the way the sun used to catch on the stained-glass windows. But those memories are vague, shadows of a time I can barely grasp.

The day my powers first manifested, there was an incident—a brush with death when vampires descended, drawn by the scent of magic in my blood. I nearly died that day, and I bear a four-inch scar above the outside edge of my right eyebrow that ends in my hairline, as a reminder.

I remember the touch of the young vampire's hand on my skin— how it felt like fire, as if his touch burned right through me. The sensation was so intense that it sent my body into shock, and I thought I would melt under the heat of it. My skin seared with the kind of agony I couldn't describe. And then, as I gasped for breath, there was a flash—a brilliant, white light that blinded me, swallowing everything in its path. I could feel the magic within me, surging uncontrollably, wrapping around the vampire like a vice, pushing him back. It was as if the very air itself was fighting to protect me.

I don't know how I survived, but I did. And now, with that scar and the memory of that blinding light, I know something within me is different—changed. What I don't know is whether that light saved me… or if it marked me.

After that, my parents brought me back to the palace, and I never returned to the academy. They told everyone I had died, weaving a lie to protect me and my magic. From that day on, I was hidden from the world, an unknown daughter in a wing of the palace where only the most trusted servants were allowed to serve me. Some of those servants disappeared over the years, vanishing without a trace, and I couldn't help but wonder what they had seen or heard that sealed their fates.

I suspect—though I've never had the courage to ask—that my parents had them killed. The thought unsettles me, twisting my insides into a tight knot. Why else would they vanish, erased from existence as if they had never been here at all? If they knew too much, if they were a threat to my safety, that would explain their fate. And if that's true, then my parents really were willing to go to any lengths to protect me.

But why? How dangerous are my powers if they would resort to such extremes? The idea that my very existence could put others in danger—especially those who serve me, those who try to help me—makes my blood run cold. I can't help but wonder if the blood in my veins is more of a curse than a gift. It's a chilling thought that keeps me awake at night, the unsettling suspicion that if my own parents would go so far to keep me safe, maybe I'm more of a weapon than I ever realised.

My parents feared that my magic would make me a target, a tool for those who wished to control or destroy me.

They whispered of dangers lurking beyond the palace walls, of vampire kings who would come for me if they ever learned the truth. They were right. Draven found me anyway. And now I'm here, in this beautiful cage, because of a prophecy I never asked for, under the watchful eyes of a man who views me as both a prize and a threat.

But I'm not powerless, no matter how much they want me to believe I am. Every day, I collect scraps of information, piecing together the secrets of this place. I listen to the servants' idle chatter about the political climate and which lords hold grudges. I watch the guards' shifts and note their moments of distraction or fatigue. I study the movements of envoys, courtiers, and visiting dignitaries, taking note of who they speak to and what expressions they wear when they leave Altair's chambers. I overhear mentions of trade routes, border conflicts, alliances that are strained or strengthened, and whispers about hidden rebel factions in the south.

I gather these fragments like weapons, storing them away, waiting for the moment when I can turn them to my advantage.

Or find a way out before this place becomes my tomb.

CHAPTER FOUR
Altair

Gods, the fury.

It is a living thing, a serpent coiling around my heart, squeezing tighter with every breath. An unrelenting blaze, burning through every fragile thread of decency I still cling to. I can feel it in the thundering pulse at my temple, in the darkness crawling up my throat, threatening to choke me with its bitterness.

He touched her… he laid his filthy fucking hands on my wife.

The audacity of it… the sheer, reckless audacity.

I have been gone too long it seems, allowing the Lords to become complacent. The council feels different now, the air thick with their arrogance and unchecked ambitions. My absence, however necessary, has come at a cost. King Sovran's forces had sparked a skirmish to the southeast, a calculated move that hinted at more than just territorial posturing.

He knew.

Somehow, Casius had found out about Olwyn.

The news had reached me swiftly, and the battle had demanded my attention, ensuring that I remained away from the heart of my kingdom longer than I should have. The clash had been fierce, a reminder that Sovran would not stand idly by while I held such a potent advantage. The realization of how precarious my hold on power truly is gnaws at me now.

The lords may have grown bold in my absence, but I will remind them where true authority lies—and that any disruption to my plans, or my claim over Olwyn, will be met with unyielding force.

Every instinct I possess tells me to hunt down Dazeem and finish what I started. It gnaws at the bars of my control, its growl echoing through my mind, threatening to break free. I wanted to let it loose, to let that dark force within me—an ancient, forbidden power—consume him, to strip his flesh from bone until nothing remained of his insolence.

But there's also a part of me that wants to shield Olwyn from the ugliness of my world. A part that fears what she would think if she saw the true depths of my darkness. I want to keep her safe from the brutality, to preserve her innocence a while longer. To be seen as something other than a monster… not yet. Not by her.

Dazeem is a necessary evil, a linchpin in my delicate political web. He has connections to the vampires in the Faerie realm—those that live in the Unseelie court. They may not be pureblood vampires, but there are hundreds that live there. And those numbers could always come in useful in the future.

So whilst I let the snivelling coward live, even as he bared his fangs at me, Ailith had gotten such pleasure from handing me her blade to remove his hand.

"I think that went well?" She smirks once she finds me after removing Dazeem from my presence.

I growl in response.

"But not so much with Olwyn, hmm?"

It probably went better than it could have, but I suppose she had been in shock. Shock at being manhandled by a male that would tremble at her feet if she used her power, and for seeing me return to the palace.

Iolas has taken her back to her chambers, yet her scent lingers in the room, a delicate blend of jasmine and something uniquely hers— warmth, perhaps, or the sweet hint of fresh rain on earth. It tightens in my chest, constricting my breath with a heady mix of longing and something darker, a craving that goes beyond a mere thirst for blood. I could practically taste it on my tongue when I had been so close to her. Able to touch her, even if it had been under the guise of checking her injury.

Injury.

The thought sends another wave of rage blasting through me, my shades darkening the room around me.

"Stop that shit," Ailith commands. "You'll suck the light from the entire palace."

I force my shoulders to relax, taking another deep inhale of the remaining scent of jasmine in the room.

"Sorry," I mumble.

"I think she actually took your return rather well." Ailith waves a hand flippantly through the air. "She didn't scream… or run from the room."

"I think that was preservation. Iolas has told her not to run from our kind."

Ailith purses her lips, knowing how strong the *hunter* urge can kick in. Ailith has always been my confidante, ever since we grew up together. She's one of the only people—besides Iolas—who knows the depths of my darkness and yet remains unafraid. She's seen me at some of my worst, and still, she stays by my side, offering her counsel with a bluntness that others would never dare.

Under different circumstances, I know she and Olwyn would get along. Because under Olwyn's fear, I sensed something else... A bravery I had seen that first night I took her. Even though I could sense her unease at my closeness. Could still feel her disgust at the sight of my teeth, which I retracted as soon as I could. But she didn't flinch, and I still caught her looking.

Her green irises had been so bright… and *looking*. As if really seeing me.

It makes me want to hide.

It makes me want to hide *her* from all the cruel truths in the world and the wrenching hurt that could fill her heart.

But I will take her anger. Her hate.

"She's more rebellious than I anticipated," I admit, my voice low. "Stronger."

When she snapped at me, it had taken me by surprise. So brave. So reckless.

"Staying?" she had asked, her voice raising just ever so slightly.

Ahhh. So she was curious.

And I wanted to know how much.

Ailith raises an eyebrow, "And that surprises you? Did you expect her to be a wilting flower? You took her from her home, after all."

"I took her to save her," I snap, turning back to face Ailith. "To protect her from the lies she's been fed, from the life she's been forced into."

Ailith tilts her head, her gaze softening slightly. "And yet, she doesn't know that does she? She sees herself as a caged bird. Do you think that's how she should feel?"

My jaw tightens. "No. She is my queen, not my captive. I want her to see that. To embrace it."

Ailith chuckles softly, running a dark hand over her shaved head. "Without knowing everything? You may need to do more than just tell her that, Altair. She's not going to believe words alone. Actions, dear king, speak much louder."

It's dangerous if she begins to voice the questions I can already see flickering behind her eyes, questions that could unravel more than she's ready to confront. Yet, that curiosity is also illuminating—it shows me a path into her guarded mind. I noticed how she hesitated when I suggested dinner, how she looked poised to argue, the defiance sparking in her expression. But she chose to hold back, a decision that intrigued me more than I cared to admit.

If she had refused my request for dinner, I would have pressed the matter, not from a need to assert my authority, but from a genuine concern to ensure she was taking care of herself. Her agreement, however reluctant, suggests there's a part of her that wants to understand me as much as I want to understand her.

I let out a slow breath, running a hand through my hair.

Ailith steps closer, her voice gentler and dark red eyes soft. "She's been through a lot. You can't expect her to trust you immediately, especially given the circumstances of her arrival. You need to find a way to show her, not just with words, but with deeds. You've only been back a day. Make her see that this can be her home, too."

"I thought she might have realised that whilst I was away," I mutter, frustration edging my tone. "But now I'm worried she'll always see me as her captor."

Ailith places a hand on my arm. "Then change her perception. Show her something different. Take her outside the palace, let her see what life could be like. How it actually is. Give her a choice, Al."

I chew on her words, but something gnaws at me, deep in my gut. It's not that I haven't tried to ensure she had comforts. I ordered my men to treat her well, to keep her safe. I gave instructions for her to be respected, to be treated as my queen. Yet somewhere along the way, something went wrong. My absence, my forced detachment from her... it all feels like it's torn down any chance for trust.

I left her here, alone, with only orders and empty promises. I assumed she'd understand that I couldn't be there. That I was doing what needed to be done for both our kingdoms. But I failed to realise just how much that absence would weigh on her. I never stopped to think how terrified she'd be, left to navigate a world full of people who might see her as nothing more than a prisoner, just another pawn in this game I never wanted her to be part of.

If I had only been there—if I hadn't abandoned her in that cold, empty space... maybe things would have been different. Maybe I wouldn't be standing here now, feeling like a stranger to her, watching her resent me for what I thought was her protection.

Ailith is right. If I want to change things, I can't keep pretending the past is something I can't fix. I have to take action, to show her that I'm not just a shadow in her life. I need to prove to her that she's more than just a forced marriage, that she's more than just a prisoner in this gilded cage.

But how do I undo the damage I've done by staying away for so long? How do I make her believe that I'm not the same man who captured her and left her to fend for herself in a place where no one understood what she needed?

I shake my head. "You know what's out there. How do I show her freedom without letting her go?"

Ailith gives me a small, knowing smile. "Ah, but that's the trick, isn't it? Freedom isn't always about leaving. It's about knowing you have the choice to stay."

I turn back to the window, my mind spinning with possibilities. "I can't let her leave the palace. Not yet. She needs to feel capable, strong. She needs to know she can stand on her own before that happens."

Ailith nods. "Iolas said she's improving, and by the Gods she looks better than when we found her. Find ways to push her, to surprise her."

She's right. Olwyn has improved since I last saw her, eight moons ago. Her skin, which had been pale and drawn, now glows with vitality. The faint hollows beneath her cheekbones have filled, replaced by a healthy flush of colour that makes her look almost… content. Her body, too, has changed—her figure filling out with strength, no longer too thin for the beautiful clothes she wears.

The clothes that fit her like a second skin, mould to her form, accentuating every curve and line with a precision that borders on the divine. I'll have to remember to pay Thalia and Sera extra for all the work they've put into making her outfits.

But it isn't just her appearance that strikes me. Her posture is different—more assured, even after all she's been through. Perhaps it's the training with Iolas, or perhaps it's a remnant of the strength she carried in her daily life before I disrupted everything. She holds her head higher now, her shoulders squared despite the burdens pressing down on her, the pressures of being the only human at court, and the trauma of being torn from her home. Yet, there remains that quiet defiance in her green eyes, like a hidden flame refusing to be extinguished.

I need to understand that fire. I want to see how far it can burn.

"I'll find a way," I say quietly, more to myself than to Ailith.

"Good," Ailith replies. "Because she needs to see that you're her ally."

I nod, feeling a small spark of hope ignite within me. It's time to change the game. To show Olwyn that she has a place here, with me.

She plays the card well, even if she doesn't know its true value.

CHAPTER FIVE
Olwyn

I have barely been back in my suite for an hour when a team of maids arrive, seemingly impervious to my protests.

They swarm around me, primping and fluffing, their deft hands dressing me.

The dress is a breathtaking sight in a delicate shade of light blue, reminding me of the clear sky on a crisp morning. It clings to my figure perfectly, accentuating curves and movements with graceful precision. Eating hearty meals and being able to snack has been an improvement from the smaller morsels I was given back home—yet another reminder of the poverty even royalty live in whilst vampires flaunt their wealth.

The bodice is adorned with intricate, silver-threaded embroidery that seems to shimmer like starlight. A narrow waist gives way to a flowing, layered skirt that billows with every step, each layer a shade lighter than the one above it. The fabric cascades like a gentle waterfall, the hem brushing the floor as I move, creating an illusion of walking on air.

The dress is completed with dainty straps that adorn the shoulders, leaving the back exposed in a sensual way I am certainly not used to. I feel like the princess—queen—I am. Yet, despite the maids' insistence, I absolutely and vehemently refuse to wear the silver crown they have brought.

I cast a glance into the tall leaning mirror, and I am suddenly grateful for the maids' presence. The reflection that stares back at me, draped in this gown, looks almost supernatural.

The subtle makeup applied by the skilled hands of the maids has worked a kind of magic on my features. My olive eyes, usually understated, now seem to shimmer. My lips, painted in a soft shade of pink, have taken on a natural, healthy glow, and they glisten with a dewy sheen.

My long silver hair, which cascades down my back in curls I could never accomplish on my own, has been woven with small braids along the sides, just above my ears.

A low whistle breaks the room's silence. Turning, I find Iolas leaning casually against the doorframe, hazel eyes alight with mischief. His curls catch the waning light, framing sharp cheekbones and a roguish smile that could make even the most composed heart flutter.

"You certainly clean up *very* well. Is it just for show, or is there a reason you're trying to distract me from my role as your most trusted guard?"

"Compliments from the court's rake, how novel," I say, the sarcasm dripping from my words like poison from a blade. I've seen so many members of staff lust after this male as we walk past, that I'm almost bored of it. He *is* hard to ignore as he's often the tallest person in any room, his chest broad and muscles demanding attention. I seem to draw the majority of his flirtatious behaviour, and I'm convinced it's because I don't fall for it.

Or maybe he knows he's my only companion in this place and he's trying to be nice.

"As if I need a dress to distract you. And you're my *only* personal guard," I point out.

I storm past him and his dark laugh follows me, echoing in my mind as we silently tread through the labyrinthine corridors of the palace.

The grand dining room is an extension of the palace's breathtaking elegance. High, arched windows stretched from floor to ceiling, their stained-glass depicting scenes of mythical creatures and beautiful landscapes. Gossamer drapes billow gently, caught by the gentlest breeze, offering glimpses of lush gardens beyond.

The walls are covered with intricate tapestries that seemed to come to life in the soft, golden glow of ornate chandeliers, casting a warm ambiance over the room. The dining table is a masterpiece, an immense slab of shimmering crystal that seems to have been carved from a frozen waterfall.

As I enter with Iolas, the king is already seated at the head of the table. He wears an exquisite suit of dark green, the colour accentuating his dark features.

His eyes raise but give nothing away as he watches me enter. I swear I see his gaze linger on my figure and the darkness in his eyes diminish a little as they meet mine, but with a blink I realise I am wrong.

For months I have taken my meals in this room on my own, with only Iolas to keep me company. Iolas who walks forward to *stand* by the chair at Altair's side.

I had gotten used to it just being us two. Had grown accustomed to it. Suddenly, I feel like that nervous princess again.

I start to take my seat at the opposite head of the table, the soft rustling of my elegant gown accompanying my movements. Altair clears his throat, diverting my attention. He points to the seat at his right side, a silent invitation. My brows furrow at the unspoken request, and I roll my eyes in a mock display of annoyance.

Nevertheless, against my initial resistance, I give in, hoping to get this over with as soon as possible.

Iolas smirks. Amusement dances in his eyes as he watches my strides, and my graceless descent into the indicated chair.

While my knowledge of the king is limited, I can discern the irritation in his cold gaze, even as his eyes harden at the sight of the bruise on my chin from Dazeem's disgusting fingers.

I sit, folding my hands in my lap to quell their desire to fidget.

Iolas continues to stand, and I glance at him, confused.

"Are you not eating with us?" I ask.

He suppresses a smile and shakes his head.

"Why?" I press.

"*Has* he been eating with you?" Altair draws my attention, his head tilts to the side as his gaze shifts from my face to Iolas behind me.

"Well…" I hesitate, realising I might have misspoken. Too late now. "Yes. When else would he eat considering he spends *all* his time guarding me?"

Iolas snorts, quickly masking it with a cough.

The king's cold eyes fix on me, and his voice cuts through the air like a chill wind. "It seems you two have become quite familiar."

"You know how it is, Your Majesty," Iolas banters back, his tone light. "Guarding Her Highness day and night, one becomes practically family."

I suppress a gasp, astonished at the audacity with which Iolas speaks to the king. Altair's expression hardens, a flicker of irritation crossing his features.

"Iolas," the king warns.

Iolas chuckles, seemingly undeterred. "Just doing my job, Your Majesty. Making sure no harm comes to our beloved queen."

"Yes, well. Your job is protection, not commentary."

"Of course, Your Majesty," Iolas replies, inclining his head in a gesture that might have been respectful if it wasn't for the mischievous glint in his eyes.

I bite the inside of my cheek, fighting back a smirk, despite the worry that surprisingly blasts through me. I do not want to see Iolas get into trouble.

The king's scowl lingers on Iolas for a moment longer before he turns his attention back to his plate. Without another word, he raises his hand and clicks his fingers, and like magic, food materializes on the plates in front of us. The sudden appearance of the sumptuous feast is a startling sight, momentarily distracting me from the tension that grips the room.

I can't hide my surprise. I've never seen Altair use his magic beyond the shadows that seem to slither and coil around him like living extensions of his will—cold, dark tendrils that seep from the corners and writhe when he's angry. But this? This is different. This is refined, effortless.

Magic here is tied to bloodlines, each house wielding unique powers passed down through generations. Altair's command overshadows is infamous—a power said to come from an ancient ancestor no one remembers, but one that marks his bloodline as both revered and feared. But conjuring food with a simple snap of his fingers speaks to an even higher level of power, something only the most elite of vampire nobility can do.

A chill runs down my spine. If Altair can do this without a second thought, what else is he capable of?

I turn my head, and Iolas shoots me a quick, mischievous grin. He doesn't seem scared of him at all. Confusion runs through me at the thought, as I try to reconcile what I've just witnessed. How could the king swiftly punish Dazeem, yet allow Iolas to speak so boldly without consequence?

A spark of hope flickers in me despite my better judgment. If Iolas can joke and jest with Draven without facing violence, perhaps there's a chance the king's temper isn't as uncontrollable as I feared. Maybe one day, I could navigate this life without the constant worry of triggering his wrath.

But still, a reminder lingers in the back of my mind—I don't truly know who the king is. Growing up, I had been fed stories of his merciless rule, tales that cemented his reputation as cruel and power-hungry, especially after he took me from my home by force. That memory holds strong, but seeing Iolas's ease around him cracks the certainty of my belief. I may not be ready to trust, but maybe, just maybe, there's more to Draven than the monster I imagined.

The scent of roasted meat and freshly baked bread fills the air, but I can hardly taste anything as I pick at my food. My hands feel cold despite the warmth of the room, and each bite is a struggle as my thoughts whirl.

I wonder how the king would react if I demanded Iolas be fed.

Probably not well.

But the silence ends as soon as the king finishes eating.

The king wipes his mouth with his napkin, placing it on the table. "I need to tell you something."

I sit back in my chair, my heart pounding in my chest. What could he possibly need to tell me? Are my parents dead? Has something happened to them? The uncertainty gnaws at me, and I struggle to maintain a composed facade. "Go ahead," I manage, my voice steady despite the turmoil inside.

"We shall be treating with the vampire king of the west. We have entered into peace talks. He'll be visiting us here, at the palace."

That's possibly worse than anything I was imagining.

The vampire king of the west.

Casius Sovran.

The name alone sends a chill through my veins, conjuring images of the monster from the stories I've heard in hushed whispers. They say his cruelty knows no bounds, worse than Altair, and that even the most hardened vampires trembled at the mention of his name. And now, he is coming here. My pulse quickens, not just at the thought of his arrival, but at the uncertainty of what his presence will mean for me—and for the fragile peace I am desperately clinging to whilst captured.

I swallow hard, my fingers tightening around the fabric of my gown. My eyes darting briefly to the exit, then back to Altair, the faintest tremor in my hands betraying the calm facade I try to maintain.

Peace talks between the vampires. I had never heard of such a thing.

Never thought it was possible.

"Why?" I ask, clearing my dry throat.

"Pardon?" Altair's brows rise an inch. "Does this not please you?"

Two vampire clans who have long been at war with each other coming together. For what purpose?

No. This does not *please* me. At least, not without further context.

"Yes, very delightful," I manage, my voice laced with a sarcasm too sharp to be mistaken for genuine enthusiasm. My hands clench into fists beneath the table, nails digging crescents into my palm—the only outlet for the terror I feel.

I hesitate, the room's tension pressing down on me. My heart thunders as I think of my parents, but I force myself to broaden my focus. The fate of the humans isn't just about them—it's about all those whose lives are now under Altair's control, threatened by uncertainty. I meet his gaze, trying to summon more strength than I feel.

"What of my kind?" I push, my voice tight. "What is to happen to the humans in Avantra? Have they been discussed at all?"

Something flickers in his eyes, a momentary crack in his detached demeanour. He glances once more at Iolas before returning his attention to me.

"It has yet to be decided."

A chill runs down my spine. The ambiguity twists in my gut, heavy and foreboding. My mouth opens, then shuts again, indecision clawing at me. His brow rises, as if amused by my hesitation.

"What about my parents?" I finally ask, the tremor in my voice betraying the desperation I can't fully mask.

"They are where I left them," Altair replies, the coldness in his tone like a blade. He lifts his goblet, dismissing the gravity of my question with practiced indifference.

"And I am hoping that is *alive*?"

"Perhaps not deservedly so, but yes," he replies with more than a hint of disdain.

I clench my teeth, anger boiling inside me. "They remain in their palace?"

"Yes. They are still living out their pitiful existen—"

"Enough," I interrupt, my tone firm and hands feeling warm. "I am not in the mood to be subjected to your callous disregard. My parents deserve more respect than your scorn."

"Your *parents* deserve the sharp edge of my—"

Before he can finish, I reach down, fingers brushing the hem of my gown as I pull the dagger from the sheath strapped to my thigh. The motion is quick, almost instinctual. In one fluid move, I raise it and send the blade hurtling forward. The metallic thud as it embeds itself into his hand reverberates through the room.

A surge of satisfaction courses through me, brief and fierce. But as Altair's two-toned eyes lift to meet mine, a glint of cold, calculating surprise flickering in their depths, the satisfaction drains away, replaced by a wave of sickening fear. My pulse pounds, realization hitting me like a blow.

What have I just done?

My eyes drop to the dagger I just embedded in his hand, and I wait for the repercussions of my act. But the king's gaze merely lifts from me, turning and meeting Iolas.

"You gave her a blade." The king's voice carries a mix of surprise and accusation, directed at my vigilant guardian.

Iolas sounds like he is trying not to laugh. I do not turn to look. I dare not take my eyes away from the king. Not after what I have just done in temper.

"Well, someone had to teach her proper knife handling. Otherwise, her poor table manners would be the talk of the kingdom." My lips twitch. "Don't want her *accidentally* stabbing you."

"Just intentionally?"

"I think it was a good decision after what happened with Dazeem, don't you? Even if she didn't even attempt to use the dagger."

"I was just about to before Altair came in!" I protest.

The king's gaze shifts from Iolas to me, assessing the situation with a calculating eye. Without a word, he rips the blade free from his hand, and I swallow hard. He inspects the bloodied weapon with a cold gaze… before licking the crimson from the end it.

I glance down, watching as the edges of his wound stitch themselves together, leaving barely a red mark upon his hand.

I struggle to keep myself from wincing, clenching my teeth.

Placing the blade on the table, Altair nods. "Good. She should know how to defend herself."

What?

"Just don't give her a witch blade," he hisses slightly at Iolas, and I fight to hide a smug smile. "I had planned to train you upon my return. I'm glad you had a head start, even if you are sloppy in your movements."

"*Sloppy?*" It slips out, a bite in my tone.

"Yes," the king *smirks*. "But we can remedy that."

Before I can react, his hand darts across the table to grip my own, holding it flat against the polished surface. The unexpected contact sends heat through my arm.

I might as well have all the strength of a newborn. His grip is firm, unyielding, the warmth of his hand seeping into mine even as the cold steel of the blade grazes my skin. The sensation is electric—half pain, half thrill—as the tip of the dagger presses down just enough to quicken my pulse but not enough to break the skin. I can't tear my eyes away from his, the dark depths promising both danger and something far more unsettling.

He moves the cold blade until it rests on the fleshy part between my thumb and forefinger. Fearful anticipation runs through me as his lips part, his fangs now on show.

"Al—" I hear Iolas say cautiously.

"If you wanted to truly make me bleed, this is where you should have struck." He speaks, his voice low and intimate.

My hand remains captive under the king's firm grip, the cool steel of the dagger tracing a delicate path across my skin. I resist the urge to pull away, meeting his darkened gaze with a mixture of defiance and curiosity.

"If you wish to be a queen who commands respect, you must learn to wield more than just words," the king murmurs, the blade lingering at a point where my pulse quickens beneath. "You will continue your training. Especially with King Casius coming."

I don't argue.

I nod, acknowledging the truth in his words even as the sharp edge of the blade dances along the delicate surface of my skin. The king's gaze, now fixed on my eyes, holds a challenge and a promise of a different kind of training than what I have been doing with Iolas.

Finally, he releases me, and I sit back in my chair hastily, rubbing a finger over the back of my hand—no mark to be seen.

"When will he arrive?" Iolas asks, his voice low but steady. I know he is only asking for my benefit. It is likely he and the king have already had this conversation, and yet, I find myself clinging to the shred of clarity his question provides. I am grateful all the same. I am glad Iolas doesn't try to keep information from me. He can probably tell I am panicking. Can tell I want to run away.

Altair answers with a calm, matter-of-fact tone, "In one moon's time."

The words hang in the air like a heavy weight. A single moon, and everything could change.

Better the enemy you know than the one you don't.

That's why the idea of Casius terrifies me. With Altair, as volatile as I believe he is, I always felt there was some safety in his palace. His power and position acted like a shield, keeping the other vampires at bay, at least until today with Dazeem.

But now? He is home and that feeling of security is gone.

My mind wanders as they speak, and I know I should be listening. But—oh Gods above.

Now he is home, am I expected to uphold a… *marital* role?

My thoughts drown out the sound of their conversation.

There is no way in Noctura that I will be going anywhere near the man. Gods know what depraved things he is into. I will be keeping my body *and* my blood to myself.

I had a lover once, back when I still sneaked out of my palace room on the odd occasion, looking for a brief escape from my cage. A fleeting, stolen pleasure before everything changed.

Not that Altair has tried yet. Small touches here and there, like when he held my hand against the table. But in the short time I have spent with him, he has never even expressed an interest in my blood—even with its magical properties.

I have been the first human born with the ability to use magic in centuries. No one knows why. Not my parents, or the priests they often summoned from all over the human realm.

"No wonder she doesn't like vampires," the king's voice breaks through.

"I think she at least likes one vampire," Iolas grins as he steps more into view beside my chair.

My mouth parts, about to ask what they were talking about, but then I swallow my words.

Doesn't like vampires?

I used to.

My mind drifts once more. Back to a large classroom, and a little boy with green eyes. Vampires I played with. A loud noise. Lots of light.

And then no more classroom.

Spilled blood all over the floor.

Screaming.

I blink a few times and shake my head. Altair's head tilts like a feline, his eyes knowing.

"Where did you just go?" he asks.

"What do you mean?" I blink, glancing away and not meeting his eye.

"Where did your thoughts go?"

"That… that is personal. And it doesn't matter."

He leans back in his chair, his expression waiting.

I huff. "I don't dislike *all* vampires." I tell them, and Iolas's brows reach his hairline.

"I… I think I used to be friends with some when I was a little girl."

They share the same surprised expression, perhaps shocked at my use of the word 'friends', before Altair recovers.

"Well, well, well," Iolas chuckles. "Will you look at that, Al—"

The room darkens slightly as Altair shoots Iolas a warning look, and the latter's mouth snaps shut. I've never seen Iolas silenced so quickly, but Altair sees the questioning look on my face.

"Is there something you wish to ask me?" He says.

"I want to know why," I say, my voice steady and sharp, cutting through the air. I'm done being passive. Done being the docile little captive he probably expects.

"Why?" he repeats, his feigned ignorance only irritating me further. "Why what?"

I don't hold back. I narrow my eyes, my suspicion bubbling to the surface, smothering any trace of curiosity I had. "Why you brought me here and then left. Why you've kept me like some kind of prize. What do you want from me?"

The words fall from my mouth, deliberate, defiant. No more polite questions. If he's going to play his games, I'm going to make sure he knows I'm not some fool to be manipulated.

He chuckles softly, the sound sending a shiver down my spine. It unsettles me, and I can't ignore the flicker of uncertainty it stirs within me.

"Must there always be a reason?" he counters, his tone almost mocking. "Perhaps I truly just wanted to punish your parents for them hiding you."

"Men like you always have reasons," I reply without hesitation, my voice firm despite the nervous flutter in my chest.

"Men like me?" He arches a dark eyebrow, his amusement clear. "There are no men like me. But please, what sort of man do you think I am, Olwyn?"

A monstrous one.

A violent one.

For a moment, I hesitate, weighing how bold I can be. "A dangerous one," I finally say. "A man who takes what he wants."

He leans closer, lowering his voice to a conspiratorial whisper. "And what if I told you that what I want is you?"

My breath hitches. But I quickly mask it, lifting my chin defiantly. "Then I'd tell you that you'll have to do better than cryptic games and half-answers," I reply, trying to keep my voice steady. If he wants my blood, I'd rather him just tell me outright. Get it over with.

He laughs then, a genuine sound that takes me by surprise. "Fair enough," he concedes. "But I think you underestimate the value of a good mystery."

I roll my eyes, an action I'm so used to doing to Iolas, but feels expectedly rebellious towards Altair. "Or maybe I just don't like being kept in the dark," I retort.

"Oh, I'm starting to realise that," he says his amusement fading into something more serious. He watches me for a long moment, and I can sense his scrutiny. He seems both irritated and captivated by my defiance, I can tell. The king lets out an exasperated breath, his gaze glancing at my plate before standing.

"You can go back to your room," he orders.

I jerk back in my seat slightly. "Is that really necessary?"

He leans forward, his voice laced with an underlying tension as his eyes flash. "Entirely."

Suddenly I remember who sits beside me. The predator has bared its teeth, and I know I shouldn't push him. I know I should just do as I'm told and keep my head down. But something inside me refuses to back down, refuses to let him think he can control me so easily. Maybe it's foolish, maybe it's dangerous, but I can't help it. I've spent too long hiding, too long being told what to do even before I met him. If I don't stand up to him now, I'll never have the chance again.

Plus, Iolas hasn't eaten yet.

I square my shoulders, not one to easily back down. "And if I refuse?"

Altair scowls, his knuckles turning white on the arm of his chair. "Do you want to stay with me in *my* room?"

I hesitate, contemplating the fact that I don't even know what his room looks like. The thought of venturing into that unknown territory holds a certain level of fear I don't even want to acknowledge. Finally, I answer, "No."

His lips curve into a small, almost amused smile. "Then return to your room. Iolas will accompany you and remain guard outside."

I turn to find Iolas smiling at me, showcasing perfectly white teeth.

"Iolas needs to eat," I say with a sniff.

"I will have some food sent up for him." Altair says between clenched teeth, his patience wearing thin.

"I am fine, little witch." Iolas assures me.

"Little witch?"

I rush to distract Altair from Iolas' nickname for me. "Or we could stay here whilst he eats—"

"Olwyn." Altair bites out, and my mouth clamps shut.

My heart beats faster as I process the sound of my name on his lips, completely unexpected.

And then I realise they can hear it. Heat floods my face.

"I think I shall return to my room." I stand, the chair legs scraping obnoxiously against the floor.

Iolas snickers. "I, of course, shall join you, Your Majesty."

"Don't get too excited. I merely tolerate your presence," I tell him.

"I think you'd like to do more than just tolerate my pres—" he begins to joke.

"Iolas," Altair snaps, and for some reason it sends a wave of irritation through me.

Iolas has a glint in his hazel eyes. "As you wish, Your Majesty."

Ignoring them, I lean forward to pick up my dagger from beside the king.

I don't give him a warning before raising a leg, smirking as both of his own shot apart and the heel of one of these stupidly high heels digs hard into the chair between his legs. The sharp click of the heel on the chair's surface is almost audible in the tense silence. My fingers brush against the cool steel of my dagger, and I see Altair's eyes darken as I slowly, deliberately sheath it on my thigh.

I feel the heat of his stare, the way it burns through the fabric of my dress, and it takes everything in me to keep my expression neutral. But I know he sees the fire in my eyes, and for a moment, just a moment, I think I see something like respect flicker in his. Or maybe it's just my imagination.

When I am done, I move without a word, walking out and refusing to look in the king's direction, though I sense his gaze burning into my back.

The rhythmic echo of Iolas' footsteps follows me as I make my way through the palace.

"He's gonna make you pay for that in training tomorrow," Iolas says from behind me, amusement clear as day in his tone.

I swallow hard, suddenly regretting my actions.

Now, the prospect of returning to my room holds relief.

Dinner wasn't what I expected. It wasn't as… unpleasant as I thought it could be.

I wasn't drained for starters, so that's always going to be a plus.

Gods.

I stabbed the king.

I fight hard not to hyperventilate, considering myself fortunate to be alive. Had I done that in front of his lords or his subjects… I'd likely be bled out all over the floor.

I maintain composure as we walk up the spiral staircase.

Upon reaching my suite, I turn to Iolas, with only a slight quiver in my voice. "Thank you for the company, even if it's forced upon me."

He snorts, his eyes sparkling. "Anything for you, little witch."

I huff at his choice of nickname but open the door to my room nonetheless.

Iolas's lips curl into a wicked grin, and there's a mischievous glint in his eyes. "I hope you're ready for tomorrow," he says, and my grip on the door frame tightens.

"Tomorrow?" I echo, a knot forming in my stomach.

"You heard Altair. Tomorrow, you start training with *him.*"

I slam the door without another word, hearing Iolas's deep laughter echo behind it.

Shit.

CHAPTER SIX
Altair

"**I think tomorrow's going to be entertaining.**" Iolas tells me when he swaps shifts around midnight. When he isn't able to protect her himself, I have two guards take his place outside Olwyn's room.

I grunt in response. Underneath my gruff exterior, there's a simmering pressure that makes me want to crawl out of my skin. I can't shake the image of her face when I brushed the dagger over her skin—her eyes widening, a flicker of raw emotion breaking through her otherwise guarded demeanour. I had intended to test her, to see how far her bravery would stretch, but the intensity of her reaction had cut through me in a way I hadn't anticipated.

"Come on, don't be sore, Al. Your hand is surely sore enough." The bastard laughs, glancing at my hand—the very one Olwyn had stabbed. I lift it up, flexing my fingers as if to test the tendons. No evidence of her blade remains, but there's a phantom ache, a lingering sensation where the metal had bitten into my flesh.

My brave wife.

"She's grown bolder under your training," I mutter, not bothering to hide the admiration in my tone.

Iolas snorts. "She was always bold. Or have you forgotten that you found her, wed her, and left her all in the same night? Didn't take her for a timid flower then, did you?"

I glare at him, my patience thinning. "Like I had a choice to leave her."

Iolas shrugs, but there's a hint of understanding in his eyes. "I know, I know. I swear Casius always has perfect timing for ruining your moods, doesn't he?"

I grumble under my breath, unwilling to admit just how much truth there is in his words. Casius had started a skirmish to the east, in the human lands. I felt bad for the innocents that had been slaughtered in the countless battles over those months, but the vampire was nothing if not unhinged. I shake my head of the memories. "What have you been teaching her in hand-to-hand combat?"

Iolas's expression shifts, becoming more serious. "The basics, to start. She was hesitant at first, but she learns quickly. I've taught her how to throw a punch properly, how to keep her balance. She's not as strong as a vampire, obviously, but she makes up for it with speed and agility. She's got a natural instinct for it, too—knows when to dodge, when to strike."

"Small knives?" I ask, my curiosity piqued despite myself.

"She's good with them," Iolas admits, and there's a hint of pride in his tone. "Really good. Better than I expected. Her aim is decent, and she has a knack for using her surroundings to her advantage. I've been teaching her how to throw them accurately and how to use them in close quarters. She's still hesitant when it comes to aiming for vital spots, though. Needs more confidence in her strikes."

I nod, absorbing this information. "Any flicker of magic?"

His smile fades. "No."

I exhale, my frustration growing. It's more than just the absence of magic; it's the potential that's slipping through our fingers. She has the power, I know it. But she's holding it back. Whether it's fear, ignorance, or something else, her reluctance to let it surface could be our undoing. I glance at the floor, wrestling with conflicting emotions. I'm unsure whether her lack of control is a blessing or a curse.

The truth is, I married her for more than just the political advantage, though that's what I tell my lord and ladies. I needed something more—*control* over her training. I had no other choice. It wasn't just about binding her to me with the vows; it was about binding her to the purpose she doesn't know about. She can't be left unchecked. If she can't learn how to control her powers—how to *use* them without hurting herself or anyone else—then she's just a ticking time bomb. And as much as she resents it, I can't let that happen.

Her abilities are dangerous. She doesn't understand the risks yet, but I need her to be able to protect herself, to face the enemies who might come for her, or worse, come for me through her. But most importantly, I need her to control those powers before they consume her—or worse, those around her. That's why I married her, whether she believes it or not. I need to be the one to guide her, to make sure she doesn't break before she becomes what she's meant to be.

"And what does she need to improve?" I ask.

Iolas leans against the wall, crossing his arms. "She's holding back. Afraid to fully commit to a move. It's like she's scared of what'll happen if she does. She needs to learn to trust her instincts more, to take risks. Right now, she's predictable, too cautious. She needs to learn to be more… spontaneous."

"Spontaneous?" I raise an eyebrow.

"Yes," Iolas smirks. "You know, less thinking, more doing. She's too busy second-guessing herself. She needs to surprise her opponent, catch them off-guard. Right now, it's too easy to see what she's going to do next."

I consider his words. "I will test her myself tomorrow. See if she can handle being pushed out of her comfort zone."

Iolas grins. "Oh, I'd pay to see that. But she might just surprise you."

I can't help the small smile that tugs at the corner of my mouth. "She already has," I admit, thinking back to the sting of her dagger and the fierce look in her eyes as she faced me. "I think I'll enjoy testing her limits."

Iolas chuckles. "I have no doubt about that."

My mind drifts to the way she looked tonight—more radiant, more self-assured, and yet… there's a fragility there that makes my chest tighten, like a string pulled taut. I noticed the slight hesitation in her step when I gestured to the seat beside me, the flicker of uncertainty in her gaze before she quickly looked away. But she belongs at my side, not at a distance. I need to make her see that.

"I've noticed," I begin, my voice more subdued. "How close you've grown to her."

Iolas's gaze flickers, and he grins with a hint of his usual mischievousness. "Oh, come on, Al. She's something else, isn't she? She's been through the wringer and still manages to give me that fierce look every day. It's hard not to get a little attached. But hey, if I start writing poetry about her, you'll know I'm in trouble."

I study him, noting the way he tries to downplay his feelings. "Just don't get too wrapped up in it, Iolas. We both know how complicated these attachments can be. Especially with someone in her position. I just don't want you to be caught off guard. Emotions can cloud judgement, and we can't afford that."

Iolas gives a mock salute, his tone playful. "Noted. I'll keep my emotions on a short leash."

But perhaps I'm too late in saying this.

The truth is, there are dangers to these connections that go beyond just the personal. *Vampires*—we live for centuries. Time doesn't affect us the way it does humans. We can lose ourselves in relationships with mortals, fall in love with them, even grow obsessed, but it's all temporary. *Their* lives are fragile. A few decades, a century if they're lucky. And when they die, we're left with the aftermath. The grief. Knowing we'll outlive them, again and again. It's a constant ache for our kind, one that many of us try to avoid, consciously or not.

But what surprised me most was the affection Olwyn seems to have grown for Iolas. For a *vampire*. A soft smile here, a knowing glance there. He's always been the more 'human' of my friends—the one who laughs easily, who delights in testing boundaries and pushing buttons. A game he's been playing for far too long. He's my oldest friend, besides Ailith, so he gets away with a lot. Plus, he's loyal, and I can see he cares for her in his own way. That much is clear. And she cares for him.

My jaw clenches at the thought. And I realise it's jealousy. The familiarity between them—it irks me. Not because I fear losing her to him, but because it's a reminder of how little time I've spent with her. She's grown accustomed to Iolas, while I've been nothing but a shadow in the background. I should be the one she confides in, the one she looks to for comfort. But I'm not.

I want her affection for myself. Not just her compliance or her presence in my court, but the warmth of her smiles, the ease of her laughter. I want to be the one who draws that light from her, who sees the softness in her eyes.

But all I can think about when she looks at me is: is she afraid of me? Does she hate me? I can't blame her if she does. I've given her every reason to. I can see the guardedness in her every movement, the way she holds herself like she's always ready to flee. I know she hates me for what I've done, and perhaps she should. But there's something else in her eyes, something I can't quite place. It's not just fear—it's curiosity, maybe even confusion.

Seeing it written in her expression across the table tonight, I felt a stir of something I hadn't in months. I want more than just her to be safe; I want to understand her, to learn every nuance of her thoughts, her fears, her dreams.

Iolas's voice, light and teasing as always, had grated on my nerves more than usual today. And I know why. He's getting closer to her, and I find myself wanting that. I find myself questioning whether I can drop the cold exterior to try and win her over.

It's maddening how easy it always comes to him.

She does not see what I see—the way he provokes and teases, but always with a keen eye on her safety and well-being. He's woven himself into her daily life, and I fear she might think he's the one she should trust.

I want to be the one who earns her trust, even if it takes time. Even if it means showing her that she belongs here, with me. Not because of some prophecy, not because of some war, but because of something else entirely.

No matter how long it takes, I will earn it. I will earn her.

She is my queen, my responsibility, and I will protect her.

CHAPTER SEVEN
Olwyn

The first glimpse of dawn barely whispers through the window, casting long, slender fingers of light that claw across the stone floor of my chamber.

It is a mockery of the sleep that escaped me last night, my mind constantly reminding me that I'd be subjected to spending time with the king today.

I drag my feet towards the dresser, where a small breakfast is waiting, but my eyes immediately fall on a set of training leathers neatly arranged on the chair next to it. I've seen some of Altair's guards wear them on their way to their training arena beyond the courtyards.

But the realisation that someone has entered my room without my knowledge during my sleep seriously pisses me off.

I hope it was Iolas… if it had to be anyone.

With a yawn, I resign to the fact that I probably won't get away with skipping breakfast *and* training, so I approach the chair, eyeing the outfit with disdain.

Picking it up, I can't help but note how different they are from anything else I have ever worn. The thicker material feels foreign against my fingertips, and a silent commentary runs through my mind about how uncomfortably tight they will likely be on my frame. It is a stark departure from the looser breeches and shirts I have become accustomed to when training with Iolas.

I can't shake the feeling of dread settling in my stomach as I slip into the training leathers. The material is tight, restricting. I try to steady my breathing, but the thought of spending time alone with Altair sends my mind racing. What if I can't keep up? What if he's pushing me for a reason? My fingers tremble slightly as I finish fastening the last strap, and I can't help but think that this training isn't just about learning to fight. It's about proving myself—to him, to Iolas, to myself.

Opening the door, I almost slam into the chest of all six foot seven of an imposing vampire.

"Good morning!" Iolas chirps, his hazel eyes bright with energy as his hands gripped my shoulders to right me.

I raise an eyebrow at his enthusiasm, unimpressed.

"Did you eat?" I ask.

He nods, and then his eyes widen when he takes in my attire, his gaze travels down my form… slowly. "Looking good little witch," he remarks casually, though his tone has lowered. "I'm here to escort you to training," he says, oblivious to my evident lack of enthusiasm.

I sigh, resigning myself to the inevitable. "Fine, let's get this over with," I mutter, stepping out of my room.

"Uh uh," Iolas raises a hand to stop me, before circling his finger in a bid to get me to turn around.

"What?" I jerk my head at him.

This time he rolls his eyes at me, grabbing me by the shoulders and turning me, before taking a hold of my hair.

"What in the gods name are you—"

"Your training with me has been child's play." He interrupts, tugging at my silver strands. "And training with Altair is no place for a mane such as yours to fly free," he murmurs as he leans down, his breath warm against my ear. "You wouldn't want it to be an advantage to your opponent, would you?"

"Since when do you care about advantages in training?" I counter, trying to ignore the way his proximity to my neck sent a shiver down my spine. Iolas has always used dirty tactics to knock me on my ass.

"Since always, little witch. You know I'm here to protect you, even from yourself."

"Protect or control?" I shoot back, though the bite of my words is softened by the rhythmic pull of his hands as he starts to secure the braid.

Iolas breathes out, turning me around. "Is there a difference in your eyes?"

"Always," I reply, meeting his hazel gaze squarely as his chest expands.

"Good to know," he says with a step back, as if needing space.

My fingers play with the end of the braid; the leather strap tying the end.

"So what? Altair is going to pull my hair if I don't tie it back."

Iolas releases a dark laugh that makes me clench my toes. He pats the top of my head before clasping the tops of my shoulders.

"Only if you ask nicely, little witch."

He uses his vampire speed to dash away from my carefully aimed punch, and I throw the very well-done braid over my shoulder.

"Where did you get the strap from?" I ask, my fingers itching to touch the smooth leather again. I can't imagine he keeps many around, seeing as his hair is too short to tie.

"I have my ways. You never know when a leather strap might come in handy." He winks and I scoff, pushing him aside to walk down the hallway.

As we stroll through the palace, passing by various members of the staff, I can't shake the feeling of unease gnawing at me.

I know I should just follow his orders, keep my head down, and get through this training session without causing any trouble. But something inside me rebels against the idea of being so compliant, so passive. Iolas may be protective, but I can't rely on him forever. I need to prove to Altair that I'm not just another pawn he can control. If I'm going to survive in this palace, I have to show him that I'm stronger than he thinks—even if that means risking his wrath.

We arrive at the training room tucked away towards the back of the palace, the heavy wooden door, reinforced with iron and etched with runic symbols of protection, creaks open to reveal an expansive space dedicated to martial training. The room is dimly lit, with the only illumination coming from flickering torches mounted on the stone walls. Their golden light casts long shadows that dance across the floor, adding an eerie ambiance to the otherwise utilitarian space.

The floor is made of smooth, polished stone, with two large training mats resting against it, designed for ease of movement and to endure the wear of combat. Along the walls are various training apparatuses: wooden dummies, practice swords, and racks of weapons from different eras.

The air is tinged with the faint scent of sweat and leather, a testament to the countless training sessions that have taken place within these walls. Several weapon racks stand against the walls, their contents neatly arranged yet ready for quick access.

My eyes immediately seek out the figure waiting inside. I pause for a moment, my gaze lingering on his relaxed posture and the effortless grace with which he carries himself. The shadows don't seem to be present at this moment, and he almost looks human… besides his pointed ears.

Until I notice he is wearing casual breeches and a loose linen shirt.

"Why do *I* need leathers?" I finally voice the question—perhaps a bit too loudly—that has been nagging at me since I first laid eyes on the training outfit.

"You're the one who needs protecting," Altair replies without looking in my direction.

My eyes narrow in his direction, the implication not lost on me. "And you don't?" I challenge.

I swear I see the corners of his mouth turn up before I blink. But nope. That familiar scowl remains on his face.

But his eyes seem a little lighter. "I assure you, I am more than capable of taking care of myself."

I am unimpressed by his arrogance. "Funny, I seem to recall a certain incident involving a dagger and your hand," I retort, unable to resist.

The lightness in his gaze falters slightly, a flicker of annoyance crossing his features before he regains his composure. "Ah, yes, that," he says, his tone tinged with mock seriousness. "Merely a momentary lapse in judgement."

I can't help but smirk at his response, feeling a small sense of victory. "Well, let's hope today's training doesn't involve any more 'momentary lapses' on your part," I quip, earning a chuckle from Iolas who is standing close behind me.

Altair's jaw tenses, a subtle sign of his growing impatience, but he maintains his composure as he gestures towards the training square in the centre of the room. "Iolas, you may leave." he says, his tone clipped.

"What?" I blurt out. Altair pauses. So does Iolas. "Is Iolas not staying?"

The tension in the room escalates as Altair's gaze bears into mine, his expression unreadable. "Are you questioning my ability to keep you safe?" he asks, his voice low and dangerous.

I square my shoulders, refusing to back down. "Yes," I reiterate, meeting his gaze head-on. "After all, I was the one who stabbed you, remember?"

Now this time my eyes do not deceive me. A hint of a smirk plays at the corners of his lips. But his eyes remain steely, so it does nothing but unnerve me. "Fair point," he concedes. "But you have my word. I will not hurt you… much."

With a sceptical glance, I glance towards Iolas, who stands nearby, his expression carefully neutral. Iolas has become a companion, perhaps even a… friend. But would he stand up against the king if he chose to take a bite?

"You'll be just outside?" I ask, seeking reassurance.

Iolas nods. "Of course, Your Majesty," he replies, his tone respectful for once, yet tinged with a hint of amusement.

Altair's casual posture doesn't fool me. I know that beneath his calm exterior lies a dangerous predator, one who's more than capable of pushing me to my limits. As he gestures towards the training square, I feel a knot tighten in my stomach. This won't be like training with Iolas—there won't be any playful banter or gentle corrections. Altair is here to test me, to see how far I'm willing to go to prove myself. And I can't afford to fail.

"Shall we begin?" he asks, and perhaps I should have thought before speaking, because now he seems agitated. He shares a look I can't decipher with Iolas, before the latter leaves the room.

We're alone.

A wave of fear washes over me. Despite my attempts to appear composed, the prospect of training alone with the king makes my stomach churn and goosebumps cover the flesh under the tight leathers.

Who is going to stop him if he decides to tear into my throat?

Suddenly I want to run from the room.

But one of the things Iolas taught me in our sessions was that running from a vampire was one of the worst things you could do. Their natural instincts love a hunt, and a warm-blooded human was the best prey.

It's a good thing my feet feel frozen to the floor.

Altair stretches his neck to the side, his voice breaking through my thoughts, pulling me back to the present. "We'll start with something simple," he announces, his tone authoritative. "Iolas has been training you with a dagger. Today we'll practise hand to hand."

That doesn't sound too hard.

Iolas has been training me for months now and I have gained some skill with my fists and with a small blade.

I feel a moment of relief.

Before I realise that means Altair will likely be up in my personal space.

And closer to my neck.

Knowing there is no way out of this I nod, acknowledging the king's instruction, trying to push aside the nerves that threaten to overwhelm me. "I'm ready," I tell him, forcing confidence into my voice despite the doubts swirling in my mind.

I definitely am *not* ready.

As Altair nears, a surge of adrenaline courses through my veins, my fingers itching to draw my blade from its sheath. Determined to get him away from me. Memories of our previous encounter at dinner fuels a reckless urge to strike out again. Why not? I've already wounded him once before.

I raise my fists instead, positioning them defensively in front of my face as Iolas's lessons whip through my head. With a swift movement, I launch an attack as soon as he comes within striking distance, but he effortlessly sidesteps my blows. Undeterred, I press forward, launching a barrage of punches, each one aimed at him with increasing determination.

It is the tipping up at the corners of his mouth that spurs me on.

The slight smirk that causes my fear to bleed into anger.

But I watch him as much as he watches me.

He is like a dancer, as he effortlessly blocks each punch I aim at him. Without raising a single hand. With each evasive manoeuvre, I feel a growing sense of inadequacy creeping in, a gnawing doubt that I could ever meet his skill and precision. It makes me feel like Iolas has been babying me.

Makes me doubt that I could ever be strong enough to protect myself.

Every blocked strike heightens the tension in the air, fuelling my determination to prove myself, even as I struggle to keep up with his relentless pace.

But even though I couldn't land a single punch… I quickly realise that Altair is holding back, his movements slower and less forceful than I have anticipated. He is avoiding, but he isn't advancing. A frustrated huff escapes my lips as I struggle to understand how I am supposed to improve if he continues to pull his punches.

Continues to treat me like a fragile human. A human who is surrounded by vampires.

"Why are you going easy on me?" I demand, straightening and dropping my arms. My chest heaves slightly from the effort I have already exerted. I know I am being bold, questioning him with irritation lacing my words as I meet his gaze, searching for an answer.

"I am merely assessing your skills," he says with that infuriating calmness that seems to cloak him like a second skin.

"By treating me like a child wielding a stick instead of a sword?" Anger simmers beneath my skin, begging for release.

For a brief moment, surprise flickers across the king's features before the mask slips, revealing a glimpse of the storm beneath. His next strike comes swift as a falcon's dive, forcing me to deflect with an urgency I haven't needed until now.

It becomes evident that he *had* been holding back, and now he is challenging me to keep up. With each step, each feint, he tests my reflexes and endurance, urging me to match his pace.

Each evasion by him results with a flick from his finger where I've left myself vulnerable—which happens to be a lot of places, judging from the number of times I feel the slight sting from the flick of his fingertip.

He's toying with me. The realisation hits like a slap, stoking the fire of my anger. Every movement, every flick of his fingers is designed to frustrate and provoke me. I grit my teeth, refusing to be treated like some fragile human who can't handle the fight. If he thinks I'm weak, I'll show him just how wrong he is.

"Your anger is a blade, Olwyn," he says, his voice a low hum that vibrates through the tension between us. "Yet unsharpened, it lacks direction."

His words are like the bite of winter wind, cutting and cold, designed to provoke. I can feel the simmering heat of irritation rise within me, fuelled by his deliberate goading.

Every blocked strike sends a jolt through my arms, the impact reverberating down to my bones. My breath comes in ragged gasps, my chest heaving as I struggle to keep up with his relentless pace. Sweat drips down my temple, stinging my eyes, but I force myself to focus, to push through the burning in my muscles. I can't afford to show weakness now.

After several attempts at striking him, he shifts his tactics. As I lunge forward with a punch, he sidesteps gracefully, seizing my wrist with a grip that feels like iron. Panic flares in my chest, but an instinct I didn't know existed surges within me.

I twist my body beneath his arm, using the momentum to spin out of his hold. My shoulder protests the sudden movement, but I push through the pain, bringing my leg up in a sweeping arc aimed at his knees. Altair moves like liquid, releasing my wrist and leaping back just in time to avoid the blow.

I blink.

I blink some more.

My own surprise is drowned out by the vicious satisfaction I feel at seeing the same shock on his face.

"That was… unexpected," he remarks, his voice tight with restraint.

A few months ago, I wouldn't have even attempted that move. I would have hesitated, too afraid of making a mistake. But now, as I stand facing Altair, I feel something shift inside me.

As my hand finds the handle of my dagger, ripping it from its sheath, his chin lowers, his dark eyes stormy as the room darkens slightly. "I said—" he starts to warn me.

Undeterred, I swing my arm up, aiming to carve a hole in his smug, assured expression, determined to unsettle him as he has done to me.

His open palm collides with my wrist, sending a shockwave of pain shooting up my arm, but I clench onto the dagger despite the agony coursing through my bones. Altair winces, his arm dropping slightly, but I growl in frustration and lash out, aiming to stomp on his irritatingly graceful feet.

Suddenly, I find myself pressed against him, his firm grip holding my arm. I gasp, looking up and seeing nothing but swirling darkness in his eyes as I feel the heat emanating from his body through the thick leathers I wear. It ignites a blush on my cheeks. A flash of light blue sweeps across his dark eyes as the shadows flicker, sending a shiver down my spine.

"I told you—" Altair begins, but the blade at his throat silences him. He remains still, his fingers releasing their hold on my arm as I step back, lowering my blade.

Because how badly will I be punished if I open his throat right here?

He will heal, and quickly… this blade will not kill him. But it will still hurt, and he will bleed out until the wound closes.

I can't imagine that would be comfortable.

I need air.

I turn away without thinking, but his touch again on my arm makes me whirl around, anger pulsing through me and warming my hands. I scream in anger that almost blinds me as my free hand shoots up, palm open, poised to strike, but it stops inches from his face… and nothing happens.

What was that?

It was instinct—a reflex—I don't understand.

Yet Altair looks victorious, reaching to grab my wrist, holding it steady in front of his face. And there is something more there. Something guarded behind his dark gaze.

Like he had expected *this*.

I was sick of feeling like I was predictable.

Like I was *known*.

His shadows peel away from the objects in the room and dance around us, shifting like living entities, drawn to Altair's presence. And I realise they hadn't been present until now. But they coil and twist, forming a barrier between us and the rest of the world—a private stage. I can feel their cold tendrils brushing against my skin, as if urging me to give in, to let the darkness claim me.

"Go on, I dare you," he whispers antagonistically, his breath a caress against my skin, sending a shiver down my spine. His grip on my wrist tightens ever so slightly, urging me forward.

"I-I… I don't—"

"You do. You know what this is. Do it."

Magic.

The magic I had been coveted for. The magic the prophecy has promised. He thinks I am hiding it. This whole time, he has been trying to bring it out of me.

My eyes lock onto his, a swirling maelstrom of emotions hidden beneath the surface as his calm mask has slightly slipped from his face. I am tired of these games, tired of being seen as something I am not.

"I *can't*," I whisper, the admission tasting like ash on my tongue.

A twisted smile appears on his lips, fangs glinting in the dim light. "Can't or won't?" he questions me. "You have the power within you, waiting to be unleashed. You know exactly what to do with it."

My nose scrunches up in irritation. "Don't you think if I knew how, I would have rid myself of you already? Would have escaped?"

His eyes gleam with a victorious glint. "I think if you truly wanted to get rid of me, you could have done it by now. I know you know how to, *little witch*."

My patience wanes, hating the way Iolas's nickname for me sounds from his lips. How he says it was like an insult, and not a term of endearment. From the only friend I have had in the palace for months.

I snap. "You don't call me that!"

With his hand a blur, he moves to hold the back of my neck, his fingers wrapping in the strands of my hair, pulling it back ever so slightly.

It will only take one small twitch of his hand. One small, *effortless* movement for him to bend my head, expose my neck and sink his teeth into my skin.

But his eyes flash in what seems like awareness, and he only pulls me closer, his breath mingling with mine.

"I'm not going to bite you, Olwyn."

The atmosphere feels wholly different now.

I don't believe him, even if his voice sounds heartbreakingly honest. I want to scream, to lash out, to do anything but stand here and feel his grip tighten around my neck. But a part of me—an infuriating, traitorous part—wants to give in, to see what would happen if I let the magic he claims I have surface.

But I can't. I don't know how, and even if I did, I'm terrified of what it might unleash. The thought of losing control, of becoming something I don't understand, freezes me in place. I could use my blade. Could stab him with it. But what is the point when I know it won't hurt him—will only piss him off more.

"Just let me go!" I shout at him, and it sounds like I mean right now, but he works out my true meaning.

"When you really think about it, do you really want to escape? You are well fed. Corph knows you look a hell of a lot better than when I first claimed you, especially in these Gods forsaken leathers. You aren't restricted to your suite, or micro-managed on how you eat. You are stronger, healthier, and dressed in the finest clothes I can obtain. You can train and harness your powers…"

My back stiffens. How could he know how I had been living back home in Avantra? The memory of being confined to my suite there, a room hidden away from prying eyes, feels like a ghostly echo now. In Avantra, my existence was limited to that small, secretive space, accessible only through a concealed doorway that was known to a select few. The room itself was dark and cold, with heavy drapes that blocked out the sun and a single, narrow window high up on the wall, providing little more than a sliver of the outside world.

Food was a rare and controlled luxury, delivered by servants who were permitted to enter only at specific times. But I never complained, I knew the city suffered from hunger due to the vampire's restrictions on food imports. My parents had told me so.

Altair continues. "You have a much easier life. Do you really think you could go back to living in Avantra?"

The contrast is undeniable. Here, in this palace, I have more freedom than I ever dreamed possible in Avantra. I have access to training and resources, a marked improvement from the scarcity and isolation I experienced. Yet, the cost of this freedom is not lost on me. His words and proximity flare up a reckless version of me as my chin tips up, daring to expose more of the slope of my neck. "I think that you can feed me and dress me in whatever you want. A pretty pet is still just that. A *pet*."

The darkness around him pulses and he bares his fangs, my stomach dipping uncomfortably at the action.

"You are not a *pet*!" He is breathing heavily now, his eyes wild. "You are my wife."

His words hang in the air, heavy and urgent, but there's something about them that makes my chest tighten, and my breath catch. I don't know if I should feel grateful or more trapped than ever.

"Remember, Olwyn," his voice is low, almost too soft, and it catches my attention like a thread I can't ignore. "I chose you. Not as my prisoner. Not as my pet. *As my queen.*"

His eyes lock onto mine, and for a moment, it feels like he's stripping me bare, like he can see every thought, every fear, and every doubt I've hidden so carefully. I swallow hard, fighting the urge to look away, to retreat back into the walls I've built around myself.

He continues, and his words hit harder than I expect. "If I wanted you for food, or to prevent a prophecy from coming true, I could have drained you the moment I saw you."

I flinch. It's not what I want to hear, but it's the truth, and I know it. His presence in my life has never been as simple as I assumed. Not just the king, not just the monster—there's more to it, more to him than I've let myself see.

"But if you want to stroll around this palace feeling like a prisoner, unable to make more for yourself... that is your doing, not mine."

His words hit harder this time, and I feel the weight of them. I open my mouth to speak, but I don't know what to say. I've been so focused on feeling trapped, so consumed by the feeling of helplessness. But what if he's right? What if I've been keeping myself in this cage, instead of trying to find a way out?

"You have plenty of opportunities laid before you, *all* you must do is ask."

I almost laugh bitterly. Ask. For what? For freedom? For control? For some semblance of the life I used to know? I've been asking for too long, and all I've gotten is silence in return. But then, his words echo again, louder this time. *You have plenty of opportunities.* Maybe I just haven't been asking the right questions.

"You are destined for more than you realise," he says, his voice calm, but the pressure behind it is undeniable. "Embrace it or fight against it. The choice is yours, Olwyn. But you *will* choose."

I blink, feeling like the ground beneath me is shifting, like the walls I've built around myself are starting to crumble. I want to fight him, to tell him he's wrong, that I *didn't* ask for any of this. That I never wanted to be his queen, never wanted to be trapped in this world of politics and magic. But something in his words makes me stop.

He's giving me a choice.

I can't remember the last time anyone did that. He doesn't want me to be his puppet, but his equal. Or at least, that's what it sounds like.

I'm not sure if I'm ready to embrace it, not sure if I *want* to embrace it, but as his gaze holds mine, I know something has changed. Maybe it's not just him. Maybe it's me. Maybe I've been too afraid to take control of my own future.

But now, standing here in the silence that stretches between us, I realise—this choice is mine, whether I'm ready or not.

But this *magic* he wants me to show him… it isn't there.

"I can't," I whisper, the words escaping my lips before I can stop them. His eyes drop to my lips for a moment, a flicker of disappointment passing through his gaze.

But then, as swiftly as the storm had come, it passes. One second, his presence is all-consuming, his grip a vice around my neck and wrist, and then—it's gone. The shadows retreat, dissolving into the corners of the room as light floods back in. I'm left standing in the aftermath, the ghost of his touch lingering on my skin, my pulse still racing as if my body can't quite believe the danger has passed.

"Fine," he mutters, his voice low. "Have it your way."

Without another word, he turns on his heel, flexing his hand. He stops once he opens the door. "Consider what binds you, Olwyn," he says over his shoulder, his silhouette framed by the doorway. "Is it your *captor's chains*, the limits you place upon yourself? Or perhaps something else?"

I stare at him, struggling to process the sudden shift. The room feels emptier, colder, without the oppressive weight of his presence bearing down on me. But his words echo in my mind, refusing to be ignored. I should be relieved that it's over, but instead, I'm left with a gnawing sense of unease.

Why didn't he bite me? If my blood *is* so potent with magic, why hasn't he taken it for himself?

His words make it seem like he knows more about the bigger picture. If I am such an important part, why won't he share it with me?

It is beginning to become a bit overwhelming. Before he had returned, I could just play pretend. I am no longer the girl from a crumbling kingdom. I am a queen—a captive in a luxurious prison—even if every move is under the watchful eyes of the vampires around me.

For whatever motives the king has, I need to play the game at the moment.

So, if he wants me to train, I will. To learn my magic and release it. I will.

If he is going to help me get stronger, I'd let him.

But first I'm going to get answers.

CHAPTER EIGHT
Altair

She thinks she is a pet.

The words bounce around in my brain, refusing to settle. Is that truly how she feels? Does she see herself as a caged animal, something to be kept and tamed? A rush of frustration surges through me, but there's something else beneath it—something more vulnerable, something I can't quite name.

I've tried to ensure her comfort here, to give her every luxury I could. I left orders before I left, assurances that she would be well cared for in my absence. But even I know that's not enough. I wasn't here. I don't know how she was treated while I was gone. I don't know if those orders were even followed, or if someone in this damned court took advantage of her isolation. I don't know what happened in the time I was absent, or how my absence might have shattered any sense of trust I'd tried to build.

I married her, then walked away, expecting her to simply accept it, to accept *me*, without ever truly considering how my absence could have affected her. I thought my gifts and my words would be enough, but I see now that they weren't. I should have been here. She needed me here. And if she feels like a prisoner, like she's nothing more than something to be controlled, then I've failed her.

I watch her, the way her chin lifts, the slope of her neck exposed—a dare, a challenge that makes my blood sing and my fangs ache.

But behind her bravado, I see the flicker of fear, the uncertainty that shadows her green eyes. Her pulse races beneath her skin, and I'm keenly aware of every rapid beat. It's a drumbeat echoing my own rising frustration.

She is more than a pet. She is my wife. *My queen.* How can she not see that?

The shadows around me pulse, mirroring the anger that coils tighter and tighter within me. I bare my fangs, my voice coming out rough, more growl than words. "You are not a pet," I declare, my breath hot and ragged, the truth of it burning in my chest. She flinches but doesn't back down, and a part of me thrills at her courage, even as my mind twists with anger.

I need her to understand.

I tighten my grip, feeling the delicate bones of her wrist beneath my hand. A warning? Perhaps. But also, a tether, an anchor. If she pulls away, I'll lose everything? I lean closer, my breath brushing against her skin, and for a moment, I see a shiver run through her—a tremor I can't quite tell is fear or some other emotion. Her eyes, bright and defiant, meet mine, and I see myself reflected in them—wild, desperate, afraid.

I try to steady myself, but what I've kept from her presses down on me. The truth—*my truth*—is so much more complicated than I've let her see. She doesn't even know the full extent of her power, how dangerous it could be if it's unlocked too soon, if she loses control. I can feel the tremor in my own gut at the thought. If she finds out what I've been hiding, and she doesn't understand her power or how to wield it… if she lets her emotions run unchecked—she could destroy herself.

She has no idea that she is already a danger to herself. I fear the moment she discovers the truth, the moment she realises how much power she holds and how little control she has over it. Will she lash out? Will she trust me, or will she turn that anger on everything around her, including herself?

The conflict rages within me. I want to protect her, to guide her through this—*but she has to be ready*. She has to learn to control herself, to understand her magic, before she can ever truly know the truth. But how can I keep it from her any longer, when everything in me is screaming that she needs to know, needs to be prepared?

I want to be the one she trusts, the one who can show her how to wield her magic, how to protect herself. But if I want that trust, I know I need to change. I need to give her something—*something real*—to show that I'm not just the king who married her out of convenience, who left her to fend for herself. If I am going to ask her to trust me, to help me guide her, I have to start by offering her something she's never had from me: honesty, transparency, and maybe even a bit of compassion.

The thought nags at me, but I know it's the only way forward. If I want her to trust me enough to let me help her, I need to show her that I'm not the enemy—*I need to be someone she can believe in*. But is that even possible after everything I've already done?

"Remember, Olwyn," I whisper, my voice low, urgent, yet softer than before. "I chose you. Not as my prisoner. Not as my pet. *As my queen.* If I wanted you for food, or to keep a prophecy from coming true, I could have drained you the moment I saw you." I pause, letting my words sink in, knowing the weight they carry. My hand loosens from her wrist, allowing her to pull away if she chooses, though part of me hopes she doesn't. "But if you want to stroll around this palace feeling like a prisoner, unable to make more for yourself... that is your doing, not mine. You have plenty of opportunities laid before you, *all* you must do is ask."

I take a step back, giving her space, but keeping my gaze locked with hers. The tension between us is thick, but I know this is necessary. She needs to hear the truth, even if she doesn't want to accept it yet. I realise now that I can't simply dictate her path—I need to give her the tools to decide it for herself. I can't protect her from everything, especially not from the truth of what she is capable of.

"You are destined for more than you realise," I continue, my voice steady, even as the urgency still presses in my chest. "Embrace it or fight against it. The choice is yours, Olwyn. But you *will* choose." I let the words settle between us, my own heart beating heavy in my chest. For the first time, I'm not speaking as her king, but as someone who sees her potential—someone who wants to see her become who she is meant to be, not what I've forced her into.

I wait, watching her, hoping—praying—that she hears the meaning behind my words. That she understands I'm giving her more than just control over herself, but control over her future. Over *her destiny.*

She hesitates. "I can't," she whispers, the words barely audible, but they hit me like a punch to the gut. *I can't.* Why can't she? Because she doesn't trust me? Or is it something deeper, something I'll never be able to reach?

I let the shadows slip away, retreating to the corners of the room like a scolded dog. My grip loosens, and I step back, my anger cooling, replaced by something colder… something emptier.

"Fine," I mutter, the word feeling like a stone in my mouth. I turn, opening the door, but I can't help myself—I glance back. "Consider what binds you, Olwyn," I say, my voice softer, yet sharp as a blade. "Is it your *captor's chains*, the limits you place upon yourself? Or perhaps something else entirely."

As I leave, I try to shake off the feeling gnawing at me, the echo of her heartbeat still pounding in my ears. *Am I any better than those who kept her in Avantra?* Have I merely replaced one prison with another?

But then I remember her defiance, the way her eyes blazed with anger. She's stronger than she knows. And maybe… just maybe, she'll realise that here, with me.

I stalk past Iolas, feeling his curious eyes on my back. For once, he doesn't say anything. Smart man. He knows better than to provoke me when I'm like this. I don't even bother glancing his way; I feel the restraint in his stance, the tension that holds him in place. Good. I'm not in the mood for his quips or his questions.

"I'll be in my study," I mutter, my voice flat, barely a breath above a growl. I feel his gaze linger on me as I leave the training room, leaving Olwyn behind.

She needs some time alone, to think, to breathe. And so do I.

I wish I could be as aloof with her as Iolas is. Wish I could call her by any other name.

CHAPTER NINE
Olwyn

I feel like I have been kicked by a horse. Shit, by two horses. As I stretch, my muscles scream in protest, the soreness radiating from my shoulders down to my legs. Every movement is a reminder of yesterday's training, and it takes all my willpower not to wince.

Fuck Altair. Fuck his training.

The sun shines through the gap in my drapes and seems to be mocking me with its cheeriness, but it reminds me of my plan to get answers.

I can't afford to show weakness—not in front of Iolas, and certainly not in front of Altair. I force a smile, pretending the pain doesn't exist, even as it gnaws at the edges of my composure.

"Morning, little witch," Iolas greets, strolling into my room after I finish dressing. He leans against the stone doorway, his honey-brown curls an unkempt crown, his hazel eyes travelling from toe to head, as if trying to catalogue injuries that aren't there. After my session with Altair yesterday, I think Iolas could sense my mood, remaining quiet as he escorted me back to my room, still saying nothing as I slammed the door and screamed out in frustration.

He leans into the room, placing a small, sealed pot on my dresser. "A balm from the kitchens. For your aches."

Well… that is quite sweet.

"I don't know what you're talking about. I feel fine." I stretch with deliberate smoothness, suppressing the urge to clutch at my sore sides.

He smirks. "Sure you do."

It's not the first time he has brought me some. But I thought I had been getting stronger. Training with Altair has made me feel like I'm back at the start. I walk past Iolas, leaving him to follow behind. With each step towards the great hall, I can feel his gaze on my back, heavy with questions and concerns I can't afford to entertain. Not now, not when there is a kingdom to run and a game of deception to play.

Altair isn't in the hall when we arrive for breakfast. I take *his* seat at the head of the long, mahogany table, surprised when Iolas takes the seat to my right.

His lips press together in amusement when he notes my raised brow. "Gods, one dinner with Altair and you want to banish me from the table forever."

My cheeks flame. "That's not what I want. I was surprised, that's all. Altair won't mind?"

"Oh, I'm sure the king won't mind." Iolas leans forward and elbows my arm gently. "He knows how much you enjoy my company. Plus, I think he'll be too distracted by where you're sitting."

I huff at him, reaching forward to claim a piece of fruit, my stomach grumbling at the food already laid out. The scent of fresh bread and spiced fruits wafts in the air. I take a plum, the purple skin gleaming like a bruise against the white cloth, and sink my teeth into its flesh, relishing the sweetness that bursts onto my tongue.

"Good morning, Olwyn," comes Altair's voice, smooth as velvet as he saunters into the room. I almost can't control how my eyes roam over the tight fit of his courtly attire. The cut of his shirt over his muscled chest, the top few buttons undone. My gaze flickers up to meet his shadowy eyes, and my face flames again, feeling caught in the act.

There's a brief look of confusion on his face, and I feel as though he is sifting through my thoughts like one would sift flour for impurities.

"Morning," I reply, my tone light and airy—perhaps a little too breathless—as I ignore the tension that tightens my shoulders. "I trust you slept well?"

His eyes linger on me, and I can feel the heat rising to my cheeks, but I refuse to look at him again. I focus on buttering my bread, trying to ignore the way his presence fills the room.

Sitting in Altair's seat is a small act, a way to remind myself that I still have some control in this twisted game we're playing. But as I feel his gaze on me, I wonder if I've overstepped. His silence is heavy, charged with a tension that makes the air feel thick. For a moment, I expect him to order me to move, to put me back in my place. But when he sits down next to me instead, I can't help but feel a small, unexpected thrill of victory. Maybe I'm not as powerless as I thought.

"Very well, thank you," he says. I can sense his curiosity, the slight narrowing of his eyes as he tries to decipher my unusual cheerfulness. The image of resilience, I remind myself.

Iolas breaks the silence. "You two are positively chipper this morning. Did something happen during training that I should know about?" His hazel eyes dance as he leans back in his chair, the corners of his lips twitching with barely contained laughter.

Altair's expression remains impassive, but the flicker of something unreadable in his eyes betrays his thoughts. "Nothing of consequence," he replies smoothly, though his tone holds a hint of steel.

I fight to keep my composure, plastering on a smile that feels too tight on my face.

Fortunately, Altair changes the subject, talking to Iolas about changing up the guard rotations. As breakfast progresses, I find my cheeks hurting from smiling. The fake nicety as I nod along to Iolas's chatter when he addresses me.

Once I have eaten as much as I can, I decide it's time to start putting my plans into place. I set the knife down with deliberate care, my fingers lingering on the hilt for a moment as I prepare myself. "I was thinking," I begin, my voice steady but laced with an underlying edge, "with King Casius's arrival approaching, perhaps I could help with the preparations?" I try to keep my tone casual, maintaining the facade of eager involvement. "It would be a good way for me to learn more of the palace's operations."

Altair's fork freezes midair, and his gaze snaps back to mine, a flash of surprise flickering in his eyes. "You wish to be involved?"

I nod, offering the brightest smile I can manage, even though I can feel Iolas's intense gaze from my side, as if he's waiting for my next move. "Yes, of course. It's important that everything goes smoothly for his arrival, isn't it? I could help plan the ball." The words leave my mouth with more confidence than I feel, but it's the first step. I need to be involved, to learn everything I can. The closer I get to the heart of this place, the more control I can take back.

Altair's brow furrows for a moment, as though weighing my words, but after a beat, he inclines his head with a slight tilt of his lips. "Very well. I will arrange for you to meet with the staff. They will show you what needs to be done."

I'm taken aback by how easily he agrees. I was prepared for resistance, perhaps even a refusal, but here he is, offering his approval. My heart beats a little faster, and for a moment, it almost feels like I've won something—like I've made a step forward in this chaotic game. Gods above, he says yes.

"Thank you," I say, my voice softer than I intended. I can't stop the relief from spilling out, and I feel a sense of accomplishment flood my chest. Step one of the plan: infiltrate the inner workings.

But as the excitement dies down, I realise I've used this opportunity to push forward—but it's not enough. My mind races, questions bubbling up that I can no longer keep at bay. It's time I got some answers. I turn to Altair, the words already forming in my mind.

"I also think it's time I had some answers," I say, my voice firm, my gaze unwavering. I meet his eyes, locking onto him. "Why did you take me?" I pause, feeling the question hang between us. "Was it solely for the prophecy?"

Iolas stiffens, but Altair doesn't look away. Instead, he shares a brief, knowing glance with him, the unspoken communication flickering between them like a silent exchange. For a heartbeat, I wonder if Altair will try to avoid the question, sidestep it like so many others. But then, to my surprise, he answers.

"I took you because you are a part of something much larger than all of us," Altair says quietly, his voice laced with an edge I can't quite decipher. "The prophecy... yes, it played a role. But it wasn't the only reason." His gaze darkens slightly, and I see something in his eyes—something that looks almost like regret. "But the truth is, Olwyn, there are many things I can't tell you. Not yet. For your safety."

I open my mouth to protest, but he raises a hand, silencing me before I can speak. "Please. You must understand," he continues, his voice low and earnest, "this world, our world, is dangerous. There are people—forces—that would use you, manipulate you, destroy you to keep things as they are. The prophecy, your role in all of this... it's a weapon, one that could bring about peace—or more war. But there are dangers in it that even I can't fully predict."

The raw honesty in his voice stirs something deep inside me—something I hadn't expected. I've always seen him as the enemy, the one who took me, forced me into this situation. And I never anticipated he would be this open with me. But now, I wonder if he's just as trapped as I am. His eyes meet mine with a weight I can't ignore, and I realise that whatever this is between us, it's far from simple.

"I need to know more," I say, my voice barely above a whisper. "I need to know why I'm part of this, why I'm stuck in this game. If I'm going to trust you, I need to understand."

Altair's gaze softens just a fraction, the storm in his eyes clearing for a moment. "I will tell you more," he promises, his voice low. "When the time is right. But you need to trust me now. Trust that what I'm doing is for your protection."

For a heartbeat, silence stretches between us, thick with his words. I want to argue, to demand more answers. But I hold back. He's offering me a piece of truth, something I didn't expect. Perhaps that's all I can get for now.

"Then you need to stop treating me like I don't have a say in any of this," I tell him, my voice steady despite the uncertainty swirling inside me.

Altair regards me quietly, his expression unreadable for a long moment. Then, he nods once, sharply. "Agreed."

The room seems to take a collective breath as Altair smiles lightly at me before turning to Iolas. "I need to speak with you after breakfast."

Iolas grunts through a mouthful of food, before swallowing.

"I'll take the little witch to her room then meet you in the study?" His eyes flick to me.

I pre-empt him, standing up quickly. "No need," I say. "You go ahead and speak with Altair. I know my way by now."

Iolas hesitates, his eyes searching mine. "Are you sure?"

"Absolutely." I laugh, hoping it sounds genuine. "I promise I won't get lost, not with the guards. And when you join me after, I'd like to visit the library."

He looks towards Altair, who appears conflicted for one moment, before he nods, though the reluctance in his eyes is clear as he waves a hand to the two guards stood by the double doors to escort me.

"Very well."

With a final nod to both men, I turn and walk out of the hall, the echo of my footsteps bouncing off the stone walls as the royal guards follow me. As soon as I am out of sight, I let my smile drop, my mind already racing with the possibilities of the information I could gather while helping the staff prepare.

The guards escort me directly to my closed door, only one other room in the corridor—the door always locked.

I give them a nod and push open the door to my chambers, my mind still buzzing with plans as I hear them retreat down the staircase. But the moment the heavy door clicks shut behind me, a chill runs down my spine and my hands feel warm. Something is wrong.

The room is dim, the drapes pulled halfway across the windows, casting shadows that dance eerily across the walls. My eyes flick around, searching for what has set off the alarm bells in my head. And then I see him.

A large man, his frame filling the space between my wardrobe and the window, steps forward. His face is obscured by a hood, but I can see a cold glint of silver in his eyes beneath it.

I take a step back, my hand reaching behind me to reach for the doorknob.

But he launches for me, moving with terrifying surety, closing the distance between us in a few strides. I catch a faint scent of sweat and leather, mingling with something metallic as I open my mouth to scream.

But my mind races as his hands close around my throat, panic clawing at the edges of my consciousness. This can't be happening. Not here, not now. I struggle to breathe; to think, as black spots begin to cloud my vision. Every instinct screams at me to fight, to survive, but my body feels sluggish, unresponsive.

I can't die here.

His grip is like iron, unyielding, and no matter how hard I claw at his hands, he doesn't flinch. Panic rises, thick and choking, as my strength ebbs away. I've fought before, but this is different—this is raw, brutal survival, and I'm losing. My nails dig into his skin, but it's like trying to break stone. I instinctively reach down to where my dagger is sheathed at my thigh, my fingers brushing the cold metal. But it's too far, and I can't quite grasp it. For a moment, pure terror floods me, my breath quickening, but then instinct takes over.

Iolas's voice echoes in my mind: *"Always aim for the weak spots— eyes, throat, groin. If they're stronger, use their strength against them."* I force myself to remember, to focus, even as the world narrows to the crushing pressure on my windpipe. My body moves on instinct, driven by desperation.

I swing my knee up, aiming for his groin. It's not as hard as I like, but I am still aching from training. He grunts, loosening his grip just enough for me to suck in a desperate breath. I take the opportunity to strike him in the face, feeling the satisfying crunch of his nose under my knuckles—just as Iolas has shown me.

He roars in pain, but his grip tightens again, crushing my windpipe. Black spots dance in my vision. Desperately, I reach for the dagger strapped to my thigh, managing to unsheathe it with trembling fingers.

I need to get him away from my neck.

With a surge of adrenaline, I drive the blade towards his side, but he is quicker. His hand shoots out, knocking the dagger from my grasp. It clatters to the floor, skidding out of reach.

Terror grips me as he shoves me back, my head slamming against the wall. Pain explodes behind my eyes, and I taste blood in my mouth. I try to scream, but we both drop to the floor, his grip on my throat once more turning it into a strangled gasp.

His eyes bore into mine, and I see a flicker of triumph in their cold depths. He leans in closer, his breath hot and foul against my cheek.

"Time to die, princess," he growls, his voice a low, menacing rumble.

Princess?

Iolas's lessons scream in my brain and with the last of my strength, I swing my arm up, jabbing my fingers into his eyes. Hard. He howls, jerking back and loosening his grip just enough for me to suck in another breath. I kick out wildly, my foot connecting with his knee, and he leg slips out from under him.

Gasping for air, I scramble back for the door, my heart pounding in my ears. I must get out; I have to find help. Regret pierces through my panic—I should have had Iolas escort me to my room. But as I reach for the handle, he recovers, lunging toward me with a grunt and pulling me away.

He's squeezing the life out of me. My strength is fading, and a dark, cold edge begins to creep into my mind, whispering that this is the end.

CHAPTER TEN
Altair

"**You look like the cat who got the cream.**" Iolas teases, his tone light, but I see his eyes probing, searching for my reaction.

I don't respond immediately, my mind still half-occupied by the image of Olwyn's determined expression. Finally, I turn to Iolas. "She wants to be more involved," I say, a hint of surprise creeping into my voice.

"Hmmm," he replies, smirking wider. "Didn't expect that, did we?"

I shake my head, a quiet chuckle escaping my lips. "No… but maybe this is the start of her understanding her place here." I narrow my eyes thoughtfully. "A way for her to find her purpose."

"Or a way for her to find out more about why you took her in the first place," Iolas counters, crossing his arms. "Are you certain this is wise?"

My smile fades slightly, replaced by a contemplative look. "I'll tell her everything eventually. Until then she deserves some freedom… and if she's going to stay, she must feel she has a stake in this place." I sigh, running a hand through my hair. "If that means letting her help with the preparations, so be it."

Iolas raises an eyebrow. "And what do you think she'll find? Or what do you want her to find?"

I glance at him, a shadow of a smile playing on my lips. "Perhaps she'll find that life here isn't what she's been taught to believe. Maybe she'll see that she has a choice… to trust me."

He nods, but his expression remains cautious. "You think allowing her to get involved will convince her to trust us?"

I shrug. "It's a start. But—" I take a deep breath, my mind already shifting to the next conversation. A sudden shift in the air catches my attention—a foul stench, like human flesh mixed with sweat. I stop mid-speech, nostrils flaring.

"What is it?" Iolas asks, instantly alert, and lacking the superior senses and magic that I have as king.

I feel my eyes darken, my expression hardening. "Human," I say, my voice low and tense. "An unfamiliar one. In the palace."

Iolas's eyes widen, and he straightens, his hand moving instinctively to the hilt of his sword. "Olwyn," he breathes.

Without another word, we both burst into action, moving down the corridor. The stench grows stronger, mingling with the faint scent of jasmine that still lingers from Olwyn. Panic grips my chest, my shadows coiling around me like a second skin as I rush toward her chambers.

They are in her room. Rage almost blinds me.

Iolas reaches the door first, slamming it open with a force that sends the wood splintering. I linger behind, aware that she is safe with him there and that if I enter in this form, I will scare her. My body is nothing more than shadow and nightmares, enraged by the fact someone has made it into her chambers, either planning to take her or harm her. I take a breath, forcing the shadows to recede and my normal form to take its place.

"How did you get in here? Who sent you?" Iolas demands, his voice a guttural growl, echoing off the stone walls. A man—a human, foul and unwashed—is clamped in Iolas's grip, his feet dangling inches from the ground.

The intruder struggles, his face turning red as he claws at Iolas' iron grip, but even in his fear, there's defiance in his eyes. "You know who," he chokes out. "Vampire scum."

I enter and my gaze snaps to Olwyn, who is on the floor, gasping for air, her throat red and bruised. I see her back hit the wall as she scrambles away, her eyes wide with fear.

I step further into the room, and immediately, the temperature drops. My shadows twist and writhe eager to wrap around the man. The air hums with dark energy, crackling with power that I hold effortlessly in check, despite my urge to unleash it.

Iolas drops the man to the floor, stepping back but keeping his muscles coiled, ready to strike again if needed. The shadows inch closer, creeping across the floor. I feel one tendril brush against Olwyn's ankle, as if curious, seeking her warmth. My eyes, now fully darkened, lock onto the intruder.

"You will speak," I say, my voice a deadly calm, dripping with menace. "Or you will suffer a fate far worse than death."

The man shivers, but I see a flicker of rebellion in his eyes, a spark that refuses to die. He spits blood on the floor, his gaze meeting mine with a challenge. "Do your worst," he rasps. "I will die before I betray my people."

I step closer, and the room darkens further. The shadows stretch and twist like living things, feeding on the fear emanating from him. I feel Olwyn's fear too, sharp and potent, mingled with something else. I push it from my mind for now. There is a job to do.

"You misunderstand," I say softly, each word a promise of pain. "Touching her means death is a mercy you will not receive. Not until I have what I want. And not until she says you can be granted peace."

"You can kill him."

My heart skips a beat. Clenches painfully in my chest as I hear her say the words. I don't want to give him that peace. But I hear the bloodlust in her words, even as they sound weak, and I feel almost… proud of her.

The man's bravado falters, his face paling as he finally understands the gravity of his situation. Iolas moves to kneel by Olwyn's side, his hand brushing against her neck. I see her wince, and something in me tightens, a deep, protective rage simmering beneath the surface.

"Come on, little witch. You don't need to see this," Iolas murmurs gently, wiping away her tears.

This scum made her *cry*.

Rage seethes within me as I turn on the two guards who enter her room.

"Why didn't you check her room before she entered?" My voice thunders through the space, vibrating with fury.

The guard's face drains of colour as he stammers, "Your Majesty, we didn't think— I'm sorry. We assumed everything was secure."

My glare sharpens, slicing through his weak excuse. The tension thickens as the guard shifts nervously under my scrutiny and I rein in the urge to lash out further.

Turning my gaze to her, I catch the pain and fear etched in her features, a sight that makes my chest tighten uncomfortably. I look away, a muscle ticking in my cheek. "Take him to the dungeons," I bark as the guards scramble into action, seizing the man by his arms. "We will continue this conversation there."

I watch as the guards drag the man from the room. I should have ripped his throat out the moment I entered, but I need to know more. My gaze shifts to Olwyn. She sits there, trembling, touching her bruised throat, her eyes wide and filled with something beyond fear—betrayal, maybe. Confusion. I can't be sure, but I can feel it like a blade twisting in my chest.

I glance at the shattered remains of her wardrobe, splintered wood scattered across the floor like bones, and I feel a fresh wave of rage boiling beneath my skin. My shadows pulse, eager for release, but I force them back. I need to keep my calm, to stay composed, for her.

I move closer, kneeling beside Iolas. The sight of Olwyn's fragile frame, her eyes darting around as if searching for some escape, causes my chest to tighten. Here, in the one place I should have been able to protect her… I have failed. I try to soften my expression, to dim the darkness that always seems to lurk in my gaze. "Where does it hurt?"

She shakes her head, her voice hoarse and strained. "I'll be fine," she insists, but I can see the lie in her eyes, the way her fingers still tremble against her throat. The way she doesn't trust me to comfort her.

My jaw tightens, the shadows in my eyes darkening again. I look at Iolas. "Will you stay with her?"

"Al, maybe you should wait—"

"Will you?" I cut him off, my voice sharp, barely holding back the command. I need him to understand this isn't negotiable. Not now. I can't be near her and keep control. I need to release the darkness before I scare her further.

Iolas nods, his jaw clenched, eyes meeting mine with an understanding that goes deeper than words.

I stand, my movements stiff, fighting the urge to destroy something, anything, to let the fury that thrums through me out. I turn to leave, needing distance before I lose control, when I hear her voice, faint but firm.

"He called me princess." Her voice is a whisper, but it stops me in my tracks. I turn back, meeting her gaze. Her confusion and pain are clear, and it almost ends me.

I force myself to remain composed, though my mind races. Her eyes search mine, desperate for answers. Answers I cannot give her right now.

"Why did a human try to kill me?" Her voice is cracked, strained, but there is a fragility there that I have never heard. I glance at Iolas, and he meets my gaze with a flicker of resignation.

"Because you are no princess. You are a queen," I say, the words leaving my mouth heavier than I intended.

Her brow furrows in confusion.

"A queen of what? A title and land I didn't want?" I feel the sting of her words and doubt like a lash across my skin. She doesn't understand, of course. How could she? To her, the title feels like a curse, a burden she never asked for. And yet… she is so much more than she realises, more than she dares to believe.

I turn, my steps deliberate as I leave the room. My chest tightens with every step away from her, my mind already calculating how I will tell her. How I will upend her world again.

A choked sob reaches my ears, and I pause for a moment in the hallway, my fists clenched at my sides. I want to go back, to tell her… tell her what? That I won't let anyone hurt her? That she isn't a prisoner here, not truly? But I push the thought away. She needs time. And I need to give her answers.

I can't help but feel it. A pang of guilt, unexpected and unwelcome, twisting in my chest like a blade. I head for my study, needing a moment to gather myself. I can't afford to let her see me weak. Not yet.

I hated to leave. But I had to before she saw the monster.

CHAPTER ELEVEN
Olwyn

Iolas, his face tight with concern, leads me down to the small infirmary room tucked away on the lower level of the palace.

The air here is cool and still, a stark contrast to the chaos of earlier. The walls are a sterile white, and everything about the room feels too calm, too clean for the bruises and panic still pulsing through me. Shelves stocked with jars and vials line the walls, and a large wooden table holds an array of medical supplies.

I'm still catching my breath when we find Ailith already waiting, leaning against the wall with her arms crossed like she's been expecting us.

I sit on the edge of the bed as Iolas tells her what happened, my hands gripping the crisp linens. They feel too fresh, too pristine against the violence I've just faced.

Without a word in response, she gives me a quick once-over, her sharp eyes lingering on the bruises already forming along my neck and arms.

"You can go," she tells Iolas with a casual wave, not even sparing him a glance.

Iolas hesitates, his jaw tightening. I can tell he doesn't want to leave, his eyes flickering with something like regret. But Ailith's tone doesn't leave room for debate. He presses his lips together, gives me one last look, and then turns to leave—probably to find Altair.

As soon as the door clicks shut, Ailith steps forward, her movements efficient, businesslike. She dips her fingers into a jar of salve, rubbing it into my neck with the same clinical precision as someone polishing a sword. Her touch is firm but not painful, and the cooling sensation of the salve soothes the bruised skin.

"Let me guess," she says, her voice flat as she works. "Didn't see him until it was too late?"

I wince as her fingers press into a particularly tender spot. "Yes," I mutter.

"Thought so." Her red eyes narrow, not in sympathy but in scrutiny. "What the hell happened?"

"You already know." I can't help the sharpness in my voice. Iolas had updated her the moment we walked in.

"I know what *he* said," she replies, her tone dry. "But I want to hear it from *you.*"

There's something about her directness, her blunt, no-bullshit approach, that makes it impossible to evade her questions. I sigh, feeling the weight of her stare, and recount the attack. "I didn't see him right away," I admit. "He was fast, and I think I tried to defend myself, but…"

Ailith raises a brow, her hands never slowing. "*Tried* isn't good enough, sweetheart. Focus. What did you do?"

Her interruption is firm but not unkind, pushing me to think, to relive it more clearly. I close my eyes and force the words out. "He grabbed me before I could react. I fought back, but he was stronger. I hurt him, but… not enough."

She hums under her breath, applying more salve to my neck, her fingers moving to my shoulders. "And how are you feeling now?"

I let out a frustrated breath. "I don't know," I admit, the words spilling out in a rush before I can stop them. "Angry. Confused. He was human, so I'm assuming my own kind are less than happy about my *union* with Altair. But I never thought they'd try and kill me for it."

Ailith steps back for a moment, considering me, her sharp gaze softening ever so slightly. "There's always a reason," she says, her voice a bit quieter now. "It might not be clear yet, but Altair will figure it out. There's always a motive behind these kinds of attacks. Always."

"Do you think it's random?" I ask, biting the inside of my cheek. "Or do I need to worry about a larger group?"

Ailith meets my gaze, her expression unreadable. "Maybe. Maybe not. Could be an isolated attack. Could be someone else with their own agenda. You're in a dangerous world now, girl. People will want to use you, manipulate you."

Frustration surges in my chest, hot and relentless. I clench my fists until my nails dig into my palms. "Why me? All because of a prophecy I never asked for. A power I don't even understand. I've been locked away, hunted, captured, and forced into a marriage that wasn't my choice—all for what? I'm tired of being a pawn, of being controlled by something that's dictated my life since the moment I was born."

My voice rises, shaking with rage as I stare Ailith down. "If this is what they want, then let them come. I won't stand by and let anyone decide my fate anymore."

Ailith finishes with the salve and steps back, wiping her hands on a cloth. Her gaze is steady, unflinching. "Maybe it's that prophecy, maybe it's your union with Altair, or maybe it's something entirely different. It doesn't matter right now. What matters is that you don't let this break you. You stood your ground today, and that's more than most would dare."

I let out a hollow laugh, the sound bitter and raw. "Then why does it feel like I've already lost?"

Ailith's eyes harden, and she leans forward. "Because you didn't finish him."

The bluntness of her words makes me flinch. "I didn't—"

"No," she interrupts, her voice edged with steel. "And that's fine—for now. But next time? You'll be ready. You'll be faster, stronger, and willing to do whatever it takes. Because you'll need to be."

Anger flickers beneath my skin, coiling tight with frustration. I stare at her, absorbing the truth in her words even as part of me resists it. "I don't know if I have that in me," I say, my voice thick with doubt.

Ailith's expression softens just enough to show a glimmer of understanding. "You do. You're more than just a pawn, Olwyn. But if you don't fight, if you don't become who you need to be, they'll tear you apart. And I'm not just talking about today's attackers or the lords circling like vultures. I mean everyone."

Her words settle into me like a heavy weight, harsh but true. I draw in a breath, feeling something shift inside me—a resolve born from rage and exhaustion. I nod, this time with more conviction.

Ailith's lips quirk into a smirk. "Good. But don't thank me yet. You've still got a long way to go. And I'll make sure you survive long enough to finish what you start."

CHAPTER TWELVE
Altair

The room is thick with the scent of blood and fear.

I stand at the edge of the shadows, letting them ripple around me in dark, undulating waves as they whisper and coil, wrapping themselves around the man strapped to the chair. He's human, but he's lasted longer than most—his breath comes in ragged gasps, but his eyes still gleam with defiance. That's fine. I like it when they last.

"You know who wants her dead. After all, it's your fault she's now a target. Perhaps you should have left her alone," he laughs, his voice hoarse but mocking, as if he knows something I don't. His lips curl up into a twisted grin, teeth stained with blood. "Doesn't matter what you do to me now. Everything is already in motion."

I don't respond immediately. I let the shadows creep higher, their cold touch crawling up his legs, wrapping tighter and tighter, until I hear his bones creak under the pressure. He grunts in pain but refuses to scream. His defiance amuses me—for now.

The shadows are eager, hungry for more, whispering dark promises in my ear as they dance along his skin, teasing the edge of his endurance. I've held back with him, just enough to keep him conscious, just enough to keep him talking. But the patience I'm exercising is a fragile thing.

"And when they learn you have failed, who will come for her next?" I ask, my voice soft, almost gentle—a stark contrast to the raw power thrumming in the air around me. I need to know. I know deep down who has sent him, but I need him to confirm if there will be more. "I might consider ending this quicker if you tell me."

His eyes flash, and a rasping chuckle bubbles from his throat. "F-fuck you." He pauses, spitting blood onto the floor, and his eyes meet mine again. "Vampire scum."

The shadows react to my irritation before I even have to lift a finger, tightening their hold on his limbs, slithering around his neck like a noose. His body jerks involuntarily, and finally—finally—he lets out a strangled cry of pain.

"Speak clearly," I murmur, my hands clasped behind my back as I watch him squirm. "Or I'll make sure your death is very slow, and very painful."

"You think this is about pain?" he gasps, his body trembling as the shadows close in tighter. "You think anything you do to me matters? I'm already dead." He laughs again, weaker this time, but there's still a hint of madness in his silver tinted eyes, a flicker of twisted satisfaction that makes my jaw tighten. "They'll come for her. *She'll* come for her."

Atha.

I take a slow step forward, the shadows responding to my unspoken command, swirling and gathering, tightening around him in a violent, cold embrace. Atha. A powerful sorceress, a queen in the human realm—one Olwyn has never been told about. She's the one pulling the strings from the shadows, the one who's sent this assassin, and will likely send more.

She knows the prophecy—she's the one who foretold it after all—and she knows that the path Olwyn is on could lead to peace between vampires and humans, and that is the last thing Atha wants.

She had her *subjects* keep Olwyn hidden and neglected in Avantra, hoping to use her for her own gain when she was ready. But Atha lost all control when I found Olwyn.

Atha wants to keep us at war, wants to see the bloodshed and the strife continue because it feeds her. Peace between our worlds would undermine everything she's worked for, all her control.

She is ruthless. She'll do *whatever* it takes to ensure her vision of the world remains unchallenged. The proof of it is scarred upon my face.

"Where is she?" I ask, my voice sharper now, my control slipping ever so slightly.

His chest heaves, sweat and blood dripping down his face. His mouth opens, but instead of the answer I want, he gives me a wild grin, teeth bared in a sick, gleeful expression. "You're too late. She's already marked. Her fate's sealed."

The shadows react before I do, slipping into his mouth, silencing him. For a moment, I consider letting them finish him here and now, to drown him in the dark. But no. That would be too easy. He's playing a game, and he thinks he's winning.

I reach out, brushing a hand against the edge of one of the shadows. Instantly, they retract, pulling away from his face and slithering back into place around his body. He coughs violently, sputtering blood onto his lap, his chest heaving as he gasps for air.

"I'm losing patience," I warn, leaning closer. "Tell me where Atha is, and I'll make sure your death is clean. A mercy, considering what I could do."

For the briefest second, something flickers in his eyes—fear, maybe. But it's gone as quickly as it came, replaced by that same twisted grin. "You'll never get the chance," he whispers. "Olwyn belongs to *her.*"

My jaw tightens, and the shadows pulse in response to the fury building inside me. But still, I keep my voice calm, controlled, even as the anger coils like a serpent beneath my skin. "*Where?*"

The man's laughter fills the room again, low and broken, each chuckle followed by a cough of blood. "You'll find out soon enough."

I don't let him finish the laugh.

The shadows surge forward, enveloping him completely in a crushing wave of darkness. He gasps, his eyes wide with terror, but I don't stop. I let the shadows squeeze, tighter and tighter, until there's a sickening crack. His body jerks once, and then goes limp. His head lolls forward, blood dripping from his mouth.

For a long moment, the room is silent, the shadows receding as I step back. I let out a slow breath, willing the anger to ebb away, though the man's final words still echo in my mind.

She belongs to her.

I curl my fists, feeling the raw power of the shadows still humming through me. I thought I could protect Olwyn by keeping her here, keeping her knowledge limited. I now fear I'm no better than those who hid her away. Everyone, including me to some extent has thought they could use Olwyn as a pawn in their game.

They were wrong.

I'll find Atha, and when I do, there won't be any mercy.

As I turn away from the lifeless body slumped in the chair, my thoughts drift to Olwyn, alone in her chambers, unaware of how deep this danger truly runs. Of how much worse it's going to get.

But I'll protect her. No matter what it takes. No matter who stands in my way and who I need to root out of my kingdom. But first, I'll start by being honest, as much as I can.

She doesn't belong to *her.*

She belongs with me.

And Gods help anyone who dares to think otherwise.

What I'd give to tear the nightmares from her mind.

CHAPTER THIRTEEN
Olwyn

I wake to screaming.

The screaming is my own.

I thrash against the warm sheets tangling around my legs, unseeing besides the flashes of dirty hands reaching out to wrap around my neck. The coarse splintered wood on the floor.

I flinch as warm, calloused hands take a gentle but firm hold of my arms.

"Olwyn," the voice is soft, coaxing me out of this dream I seem to be stuck in whilst awake, like some tortuous mirage I can't escape from.

"Come back, love," it calls me gently.

I sob, but my breathing steadies as I slowly suck in each gasp to calm my racing heart.

"That's it," the voice sighs in what sounds like relief.

I become more aware of my body. The silk sheets underneath my clammy sweat-soaked skin. The soft fabric of my camisole as it sticks to me. The gentle but calloused hands now holding mine.

I know my eyes are probably wild. But Altair doesn't react as I sit, dragging my sharp dagger from underneath my pillow and holding it against his throat. He just stares, with that infuriating calm expression, waiting…

"What are you doing here?" I ask, as if this whole palace doesn't belong to him. But he has invaded what is supposed to be *my* sanctuary. My safe place. Although it has felt nothing but ever since that man violated it a few days ago.

"Olwyn," Altair says quietly, some tendrils of shadow brushing over my arms gently, in a soothing caress that makes me want to move away. But I do not take my eyes off the man sitting beside me on my bed, wearing nothing but a loose pair of dark bed trousers.

I tighten my grip on the dagger, needing to feel some sense of control, some power over this man. But even as the blade cuts into his skin, drawing a single drop of blood, he doesn't flinch. His calm, measured gaze makes me feel like a child throwing a tantrum, and I hate him more for it. I want to hurt him, to make him feel as helpless as I do, but I know—deep down—that he's the one with all the power.

My teeth clench. "What are you doing here?" I repeat.

My eyes dart to the open door behind him, the one that I have tried countless times to open… that leads to a room I didn't even know existed—a room that's been next to mine this entire time. The thought of him, just a few steps away every night, makes my skin crawl.

"Your room is next to *mine?*"

His brows fall into a frown. "You are my wife. What makes you think I wouldn't stay close to keep you safe?"

I feel sick.

He heard my nightmare. Felt like he could enter my room to wake me. He must have heard me every night since the attack.

My heart pounds, not just from the remnants of the nightmare, but from the realisation that this man, this vampire, has been just a wall away from me all along. Part of me wants to shove the dagger deeper, to make him feel even a fraction of the fear that courses through me unchecked as the adrenaline from my nightmare still eats away at me. But another part—a traitorous part—whispers that maybe, just maybe, he's telling the truth. That he wants me safe. And that scares me more than anything.

"I'm sorry for disturbing your sleep, *Your Majesty*." I hiss.

"That's not why I—"

"Sorry that I was assaulted in *your* palace. Perhaps if you hadn't taken me from my home, it wouldn't have happened," I spit out, too angry and upset to hold the words back.

His eyes darken. "I think you have no idea what position you'd be in right now had I not taken you from Avantra."

"Oh yes. Because I'm much safer in a palace full of vampires who'd love nothing more than to drain me, without another human for hundreds of miles around."

He snarls. "The vampire staff in this palace wouldn't dream of hurting you, I trust all of them with my life—save for the Lords who I *have* to entertain for political reasons. And there are humans in the next wing of the palace!"

What?

He sighs.

"What is that supposed to mean?" I ask harshly. My mind conjuring rooms filled with living blood bags.

"It means, Olwyn, that there are human staff here. Working, living, thriving."

I shake my head. "I don't believe you."

"You can meet them."

Humans. Living here, in this palace. The idea is so foreign, so contrary to everything I've been told, that it feels like a punch to the gut.

"Why haven't I seen them before now?" I demand. "Because they're nothing more than blood bags?"

He sneers. "Don't be so crass. It's because I didn't want to overwhelm or confuse you so soon. I wanted to ease you into how different things are. How much you've been abused and brainwashed."

"My parents never abused me," I say in outrage.

Never.

His gaze flashes furiously. "I think you are blinded by the conditions you were kept in. If I hadn't arrived, you would have continued to weaken, kept from good food and light until you started to wither." The thought alone is outrageous, and yet… there's a sliver of doubt, a nagging question that's been there since the moment Altair took me from Avantra, but before it can flare into something more, he continues. "Something that would have pleased the king and queen immensely."

I jerk back, pulling the dagger with me.

It is a mistake.

The dagger is out of my hand before I even realise it, Altair's grip firm yet oddly gentle as he places it on the bedside table. I feel the loss of that small weapon acutely, like the last vestige of control slipping away. He's too close now, his presence overwhelming, but instead of backing away, I hold my ground.

"If I was kept from good food, it was only because the vampire kings are the ones who stop Avantra being fed!" I accuse him.

He laughs darkly. "More lies. Are these lies you tell yourself? Because you don't want to acknowledge what has clearly been right in front of your face? Or are these stories that have been ingrained in you from a young age?"

"You have no fucking clue what you are talking about! My parents wouldn't treat me like that!"

"But they did!" he roars, his face coming to inches within mine.

I blink.

What is he talking about?

Altair's anger flares, but beneath it, I see something else—a deep-seated frustration, maybe even guilt. His face is a mask of control, but his eyes… his eyes betray a conflict, something that he's desperately trying to hide.

Why does he care so much about what I believe? What's driving him to protect me, to keep me safe even as he keeps me in the dark? For a moment, I almost feel sorry for him, but then I remember who he is— what he's done.

"Don't you ever wonder why your parents didn't wither and lose weight as you had? Didn't you ever stop and consider the fact that they were keeping food from you? To weaken your access to your magic."

I shake my head... even if he has a point. My father was gluttonous, and often drunk off ale and wine I did not see. There were… inconsistencies. I push the thought away, refusing to let it take root. But the seed of doubt has been planted, and it's growing, no matter how hard I try to ignore it.

"They kept you weak. They kept you controlled."

"That is a lie," I sob, realising I am crying, but he continues.

"They kept you hidden and away from anyone who would have stood up to take care of you, because they wanted you weak."

"You lie!" I scream in his face, tears streaming down my face. "If this is true, why haven't you told me before now? Why leave me in this palace by myself the night you took me?"

His eyes soften, like he has come to a realisation I have yet not. "I knew you would be looked after, more than in your old home."

"This is not my home!"

Why does he look hurt? "This is more of a home than you had with them! Whether you want it to be or not. You have never looked healthier, and you are starting to get stronger."

"Only because you want to use me for my magic."

He laughs again, the sound cold and cruel. "If that is genuinely what you believe, you might as well take that dagger and draw it across my throat to shut me up. Because nothing I say will make you believe me." His fingers run through his hair in frustration, his voice soft but firm. "I know I've taken you from everything familiar, but this isn't about cruelty.

There are reasons, personal and complex, that you may not yet understand."

His words cut deep, but the pain they bring isn't just from the accusation—it's from the gnawing doubt that has been growing inside me since he came back. Why hasn't he killed me? Fed from me? Could everything I've believed be twisted? But no—this is Altair. The vampire who tore me from my home. How could I ever trust him? Yet, the honesty in his voice, the way he looks at me… I hate that a small part of me wants to hear him out.

"You say that, but all I see is that you've ripped me from my home and thrown me into a world I don't belong in."

Altair sighs deeply, turning away to stare out the window, the moonlight casting shadows on his face. The sight of it looks like an image made by a master painter, and I must stop my breath hitching at the sight,

It's cruel that someone could be that beautiful.

"I can't explain everything right now. Some truths are too dangerous to reveal too soon."

That's bullshit.

"So, I'm just supposed to accept that you've upended my life with no explanation? Just for some diluted magic that runs in my veins, but I can't use. Is this about Casius?" My voice trembles.

His shoulders slump, eyes closing briefly. "I wish I could tell you everything, but there are forces at play that go beyond what you see. What I can promise is that my actions are not driven by malice." He turns back, his gaze locking onto mine with what looks like a mix of regret and earnestness. "If you knew everything, you might understand why this was necessary."

I tilt my head. "And when can I know? When will you trust me enough to tell me?"

"In time. I need you to trust that I'm trying to protect more than just myself in this. Trust is not given lightly, but it is earned. I hope to earn yours by proving that my intentions, however misguided they may seem now, are for the greater good."

I take a measured breath, actually feeling grateful we are having this conversation. He genuinely seems to feel like keeping me in the dark is for my own good. "And what if I can't trust you? What if I can't see past the way you've treated me?"

"Then I must ask for patience. I hope you can reflect on the fact that whilst I did take you, I have never intentionally hurt you. I have not degraded you, demanded much from you or fed from you. And I never will."

Why do his words sound like the truth?

"I am willing to show you through my actions that your well-being is important to me, even if the full story remains untold for now."

My fingers fidget with the sheet covering my legs as I look away, a little bit scared of the intensity in his eyes. "Actions speak louder than words."

Altair nods, a small, almost sad smile tugging at the corners of his mouth. "I'll do my best to show you that despite the harshness of my decisions, I have reasons that might, in time, make sense. For now, I hope you can see the care underlying them." He reaches out again, this time gently placing his hand on my shoulder. I don't jerk away from the movement.

"Can you show me anything now?" The request shocks me as much as it shocks him. I don't fully believe what he has told me. But if he can offer proof, I will consider it.

"I can't do that," he says, looking away, his jaw tightening. It's not just concern in his eyes—there's something else, something darker that he's trying to keep hidden. Is it fear? Regret? The silence between us stretches, and I wonder what secrets he's guarding so fiercely that he'd rather risk my mistrust than reveal them.

"Why not?" My voice lowers.

He looks at me, head tilting as he considers me. It's hard not to feel self-conscious under his gaze. His fingers brush the healing bruises on my neck, and I force myself to stay still, to not flinch. The touch is tender, almost reverent, but it's also a reminder of how easily he could hurt me if he chose to. His gaze locks onto mine, and for a moment, it's like he's searching for something—some sign that I trust him, or maybe that I don't. The space between us feels charged, like the air before a storm, and I can't decide if I want to lean closer or pull away.

"Because I won't do anything to put you in a position where you could get hurt again."

"Because you need me." I nod.

"No, Olwyn," his eyes pin mine. "Because I want you."

My eyes widen and he coughs.

"Uh, I want you to be safe."

I huff. His full lips part for a moment, before closing in a small smile.

"But if I want you to trust me, I need to trust you with some truths too." He nods, although he seems reluctant.

"Truths?" I ask, almost too eagerly, as if waiting for the other boot to drop.

"I will allow the human staff to go about their usual duties, and I have a plan to prove that it isn't my kind causing all the neglect. But you must do as I say."

I raise an eyebrow, my gaze narrowing. "I want to speak with them," I say, cutting him off before he can finish. "I want to talk to the human staff directly, openly. If you want me to believe you, then I need to hear it from them."

He meets my gaze for a long moment, his eyes softening as if he's finally seeing the weight of what he's kept hidden. Finally, he exhales slowly, almost as if the words are a weight lifted off his chest. "That's a valid request. I'll make sure they're available for you."

"I regret not showing you this from the start," he admits, his voice quieter now, a hint of vulnerability threading through it. "Maybe if I had, you could have seen me as something more than a monster. The humans live here, too. I should have trusted you with that from the beginning."

I don't know what to do with his admission, it so at odds with how I thought this conversation would go.

"All right," is all I say.

"Give me two weeks," he asks. "Two weeks to continue your training myself. Stick to it and I'll *show* you."

That didn't sound too bad. I wanted to continue my training anyways. I didn't want to be weak again.

I nod. "Deal."

I've just willingly made a pact with a vampire, one who claims he's trying to protect me, but I can't shake the feeling that I've stepped onto a path I might not be able to turn back from. Better the demon you know, I remind myself. But what if that demon is more dangerous than I ever imagined?

CHAPTER FOURTEEN
Altair

The soft murmur of voices drifts through the hallway as I step into the morning light.

The staff are already bustling about, preparing for the day. A few humans I know by name offer nervous glances my way, wondering why the change. They've been restricted from certain parts of the palace for too long, avoiding Olwyn's side of the palace.

But now, that changes. I promised her I'd show her the truth.

I stride toward the kitchens, the cool stone underfoot barely making a sound as I enter the wide, sunlit room. The scent of bread baking fills the air, and various members of the staff—vampire and human alike—are already working, side by side.

Crista, my head of staff, spots me the moment I walk in, her sharp eyes flicking toward me with a readiness I admire. For a human, she commands respect. The vampires under her charge, though naturally more powerful, heed her as if she were their superior. It's how I run my house. Rank through merit, not strength.

"Your Majesty," she greets me, bowing her head slightly. "Is everything in order for today?"

I give a brief nod. "It is. But we're making a change." My eyes sweep over the human servants who pause in their work, their postures stiff with caution.

Crista raises an eyebrow, but says nothing, waiting for me to continue.

"The human staff," I say, my voice carrying through the room, "can all return to their usual duties. There's no need for you all to keep your distance any longer."

A ripple of surprise passes through the humans, a few glancing nervously at one another. They've become accustomed to staying away from the eastern wing, away from Olwyn. But now… now, she needs to see it. To understand.

One of the older human servants clears his throat. "Thank you, Your Majesty."

I nod, acknowledging the sentiment. "You've all been more than patient. I appreciate that."

I turn back to Crista. "Make sure the human staff are fully integrated today. Let them move freely throughout the palace."

Her brow furrows slightly, but she nods. "As you wish. Anything in particular you want her to be shown, Your Majesty?"

"No," I reply. "I want them to go about their usual duties without hesitation. Let her observe. The less pressure, the better."

Crista purses her lips, considering my words before nodding in understanding. "I'll make sure everything goes smoothly."

"Good," I say, then step closer, lowering my voice so only she can hear. "I want you to make yourself scarce for the day. If she feels too watched, she might withdraw. I need her to feel comfortable enough to see what's truly happening here, without the feeling of being managed." Crista is known to be… stern. Perhaps too much. But she gets things done. Today, however, I don't want her demanding nature to be too much for Olwyn. I think introducing Olwyn to the staff—who will be more relaxed without Crista around—would make this easier.

Crista's sharp gaze meets mine, and though she's not one to leave her post easily, she understands. "Understood. I'll find something to occupy myself with elsewhere."

I nod, my thoughts already turning inward as she leaves the room. The clatter of dishes and quiet conversation resume behind me, but it's distant now, fading into the background as I focus on the conversation I had with Olwyn the night before.

Her nightmare still lingers in my mind, the way she had thrashed and cried out, her pain so raw, so real. It had torn through me like a physical wound. And yet… when I entered her room, the way she held that dagger to my throat—brave, terrified but refusing to show weakness—it stirred something deeper in me. Her strength. Her resilience. Even after what happened in her chambers with that assassin, she hasn't broken. She's not cowering in her room, nor is she looking for pity. She's fighting—internally, externally. She's refusing to let fear define her.

That forest fire in her eyes was still there. A refusal to be a victim, even when everything in her world seems to be falling apart. It takes a certain kind of courage to keep going after something like that. Not everyone would.

I promised her I'd show her the truth. That this world—her world—isn't what she's been taught to fear. But I also told her that she had to give me two weeks. Two weeks to keep training, to stay focused, to not let fear rule her decisions.

And she agreed.

That, more than anything, tells me there's hope for her to see things differently. Despite the doubt, the anger, the fear, she's willing to trust me. Just a little. That's enough—for now.

I walk out of the kitchens, my thoughts drifting back to her again. Last night, after our talk, I couldn't sleep. Every time I closed my eyes, I kept hearing her breathing, seeing the shadows in her eyes from that nightmare, even if I could hear her settled heart beating in the room next to mine. It's not just the attack that haunts her, it's her entire life up until now. Every lie, every fear that's been fed to her since she was a child. Her mind is a battleground, and she's fighting enemies that don't exist—at least, not in the way she believes they do.

As I make my way through the palace, heading toward the water gardens, I think about how hard it must be for her. It's no wonder she's struggling. But she's strong. And if anyone can survive this, it's her.

She's not like anyone else. I remember that.

And maybe… just maybe, she's starting to remember it too.

The most dangerous thing in this world to have is hope.

CHAPTER FIFTEEN
Olwyn

Altair stayed true to his word.

He arranged for me to meet with the members of staff in charge of planning the ball for King Sovran's arrival.

The *human* members of staff.

I never really knew what planning a ball entailed. Since my parents kept me hidden, I had never attended one back home. I used to sneak out though, like the times I had into the city to explore. I always remained in the upper levels, watching secretly as couples danced, and people drank. I always wondered how my parents could afford to throw such events when our people and I were hungry. After being told food had to be rationed to last.

Yet our guests drank like there was an infinite amount of wine.

The guests fornicated upon the lavish rugs. Soft flesh on display for the whole room to see.

It reminded me of Altair's words, and I started to question everything.

Sera and Thalia—two of the *human* members of staff that I can engage with now—really take their role seriously. I've never seen so many different samples of fabric, flowers or different types of crockery.

There are other staff in here, measuring various things and pointing around the walls. They are vampires.

It astounds me that they are interacting together without malice. Without any fear or anger.

It's a little overwhelming if I'm honest. And I haven't gathered any valuable information from it yet at all.

Other than what dress the ladies want to put me in.

"It has to be this colour," Sera pulls out a swatch of deep emerald green. "It will go beautifully with her eyes." She looks at Thalia like it's the most obvious option in the world. She smiles at me softly. "You really do have stunning eyes."

"Thank you," I mumble.

"It has to be this one. Because… well it just does." Thalia grins, holding out a piece of charcoal black silk. There are tiny shimmers of silver throughout the fabric, and it looks like starlight.

"I-I really like the black," I mutter, hating the way Sera pouts as she fidgets with the end of her dark brown braid.

Maybe I preferred it when I was mostly by myself.

"But how about you pick the jewellery I wear with it?" I offer, and Sera smiles.

"Definitely. Have you decided which crown you're going to wear?" She asks.

"Crown?" I ask.

They share a look and then give me a similar pointed expression.

"You'll need to wear a crown, Your Majesty," Thalia says, and Sera nods eagerly next to her, her blue eyes wide. "This may be a joyous occasion, but it's still a show."

"A show?"

"To King Sovran," Sera tells me. "King Altair will want to show King Sovran how united you are in your marriage. How you will be the power couple to end the war."

I want to laugh at that. If that was ever Altair's goal, he certainly hasn't told me that. But maybe that's what everyone thinks.

"Why do we care what King Sovran thinks?" I ask.

Thalia laughs, brushing her long red hair away from her face.

Sera looks at me with what could be pity in her brown eyes. "Everyone knows of the prophecy. If Altair hadn't asked for your hand in marriage, no doubt Casius would have found you and claimed you like the savage he is."

United. That's what Sera and Thalia believe my marriage to Altair represents—a union of humans and vampires, a beacon of hope. But how can I be the symbol they want me to be when I can barely hold myself together? They clearly don't know the truth—that this marriage was forced upon me, that I was dragged from my home and thrust into a world I don't understand. And I wonder why Altair hasn't divulged that. Hasn't boasted about kidnapping the human queen as a show of power.

"What is his court like? I've been told he's a savage. But news wasn't always trustworthy where I came from," I say. I have heard whispers of King Casius Sovran whilst living back with my parents, but nothing solid other than horror stories. If I can learn more about the rival vampire king, I will—especially if I am going to meet him.

Thalia looks around, making sure we are alone before leaning forward over the fabric covered table. "I heard his lovers never leave his chambers alive once he's done with them, but women still throw themselves at his feet for a chance of one night with him."

My eyes widen.

Sera scoffs. "Those stories are obviously exaggerated," she says before sighing longingly. "I'd throw myself at his feet for one night with him."

"Sera!" Thalia swats her arm.

"What?" Sera laughs. "I heard he likes knife play. Don't shame me for my kinks."

I blink, looking between the two.

Thalia looks at Sera, and back at me.

"Oh!" Sera blushes. "Sorry, Your Majesty. Ignore me. I need to stop reading those romance novels."

I just nod.

The conversation shifts, but my thoughts linger on what they've said about King Casius. My heart beats faster at the idea of meeting him, an undercurrent of fear mixed with a strange curiosity. I imagine his palace, dark and foreboding, and wonder what it would be like to face a man with such a fearsome reputation.

But then I always imagined Altair to be a monster, and he hasn't done anything too monstrous towards me… yet.

As I watch the intricate lacework being sewn into the tablecloths, I realise that this ball is more than just a celebration—it's a stage. A stage where I'll be expected to perform, to prove my worth as Altair's queen, to show the kingdom who I am.

What have I been forced into?

Sera and Thalia bring out a large wooden jewellery box, filled with shimmering pieces. Diamonds, rubies, emeralds—all glittering temptations. They debate over which would best compliment the dress, holding each piece up to my neck. I can see my reflection in the polished silver of a mirror across the room, adorned like a doll for display.

As they finally settle on a set of emerald earrings and a matching necklace, Sera's words about the prophecy echo in my mind. I wonder what my parents would think if they saw me now. Would they be proud that I have become the sacrifice that has saved their city? Or horrified at the role I'm being forced to play?

Do they even care that their extra mouth to feed is gone? Was feeding me ever really a burden? Could Altair be right?

The room starts to feel stifling, the burden of the crown I'll wear at the ball pressing down on me even though it hasn't been placed on my head yet. I take a deep breath, trying to steady myself. This all seems like a test, a performance where I must play the part perfectly. Even though I asked to be a part of it.

But if what they say is true, what Altair is trying to do is sow peace between vampires and humans… For my sake, and for the sake of those who still believe in peace, perhaps I should… try?

"Are you all right, Your Majesty?" Thalia asks, her voice gentle.

"Yes," I reply, forcing a smile. "Just a lot to take in."

She nods, her eyes understanding. "We'll make sure everything is perfect. You'll be the most stunning queen anyone has ever seen."

As they continue to fuss over the details, I steal a glance out of the window, where the twilight sky is painted in hues of purple and gold. Somewhere out there, King Casius is preparing for his arrival, and I can't help but wonder what fate has in store for me when we finally meet.

I wonder if these peace talks will result in something positive for all of us.

I wonder what Casius will make of me.

I wish I could tell her everything, but first I need her to trust me.

CHAPTER SIXTEEN
Olwyn

The shadows stretch longer as dusk settles over the palace, the warm light from the sconces casting flickering patterns on the stone walls.

I find myself wandering through the corridors, lost in thought, two royal guards walking silently behind me. The conversation with Sera and Thalia plays on a loop in my mind, their words about King Casius intertwining with my own fears and curiosities.

As I approach the dining hall, the scent of roasted meat and fresh bread fills the air, my stomach rumbling with hunger as they momentarily distract me. The guards who have been escorting me push open the heavy oak doors and I step inside. Altair and Iolas are already seated, deep in conversation. Altair's dark hair falls across his forehead, his sharp features tense in the candlelight. Iolas, in contrast, is more relaxed, waving his hands about as he talks excitedly.

Both their gazes dart to me as I approach. I smile lightly, taking my seat. Altair continues to talk to Iolas but leans over to fill my plate with a variety of food. As I pick at it, the earlier conversation keeps intruding, making it difficult to focus on the present. Altair and Iolas exchange glances, but I eat, my brow falling more and more as I remember the conversation with Thalia and Sera earlier.

Altair and Iolas converse back and forth, the latter's eyes drifting over me curiously—probably wondering why I am being quiet.

Altair apparently has the same thought. "Everything all right, Olwyn?" He asks as Iolas takes a mouthful of his wine.

"What's knife play?" I ask, my head tilting.

Iolas chokes, dribbling the drink down his white shirt before coughing. "Fuck me," he laughs.

Altair stares at me wide eyed, the skin of his cheeks and neck darkening. He clears his throat. "Um, who have you been talking to?"

Oh no.

Is this something that will get Sera and Thalia into trouble? "I overheard some of the staff talking," I quickly take a bite of my food and Altair's eyes narrow at me.

"Hmmm," his lips purse, and he meets Iolas's gaze.

Iolas is enjoying this. He looks positively delighted.

"Do you want to explain?" Altair asks him, and he sounds uncomfortable. I look between the two. Iolas crosses his thick arms over his wine-stained shirt.

"No, no. I'll leave this one to you, Your Majesty." Iolas's grin is wicked, I can't help but notice the flush on Altair's cheeks, the way his fingers fidget with the laces of his shirt. It's almost… human. And so endearing.

"It's a sex thing," is all he says. And bluntly, like he needed to say it as quickly as possible.

But I'm now more intrigued.

"A sex *thing*?" I ask. Iolas chuckles, and a muscle in Altair's jaw ticks, before he nods.

I shake my head pointedly at him, wanting more information.

He huffs exasperated. "It's when someone uses a blade during… *intimacy*, to elicit pleasure."

"Cutting?!" I ask, horrified.

"No, that's blood play," Iolas chimes in.

"Iolas!" Altair's eyes snap to him, before meeting my wide-eyed gaze. "No cutting. Just scratching or using one to remove clothes. They use it to provide sensual stimulation."

I look away from his intense eyes. My mind drifts off on its own, uncontrolled, remembering when Altair brushed the edge of my dagger over my hand against this very table. I press my thighs together, feeling a heat build between my legs, one that I'm not sure how to handle or even acknowledge at this moment in time.

Iolas sucks in a breath, and I see Altair stiffen, his eyes darkening.

"Oh," I say, realising they have been waiting for me to respond. I glance at Iolas, curious after his amusement at the question. "Is that something you've done?"

Iolas's face goes bright red. "Uh, not usually my sort of *thing*."

For some reason that feels like it makes sense, and then I think about asking him what his 'thing' is. My gaze moves to Altair, and I have to school my expression as I see his black eyes.

"And you?" I ask, suddenly regretful as I hear how breathy my own voice sounds.

Altair pulls at his laces once again. "Why?" he asks, his voice rough.

I shake my head. "I just hadn't heard of it. Curious, I guess."

Iolas shifts in his seat, with a hoarse laugh. "Innocent little witch."

I glare at him. "Who said I was innocent?"

The shadows in the room deepen, pooling around Altair like they're drawn to him, feeding off the tension in the air. The flickering light from the sconces casts long, wavering patterns on the stone walls, making the room feel smaller, more intimate. It's as if the palace itself is holding its breath, waiting to see what happens next.

I look at Iolas, noting his wide eyes and now pale face.

"I'm just gonna—" He trails off, jerking a thumb over his shoulder as he makes to stand from his seat.

"Sit," commands Altair, and I've never heard his voice so low, but his shadow-filled eyes have not left my face, which I can feel flame under his scrutiny.

"If my dear wife feels comfortable enough to ask if I've fucked anyone whilst using a blade, then surely she can share more about her own *experiences.*"

Oh my.

CHAPTER SEVENTEEN

Altair

I see the panic flicker across her face, and it only stokes the fire in my chest.

The shadows feed off my emotions, swirling tighter, darker, as they creep closer to her legs. I want her to squirm. I want her to feel the same burn I'm feeling.

"T-that's really none of your business," she stammers, her voice trembling.

I lean forward, my eyes locking onto hers, the darkness in them swirling like a storm. "Oh, I think it is, love," I whisper, my voice rough. "After all, you are my queen and wife, so perhaps I should know who has spent time between those lovely thighs of yours."

Her gasp is delicious, before she clamps her mouth shut. I glance quickly at Iolas, who stares pointedly at the table, his face tight with discomfort. But I don't care. I want to know. I need to know.

"Well?" I ask again, my voice low and dangerous. A tendril of shadow slips higher, brushing the back of her knee.

"It was the baker's boy!" she blurts out, her leg jerking as the shadows retreat slightly.

I narrow my eyes, taking in her flushed face, her wide eyes. "The baker's boy?" I repeat, disbelief colouring my voice.

Her cheeks flush even deeper, and she nods quickly. "It was years ago, when I used to sneak into the city after dark. He never knew who I really was. I'm assuming he still doesn't."

I feel Iolas shift beside me, but I don't look at him. My focus is entirely on her—on the way her breath quickens, the way her chest rises and falls with each rapid inhale. My shadows retreat slightly, giving her some space, but they linger just beneath the surface, waiting.

"Did he look after you?" Iolas asks, his voice soft, serious.

Olwyn blinks, her throat working as she swallows. "He did. He was gentle."

My jaw tightens, the shadows curling possessively around me, but I force them back. Past the jealousy, I am glad there was someone who was her choice. Someone who didn't take something else from her. I force myself to breathe.

"Very well," I say, though my voice is strained. "He may live."

Iolas snorts, but quickly quiets Olwyn glares at me, her defiance sparking again.

"He was gentle *many* times," she says with a coy smile.

The room goes deathly quiet. Iolas's laugh fades as I stare at her, my nostrils flaring, shadows flickering wildly around me.

"Many times?" I repeat, my voice soft, dangerously so.

"Yes," she nods, her eyes locked on mine, and something inside me snaps.

I stand abruptly, the force of my movement causing the table to shake, the cutlery rattling in the sudden stillness. Iolas murmurs my name under his breath, but I don't care. I'm done with this conversation. I'm done with her testing me, though I know it's my jealousy riding me.

"I will not have my queen reminiscing about another man's touch," I say, my voice firm, my body rigid. The shadows ripple in response, moving faster now.

Olwyn meets my gaze, the fire in her own burning, but I can see the flicker of uncertainty in her eyes. She's testing me, pushing boundaries she doesn't even realise are there.

"It was before I even knew you."

"That does not matter," I snap, taking a step towards her, my mind irrational. "We are together now, and I will not share you with a man in your memories."

The fire blazes in her eyes, and I know I sound ridiculous.

"You asked!" She shoots back, not even flinching.

"You will forget him, Olwyn," I say, leaning down and taking a gentle hold of her chin, my heart skipping at touching her. "I want you to forget every touch, every whisper. Do you understand?"

She wants to fight me. I can see it. And that hunter instinct inside is screaming for it.

Fight me. Please, fight me.

Her voice comes out steady, but fierce. "No. You may have some control over my present. But you don't control my past. So, if I want to, I'll hold onto those *fond* memories closely."

She holds my gaze, refusing to move even when a shade tickles over the skin of her wrist.

The tension thickens between us, but something sharp claws at my insides, cutting through the fire of my anger. And I know my blue eye has darkened.

Her eyes widen, like she's come to a realisation, and she leans in slightly, tilting her head. "You're jealous," she says, her voice low but clear, daring me to deny it.

And I can't. I find I don't want to. I want her to know that I am jealous.

That I crave that part of her. Crave her against me, under me, riding me.

Rein it in.

My grip on her chin tightens slightly, but the flicker in her eyes tells me she knows she has hit the mark.

Jealousy. Pure and raw.

And now she sees that I want her.

"Jealous?" I repeat, my voice low and tight, the words edged with something raw. My gaze drops to her lips, lingering there for a moment too long before snapping back to her eyes, my jaw clenching and teeth aching. "Yes. I'm jealous."

I can feel the desire coursing through me, stronger than ever. It's a dangerous mix of jealousy, possessiveness, and lust, all swirling together, threatening to overwhelm my control. I'm barely holding on, the shadows feeding off my emotions, growing darker, hungrier.

I let go of her chin, my hand dropping to my side as I take a step back. She watches me, her eyes wide, uncertain, and something about the way she looks at me—so vulnerable, so unsure—makes me want to pull her back into my arms, to reassure her that she is mine and no one else's.

But I don't.

Not yet.

"May I be excused?" Her voice is steady, but I can hear the tremble beneath the surface. "I'd like to return to my chambers."

I don't stop her. I know I want to, but I need space, too. Space to cool off, to clear my head before I do something rash. Something I can't take back.

"You don't need to ask, Olwyn," I say, my voice a little too rough, but I force myself to stay composed, to hold back the storm brewing inside me.

She nods and stands, giving a quick glance to Iolas, who looks just as conflicted as I feel. He offers her a small smile, reassuring her in a way that I can't right now. Not when I'm on the verge of losing control.

Two new guards—ones I have chosen myself and trust to escort her properly into her room—peel away from the double doors to join her. As she turns to leave, I can't help myself.

"And Olwyn," I call after her.

She stops, turning to look at me, her eyes filled with confusion and something else… something raw.

"If you find yourself craving a touch a little less gentle," I say, my voice dropping to a low growl, "you need only ask."

Her eyes widen, a flush creeping up her neck and into her cheeks, but she doesn't say anything. She just nods once, her lips parting slightly before she turns and leaves the room.

The moment she's gone, I feel the weight of Iolas's gaze on me.

"Al…" he begins, his voice low, cautious. I can hear the warning in his tone, the concern.

I don't look at him.

Instead, I take a deep breath, forcing the shadows to retreat, pulling them back inside me, reigning in the darkness that still claws at the edges of my control. I can't afford to lose it now. Not when I'm so close to unravelling everything.

"What the fuck are you doing, Al?" Iolas finally asks, his voice tight with frustration. He doesn't sound angry, though. Just... worried.

I turn to him, meeting his gaze, and for the first time, I see it. He knows what I'm feeling. The guilt. The shame. The regret. He knows I'm torn between wanting to protect her and wanting to claim her. And he knows that it's tearing me apart.

But I don't have the answers. Not now. Not when everything is so tangled, so messy. When my own feelings are a knot I can't seem to untangle.

"I can't lose her," I admit, my voice barely more than a whisper.

Iolas's eyes soften, his posture relaxing slightly as he takes a seat across from me. "We're not going to lose her, Al," he says quietly. "But you've gotta be careful. She's still figuring things out. She's… fragile."

Fragile.

The word grates against my nerves, and the shadows flicker in response, like they're reacting to the idea of her being anything less than strong. Anything less than resilient.

"She's not fragile," I snap, my voice harsher than I intend. "She's stronger than you think."

"I know that," Iolas says quickly, holding up his hands in surrender. "But she's also human, Al. And you've gotta remember that. You can't treat her like one of us. When she finds out about Atha and everything… it's gonna be a lot."

I run a hand through my hair, frustration gnawing at my insides. I know he's right, but it doesn't make this any easier.

"I just…" I trail off, unsure of how to articulate what I'm feeling. How do I explain that I want to protect her, but I also want her? That I crave her in ways that scare me because it's not just about her blood, it's about her—her strength, her fire, her defiance.

Iolas watches me for a long moment, then sighs, leaning back in his chair. "You're in deep, aren't you?"

I don't answer. I don't need to. He knows.

"It's because I remember," I whisper, my mind drifting back.

Bright green eyes, a blinding white light. Destruction everywhere. For a moment, there's only silence between us, until I shake the memories away.

The shadows have calmed, retreating into the corners of the room, no longer feeding off my emotions. But I can feel them waiting, always ready to surge forward at the slightest provocation.

Iolas stands, placing a hand on my shoulder. "Just… don't push her too hard, too fast…"

"I won't," I cut him off, my voice firm. I won't let that happen. I can't.

He gives me a nod, his hand squeezing my shoulder briefly before he turns to leave. But before he steps out of the room, he pauses.

"By the way," he says, glancing back at me with a smirk. "If you ever decide to try that knife play thing... let me know how it goes."

I glare at him, but he just chuckles and disappears through the door, leaving me alone with my thoughts.

And the shadows.

I sink into the chair, resting my head in my hands.

All I can think about is her.

Olwyn.

My queen.

My wife.

The desire... it's overwhelming. It's like an ache that never goes away, a hunger that deepens the more I see her, the more I hear her voice, the more she *exists* in the same world as me. She's everything I never knew I needed, and it terrifies me. Because I know if I fall too deeply, too quickly, I'll lose myself in her. And once I do, I'll be *lost*.

I'm not afraid of *wanting* her. I'm afraid of what it will do to me when I realise I can't live without her. That if I let myself care, let myself get too close, she'll tear my heart out the moment she knows the truth—or worse, she'll be *taken* from me.

Her scent drives me mad. It makes me lose control.

CHAPTER EIGHTEEN

Olwyn

It always surprises me how soft underfoot the mat in the training room is… considering how many times I have been thrown onto it—it feels a lot harder.

Iolas stands opposite me, a playful grin on his face. His stance is relaxed, his body language inviting and teasing.

"Ready?" he asks, twirling a small throwing knife between his fingers.

I nod, trying to ignore the fluttering in my stomach. "Always."

He laughs, a sound full of warmth and mischief as usual. I'm just grateful he's not bringing up the knife play talk. "Good. Let's see if you remember what I taught you last time."

We begin to spar, the clinking of our blades filling the air. Iolas is quick for his size—even though he's tuning his vampire speed down—his movements fluid and graceful despite his broad frame, and I really do need to concentrate to keep up. He moves with the ease of a predator, circling me with an almost playful lightness. His strikes come swift and precise, yet there's a teasing quality to them, as if he's testing my limits, pushing me to react faster, to counter with more force.

His eyes gleam with amusement every time I manage to block his strike, his grin widening as he effortlessly evades my counters. His confidence only spurs me on.

I can't shake the thought that I need to be better—stronger. Especially after what happened in my room. Iolas's blade glints in the sunlight as he steps forward, quick and sure. I counter, muscles burning with the effort, but he's faster—always a step ahead. I pivot, blocking his strike, but he's already moving, the smirk on his face widening as he presses me back.

He circles me, his movements a blend of ease and command, and I'm reminded how easily he could overpower me if he wanted to. The realisation sends a thrill through me. I'm not just sparring with Iolas—I'm testing my limits, seeing how far I can push before he pushes back.

After a few rounds, he steps back, a sheen of sweat glistening on his brow. With a quick, practised motion, he grabs the hem of his shirt and pulls it over his head, revealing the broad expanse of his chest. His muscles ripple under the sunlight drifting through the windows, the ridges and planes of his torso defined with the strength of a warrior.

My mouth dries, the words I was about to say slipping from my mind. His skin glows with a faint sheen of sweat, highlighting every contour of his powerful frame. The playful grin never leaves his face, as if he knows the effect he's just had on me, and it only makes my heartbeat faster.

And he can hear it.

Cheeky bastard.

"You play dirty," I narrow my eyes at him.

Iolas's grin widens. He twirls the blade in his hand, taking a step closer. "Only when it gets me what I want," he purrs.

"And what if I did the same?" I tilt my head, enjoying the way his full lips fall a little as he thinks about it.

He stops twirling the blade, gripping it tightly as his gaze locks onto mine, the playful glint in his eyes replaced by something else as he growls slightly. His voice drops.

"Careful, little witch." He steps even closer, the heat radiating off his bare skin palpable in the narrow space between us. "You might not be familiar with knife play but keep teasing me like that and we'll play a little game of our own."

There it is.

My breath catches in my throat, the charged air between us sparking with a heat that has nothing to do with training. Iolas's eyes darken, his gaze dropping to my lips for just a second before sweeping over the rest of me, lingering where my pulse beats visibly at my neck.

I can't move. I don't want to.

What is going on with me lately?

My heart pounds so loudly, I'm sure he can hear it, and the space between us feels almost unbearably tight. Then, almost as if waking from a trance, Iolas blinks rapidly and steps back, his expression twisting into something between frustration and restraint. He swipes a hand over his face, shaking his head as if to clear it, and I feel the cool rush of air fill the space between us once more, breaking the spell.

"Enough of this," he says, his voice gruff as he forces a smirk back onto his lips, though it doesn't quite reach his eyes. "Come on, Olwyn. Another round. Let's see if you can keep up."

I nod, swallowing the lump in my throat, and take my stance, willing my heart to steady itself. But beneath my focus, there's a simmering awareness of his every movement, a pulse of something more than just adrenaline. I push it down, reminding myself that this is just training... even if it doesn't feel that way.

"You're getting better," he compliments, his eyes sparkling with amusement.

"Trying to flatter me?" I retort, blocking his strike and pushing him back. "Distract me?"

"Is it working?" he asks, his voice a purr that sends a shiver down my spine. I tighten my grip on the blade, refusing to let him see the effect he has on me. I meet his gaze, my breath steadying as I force a smirk.

"You wish." It is working.

The door to the training room opens, and Altair strides in. His presence immediately changes the atmosphere, and I straighten, the air growing thick, especially after dinner last night. He watches us for a moment, his expression unreadable.

Why do I feel guilty?

"Iolas," Altair says, his voice calm. "I'll take over from here."

Iolas gives a mock salute before brushing his hair out of his eyes, stepping back with a wink at me. "Good luck, little witch. Don't miss me too much."

I barely have time to process his words before Altair steps onto the mat, a set of small throwing knives in his hand. His eyes meet mine as he pulls one out, discarding the others and I feel a shiver run down my spine.

But I must see this through. He'll only show me more if I keep up my side of the deal.

"Let's see what you've learned," he says, his tone challenging.

We begin to spar, and it seems so much easier in my training gear now. Or perhaps I am getting stronger. I notice the difference with every session.

Altair spars differently. His movements are precise and calculated, his strikes carrying more weight and intention. But he glides through the space like a dancer, or a large feline, like it's only natural to him. He doesn't hold back, pushing me to my limits. Each time I manage to block his attack or dodge his knife, he presses harder, his eyes never leaving mine.

"You're holding back," he accuses, his voice low and intense.

"I'm not," I reply, panting slightly. "You're just better."

I am definitely holding back, always feeling unnerved in his presence. Scared to get too close, but now I can't for sure say why.

His lips curve into a small, predatory smile. "You can do better than this, love. Show me your strength. Or has your fragile human body reached its limits?"

Prick.

I grit my teeth, determined to prove myself. I throw my knife at him, but he dodges effortlessly, closing the distance between us. Before I can react, he sweeps my legs out from under me, knocking me onto my back. I gasp as the air is forced from my lungs.

Altair straddles me, pinning me to the mat. His weight makes me gasp, the heat of him penetrating my leathers and feeling like it soaks into my already warm skin. He holds a knife in his hand, spinning it in his hand as the blade glints in the dim light. "Pay attention," he instructs, his voice a low murmur. "You're not going to do any damage aiming where you are."

He drags the flat of the blade lightly over my skin, starting at my throat. The cold metal sends a shiver through me, and I feel the sharp contrast between the blade and the heat of his body above me. "This," he says, his voice barely more than a whisper, "is a prime point. A quick slice here with witchsilver, and it's over in seconds."

He moves the blade down to my collarbone, tracing a slow, deliberate line along the bone. "Here, the subclavian artery. A precise cut can incapacitate almost instantly." His eyes flick up to mine, watching my reaction closely.

My breath catches in my throat as he continues, the blade gliding down to my wrist, just above the sleeve of my leathers. He turns my hand palm-up, exposing the delicate skin.

"The radial artery," he explains, pressing the flat of the blade against my wrist. "Cutting here is effective, but slower. It takes time for the blood to drain."

I nod, my heart pounding in my chest. His touch is both electrifying and terrifying, and it reminds me of the power a vampire could have over me.

But he isn't done.

Altair shifts his weight slightly, and the blade moves to the inside of my elbow, over my clothes. "Another vulnerable point," he murmurs, the tip of the knife tracing where the vein rests underneath. "Easier to reach in close combat."

He continues down my body, the blade moving with practised ease. He slides it over my ribs, stopping just below my left breast and I inhale. "The heart," he says, his voice dropping even lower and fangs on show now. "A well-placed strike here will be fatal."

His words are sharp, precise, but it's the way he lingers, the way his eyes darken as he presses the blade to my skin, that makes my breath catch. This isn't just a lesson; it's a test, and I'm not sure if I'm passing or failing.

The knife trails down to my abdomen, circling around my navel. "The aorta runs deep here," he explains, his voice almost gentle. "A strike from below can reach it, but it's risky."

He presses the blade lightly against my thigh, just above my knee. Heat floods my body, and it takes all my willpower not to flinch. His eyes darken further, the blackness swirling with something I can't quite name.

Gods I am depraved.

He inhales and his eyes flood with black. "The femoral artery," he says roughly, his eyes never leaving mine. "Sever this, and they won't be able to stand, let alone fight."

I nod again, my breath coming in short, shallow gasps. I can't tell if the shiver running through me is from the blade or the way his eyes bore into mine. There's a thrill in learning these points of vulnerability, a rush of power that clashes with the fear simmering beneath the surface.

Last night's conversation rushes into my mind, making the heat between my thighs ten times worse. I hear a small sucked in gasp from somewhere in the room, and suddenly I'm acutely aware of Iolas's presence, his eyes on us. The thought sends another jolt through me—embarrassment, fear, I'm not sure which.

Altair's fingers grip my chin, tilting my head back slightly. He drags the blade back up to my throat, resting it against the pulse point just below my jaw. He is breathing heavily, his own face inches above mine. "Understand?" he asks, his voice a rough whisper, the blade steady against my throat.

"Yes," I say in a choked whisper.

"Good," he replies, his eyes dark and intense. "Remember these points, Olwyn. They could save your life."

"How do you know so much about anatomy?" I ask him, entirely too embarrassed by how breathy my voice sounds.

He smiles. "I have books from the human realm. Our bodies are basically the same. Although I heal faster."

"The more you know about your enemy, right?"

The smile fades slightly. "Right."

For a moment, we stay like that, the world narrowing down to just the two of us. Then, slowly, Altair pulls back, helping me to my feet. "You did well," he says, his tone softer now.

I glance at him, surprised by the note of concern in his voice. "Thank you," I reply.

Altair nods, his eyes lingering on mine for a moment longer before he steps back, clearing his throat as he catches Iolas's twinkling eye . "Good. I'll leave you both to it."

I watch him leave, my mind a whirlwind of thoughts and emotions. Iolas walks back over, eyeing me knowingly and giving me a cheeky grin. "Told you it would be a challenge."

"I think I'm up for it," I say, the words feeling like a promise to myself as much as a reply to Iolas.

Iolas laughs. "But is Al?"

Fuck, fuck, fuck.

CHAPTER NINETEEN
Olwyn

The throne room hums with quiet conversation, the distant sound of shuffling feet and the low murmur of voices echoing off the high stone walls.

I sit beside Altair, a step lower on my own seat. And though the grandeur of the room surrounds us, Altair's presence makes it feel less daunting.

Altair looks every bit the king—strong, composed, and regal in the way he carries himself—but there's a warmth in his face as he listens intently to the vampire kneeling before us. His hand rests loosely on the arm of his throne, his body angled slightly forward, giving the farmer his full attention.

The man's voice is steady, though there's a nervous tremor there, not because he's afraid of his king, but simply because it's Altair. He explains something about his crops, how the weather has been unkind further north, how despite his best efforts, the soil has been slow to recover.

Altair listens carefully, his dark eyes softening. He doesn't rush the man, doesn't interrupt. He lets him speak. When the farmer finishes, there's no awkward pause, no fear. Instead, Altair leans forward just slightly, his voice steady and full of understanding.

"Have you spoken with the master gardener?" he asks, his tone gentle but direct. "He's been working on improving soil conditions after the weather you've been having. I'll send him to you, and we'll make sure your land recovers."

The man smiles gratefully, nodding with confidence. "Thank you, Your Majesty. The gardener has helped before. He's a good man."

Altair's lips curve into a small, knowing smile. "He is. We're lucky to have him. I'll make sure he visits your farm within the week."

The farmer bows his head, his gratitude clear, but there's no shock or disbelief in his expression. No wide-eyed surprise at Altair's generosity. It's as if this is something they all expect from him—kindness, support, solutions.

But as I watch, I feel a stirring deep inside, an uncomfortable twist in my gut. This is what *he* is to them—a protector, a king who doesn't just sit on a throne giving orders, but who actively *acts*, who sees their struggles and tries to ease them. And it hits me in a way I wasn't prepared for.

All this time, I've been fed a different story. My parents told me about Altair's cruelty, how he ruled with an iron fist, how the world feared him. But standing here, watching this exchange, I realise I've been lied to. And it makes me feel... unsettled. Maybe even betrayed.

I want to push the thoughts away, to hold onto the version of him I've been taught to believe, but it's hard. Because this doesn't fit with that narrative. The Altair they warned me about—the cold, heartless king— isn't the one standing before me right now.

His gestures, the way he speaks to the farmer, to the people— there's no facade here. It's real. And that realization is shaking me. Was I really that naive? Or did I want so badly to believe the lies they told me?

I can't help but feel angry at my parents for painting him as a monster. They built their walls around me and kept me from seeing the truth. But now, seeing this... seeing him care about his people, I realise just how much they've manipulated me.

A part of me wants to *demand* more proof, to challenge Altair's motives, but another part is simply... confused. How can the man who's done all this be the same one who took me from my home? Who terrified me with his shadows and cold touch?

This moment, this small act of kindness, shifts something inside me. It's like a crack forming in the wall I've built around my own heart. And the worst part? I don't know how to stop it from growing.

"Thank you, my king," the farmer says, his voice filled with a deep respect.

Altair nods. "Take care and let me know if you need anything else."

The man rises, but before he leaves, his gaze shifts toward me. I sit straighter, unsure of what to do. My hands are clasped tightly in my lap, and I try not to fidget under his gaze. Then, with a warmth that surprises me, the farmer bows deeply.

"My queen," he says with a gentle smile, his voice carrying the same respect he showed Altair.

I blink, a rush of emotion filling my chest. I'm used to hearing 'Your Majesty'—so formal, so distant—but this feels different. The way he says it, so openly, so genuinely, strikes a chord I didn't expect. It's the first time someone has called me that without hesitation, without the sense of duty.

I force myself to nod back, offering a small, uncertain smile. "Thank you," I manage to say, the words soft but sincere.

As the farmer leaves, I glance over at Altair. He's watching me with a small smile tugging at his lips.

"You're a part of this," he says quietly, his voice low and steady, meant for me alone. "They see you, Olwyn. You're as much a part of this kingdom as I am. They trust you."

His words land heavier than I expected, but not with the weight of pressure or expectation. There's a warmth to them, a sense of security that I didn't realise I needed. *The people see me?* It's an odd thought, but it's comforting, too. For the first time, I feel like I'm not just an outsider here—like I'm meant to be a part of something bigger than myself.

I look at him, a flicker of hope stirring in my chest. It's strange, but I feel... grounded.

I turn back toward the throne room as another citizen steps forward, ready to present their own request. And I realise something then.

This throne, this place beside Altair, it's not a burden. It's a role, a responsibility. One I could grow into, if I gave it a chance. Back in Avantra, I was kept so hidden, veiled away behind walls and whispers, that the idea of ruling, of standing openly before my people, was no more than a dream. I never saw a day where I could lead as freely as Altair does.

But now, here, I can see it clearly. The chance to be seen, to be known—not just as a figure, but as a force that could make a difference, to do good for them. The realisation stirs something deep within me, and for the first time in a long while, the idea of it doesn't feel so daunting. It feels right.

She's seeing. She's trying. It means so much.

CHAPTER TWENTY

Olwyn

I jolt awake, a scream tearing from my throat, shattering the quiet of my chambers.

The nightmare lingers, clinging to me like a suffocating weight. I'm gasping for air, my hands clutching the silk sheets, damp with sweat. My heart is racing, the sound of it thudding in my ears as I try to calm down, to steady my breaths.

I rid my mind of the memory of the man's scent, telling myself it isn't real, even if I can smell him as if he were led directly underneath my nose.

Footsteps echo in the room next to mine, and before I can fully collect myself, Altair comes through the door, his expression a mix of concern and determination. Shadows coil around him like a living cloak, responding to the distress that still hangs heavy in the air.

"Olwyn," he says, his voice low and steady but tinged with urgency.

"I'm fine," I croak, my voice cracking. I try to sound firm, but the tremble in my hands betrays me. "Go away, Altair."

But he doesn't listen. He strides across the room, his eyes never leaving mine, reading the panic still etched into my expression. I flinch, my pride prickling as I sit up straighter, trying to put on a brave front. "I said

I'm fine," I snap, but my voice wavers, the conviction slipping through my fingers.

Altair ignores my protests, sweeping the sheets aside. "You're not fine," he says simply. "And I cannot bear it, listening to your pain."

Before I can argue further, he bends down, effortlessly scooping me into his arms.

"What are you doing?" I shriek, pushing against his chest, my fists weakly beating against his shoulder. "Put me down!"

Altair holds me close, his grip gentle yet unyielding. "You need rest," he replies calmly, as though this is the most obvious thing in the world. "If we're going to train tomorrow, you need your sleep."

I still a little. He's not wrong.

But the sudden closeness is jarring, his bare chest pressing against me. His skin is cool and smooth, but it radiates a warmth that seeps through the thin fabric of my nightgown, sending a jolt through my body. There's an electricity in the contact, a charge that sets my nerves on fire. My breath catches, the sensation so visceral, so intimate that my instinct is to recoil, to put distance between us.

My fingers twitch, hovering near his shoulder as I instinctively try to maintain some semblance of balance. The steady thrum of his heartbeat, strong and unwavering, pulses against my side, matching the frantic rhythm of my own. The scent of him—dark and musky with a hint of something sharp, like air before a storm—fills my senses, overwhelming my resolve to stay angry, to push him away. I can feel the play of his muscles beneath my palms, each movement graceful and deliberate as he carries me across the room.

I am painfully aware of every point of contact—his arms wrapped around me, the way his chest rises and falls against mine. A blush creeps up my neck, my pulse quickening. I am caught between the urge to scream at him to let me go and the maddening temptation to sink deeper into the warmth he offers.

His grip tightens just slightly, almost possessively, and I can feel the strength he holds back, the restraint that keeps him gentle. He cradles me as if I'm something precious, and for a moment, I let myself believe it. That maybe, in this closeness, there's a truth I've been too afraid to see— that at some base level, Altair doesn't just want to protect me. The thought sends a fresh wave of confusion through me, twisting my fear into something far more complicated.

He carries me through the door connecting our rooms, each step sure, as if this is routine, as if carrying me is something he's done a thousand times before. My protests grow weaker, my body betraying me as exhaustion pulls at my limbs. I stiffen in his arms when we reach his bed.

His room is grand and impeccably decorated, dark wood furnishings and thick drapes framing a large bed in the centre. It feels warm and safe, a sharp contrast to the cold emptiness that clings to my own chambers.

"Altair, I don't—" I begin, but he cuts me off, setting me down on the bed with surprising tenderness before he tucks the blankets around me.

"Don't think too much on it," he says, brushing a stray lock of hair from my forehead. His touch is light, but it sends a shiver through me. "You need to sleep."

I feel the last of my energy slipping away. "I can sleep in my own room," I mumble weakly.

Altair steps back, his expression softening just a touch. "You'll be more comfortable here," he insists. "The outer door is already locked, and there's a bolt on this one. Use it, if it makes you feel safer."

He turns to leave, heading back towards the door. I open my mouth to argue, but the words die on my lips. A strange, unsettling warmth blossoms in my chest, one I can't quite name. I haven't felt safe in so long—not in this palace, not in my chambers, and certainly not around Altair. But the way he moved, the quiet resolve in his voice… It makes my defences wobble.

"Altair," I call after him, my voice softer now. He pauses at the doorway, glancing back at me with a curious look.

I hesitate, the words tangling on my tongue. "Thank you," I whisper. He nods once, a brief, almost imperceptible smile tugging at the corners of his mouth.

"Get some rest, Olwyn," he replies, his voice gentle. "I'll be in the next room if you need anything. And I'll make sure you're safe."

Without another word, he slips out, the door clicking shut behind him. I'm left alone in the dimly lit room, the silence almost oppressive in its stillness. I lie back against the pillows, staring up at the ceiling, my mind racing with everything that just happened.

But then his words from dinner the other night float back into my mind to add to the confusion.

If you find yourself craving a touch a little less gentle, you need only ask.

I stand, walking over and finding the bolt on the door, sliding it into place with a satisfying click. The action is small, but it gives me a sliver of control, a tiny piece of security in this overwhelming situation.

I turn back to the bed—*Altair's* bed—and the sight of it makes my breath hitch. It's absurdly large, draped in dark, luxurious fabrics that reflect the moonlight streaming in through the tall windows. The sheets are crisp and smooth, and as I slide beneath them, the lingering warmth of Altair's presence seems to wrap around me, mingling with the coolness of the silk.

The scent of him is everywhere—deep, musky, and laced with the sharp tang of midnight air. It's the scent that clings to him always, and it's oddly soothing in this space. It envelops me, filling my lungs with every breath I take. It's a reminder of where I am, whose space I've invaded, but instead of recoiling, I find myself sinking deeper into it.

It feels wrong to find comfort here, but the bed is impossibly soft, and his scent is grounding in a way I didn't expect. I press my face into the pillow, the trace of him lingering there, and I can almost feel the weight of his gaze, even though he's not in the room. My eyes drift shut, and exhaustion finally takes hold. The tension in my muscles begins to unwind, and I allow myself to relax—just a little.

Here, I feel like I don't have to be on guard. I don't have to fight, or plan, or think about what comes next. For a few stolen moments, I can simply exist, the heady mix of fear and comfort lulling me into a state that's dangerously close to peace.

For once, I don't fear the shadows lurking in the corners of the room. I don't fear the nightmares that have haunted me every night. And as I drift off, the lingering warmth of Altair's touch and the memory of his quiet reassurance wrap around me like a cloak, softening the sharp edges of my fear.

CHAPTER TWENTY-ONE
Altair

Fuck, she felt so good.

The thought slams into me the moment I step into her room, her scent in the air doing nothing to quench the fire still burning in my veins. The warmth of her body still lingers in my arms, her smell—sweet, delicate, but with an underlying strength—clinging to my skin like a brand. It took every ounce of my control to keep from holding her closer, from letting my instincts take over. The moment her chest pressed against mine, her soft breath catching as she fought to push me away, I knew I was in trouble.

I can still feel the way her fingers twitched against my bare skin, hesitant yet curious. Her heartbeat had been erratic, not just from fear. I've heard that rhythm before—it's the kind that signals confusion, tension, *desire.*

My shades pull away from objects in the room, as if in answer to my needs, brushing over my bare skin and causing goosebumps to crawl up my arms.

"Stop it," I say quietly, ignoring how I harden.

I lean against the doorframe for a moment, pressing my forehead to the cool wood as I exhale slowly, trying to get my thoughts in order. My fingers dig into the wood, as if ready to rip the door away and head back to her. I hear her soft steps as she walks over to the door.

Don't open it. Lock the door, Olwyn. I command in my head, to myself more than her. *Bolt that door so I don't kick it down.*

And she does. I hear the unmistakable click as she moves the bolt across. But I know my room will smell of her now—of her fear, her exhaustion, and something else that I'm not sure she even realises.

She doesn't trust me, I remind myself. *She's terrified of me.*

But even as the thought surfaces, I can't deny the way her body had responded when I held her close. The subtle shift in her breathing, the way her eyes flickered with something more than fear when she looked at me—*she's drawn to me.* It's there, even if she refuses to acknowledge it. But I can't push her, not yet. She's too fragile, too confused by everything that's happening around her. If I force this—whatever *this* is—too soon, I could lose her completely.

Still, the memory of her pressed against me, of her soft skin and the way she had protested weakly, knowing she didn't really want me to stop... It's driving me mad. I shake my head, trying to banish the thoughts, but it's no use. My senses are too heightened, too focused on her, as if she's branded herself into my very soul.

I pace, trying to steady my breathing.

She's safe, I tell myself. *She's in my bed, bolted in, and no one will touch her.*

I try to focus on that—on the promise I made to her earlier tonight. But then my mind drifts back to the nightmare. The way she screamed, thrashing in her bed, fighting off invisible enemies. The way her voice had cracked when she told me to go away, even though I knew, deep down, she didn't mean it. She needs me, whether she wants to admit it or not. And I... I can't stand hearing her suffer.

I want to give her a life, one full of choices and freedom, not shackled by her past or this twisted arrangement between us.

But she can't choose that yet. Not when she's still in the dark, not when everything feels like a lie. I need to show her the truth. I need to take her outside these walls, let her see for herself what this kingdom really is—

and what I really am. She's never understood the weight of what's at stake here, never understood the sacrifices made for her safety, for our future.

And after that—after she sees it with her own eyes—I'll sit with her, alone, no barriers between us, and have the conversation I should've had long ago. No more secrets, no more half-truths. I'll tell her everything. Everything I've kept hidden.

One step at a time, I remind myself. First, I'll show her the world beyond the palace walls. Then, I'll give her the truth. Only then can I start to ask for her trust. Only then can I begin to show her that, despite everything, I'm not the monster she believes I am.

One step at a time.

I glance back at the door leading to my room. She's in there, probably asleep by now, wrapped in my sheets, surrounded by my scent. The thought sends a fresh wave of heat through me, my hand drifting down, gripping my hard cock, and I bite back a curse. I need to get out of here, away from the temptation of her being so close. I can't violate her space with my urges… unless.

I breathe deep, calming myself before I leave the room, my plans already in motion.

I hope my plan works...

CHAPTER TWENTY-TWO
Olwyn

I slept the best I had in a while. Enough so that I felt better and able to join in preparing for the ball. The great hall buzzes with activity, a flurry of fabrics and flowers as the staff work tirelessly to prepare for it. I stand to the side, my fingers fidgeting in front of me, watching as the head of the staff, a stern-faced woman named Crista, orchestrates the chaos with a sharp eye and even sharper tongue. She's human, which catches me off guard, given her direct approach in a palace full of vampires.

I'm not sure I like her. Or how she speaks to the staff.

Crista directs the arrangements with brisk efficiency, her voice slicing through any chatter. "No, not like that!" she snaps at a vampire struggling to hang a garland along the wall. "Do you want the entire decoration to come crashing down during the ball? Start again, and this time, get it right."

The vampire flinches, his hands shaking slightly as he fumbles to correct his mistake. I watch in stunned silence, my mind trying to reconcile what I'm seeing. A human, reprimanding a vampire. And the vampire—the one who could probably snap her in half without a second thought—looks genuinely afraid.

It's like the world tilts sideways. I can't wrap my head around it. Why would a vampire be scared of a human?

And it's not a one off. The vampires nod in respect to her, doing her bidding.

Everything I've ever known, everything I've been taught, tells me that humans are the ones who should be afraid. That we're weak, fragile things in the existence of their predatory strength. But here, in this palace, the rules are different. They're all turned upside down.

It's very confusing… and reminds me of Altair's words about my parents.

Crista turns to me, her stern gaze still tense. "Are you all right, Your Majesty? You look pale."

I nod, but my thoughts are far away, grappling with what I've just witnessed. "I'm fine," I say, though my voice lacks conviction. "Just… thinking."

"Hmm." Crista doesn't press further. She moves on, barking orders at another member of the staff, her authority unquestioned. I watch her, the way she commands the room, the way Sera and Thalia don't approach me around her, and a thought strikes me—a memory, unbidden.

I'm fourteen again, sitting at the heavy wooden table in Avantra's palace. The room is dim, lit by the soft, wavering glow of an oil lamp. My parents sit across from me, their faces etched with anger and fear. My father's voice is slurring, as he chugs from a goblet in front of him.

"Do you remember Elderglen, Olwyn?" he asks, leaning forward, his eyes glassy. "The village in the valley?"

I nod slowly, not trusting myself to speak. I've heard the name before.

"It was a peaceful village," he continues, wiping a drop of wine that spills from the corner of his mouth. "Families, children… all living their simple lives. And then the vampires came."

My heart thuds in my chest, the familiar fear rising like bile in my throat. I've heard these stories before, but they never get any easier to listen to.

"They came in the dead of night," my mother adds, her voice trembling with barely suppressed rage. "They drained every last one of them. Not even the children were spared."

I can see it in my mind's eye: dark shapes moving silently through the village, fangs gleaming as they feed on the helpless. It's a vision that fills me with terror, a fear so deep it feels like it's woven into my bones.

"Elderglen has been left as nothing more than a graveyard," my mother says, her small fist slamming onto the table, making me jump. "And the vampires? They vanished, leaving nothing but death in their wake."

I swallow hard, trying to force down the lump in my throat. "Why would they do that?" I ask, my voice small and fearful. It's a blur, but I still remember a time when I played with vampires. When we went to the academy together.

"Because that's what they are," my mother says, gripping my hand tightly. "They're monsters, Olwyn. They have no mercy, no compassion. They see us as nothing but food."

That memory, those stories my parents told me, became the foundation of my fear and hatred of vampires, the lens through which I viewed every vampire in this palace from the moment I arrived, no matter what they actually said or did. But now, watching Crista—a human— command a room of vampires, something shifts.

The memory of my parents' words seems to waver, like smoke caught in a breeze. I see the vampire flinch again under Crista's sharp rebuke, his intimidation as real as mine was that day at the table.

What if it wasn't the whole truth? What if my parents only told me what they wanted me to believe? Maybe, just maybe, Altair wasn't lying when he said there are humans living here, thriving even. Maybe this isn't a trick. I've been so certain that I knew everything about vampires, about their cruelty, their hunger. But now, I'm not so sure.

Could it be that the world isn't as black and white as I've been led to believe? Could it be that, somewhere between the lines of my parents' stories and Altair's words, there's a truth I've been too afraid to see?

It doesn't make sense.

I shake my head, trying to dispel the doubts creeping in. But they're stubborn, and I can't quite silence them. Maybe it's time to stop seeing things solely through the eyes of fear. Maybe it's time to let Altair challenge what I think I know.

Because if vampires can flinch at a human's reprimand, then maybe—just maybe—they're not the monsters I've always believed them to be.

***

The evening sky darkens as I make my way back up to my chambers, two royal guards trailing a few steps behind me. Their presence is a constant reminder that this world is still filled with dangers lurking in its shadows. But tonight, I feel a little lighter.

I can't quite name it, but it's as if the fear that's been my constant companion, has shifted just a little. Maybe it's that flicker of doubt planted in the back of my mind, or maybe it's the way he looked at me—like he was seeing more than just a captive. Whatever it is, I'm not ready to let it go just yet.

We reach my chambers, and I step forward, expecting to push the door open. But it doesn't budge. I frown, twisting the handle again, only to find it locked.

"Is there a problem, Your Majesty?" one of the guards–Nikolas—asks, his hand already resting on the hilt of his sword.

"I... I don't know," I mutter, confused. "The door's locked."

Just as I'm about to knock, a member of staff approaches from the stairs, her expression calm and professional. "Your Majesty," she greets, bowing slightly. "If you'll follow me, please."

I blink at her, then back at the locked door. "Why is my room locked?"

The staff member offers a small, almost knowing smile. "King Altair has made arrangements for you to stay in his chambers, right next door. He wanted to ensure your comfort, considering recent events."

My heart skips a beat, and for a moment, I just stand there, stunned.

Altair... switched our rooms?

The guard opens the door to what used to be *his* chambers, and the staff member gestures for me to follow her inside. The room is grand and familiar—the same one I slept in last night—but now, something feels different. There's a softness to it, a deliberate effort that shows this isn't just any room; it's *mine* now. The bed is freshly made, the sheets crisp and smooth. The faint scent of him still lingers in the air, but this room has been prepared with care. For me.

Altair did this for *me*.

I hesitate at the threshold, my mind racing. This is more than just a switch of rooms—this is an offering. A gesture that tells me he's trying, in his own way, to make me feel... safe.

I glance back at the guards who remain just outside the door, giving me privacy, and my throat tightens with emotion. He's done this to make me feel comfortable, to give me a space that I can claim as my own, away from the nightmares that haunt me in my old chambers.

As I step inside, closing the door softly behind me, I'm overwhelmed with gratitude—an unfamiliar, unsettling feeling when it comes to Altair. But here it is, rising up in my chest, making it harder to cling to the walls I've built so carefully.

Maybe... maybe he's not the monster I've always believed him to be.

I'm not sure if she appreciated it… but she slept soundly.

CHAPTER TWENTY–THREE
Olwyn

I sit on the bench in the water gardens, the sun warming my skin as I flip through the pages of a book.

The sound of gently flowing water soothes me, and I watch as the exotic fish glide through the crystal-clear waters of the pond before me. Their iridescent scales catch the light, casting tiny rainbows that dance across the smooth stone that keeps them there.

The air is fragrant with the scent of blooming lilies and jasmine, mingling with the soft rustle of leaves from the overhead trees. For the first time in what feels like forever, I let myself relax, just a little. Besides the library, this is somewhere I can find peace.

I'm so absorbed in my thoughts that I don't notice Altair approaching until a tendril of shadow drifts over my page, making me look up. He stands there, dressed in a loose black shirt and casual trousers, looking different without the usual suits and leathers that make him seem untouchable. His hair is slightly wet and tousled, and… he is *smiling*.

"Is this your favourite spot now?" Altair asks, his voice low, almost teasing as he steps closer. The sunlight catches on the dark fabric of his clothes, making him look effortlessly regal, even without trying.

I blink up at him, momentarily startled by his sudden appearance. "It's quiet," I say, closing my book but keeping my finger between the pages. "And the fish don't seem to mind my company."

Altair chuckles, a sound that rumbles deep in his chest and sends a strange flutter through me. "No, I suppose they wouldn't." He gestures to the empty space beside me. "May I?"

I hesitate for a moment but then nod. "Sure."

He sits down, leaving a small, deliberate distance between us. His warmth radiates across the space, mingling with the sun's rays, and it makes me all too aware of how close he is. The bench feels smaller than it did a moment ago, and I fight the urge to shift closer, to close the gap that suddenly feels like a much too big divide.

"What are you reading?" he asks, leaning slightly toward me, and I catch a whiff of something warm and dark.

I glance down at the cover, my cheeks heating up. It's a collection of old poems, stories of love and loss and longing that I picked up on a whim. "Just some poetry," I mumble, feeling a bit silly for it now.

"Poetry?" Altair's brow lifts, curiosity lighting up his features. "I didn't know you liked that sort of thing."

I smirk, meeting his eyes. "Well, how would you? There's a lot you don't know about me. I'm full of surprises."

He smiles but it doesn't reach his eyes.

I sigh. "I've never really read it before," I admit, so used to reading… well, I won't admit what I usually enjoy reading. My fingers brush against the worn leather of the book's spine. "But it's… comforting, in a way."

Altair nods thoughtfully, his eyes drifting over the pond. "Comfort can be hard to come by," he says softly. "Especially in a place like this."

Our eyes meet, and for a moment, it's as if the rest of the world falls away. I bite my lip, feeling the tension in the air shift again, heavier now, like something unsaid lingers between us. I lower my gaze, focusing on the book in my lap as my mind races. Then, without looking up, I find my voice.

"Thank you," I say quietly.

His brows raise slightly. "For what?"

"For switching the rooms," I clarify, my eyes flicking back to his. "It… meant a lot. You didn't have to do that."

A flicker of surprise crosses his face, quickly replaced by something softer. "I wanted you to feel comfortable," he replies, his voice low, almost hesitant, as if he's choosing his words carefully. "It didn't seem right, you being in that room after everything."

I nod, swallowing the emotion rising in my chest. "It was… thoughtful. I'm not used to that."

He doesn't respond right away, just watches me, his gaze intense. For a moment, I think he might say something more, something that will break the tension humming between us. But instead, his hand moves slightly, brushing against mine on the bench.

The contact is brief, but it sends a jolt through me, and I freeze, my pulse quickening. I look up at him, our eyes locking. His gaze drops to my lips for a heartbeat—long enough for me to notice, long enough for my stomach to flip in response.

My breath catches, and I can't tear my eyes away from him. There's something there, something deeper than just a physical pull, and it terrifies me as much as it excites me.

"I'm glad you liked it," Altair murmurs, his voice soft but carrying weight.

I swallow hard, my heart racing, and all I can manage is a small nod, unable to trust myself to speak.

"What kind of poetry do you like?" he coughs to clear his throat, his tone casual, but there's an undertone of genuine curiosity that catches me off guard. He's not just making small talk; he actually wants to know.

I fumble with the book, running my fingers along the edges of the pages. "I'm not sure yet," I say honestly. "I guess I like the ones that… make you feel something, even if you don't understand why."

He nods, considering my words. "So, you're drawn to things that stir the heart, even when the mind can't quite grasp it. That's interesting."

I can't help but let out a small, nervous laugh. "I suppose. What about you? Do you have a preference?"

Altair leans back slightly, a thoughtful expression crossing his face. "I've always been more drawn to stories," he admits. "Tales of adventure, loyalty, sacrifice. There's something about the way a story can transport you, make you feel like you're part of something greater than yourself."

Relatable. I find myself nodding. "I like stories too. They're a kind of escape, I guess."

"Exactly," he says, his eyes lighting up as if I've just solved a riddle for him. "It's the escape. The chance to live a hundred lives and never have to leave your own."

Our conversation flows easily from there, and I find myself relaxing more than I expected. Altair asks about the books I've read; talks about the places I've dreamed of visiting—ones I've never even heard of. He even pretends to be scandalised that I've never tried some exotic vampire dish he swears is the best thing in the world.

But it's when he teases a smile and small laugh out of me that his face changes.

I don't know what it is exactly—maybe the way his eyes widen, or the way his mouth softens from its usual hard line—but there's a shift in him, like he's caught off guard. His teasing falls away, replaced by something I can't quite put my finger on. His gaze lingers on my face, on my lips as I smile, and his expression turns almost... reverent, like he's seeing something rare and precious for the first time.

The silence stretches between us, heavy but not uncomfortable, and I can feel the intensity of his stare as if it's a physical thing. My laughter dies down, replaced by a warmth that blooms in my chest, spreading out through my limbs and up to my cheeks.

Suddenly self-conscious, I bite my lip and drop my gaze, my fingers fiddling with the edge of the book in my lap. The blush creeping up my neck is impossible to hide, and I can still feel his eyes on me, watching, studying.

"You should laugh more often," he says quietly, his voice soft and full of something I can't quite name. "It suits you."

I blink, caught off guard by the gentleness in his tone. My heart skips a beat, and I look away again, my cheeks flaming.

"Well," I mumble, "maybe you should work harder to be funnier."

His chuckle is low, warm, and somehow it only makes my blush deepen.

"What about growing up?" he asks after a beat, his voice hardening slightly. "What was that really like for you?"

The question catches me off guard, and I hesitate. Memories of Avantra flood my mind—the hidden halls, the strict rules, the feeling of always being watched. I chew my lip, unsure of how much to reveal. "There were a lot of expectations, a lot of… restrictions."

He suddenly looks regretful, and he knows I am playing it down, but he nods, as if he understands more than he's letting on. "I can only imagine." His eyes search mine, and I feel the pull of his gaze like a tether. "It must have been lonely."

The honesty in his words tugs at something inside me, and I swallow hard, nodding. "It was," I admit quietly. "But I thought that was just… normal. I couldn't really remember anything different."

"I remember…" I hesitate, but he tilts his head, silently urging me on. "I do remember fun," I continue, a wistful smile tugging at my lips. "A classroom. Laughter. I remember friends. It's all so fuzzy, but it's there. I know there was a time when life was different. When I played with vampires, without fear or boundaries."

Altair's hand shifts, resting closer to mine on the bench, his fingers brushing against mine again as if by accident. The contact sends a spark up my arm. His thumb moves, just the slightest bit, tracing an invisible line along the back of my hand, and I feel my breath hitch in my throat.

"You don't have to be alone here," he says, his voice low, almost hesitant. "Not if you don't want to be."

I glance up, meeting his gaze, and for a moment, the look in his eyes steals my breath. There's a rawness there, something vulnerable and sincere, and it scares me as much as it draws me in. He's not just talking about the palace or the people in it. He's talking about himself.

"Altair…" I start, but the words trail off, my thoughts tangling into a mess. I want to tell him I want to give him a chance. A proper chance to earn my trust. I want to tell him that I am confused, and scared, but I want to try. It means stripping back everything I think I know, but I am willing to do it.

He turns to face me more fully, his knee brushing against mine in the process. The contact is brief, but I jump, and I almost drop the book. I glance down, embarrassed, but when I look up, I find Altair watching me. His gaze flickers to my lips for the briefest second before snapping back to my eyes.

"What is it?" he asks, his voice gentle, but there's a tension there, like a string pulled tight, ready to snap.

I shake my head, trying to dispel the strange, electric charge that buzzes between us. "Nothing," I say quickly, but we both know it's a lie. There's so much I want to say, so much I don't understand about what's happening. About why my heart races every time he's near, why I'm hyper-aware of every move he makes. About why his shadows don't scare me anymore, or the flash of his fangs.

So much I need to reflect on and question. But that feels like something I need to work through on my own… maybe.

Altair doesn't press me. Instead, he reaches out as if to adjust the way my book is angled, but his fingers brush more obviously against mine. The touch is light, fleeting, but it lingers, the warmth of his skin against mine searing like a brand. We both freeze, neither pulling away, and for a heartbeat, I wonder what would happen if I went against all of my old instincts to flee and just… leaned in. If I let the tension break and see where it got me.

If I simply, held his hand.

But I don't. I can't. I'm not sure if it's fear or something else, but the moment passes, and I pull my hand back, cradling the book to my chest like a shield.

Altair's expression shifts, a flicker of something— disappointment?—crossing his features before he masks it with a small, almost resigned smile. "I should let you get back to your reading," he says, though he doesn't move.

I nod, my heart still pounding against my ribs.

He rises slowly, his hand lingering on the back of the bench for a moment as if debating whether to stay. But then he steps away, the spell between us breaking as he puts distance back into our shared space. "I'll see you at training later," he says, his voice still holding that undercurrent of something unspoken.

"Yes, I'll be there," I manage, my voice steady even as my mind spins.

Altair nods, and with a final glance—one that seems to stretch longer than it should—he turns and walks away, his figure blending into the shadows of the garden's archways.

I watch him go, my fingers still tingling from his touch, my thoughts tangled. For a brief moment, I let myself wonder what it would be like to let go of my fears, to rid myself of all the beliefs and thoughts of others that I have so far chosen to live my life with, and instead… make decisions for myself. Wonder if I could reach out and take what I want. But then I shove the thought down, burying it beneath layers of uncertainty.

I pick up my book, opening it to where I left off, but the words blur on the page. My mind is far from poetry now, lost somewhere between the warmth of Altair's gaze and the lingering touch of his hand against mine.

CHAPTER TWENTY–FOUR
Olwyn

The training room is dimly lit, the early morning light filtering through the narrow windows, casting long shadows across the floor.

The air is thick with the scent of sweat and exertion, the remnants of yesterday's session still lingering as I step onto the mat, tightening the straps on my training boots.

The room is stifling, and I have taken off my full sleeve leathers, opting for a skinsuit which leaves my arms bare—able to breathe.

"Ready?" Altair asks, turning to face me. His gaze roams over my face, my arms… my chest. His unscarred eye is pitch black, but there's a glint of challenge in it that makes my pulse quicken.

"As always," I reply, trying to keep my voice steady.

We begin with the usual drills—basic blocks, strikes, and evasions. I do my best to keep up, blocking his attacks and countering where I can, but it doesn't take long before he starts to push harder, his strikes coming faster and with more force.

"Predictable," he mutters as I block another one of his strikes, frustration creeping into his voice.

I scowl, my irritation flaring. "Predictable? I've been training for a few *months* with Iolas and only *weeks* with you! How many years have you been at this, Altair?" My voice sharpens, carrying the bite of frustration and exhaustion. I dodge his next strike, barely, my muscles already burning. "And, in case you've forgotten, you're a vampire. Superior strength, speed—the whole damn package. Meanwhile, I'm only human." I grit my teeth and deflect a low kick aimed at my legs.

Altair's eyes narrow, and he steps back, lowering his hands. "Stop," he commands, and I halt, panting slightly from the exertion.

"What's wrong?" I ask, wiping the sweat from my brow with the back of my hand.

"You're holding back," he says, his voice calm but firm. "You're too focused on what you think you should do, instead of just… doing."

I frown, not understanding. "I'm trying to anticipate your moves, to predict your attacks. Isn't that what you've been teaching me?"

"Yes, but you've become too reliant on that. You're not letting yourself be free. You're not letting your instincts guide you. You're predictable. And predictability will get you killed."

His words hit me hard, a blunt assessment of my skills that feels like a slap to the face. But beneath the sting of his criticism, I know he's right. I'm playing it too safe, too cautious.

"What do you want me to fucking do then?" I ask, almost tantruming like a petulant child.

Altair's lips twitch as his eyes narrow, but his tone remains calm. "Stop thinking so much and just… act. Let your instincts take over."

"I don't know how in this environment," I tell him.

"What did you do that day in Avantra when you ran from Mikael?"

The memory of what he did to his own guard back then makes me want to smile—a much different reaction to that day. Maybe being around vampires means I am becoming desensitised to violence?

But I think about it. I didn't do anything with much thought I just…

"Acted."

"Exactly. You acted based on your adrenaline. On your instincts."

That was because I had been scar—

Scared.

The realisation hits me like a boulder. The reason I don't act on instinct when training with Altair and Iolas. The reason that lifesaving feeling doesn't run through my veins.

I'm not scared of them.

They won't hurt me.

"I want you to surprise me," he says.

I swallow hard, his words settling in. Surprise him? How am I supposed to do that when every move I make is scrutinised, analysed? How do I break free from the patterns we've established?

"Again," he commands, stepping back and raising his hands. "And this time, don't hold back."

I nod, ridding myself from my confusing revelation and steeling myself as we begin again. Altair moves with the same precision as before, but now there's an added intensity, as if he's daring me to break the mould, to do something unexpected.

I try to push myself, to be quicker, more aggressive. To try and burrow into how I found those instincts during our first session. I switch up my attacks, feinting and dodging, but Altair sees through every move, blocking and countering with ease. The frustration builds inside me, a gnawing sense of inadequacy that I can't shake.

"Too slow," he mutters as he sidesteps another of my strikes.

I growl in frustration, feeling the anger bubble up inside me. "I'm trying!"

"Don't try," he snaps, his voice sharp. "Do."

The words are like a trigger, tickling something in the back of my mind, and something snaps inside me. I don't think—I just move. I lunge forward, feinting to the left before spinning to the right, aiming a punch at his side. But he's faster, his hand darting out to catch my wrist, twisting it just enough to force me off balance.

And then, without warning, I let my body take over. I twist in his grip, using the momentum to spin around, and before I can second-guess myself, I wrap my fingers in his hair and… press my lips to his.

For a heartbeat, time seems to freeze. Altair's grip on my wrist loosens, his body tensing in surprise as I press my palms to his warm chest. The room falls silent, the only sound the pounding of my heart in my ears. My lips move against his, soft yet demanding, the heat of the moment eclipsing everything else.

And then, just as I'm about to pull back, he responds. His hand releases my wrist, sliding up to cup the back of my neck and into my hair, pulling me closer as he deepens the kiss. His tongue brushes against mine and he groans, the sound rumbling in his chest. His lips are warm and firm, and the electricity that sparks between us is like nothing I've ever felt. The tension, the frustration, the anger—it all melts away, replaced by a flood of raw, unfiltered *need*.

But I'm not done surprising him yet.

As our lips part for a breath, his eyes open, and before I can fully comprehend the light colour of *both*, I use the moment of distraction to shift my weight again. I hook my leg behind his and push forward with all my strength, using his own momentum to send him off balance. His eyes widen in realisation, but it's too late—he's already falling.

I follow him down, so that when we hit the mat, I'm on top, straddling his hips and pinning him to the floor. His back hits the mat with a solid thud, but I don't give him a chance to recover. My hands press into his muscled shoulders, holding him in place, and I lean down, my breath hot against his ear.

"Spontaneous enough for you?" I whisper, a smirk playing on my lips as I pull back to meet his gaze.

Altair stares up at me, his chest heaving beneath mine, dark eye bright with a hint of blue.

His surprise has melted into something else—something darker, more dangerous. His hands grip my thighs, not pushing me off, but holding me there, anchoring me in place. The look in his eyes makes my heart skip a beat, my pulse quickening as I realise just what I've done.

Realise what I can feel hardening beneath me, almost right where I know it would feel good.

"That," he says, his voice rough, "was definitely unpredictable."

A shaky laugh escapes me. There's no regret in his gaze, no anger—only a heat that makes my pulse quicken all over again.

"Maybe spontaneity suits you after all," Altair says with a smirk, his tone teasing but his eyes serious. My breath hitches as his hands roam further up my thighs, and I can feel the slight tightening of his fingers, and I resist the urge to roll my hips. "But I'll expect you to at least land a punch next time."

I laugh breathlessly, feeling a mix of nervousness and something I try to suppress before he senses it. "Deal. Just don't expect me to use this tactic on anyone else."

He chuckles, the sound warm and rich. It makes me want to rub my thighs together. His nostrils flare. "Good," he rasps. "Because I might get a little jealous."

My eyes roll before I can remember who lies beneath me. "I'm yours, remember."

He sits up so suddenly I would have fallen back if it weren't for his hands holding me firmly at my waist. I tense, but he isn't hurting me. His lips hover over mine. I could tip forward an inch and my mouth would touch his again.

Where his sharp canines press into the swell of his bottom lip.

"Careful with your words, Olwyn. A declaration like that might entice me to kiss you again. And my heightened sense of smell informs me how much you might just enjoy that."

I want to deny it and tell him he's wrong. But Gods know he isn't.

"And what if I were to kiss *you* again?" I boldly ask.

His breath shudders, eyes closing before he seems to pull control over himself. His eyes are completely black when he opens them, and a tingling sensation climbs up my spine as I suddenly feel like I am speaking to some dark creature, and not Altair.

"I think you'd find yourself spread out on this mat, with me buried so deep inside you, you wouldn't be able to walk from this room when I was finished."

CHAPTER TWENTY-FIVE
Altair

I've crossed a line.

She's going to run.

But I can feel her everywhere, and my whole body is on fire.

Even worse for my level of control, I can sense her arousal, the way her body *wants* mine, the way she aches for me. It's like a drug, and I am losing myself in it, in *her.*

I'm trying to gather myself, but it's impossible to shake the feeling of her pressing down on me, her weight so perfectly balanced on mine, her warmth seeping into my skin as I curse the training leathers between us.

The heat between her thighs, her quickening breath, the way her pulse flutters under my fingers. And she is just as aware of me, of what I can't hide—the way my body responds to her, hardens beneath her, so close to where it would feel *so* good.

"I think you'd find yourself spread out on this mat, with me buried so deep inside you, you wouldn't be able to walk from this room when I was finished."

The words left my mouth before I could stop them. But… she gasps, her lips parting as her breath catches in her throat, her freckled cheeks pinking just enough to make me bite the inside of my cheek to stop myself from claiming her lips again.

It's too much.

Knowing she wants it perhaps as much as I do. For a moment, I think she might kiss me again, push me further over the edge, and fuck, I would let her.

But I catch myself. Just barely.

I stand, pulling her up with me, trying to regain control. It's dangerous. So fucking dangerous. I want to take her, to feel her under me, her body trembling as I lose myself in her.

But I can't. Not like this. Not when I know what it would mean—for both of us. She knows that there is more I need to tell her. I know I am trying to protect her, but jumping into anything before I tell her everything, feels like I am being dishonest.

I need to be completely truthful with her first. I need to take her out of the palace.

I clear my throat, trying to shake off the lingering heat, the lingering need. "Let's finish up for today," I say, my voice far too calm for what I'm feeling. I have to force the words out, my body still thrumming with the tension, the desire. I watch her nod, still a little breathless, her cheeks flushed.

I've never seen her like this. So… vulnerable. So *fucking* perfect.

I clench my fists, trying to push down the overwhelming urge to touch her again, to pull her back into my arms and kiss her until she's gasping my name. But I can't. Not now.

But then the door opens, and Iolas walks in.

Fuck.

I take a deep breath, trying to pull myself together, trying to shake off the tension coiling inside me. He senses what's happened. How much she's affecting me.

And he can see how I'm holding on by a thread. I almost want to kiss *him* when he offers to walk her back to her room. I glance at Olwyn, her eyes flickering to the floor as if she's embarrassed by what just happened.

I clench my jaw, frustration and desire warring inside me. Gods, I need to pull myself together. But as I stand there, the scent of her still lingering in the air, I know one thing for certain:

I'm fucked.

It's getting harder and harder to be around her.

CHAPTER TWENTY–SIX
Olwyn

The grand hall is a flurry of movement, filled with Sera's and Thalia's chatter as they scurry about, preparing for the upcoming ball.

A cascade of flowers, ribbons, and candles adorns the table in front of me, their scents blending into something both calming and heady. The steady hum of activity around us would've overwhelmed me just a month ago, but now, it feels almost... invigorating.

I roll up my sleeves, enjoying the loose comfort of the white shirt and breeches I'm wearing, a far cry from the dresses I've grown used to. The fabric billows around me as I move between the arrangements, nodding approvingly at the work Sera and Thalia are doing.

"Your Majesty," Sera says brightly, her arms full of fabric swatches. "Which colour do you think would complement the garden roses? We're torn between the blush or the deep wine."

"Wine," I say after a moment of consideration. "It'll make them stand out more."

Thalia raises an eyebrow, glancing at Sera, impressed. "Not bad," she says with a grin. "You've got a good eye."

I can't help but laugh, the sound bubbling out of me. "Only because you've both taught me so well the last couple of weeks."

They both giggle, moving to test out the swatches against the arrangements, when I catch a glimpse of someone in the corner of my eye. A figure—human, female—standing behind them, looking as if she is working on one of the flower arrangements. I don't recognize her. She doesn't belong.

Something feels… off.

The stranger's eyes dart toward me every so often, and an uneasy feeling prickles at the back of my neck. I try to ignore it, to focus on the work at hand, but my gaze keeps sliding toward her.

She's watching me. Intently.

I glance at the strange woman, then quickly avert my gaze, hoping Sera and Thalia won't notice the growing tension in my posture. But the woman's presence continues to gnaw at me.

"Are you alright, Your Majesty?" Thalia asks, raising an eyebrow as she sets down a string of pearls meant to drape the centrepiece, and they roll off the table.

My attention falters for only a second.

But that's all the time she needs.

The flash of silver is the first thing I register—a dagger slicing through the air, aimed directly at me. My body reacts on instinct, my warm hand moving before my mind even processes the threat. I sidestep swiftly, the blade just missing my neck, and in one motion, I reach out and snatch the dagger from the air, the hilt landing perfectly in my palm.

Sera and Thalia scream, stumbling backward, but I'm already moving, the human guards on the outskirts of the room following me.

She's running.

I toss the dagger aside and take off after her without a second thought. My boots pound against the marble floor as I give chase, adrenaline surging through my veins. I'm faster than I've ever been, my body responding with newfound strength, my focus razor-sharp. *How am I this fast?* My breath comes in sharp bursts, my thoughts racing as I push myself harder. Is it the training with Iolas? My magic? Or something else? I don't know, but I can't question it now—I need to catch her.

The woman darts down the corridor, but she's sloppy, her movements frantic. I push myself harder, gaining on her with every stride. The pounding of my feet echoes through the marble halls, and yet, I feel like I'm moving faster than I should, faster than my body has ever been capable of. *This is beyond my training,* I think, *it doesn't make sense.*

As we near the grand entrance to the palace, a shadow curls at the edge of my vision.

It moves like it's alive—dark, and deliberate.

A tendril of black snakes out from the ground, wrapping itself around the woman's ankle and yanking her off balance. She stumbles, crashing to the floor with a loud thud, but she's quick. Too quick. She springs to her feet, ripping another dagger free from her belt. Several more guards from the courtyard rush forward, blocking her way forward as they point their swords at her.

I stop just short of her, breathing heavily but not winded as two guard stop behind me. The adrenaline pumps through me, making my limbs feel light, strong. I stare her down, ready for whatever comes next.

"Who sent you?" I demand, my voice steady despite the heat rising in my chest.

The woman laughs. It's a cold, bitter sound, and her eyes gleam with silver, something wild and dangerous.

Behind me, I hear the familiar sound of boots hitting the ground—Altair and Iolas, their presence unmistakable. I can feel Altair's rage boiling just beside me, his darkness reaching out like it wants to consume the woman in front of me. But even through his fury, his voice remains steady.

The guards step forward but Altair's voice halts them.

"Olwyn can handle it," he says, though there's a dangerous edge to his tone.

Iolas, however, isn't as restrained. A low growl escapes him, his fangs bared at the woman as he steps closer. His gaze flicks between me and the assassin, clearly torn between letting me finish this fight and tearing her apart himself.

The woman shifts, her grip tightening on the dagger. She knows she won't be making it home. How badly she gets hurt in the process is up to her now.

She seems to glance over at Altair, something like recognition passing through her eyes, and for a brief moment, I see a flicker of…nervousness.

"Who sent you?" I repeat, and I sense Altair stiffen.

But she just laughs again, her amusement cutting through the tension like a knife. "You think I'm going to tell you anything, little *queen*?" she sneers.

And then she lunges.

She's fast, but this time, I'm faster. My training with Iolas and Altair kicks in, my body moving with a precision and strength I hadn't even realised I'd developed. I sidestep her wild swing easily, ducking under her arm and spinning behind her. Before she can recover, I land a hard blow to her ribs, sending her staggering.

She grunts, slashing at me with the dagger, but I'm already moving again, dodging and weaving, keeping just out of her reach. She's sloppy, desperate, and that gives me the advantage. Each strike I land throws her further off balance, until finally, with a well-aimed kick, I knock the dagger from her hand, sending it skittering across the floor.

I press forward, grabbing her wrist and twisting it behind her back, pinning her against the wall. She struggles, but I hold her fast, the strength in my arms surprising even me.

"Who sent you?" I ask again, my voice low and firm.

She spits at my feet, laughing through her laboured breaths. "You'll find out soon enough."

Her tone is laced with malice, an eerie sense of certainty that makes my skin crawl. She doesn't seem afraid—not of me, not of Altair or Iolas, not of anything. And that terrifies me more than I'd like to admit.

I grip her wrist tighter, pinning her harder against the wall, trying to push down the rising panic in my chest. She struggles, but I hold her fast. She is weaker than me now. It's strange, but the thought of my strength fills me with a twisted sense of pride. But it also leaves me feeling vulnerable—because I shouldn't be strong enough to take someone like this down, not so easily. Not without years of training like Iolas. Like Altair.

A cold laugh escapes her again. "You have no idea what's coming, do you?" She sneers, and the venom in her words sends another wave of unease rippling through me. Her gaze flicks toward Altair, and I see a glint of recognition—something dark and sinister. "When they come for you… when they come for him… it'll be too late."

I don't know what pushes me over the edge, but the moment she mentions Altair, the world blurs. I can't let her live, not after she's tried to take my life. Not after she's hinted at something more, something darker coming our way.

She can't be freed. She'll come for me again. For him. For all of us.

There's only one way to ensure that doesn't happen.

I let her go.

She hisses, turning to attack me again, but I'm faster. Before she can strike, I grab the dagger from the ground. Without thinking, without hesitating, I plunge it into her chest.

The sound of metal piercing flesh is sickening—wet, final. Her body jerks, a sharp gasp escaping her lips as her dull brown eyes widen in shock. Blood spills from the wound, warm and thick, soaking through her tunic and onto my hand.

Her hands scramble uselessly at my wrist, her strength already fading, her breath coming in shallow, desperate gasps.

I stand there, frozen, watching as the life slowly drains from her eyes.

I can feel my heart hammering in my chest, and my breath catches in my throat as I realise what I've done.

She sags against me, her blood staining my hands as her body growing heavier, until finally, she collapses to the ground in a heap.

For a long moment, there's only silence. The world seems to have stopped around me, everything frozen in place as I stare down at her lifeless body. Blood pools around her, staining the ground floor beneath our feet.

My hands are trembling.

"You..." Altair's voice is quiet, soft, but there's something heavy in it, something raw and unspoken. His eyes are on me, wide with a mix of emotions I can't quite name.

Iolas, on the other hand, seems completely still, his nostrils flaring as the scent of death fills the air. He bares his teeth, his growl low and dangerous, his eyes flashing as he stares down at the corpse.

But no one speaks.

I let go of the dagger and stumble back, the sharp clang of it hitting the floor echoing in the vast hallway. I can't breathe, can't think. My chest feels tight, like there's a weight crushing me, suffocating me.

"Leave!" Altair commands his men, and they leave the three of us.

"I—" My voice cracks. I can't even finish the sentence.

Altair steps forward, his dark shadows slithering around the edges of the space, watching. Protecting. He reaches out slowly, as if afraid to spook me. His fingers brush my arm, steadying me.

"Olwyn, love" he murmurs, his tone soft now, almost coaxing. "You had no choice."

I shake my head, unable to meet his gaze. "I—killed her."

He takes another step closer, his hand resting on my shoulder. "She came to kill you. It was self-defence."

But it doesn't feel like that. The rush of adrenaline is gone, replaced by a hollow, gnawing sensation that twists in my gut. I look down at the blood staining my hands, unable to reconcile the image with the person I thought I was.

Altair's grip tightens on my shoulder, his face unreadable, but his voice low and firm. "You saved yourself."

Iolas stands a few paces back, his eyes still locked on the body. His hands are clenched into fists, and I can see the tension in his jaw, the way his entire frame is coiled like a spring ready to snap. But he says nothing.

"Let's go," Altair says quietly, taking my hand, his touch firm but gentle as he leads me away from the scene. I let him guide me, unable to find the strength to argue.

She's not ready.

CHAPTER TWENTY–SEVEN

Olwyn

ltair and Iolas had escorted me to my chambers, their presence a quiet amid the chaos still buzzing in my veins. Iolas had silently guided me to the bathroom, helping wash the blood from my hands in the basin. The water had swirled crimson as it disappeared down the drain, the faint scent of lavender soap mingling with the metallic tang that lingered in my mind. His little touches on my hands and arms reminded me to stay present, reminded me I wasn't alone.

Altair had walked in, his tall frame filling the doorway. He carried a clean pair of silk trousers and a lace-up shirt, the pale fabric so different to the dark stains on my tunic. Without a word, he set them down on the marble counter, our eyes meeting for a brief moment before they both stepped out, giving me space.

I change in the bathroom, peeling off my blood-soaked clothes and letting them drop into a heap on the floor. The cool silk of the trousers and the soft linen of the shirt feels soothing against my skin, grounding me as I take a deep breath, trying to steady myself.

Altair and Iolas wait for me as I step back into the bedroom, their eyes searching my face for any hint of how I'm feeling. Sera and Thalia are there too, standing by the window, their expressions a mix of worry and relief.

Altair clears his throat, breaking the silence. "I had them bring you some chamomile tea," he says, his voice soft but steady.

I nod, the gesture small and tired, before sinking into the chair nearest to me. The cushion cradles me, and I close my eyes for a moment, letting the room's quiet settle around me like a blanket.

The door opens, and Ailith strides in, her gaze sharp as it sweeps over everyone. She pauses, then looks at Altair and Iolas. "Give us a few minutes," she instructs.

Altair's jaw tenses slightly, checking my expression for any hesitations, but he nods, exchanging a brief glance with Iolas before they both turn and step out of the room.

The scent of chamomile wafts up from the delicate porcelain cup in front of me. I stare into the steaming tea, the liquid rippling slightly as Thalia sets the teapot down with a gentle clink.

"Shall I bring anything else, Your Majesty?" Thalia's voice is soft, cautious even, as though she can sense the thoughts swirling in my head.

I shake my head, not trusting myself to speak just yet. My hands tremble slightly as they rest in my lap, a faint reminder of the blood that had stained them less than an hour ago.

Thalia and Sera give me a small nod and exit the room, her footsteps fading into the distance, leaving me alone with Ailith.

The silence is heavy, oppressive even, and I can feel Ailith's eyes on me. She moves to sit across from me, one leg crossed over the other, her arms resting lazily on the armrests of her chair. She's wearing her body armour, which is fitted close to her form, sleek and functional, the fabric shimmering in the light as if woven from silk and steel. Despite the elegant surroundings of the tearoom, she's a force of nature—a storm in human form.

I clutch the edge of my teacup, feeling the warmth seep into my palms, trying to ground myself. But the heat only reminds me of the warmth of blood, and suddenly the memory rushes back: the dagger, the cold steel piercing flesh, the woman's lifeless body crumpling at my feet.

I killed her. I ended her life.

And it's not guilt which is making me feel sick.

The tea does nothing to soothe the nausea rising in my throat, and I force myself to take slow, deep breaths, trying to regain control.

Ailith is silent for a long moment, her eyes studying me like a predator sizing up its prey. She's waiting. Watching.

I finally speak, my voice hollow. "I killed her."

Ailith leans forward slightly, resting her elbows on her knees. "Yes. You did." Her tone is blunt, completely without sympathy.

The raw truth of her words is jarring but necessary. She's not coddling me, not pretending like I didn't just take a life. She's acknowledging it in the most direct way possible.

I swallow hard, my hands tightening around the cup. "I've never killed anyone before."

I expect Ailith to raise a brow at me, like spilling a life is nothing. But she looks away, a muscle ticking in her jaw, before leaning back in her chair. "You don't look like the kind of woman who'd spent her life gutting people."

I look up at her, startled by her casual tone, her indifference to the gravity of the situation. "How can you be so… calm about this?"

Ailith shrugs, her lips curling into a wry smile. "Because this is the world we live in, Olwyn. People try to kill you, and you either defend yourself, or you die. There's no room for sentimentality."

I blink, her words hitting me like a cold gust of wind. It's not that I don't understand what she's saying—it's just that I've never been forced to face it so directly.

"You killed someone," she continues, her voice matter of fact. "And you know what? It was necessary. She would have killed you if you hadn't acted. You're alive because you made the right choice. So, why are you sitting here like it's the end of the world?"

My hands shake as I set the teacup down on the table, my stomach still twisted in knots. "Because it feels like the end of something," I admit, my voice quiet. "I feel different. Like something's changed inside me."

Ailith's gaze sharpens, her green eyes boring into mine. "Good," she says bluntly. "It should change you. You've crossed a line that can't be uncrossed. You took control, Olwyn. You saved your own life. That's not something to feel guilty about."

I meet her gaze, the intensity in her eyes forcing me to confront the truth I've been avoiding. She's right. I acted to survive. I defended myself. But the weight of the act still presses down on me, suffocating.

"I wasn't prepared," I say softly. "I wasn't ready."

"No one's ever ready," Ailith replies, her voice sharp. "It doesn't matter how much training you do, how many scenarios you run through in your head. The first time you kill someone, it's going to mess with your head. But don't sit here wallowing in self-pity, because that won't help you. What will help you is realizing that you're stronger for it."

Stronger. The word echoes in my mind, and I try to grasp onto it, to make sense of it.

"I don't feel stronger," I admit.

Ailith snorts, clearly unimpressed with my answer. "That's because you're still letting your emotions control you. You've got the strength, Olwyn, you just need to stop letting your guilt get in the way of seeing it."

I stare at her, my mind a whirlwind of conflicting thoughts, feeling like she's talking about something else. But somewhere beneath the storm, there's a flicker of something else. Something like pride. Or perhaps relief.

I'm alive. I made it out alive.

And she's right. That woman—whoever she was—would have killed me if I hadn't acted. I defended myself. I did what I had to do. And after being attacked by that man, it's nice to feel something other than helpless.

Ailith watches me closely, as though she can see the shift happening inside me, the slow realization dawning. She leans back, her lips twitching into a satisfied smirk. "You're not the same woman who came to this palace. You're learning. You're surviving. And that's what matters."

I exhale shakily, the tension in my chest loosening ever so slightly. "I guess I am."

Ailith takes a sip of her tea, her eyes glinting with approval. "Damn right you are."

I look down at my hands, no longer trembling, and I feel the tiniest spark of confidence flicker to life. Maybe this is what Ailith meant by strength—not just the ability to fight or kill, but the ability to face the consequences of your actions and come out the other side stronger.

Ailith's smile widens, her sharp teeth flashing briefly. "You're finally waking up to who you are. There's a warrior in you, Olwyn. You just had to dig deep enough to find her."

A warrior. The thought settles in my mind, solidifying as I think back to the fight, to how I acted on instinct. To how I didn't hesitate to protect myself.

I killed her because she tried to take something from me.

And I didn't let her.

I take a sip of my tea, the warmth spreading through me, and for the first time since the fight, I feel a sense of peace. Not guilt. Not regret. Just peace.

Ailith watches me for a moment longer, and then, as if sensing the shift in my mood, she stands. "Good talk, Your Majesty," she says, giving me a half-smile that's more approving than mocking this time. "Now, stop worrying about it. You've got bigger things to focus on."

I smile, feeling a strange sense of gratitude toward her bluntness. She didn't coddle me, didn't treat me like a fragile thing. And because of that, I feel... better. Stronger. Surer of myself.

"I will," I say, standing up from the chair and straightening my posture.

Ailith nods, satisfied. "Good. Let's go."

I smile, a real smile this time, and nod in agreement.

For the first time, I feel like I'm not just surviving—I'm thriving.

I don't know what I'd do without Ailith and Iolas.

CHAPTER TWENTY-EIGHT

Olwyn

Iolas and I walk side by side down the dimly lit corridor, the sound of our footsteps muffled by the plush carpets beneath us. It's late, the kind of quiet that wraps around you like a blanket, and the palace seems to hum with an unusual stillness.

We've just finished a long day of ball prep, and my body still aches in ways I didn't know it could from the morning training. Iolas is pushing me harder now and Altair is also training me. And I really am starting to feel the difference.

"Still sore from that last sparring session?" Iolas asks, and I can sense the concern under his teasing tone.

I roll my shoulders, wincing slightly. "I'm fine. Just a little stiff."

He grins, his teeth flashing in the dim light. "I could always give you a massage. You know, to help with the stiffness. Purely professional, of course."

I glance up at him, raising an eyebrow. "Oh, I'm sure it would be *very* professional."

He chuckles, the sound low and easy. "I'm nothing if not a gentleman."

The familiar banter between us makes me smile, and I feel the tension in my body ease a little. Iolas is steady and dependable—that makes it so easy to be around him. Unlike the constant, electric tension I feel around Altair, being with Iolas is like slipping into a warm bath after a long, hard day.

"If you're hurting so much, maybe you should take a day off? Especially after what happened yesterday." Iolas suggests, probably remembering I'm human.

I feel surprisingly fine after my talk with Ailith yesterday. But I think Iolas was expecting the guilt to eat away at me for a bit longer. "It's all right. My end of the deal was to continue training. And I really want to get out of the palace and see something new, so I'll stick with it."

Iolas's feet stall. "What do you mean?" His brows fall, as if he hasn't got a clue what I'm talking about. "Get out of the palace?"

I frown at him. "Altair said I need to keep up with training for two weeks, and then afterward, he'll take me outside the palace."

Iolas's expression shifts subtly, his eyes narrowing just for a moment, though it's not doubt that crosses his face. "All right," he says, his tone easy, though I notice the brief flicker of thought passing behind his eyes. "Just, keep an open mind when you're out there."

I tilt my head, confused by his slight hesitation. "What do you mean?"

"Outside the palace," he says, his voice softer, but still firm. "It's safe enough, with Altair. I trust him completely. But you've never been to towns in the vampire kingdoms, Olwyn." He pauses, choosing his words carefully. "There's a lot to take in. And not everything will be what you expect."

The seriousness in his tone catches me off guard. "I know. That's why I want to go," I say, trying to steady my voice. "I need to see it for myself. To understand. I'm really trying," I tell him. And I am. Gone are the days when I was trying to gather information to escape. Now I'm trying to gather it to *learn*.

The spark of excitement rushes through me, carrying with it an unexpected warmth. For the first time, the world beyond Avantra doesn't feel like a distant, unreachable dream—it feels close, tangible. I want to taste freedom, not just as a way to break away from my past, but to discover what lies beyond it.

Once, freedom had only meant escape—escape from confinement, from ignorance, from the stories that had hemmed me in like thorns. But now, there's more. There's a hunger to know the truth behind those stories, to step into the unknown with open eyes and understand what it is that had been kept from me.

It's a shock to the system, realising… I don't want to escape now.

Iolas nods slowly, clearly holding something back, but when he speaks, his words are gentle. "Good. That's important. Just… if anything feels wrong, or if you wanna talk about what you see… I'm always here. You don't have to take it all on alone."

A sliver of doubt fills my stomach at his words.

"What am I going to see?"

"I don't know where Al plans on taking you, but I imagine he's going to show you what life is really like for vampires and humans here in Noctura."

Before opening my eyes to their world, I would have imagined a kingdom where vampires had a free for all on the humans that lived here. Blood and devastation. But from what I now know I'm excited to see how different it actually must be.

Iolas smiles and his silent offer of comfort means so much, and there's a warmth in his gaze that feels steady and safe, like he's offering more than just reassurance. Like he's offering a quiet place to retreat to, should I need it.

"Iolas…" I start, but the words catch in my throat. What am I even trying to say? "Thank you," I manage after a beat, feeling the sincerity of my own words. "Really."

He shrugs, but his eyes hold mine for a fraction longer than usual. "Someone's got to keep you out of trouble."

I laugh softly, and the tension between us seems to loosen a little. But even as I laugh, I can still feel his gaze lingering, the warmth of it making my pulse flutter unexpectedly. It's easy, natural, the kind of connection that feels like it could deepen without any effort at all.

"So," he says, tilting his head, his tone lightening as he shifts the conversation. "You're *really* looking forward to going out with Al? Old grump?"

"Like you aren't the same age." I nudge him and shrug, trying to downplay the surge of excitement I feel at the thought. "It's… exciting, I guess. I mean, it'll be good to see something beyond these walls. To have some freedom."

He nods thoughtfully, though there's something behind his eyes that I can't quite read. "I get that. But you know," he says after a pause, "if you ever want a break from the grand vampire tour guide, I could show you around some places instead. No pressure."

His tone is teasing, and it makes my stomach flutter. I glance up at him, and for just a second, his usual playful grin fades, replaced by something quieter, more serious.

"It's not a bad offer," I say, my voice softer than I intended.

His grin returns. "Of course it's not. I'm a much better tour guide."

I laugh, shaking my head. "I'll keep that in mind."

The moment stretches between us, the easy banter fading into a comfortable silence. I should say goodnight, should step into my room and close the door, but I don't move. I stand there, my hand on the door handle, feeling like I need to say something, especially when it looks like he's waiting for something.

"You should get some rest," he says, his voice softening again, almost a whisper. There's a gentleness in the way he says it, like he's trying to offer me more than just a simple farewell for the night.

"Yeah," I murmur, finally turning the handle. "Goodnight, Iolas."

"Goodnight, Olwyn," he replies, his voice low.

For a moment, we stand there, the space between us charged with a tension I haven't felt before. It's not the same as with Altair. With him, it's a fire, a raw, burning intensity that threatens to consume me whole. But with Iolas… it's different. Softer. Like the quiet after a storm, when the world feels still and the air is thick with possibility.

I open the door and step inside, the warmth of the room hitting me as I close it behind me. But even after I'm alone, the sound of my name on his lips lingers in the air long after the door clicks shut behind me.

And now I feel confused for a completely new reason.

CHAPTER TWENTY –NINE
Altair

ll I have thought about for two days is that kiss.
And the fact that yet another person has tried to take her life underneath my roof. The tension in my body still hasn't faded.

I haven't broached the subject, but her spirits seem lifted lately, so there a glimmer of hope in my heart that it didn't traumatise her. That she could be… happy.

I sit at my desk, running a hand through my hair, trying to gather my thoughts. But they keep circling back to Olwyn.

I need to tell her soon about Atha. That those trying to kill her are not doing so simply because she married me.

It terrifies me that she might not even choose me when she knows everything.

I clench my fists at my sides, forcing the thought away. If she chooses to leave… if that's what she wants… I'd have to accept it.

But the thought alone… it's like swallowing glass. Because I am falling so hard and fast. It's almost an impossibility at this point not to.

And I don't think I could let her return to Avantra.

Before I can think on it any longer, I hear the soft click of the training room door opening behind me. I don't need to turn to know who it is.

"Iolas," I say, my voice tight.

I hear his footsteps approach. He's not rushing, but there's a heaviness to the way he walks, like there's something weighing on him. He stops just behind me, and I turn to face him, expecting the usual teasing grin, the light-hearted banter. But there's none of that.

His brow is furrowed, his jaw set, and for a moment, I start to panic—until I see it is frustration and not concern that is set on his face.

"So," he begins, his voice low and steady, "you're taking her outside the palace."

I nod, watching him closely. I should have told him my plans. There's something in the way he's holding himself, something tense and coiled. "I am. She needs to see it. Words won't be enough to change her mind."

Iolas crosses his arms, his eyes darkening slightly as he stares at me. "You really think that's wise? Taking her out there? It's going to be a huge shock to her system seeing humans and vampires living peacefully together. Are you prepared for her to realise that you weren't lying when you told her that her whole life in Avantra was a lie? To *react* to that. What if she loses control of her powers?"

My jaw clenches at his words. I know he's right. Olwyn still doesn't know the full truth, not about the world outside these walls. But there's no other way. I can't just tell her—she must see it for herself. She has to understand.

And that's why I've waited so long to introduce her to such a different world. I wanted to ease her into it, but our timeline needs to be brought up. I know it's a risk, but it needs to be done.

"She must see what's out there, Iolas. If we keep her locked in this palace, feeding her bits and pieces of information like a prisoner, she'll never trust me. She'll never believe any of it. We need to show her. Change her perspective through action. It'll make her stronger for when she learns about Atha."

He growls. "Fucking bitch." Iolas's gaze roams over my scarred eye for a split second, before glancing away. He lets out a breath, and for a moment, I see the hesitation in his face. Iolas has always been protective of Olwyn—ever since we brought her here. His loyalty to me is unwavering, but when it comes to Olwyn... there's something different. Something personal.

"I'll be there to protect her," he says, his voice firmer now. "I'll make sure she's safe."

I shake my head, meeting his gaze. "It will just be me and Olwyn."

He blinks, taken aback. "What?"

"There can't be an escort. No guards. No added attention." I say it firmly, making it clear there's no room for negotiation. "If we show up with an entourage, it'll draw eyes. And that's something we can't afford. Not with the tension in the air. Not with Casius's visit nearing."

Iolas's brows knit together, a flicker of concern passing over his face. "You're sure about this?" he asks, voice low, but I can tell he already knows my answer.

I exhale slowly, my gaze shifting toward the window where the first shadows of dusk are beginning to creep in. "Yes. If word gets out that we're visiting, Atha won't need to search for us. We'd be handing her our location on a silver platter. And you know how quickly information spreads in the villages. A single rumour, a sighting from a wary bystander—it's all she'd need."

Iolas nods, but his jaw tightens, the muscle there flexing as if he's biting back a warning. He's right to worry; every step beyond the palace walls comes with its own risks, especially now. But this is the only way.

"You're putting a lot of trust in her." Iolas says.

"I have to," I say simply. "She's putting a lot in me."

He doesn't respond right away, but I can see the tension in his posture, the way his shoulders are tight, the way his jaw works like he's holding something back.

"You care about her," I say. It's not a question. It's a statement, one that hangs heavy in the air between us.

He meets my gaze, his expression unreadable. "Of course I do. But you know that already."

"No, I mean…" I hesitate, my brow furrowing as he looks away. "You care about her more than that, don't you?"

He doesn't answer, and I know it's for my benefit, but I can't help but notice the way his eyes lighten. And for the first time in a long while, I feel a pang of jealousy twist in my chest. Iolas has always been close to her, closer than anyone else in the palace. They share a bond, an easy friendship that comes naturally to them. He's the easy choice for her— safe, reliable, familiar.

I take a breath, forcing myself to look away for a moment.

Because I may be her husband. But I was never her choice. And I've never been the source of that ease. That simplicity. I've been the disruptor, the unfamiliar path. And as much as it claws at me to admit, I can see the way she trusts him, the way she reaches for him instinctively. It's not just habit; it's something deeper, something that makes my chest tighten with an ache I wish I could ignore.

"She cares for you, you know," I say finally, my voice steady but quieter, like speaking too loudly might break the fragile truth between us. "More than she realises."

Iolas blinks, clearly taken aback by my words. "Al—"

"It's all right," I cut him off, my tone firm. "I just want her to be happy."

I married her to keep her safe. To prevent Casius from trying to claim her himself when he found out she had been found. Vampire marriages are sacred, a bond that offers protection and power to the one who stands by your side. I thought, by making her my queen, I could shield her from the dangers surrounding us, offering her a place of safety in a world that would otherwise see her as prey.

But Iolas is more than capable of keeping her safe too. After all this is done.

For a moment, there's silence between us, my words settling like stones. Iolas's jaw works, his eyes flicking away from me as he struggles with whatever's brewing in his mind. And then, finally, he speaks again.

"I care about her," he says quietly, his voice softer now. "She's... we've become close. But I see the way she looks at you, and… you're my best friend, Al. I trust you. I trust that you'll keep her safe." He trails off.

I nod, understanding what he's not saying. There's no jealousy between us, not really. But there's something else, something simmering beneath the surface. Iolas knows me better than anyone, but Olwyn... She's different. She's the one thing we've both been drawn to in ways we haven't fully understood yet.

"I won't let anything happen to her," I promise, my voice low but steady.

Iolas holds my gaze for a moment longer, then nods, his expression softening. "I know. Just... be careful."

"I will."

Iolas knows, just as I do, that this situation with Olwyn is more complicated than either of us expected. But I trust him. I trust that he'll stand by me, no matter what.

And as for Olwyn... I'll let her make her choice. Whatever that may be.

Even if it means watching her walk away from me.

Because her happiness and safety at the end of this is all that matters.

She needs to see. It may be the only way I get her to believe me.

CHAPTER THIRTY

Olwyn

My skin prickles with anticipation, like waiting for the first drop of rain in a thunderstorm.

I stand in the centre of a dimly lit room I can't quite make out, the walls draped in shadow and flickering candlelight. Everything feels hazy, the edges of my vision soft and blurred, the dream making everything feel safe and comfortable. The carpet beneath my feet is as soft as wolf's fur, making me want to lie in it.

But someone steps out of the dark. Altair is there, his eyes like molten obsidian that gleam with a hunger that sends a thrill skittering down my spine. He steps closer, and my breath hitches, my body reacting to the mere proximity of him. The air between us crackles, and I can feel the heat radiating from his skin, seeping into my own. His gaze locks onto mine, and I can't look away.

He reaches out, his fingers brushing lightly against my cheek, trailing down to the curve of my jaw with a touch that feels both possessive and gentle. The cool tips of his fingers leave a trail of fire in their wake, and my eyelids flutter as I lean into the contact, drawn to him like a moth to a flame. Altair's lips part slightly, his breath mingling with mine, and I can feel the faint pull of his shadows curling around my ankles, and brushing up my legs, whispering promises that make my blood sing.

"Olwyn," he murmurs, his voice a low, seductive rumble that sends a shiver through me. His thumb brushes over my lower lip, and I can't help the soft sound that escapes me—a half-whimper, half-moan that makes him groan.

I want him.

I crave the darkness he offers, the consuming fire that threatens to swallow me whole.

He leans in, his mouth hovering just above mine, so close that I can feel the warmth of his breath, the barest brush of his lips against my own. My heart races, every nerve alight with the promise of his touch. His hand slides to the back of my neck, pulling me closer, and just as our lips are about to meet—

The world shifts.

I blink, and Altair's dark eyes shift, lightening into a familiar hazel. Iolas's face looms before me, his features carved in shadow and candlelight, but the energy is different. The playfulness that usually dances in his gaze is gone, replaced by something sharper, more urgent. I gasp, the sudden change jolting through me, but my body reacts on instinct, driven by the undeniable pull between us.

Iolas's hands find my waist, his grip firm, almost desperate, and a soft growl rumbles from his chest as he pulls me flush against him. My head spins, confusion mingling with desire, and I can't help the way my fingers curl into his hair, anchoring myself to him even as the world tilts around us.

The heat between us intensifies, a slow, building fire that burns from the inside out. Iolas's lips are mere inches from mine, and I can feel his breath, hot and ragged, against my skin. His thumb grazes the hollow of my throat, and I gasp, my body arching toward him, craving the release that his touch promises.

"You're playing with fire, little witch," he murmurs, his voice rough and edged with a warning that only stokes the flames higher.

I know this is wrong. The rational part of my mind screams that this isn't real, that I shouldn't be here, like this, with him. But the line between what I want and what I should do blurs, lost in the haze of heat and longing that coils in my belly.

Iolas's lips finally crash against mine, and the world dissolves into a haze of sensation—the press of his body, the taste of him, the rough drag of his teeth over my lower lip. The kiss is urgent, almost bruising, and I meet him with equal fervour, my hands fisting in his hair as if I can't get close enough, as if I need to consume him to quench the burning in my veins.

His hands roam over me, exploring, claiming, and every touch sends sparks dancing across my skin. My breath hitches, and I moan into his mouth, the sound swallowed by the intensity of the kiss. Iolas deepens it, his grip tightening, and it feels like we're both on the edge.

But then, something shifts. The taste of him changes—familiar yet darker, sharper. The hands gripping my waist feel different, slender, more possessive. It's subtle at first, like my mind is playing tricks on me, but then I realise… it's not Iolas anymore.

It's Altair.

His scent invades my senses—dark and musky, tinged with the sharp tang of a storm on the horizon. The kiss changes, too. It's no longer frantic and wild but deliberate, demanding. The way his lips move against mine, the way his tongue teases my mouth open… it's as if he's staking a claim, branding me with every kiss, every touch.

My heart races, confusion mingling with desire as I try to pull away, to make sense of the shift. But his hands grip tighter, holding me in place, his body pressing into mine with an intensity that makes it impossible to think.

"Altair?" I whisper against his lips, my voice shaky, uncertain.

He doesn't answer, just pulls me closer, his lips trailing down my neck, leaving a burning trail in their wake. My breath catches, my body betraying me as heat floods my core. Every inch of me aches for him, even though my mind is screaming that this is wrong, that this wasn't how it was supposed to go.

But he doesn't care. His hands are everywhere, claiming me, owning me. And I find myself melting into him, unable to resist the pull, the gravity of him. It's intoxicating, overwhelming, and I can't help but wonder if I'll ever be able to pull away.

And then, just as suddenly as it began, the dream fractures, the sensation of falling pulling me away from the tangled heat of their embrace. I gasp, my eyes snapping open to the still darkness of my room, my heart hammering in my chest as reality crashes back in.

The room is quiet, the shadows familiar and still, but the echoes of the dream linger, hot and heavy in the air. I press a trembling hand to my lips, the phantom sensation of their kisses still tingling on my skin. My heart is a chaotic drumbeat, caught somewhere between fear and exhilaration, and I can't quite shake the feeling that, in some way, the lines between dream and desire have blurred irrevocably.

Something's… different. Why does she blush so?

CHAPTER THIRTY–ONE
Olwyn

The breakfast table is unusually warm this morning—as usual, I sit between Altair and Iolas.

The food smells delicious, and there's a peace to the moment that feels… strange. Comforting, even. Altair's close presence is less daunting than it used to be, though I'm still hyper-aware of every glance he sends my way, every movement of his hands as they cut through a slice of fruit or lift a cup to his lips.

Iolas, on the other hand, is his usual self, casual and relaxed, though there's an edge to his smile this morning. He's been watching me closely since our conversation last night, and I feel his attention even now.

"So," Altair begins, breaking the comfortable silence. He's looking at me now, his eyes sharp but warm, as if he's about to deliver news he knows I'll like.

"As we all know, the ball is being held within the week," he says, his tone light. "I'm so happy you've been so heavily involved in the process. Your touch has truly made this event something special."

I smile back. I had been surprised by my invested interest in all the small choices going into planning a ball. Flower colours, fabrics, décor. It had been quite fun spending that time with staff.

Now the excitement of the ball, the planning, and all the details I'd worked on fill me with a sense of accomplishment. "My staff are absolutely thrilled, too," he continues, his voice filled with genuine enthusiasm. "They're excited to see all the hard work come together."

I flush slightly, my cheeks warming with his praise, a pleased smile tugging at the corners of my mouth. After months of being confined to the palace, it feels good to finally be part of something so grand, something I helped shape.

But then Altair's expression shifts again, his gaze turning more serious. "The day after the ball, we'll be holding talks with Casius," he says, his voice steady. "I want you to be present. It's important, as a show of solidarity. Your presence will send a message."

I get it. I really do.

I can hate the fact Altair wants this to look like a happy union. But I can also respect he looks very regretful about that.

I nod, my stomach twisting slightly. "Of course," I say, though the thought of dealing with Casius sends an unsettling chill through me.

Curiosity tugs at me, and I look up at him, hesitant. "What's Casius really like? I've heard the name, the horror stories, but…" I trail off, unsure how to describe the uneasy feeling swirling in my chest.

Altair's expression tightens, his jaw clenching briefly before he answers, his tone thoughtful. "Casius is cocksure, no question. He's always carried that arrogance with him." He pauses, his gaze sharpening. "But don't let that fool you. He's fiercely intelligent—strategic in a way that makes him dangerous. We can't underestimate him."

I digest his words, feeling the weight of them sink into me.

I consider his words carefully, my mind turning. "Arrogance often disguises insecurity," I say, and Altair's eyes widen in surprise. "If he's as strategic as you say, he's probably calculating his every move, making sure he never shows his weaknesses. He probably knows exactly what he wants out of these talks already. So, we need to stay two steps ahead of him."

Altair meets my gaze, his expression flickering with approval. "Exactly," he says, a rare hint of admiration in his voice. "I'm glad you see that."

I nod slowly, but then a thought strikes me, and I feel a shift inside. If I'm to be a part of this—if this is truly my kingdom as much as his—then I need to understand what we're really offering, or what we want in these talks.

I square my shoulders, pushing away the lingering unease, and meet his gaze with resolve. "What exactly are we offering in these peace talks, Altair? What do we want from Casius?"

His lips twitch, as if weighing how much to say, but then he speaks. "I'm offering peace. No more battles in the human realm, no more bloodshed in their cities. We've suffered long enough under the threat of constant war. I'm willing to end that, but only if Casius agrees to stop encroaching on our territory. We both need to be held accountable without the endless cycles of violence."

"And if he refuses?" I ask, my voice steady, though a knot of uncertainty tightens in my stomach.

Altair looks away for the first time, a muscle in his jaw clenching. "With you here he won't."

His words linger in the air, heavy with unspoken meaning. I search his face, trying to read between the lines, but it's as though he's hiding something—something more personal.

"Is it because of me? Because I'm the subject of the prophecy? Or because I'm your wife?" I ask.

Finally, he meets my gaze, and there's a vulnerability in his eyes that I haven't seen before. "Both," he admits quietly.

I sit back, absorbing his words. The implications weigh on me, but something nags at the back of my mind. I squint slightly, suddenly piecing things together in a way I hadn't before.

"You and Casius," I say, the realisation dawning on me. "You know each other, don't you?"

Altair doesn't immediately respond, his jaw tightening as though the thought of Casius is one he prefers to avoid. But I can see it now—the subtle tension, the way his voice shifts when he speaks of him.

I glance across the table, noticing Iolas has been unusually quiet this whole time. He leans back in his chair, arms crossed, watching us with a knowing look in his eyes. "Oh, they know each other all right." he says, his voice teasing but with an underlying seriousness. "Old friends," he adds with a sarcastic tone.

Altair shoots him a sharp look, but Iolas just raises an eyebrow, unfazed. Whatever has happened between them, their history doesn't seem good. But I don't want to pry if it causes Altair pain.

"So, what does this mean for the talks with him?" I ask, my mind racing as I try to understand the full scope of what we're facing.

Altair's gaze hardens again, and he leans forward, his voice lowering. "It means that it's personal. I don't trust him, and he won't trust me. But we have no choice but to meet, to negotiate, if we want to keep this peace."

I nod, my thoughts swirling.

"On a more positive note," Altair changes the subject. He's looking at me now. "Tomorrow, we're going out of the palace."

My fork pauses mid-air, and I stare at him for a moment, letting the words sink in. "Out?" I echo, unable to contain the excitement creeping into my voice.

Altair's lips twitch into the smallest hint of a smile. "Yes. I told you two weeks. And you gave me those two weeks. It's time you saw more than just these walls."

My heart leaps, and I feel a wide grin spread across my face before I can stop it. "We're really going?"

Both Altair and Iolas exchange a glance, and I catch the flicker of amusement in their expressions, though they both seem to soften at my enthusiasm.

Iolas leans back in his chair, crossing his arms over his chest. "Look at her. She's ready to burst with excitement."

I flush slightly, realising how giddy I must sound, but the excitement bubbling inside me is hard to tamp down. After months of being confined to this palace, of feeling the pressure of these grand walls closing in on me, the idea of stepping outside—of seeing what's beyond— is exhilarating.

"However," Altair says, his tone turning a touch more serious. "There is something else we need to handle before we leave tomorrow."

I pause, my fork still hovering over my plate. The shift in his voice sets my nerves on edge. "What is it?"

Altair's gaze meets mine, steady and unyielding. "I need you to attend a council meeting with me today."

I blink, feeling the excitement drain from my body. A council meeting. With all the vampire lords. The last time I was in a room with them, Dazeem lost his hand. For touching me. The memory rushes back, the feel of his disgusting fingers gripping me, and I have to suppress a shudder.

"Why?" I ask, my voice quieter now, my earlier excitement giving way to a knot of anxiety in my stomach.

Altair's eyes narrow slightly, as if reading my thoughts, sensing the hesitation. "You're my queen," he says, his voice firm but gentle. "You need to be seen as such by them. You've been too absent from their discussions since I returned. It's time you show them who they are."

Altair had never brought it up since that day in the council room, never asked me to go with him, likely knowing it would have made me uncomfortable around Dazeem. I had felt a quiet relief at that, grateful for the unspoken understanding between us that I didn't want to attend them. But now, as he sits before me, his gaze sharp, I sense the change.

I swallow hard, trying to push the rising panic down. "But Dazeem—"

"I know," Altair cuts in, his gaze hardening just a fraction at the mention of the vampire lord's name. "He'll be there. But so will I. And so will Iolas." He pauses, leaning in slightly, his voice lowering to a more intimate tone. "You have nothing to fear from him anymore, Olwyn. He can't touch you again. You could end him in a second, if you wanted to. Dazeem may be a vampire, but he's never spent a day in a training arena."

His words stir something in me—but the thought of facing Dazeem, of sitting in that room with all those vampires thinking they are better than me, fills me with dread.

Altair must see the hesitation on my face because he reaches across the table, his hand brushing mine. It's a small gesture, but it's grounding.

"You are a queen, Olwyn," he reminds me softly, his eyes locking onto mine. "And you have the power to show them just how strong you are. You've already proven that you're not to be underestimated by the way you handled that assassin, and the way you have helped organise the ball."

I nod, though I don't feel entirely convinced. My mind is still swirling with the memory of Dazeem's sneer, the way he leered at me as if I was nothing. "I'm not sure I'm ready," I admit, my voice barely above a whisper.

"You are," Altair says, his tone leaving no room for argument. "And I'll be with you every step of the way."

I glance over at Iolas, hoping for some kind of reprieve or distraction, but he's watching me intently, his expression serious. "You've handled worse, little witch," Iolas says. "Look at how you lived back in Avantra. All those lords have been brought up with a stick up their arse, believing they're better than everyone. They've never experienced a day of hardship in their lives. Well, beside Dazeem losing his hand." I laugh as he continues, and he's not wrong. "And like Altair said, we'll both be there."

His words help, but the nerves still flutter in my stomach. I look back at Altair, my fingers tightening slightly around the edge of the table. "What if… what if it goes badly?"

Altair's smirks, "If anyone tries anything, they'll have you to deal with." His gaze darkens, shadows flickering in his eyes. "And you'll see just how much power you hold here. Trust me, Olwyn."

I take a deep breath, letting his words settle over me like a blanket of reassurance. It's not much, but it's enough for now.

"All right," I say, my voice steadier than I feel.

Altair smiles, and for a moment, there's something almost proud in his expression. "Good."

I feel a mix of excitement and dread swirling in my chest—excited for tomorrow's freedom beyond the palace, and anxious about facing the lords today.

"Let's finish breakfast," Altair says, cutting through my thoughts. "We'll go soon."

I nod, but as I take a bite of the fruit on my plate, the taste is muted, the nerves twisting in my stomach too tightly for me to fully enjoy it. I catch Altair glancing at me from the corner of my eye, his expression softening just slightly, as if he can see the storm of emotions swirling inside me.

But then he returns to his meal, the moment passing as quickly as it came, and I focus on steadying my breath, reminding myself of the words he spoke.

I'm a queen.

The title still feels foreign, heavy, and cold, like a crown made of iron pressing into my skull. What does it mean to truly be a queen in this vampire kingdom where I believed at the beginning that my role was more a prison than a throne? I didn't choose this life. It was thrust upon me, a role forced into my trembling hands with little more than the expectation to survive.

Now, knowing everything I do, and having gotten… *closer*, to Altair, if I had the choice today, would I still agree to be his queen? The question sits in my chest like a stone. The truth is, I don't know. I've starting to accept this title, to wield it when needed, but not out of love or loyalty.

Not yet.

It's a mantle of survival, a mask I wear to protect myself in a court that would devour me if it sensed weakness.

But the thought of Dazeem looking down on *me*, sharpens my resolve, igniting a fire in my chest. Can I claim this role that was forced upon me and make it mine? I glance at Altair, who looks every bit the unyielding king, a man who truly believes I am capable of standing by his side as an equal.

I can face them. Even Dazeem.

The alternative is to let this kingdom crush me under its weight, to let these vampires, these nobles, and their labyrinth of power games strip me of whatever control I have left. And that… that is not an option. The thought might make my heart pound, might make the shadows seem deeper and the whispers sharper, but fear can be a weapon too.

Let them watch. Let them scheme. I'll meet them head-on.

I can't wait to see her own her title as my queen.

CHAPTER THIRTY-TWO

Olwyn

Back in my chambers after breakfast, the reality of the **upcoming council meeting starts to sink in.**

My excitement from earlier has completely drained, replaced by a gnawing pit of anxiety. I pace the room, pausing every few steps to glance at the wardrobe, as if somehow the right outfit will magically appear and give me the confidence I need.

But no matter how many times I look, no matter how many silks and satins I run my hands over, none of it feels right.

The very idea of walking into that council chamber again makes my stomach twist with dread. Last time, Altair cut off a hand in my defence. What if something worse happens this time?

A knock on the door breaks my spiralling thoughts. Before I can respond, Ailith strides into the room without waiting for an invitation.

Typical.

"Gods, you look like you're about to throw up," she says bluntly, raising a brow as she takes in my pale face and nervous fidgeting. "What's wrong with you?"

I glance at her, momentarily stunned by her entrance, but then I release a breath. "I'm about to face those psychotic lords again," I mutter, sitting down on the edge of the bed. "Including Dazeem. So forgive me if I'm not exactly brimming with confidence."

Ailith snorts, crossing her arms as she leans against the doorframe. "Oh please. Don't waste your time worrying about those self-important bastards." She rolls her eyes, stepping further into the room. "And Dazeem? That snivelling coward won't dare look in your direction without pissing himself. You've got nothing to be afraid of."

I stare at her, taken aback by her casual dismissal of my fears. But then, I shouldn't really be surprised. "It's not that simple, Ailith. What if they turn against him? What if holding a human in higher regard than one of their own makes them doubt him? Makes them doubt us?"

Ailith raises a brow, unconcerned. "They can doubt all they want, Olwyn. Let them test his resolve." She moves to the wardrobe and flings it open without a second thought. "And if they dare question either of you, let them see what happens when someone crosses you." She glances back at me, her eyes narrowing. "You're a queen, Olwyn. Act like it."

I shake my head, feeling a mixture of frustration and helplessness. "But shouldn't I be trying to earn their respect?"

Ailith lets out a harsh laugh, rifling through the dresses hanging neatly in the wardrobe. "Respect? Who gives a fuck about their respect? Make them fear you instead." She pulls out a dark blue gown, holding it up to me with a critical eye. "Respect is earned, but fear is immediate. And believe me, nothing will make those lords squirm faster than seeing you walk in there like you own the place."

I hesitate, staring at the dress in her hands. It's a deep, midnight blue with intricate silver embroidery along the edges. It's regal—commanding. It's not something I would have picked for myself, but seeing it now, I realise it's perfect.

"Fear?" I repeat, feeling uncertain. "I don't know if I want to rule by fear."

Ailith steps closer, her expression hard. "It's not about *ruling* by fear, Olwyn. It's about showing the nobles that you won't be pushed around. That you're not some weak little thing they can control or manipulate. They need to know that you're not just some figurehead queen. You're Altair's equal, and you have just as much power as any of them—if not more."

Her words hit me hard, sinking deep into my chest. Altair has been telling me the same thing, in his own way. But hearing it from Ailith, with her no-nonsense attitude and blatant disregard for what anyone thinks… it's different. She's not trying to coddle me. She's telling me to stand up, to fight, to own my place in this world.

I look at the dress again, the fabric catching the light as it shifts in her hands. It's bold. Strong. I need to be bold. I need to be strong.

"I… I don't know if I can make them fear me," I admit quietly, my fingers brushing against the soft fabric of the bedspread.

Ailith drops the dress onto the bed and steps in front of me, bending down so we're eye to eye. "Yes, you can," she says firmly. "Where's the girl that stood up to a king when she first met him? You've already survived worse than these stuffy old vampires. You made it through the attack in your room and in the courtyard. You've kept your head through everything Altair's thrown at you." She leans in closer, her voice dropping to a conspiratorial whisper. "You think Dazeem's going to be the thing that breaks you? Please. The only reason he's still breathing is because you let him."

I bite my lip, a small part of me wanting to believe her. Ailith straightens, a wicked grin on her face as she sees the doubt beginning to waver in my expression.

"You need to stop giving a fuck about what they think of you, just because you're human," she continues, grabbing the dress and tossing it at me. I catch it just in time. "You are Queen Olwyn. You've got Altair and Iolas at your side, and let me tell you, those bastards can strike fear into the hearts of gods. You're not walking into that room alone."

I blink, staring down at the dress now resting in my lap. The dark fabric is cool against my skin, and the silver thread catches the light just right, making it shimmer. It's beautiful. Powerful.

"Besides," Ailith adds, her grin widening. "You look damn good in blue."

A laugh bubbles up inside me before I can stop it, and I shake my head, feeling the tension in my shoulders begin to ease. "You're impossible."

"Thank you," she says, taking it as a compliment. "Now get dressed. Knock them dead."

I stand, feeling a little lighter as I walk toward the changing screen. "What would I do without your incredible words of wisdom?"

Ailith leans against the wall, crossing her arms with a satisfied smirk. "Probably crumble into a heap of anxiety and self-doubt. But don't worry, I'm not going anywhere."

As I step behind the screen and begin to change into the dress, I can't help but feel a small surge of confidence growing inside me. Maybe Ailith's right. Maybe I've been letting my fears and insecurities control me for too long. It's time to take control of the situation. To walk into that council room like I belong there.

Because I do.

The dress slips over my skin, soft and smooth, but it feels grounding. I stare down at the blue fabric, the silver embroidery catching the light.

When I step out from behind the screen, Ailith gives a low whistle. "Now that's what I'm talking about. Let's do your hair."

My eyes nearly pop out of their sockets at the idea of Ailith doing that. But she does, and does it with expert skill, curling it at the ends and securing a silver crown on my head.

"There. You look like a queen."

I glance at myself in the mirror, surprised by the reflection that looks back at me. I look strong. I look… powerful.

And for the first time in a long time, I believe I might actually be.

"Go give 'em shit," Ailith says, giving me a firm pat on the shoulder.

I take a deep breath, squaring my shoulders as I face the door.

I am a queen. And I want to make a difference.

It's time to act like one.

CHAPTER THIRTY-THREE
Altair

The council room is filled with the usual noise.
Low murmurs, the occasional snicker, the rustling of papers as the vampire lords settle into their seats. The air is heavy with the scent of old wood, fine leather, and a faint trace of something metallic, like old blood—probably Dazeem's.

The thought makes me smile. The vampire lords chatter among themselves, old grievances and rivalries filling the space with a tension that never quite goes away.

I sit at the head of the table, Iolas stood to my left, scanning the room with the usual calm indifference I've perfected over the years. But today, there's something else simmering beneath the surface. Anticipation. Nerves. Maybe even a flicker of excitement.

Across from me, Dazeem tries to keep his head down, his metal hand resting awkwardly on the table. He refuses to look in my direction, which is just as well. I catch the small tremor in his remaining hand as he fumbles with a piece of parchment, and the sight fills me with a dark sense of satisfaction. I've seen his eyes dart to the crack in the middle, where his body splintered it.

He's already hiding—coward. He hasn't looked me in the eye since the day I removed his hand. Since the day he touched Olwyn.

"Think they're expecting an execution," Iolas mutters under his breath, leaning slightly toward me, a smirk tugging at his lips as he watches the lords shuffle nervously in their seats. "Always makes for an interesting meeting."

I grunt in response, my eyes flicking to the door. Olwyn should be here by now. I need her here.

Two guards open the double doors and Ailith strides in with her usual casual arrogance, moving to stand by my side. Her presence, crass as it often is, brings an odd sense of comfort. She's blunt, but reliable. Always where she needs to be.

I glance at her, speaking quietly under my breath. "Is she coming?"

Ailith's lips curl into a slow, knowing smile, a gleam of mischief in her eyes. "Oh, she's coming. Give her a moment."

I can't help the small smile tugging at my own lips. "Thank you… for helping her."

Ailith shrugs, though her grin remains. "Someone's got to knock some sense into her, and you're too damn soft."

I snort, shaking my head. When it comes to Olwyn, she's not wrong. Ailith nudges my shoulder with hers before turning her gaze toward the door, anticipation flickering in her eyes.

And then… she appears.

Olwyn strides through the entrance, and everything else falls away. The council's murmurs fade into nothing, the ambient noise of the room vanishing as my focus zeroes in on her.

Gods.

She looks… *magnificent.*

Spring green eyes lined with kohl, lips rosy red. The dark blue dress clings to her figure, the silver embroidery catching the light in such a way that it almost looks like she's glowing. The fabric flows around her as she walks, something undeniably fierce about her.

But it's not what she wears that holds their attention—it's the way she carries herself, the strength etched into every line of her body.

As she walks toward me, I read every face in the room, and I know Iolas is doing the same.

Across the room, Dazeem is practically cowering. The moment Olwyn steps into the council chamber, he shrinks back into his seat, refusing to meet her eyes. His metal hand twitches on the table, the faint scrape of it against the wood the only sound coming from him. He's avoiding her completely, staring down at his lap as if hoping she won't notice him.

Good. He *should* fear her. They all know she killed the most recent assassin herself, and that she could end any one of them in a heartbeat.

But it's actually Lord Damien who I keep my gaze on. Some of the older council members exchange glances, their expressions hard. But Lord Damien's seems to be the most openly disapproving.

He's always been more vocal of his dislike of humans, even though they work in my palace and live in our kingdom, and I can see his mouth curving into a bitter line. He won't stay quiet, not when he sees his chance to undermine Olwyn.

He leans forward, resting his elbows on the table as he sighs with open boredom. "Now that your pet has arrived, can we get this meeting underway?" Each word is sharp, a blade dipped in contempt.

A murmur ripples through the council, like the rustle of dry leaves before a storm. I can feel the heat building in the room, not from anger but from something more potent: anticipation. I don't move, don't speak. As much as I'd love to rip out his tongue and serve it to Olwyn on a silver dish, today this must be her battle to fight, and I won't rob her of the chance.

Olwyn's gaze snaps to Damien, her eyes narrowing into slits of controlled fury. The silence that follows is suffocating. When she finally speaks, her voice is dangerous. "Pet?" The single word hangs in the air, and for a heartbeat, I see the first flicker of uncertainty cross Damien's face.

She steps forward, her head held high, back straight. "I stand here not by Altair's will, but by my own. I've listened to the people of this kingdom—their fears, their hopes—and I want to fight for them. If that makes me a pet in your eyes, then perhaps it's time you questioned who really has command of the room." She holds her arms out wide, and the guards around the edges of the room, Iolas included, stand to attention.

A few scattered gasps break the tension, and the corners of my mouth tug up despite myself. This is why I chose her. This is why I will always choose her.

Damien's eyes widen, the scorn draining from his face. He recovers quickly, but it's too late; the damage has been done.

"If anyone else doubts my right to be here," she continues, sweeping her gaze over the crowd, "speak now and face me."

She shifts, allowing the split in her dress to open and reveal the dagger at her thigh. It's not witchsilver, so they all know she won't kill them, but I hope their imaginations allow them to think of all the ways she could draw out their pain.

The silence deepens, shifting from doubt to something more cautious, more respectful. Even those who once glared now avert their eyes, unwilling to meet her stare.

I hold her gaze, letting her see the pride I won't voice out loud, not now. She doesn't need me to speak for her; she never did. And as the moments stretch on, the room starts to bend—not completely, not easily, but it bends, nonetheless.

Damien's jaw clenches, his fingers curling into fists on the table. But he doesn't say anything, and neither does anyone else. Some of the younger lords exchange glances, tentative nods of approval passing between them. A few heads even bow, acknowledging what she just proved.

Every pair of eyes in the room is on her, and for the first time, I think they're seeing her for what she truly is: a queen. Not just my queen. *Their* queen.

I feel a surge of pride swell in my chest. This is the Olwyn I always knew existed beneath the surface—the strength, the fire. And seeing it return after being attacked, seeing her step into this role, seeing her own her power… it's more than I could have hoped for.

To my left, Iolas stands straighter, his eyes wide with something like shock, or awe. He, too, recognises what's happening here. His gaze lingers on her a moment longer before he catches me looking, and he gives a small nod, like he's acknowledging this transformation in her.

Olwyn's strides don't falter, though I catch the briefest flicker of hesitation as she reaches the head of the table. There are no empty seats. Her gaze shifts to me, just for a second, and I can see it—the brief panic in her eyes. It's fleeting, but it's there. She's searching for where she's supposed to sit. She's already proven her strength, her confidence, but now… now, she's unsure.

And I know exactly what to do.

Before anyone can move, I stand and step away from my chair, my hand gesturing toward it. "My queen," I say softly with a bow, my voice carrying just enough authority to silence any remaining murmurs from the lords.

Her eyes widen, but only for a heartbeat. She quickly schools her expression, her chin lifting again as she steps forward and takes my place at the head of the table.

As she settles into the chair, I catch the briefest twitch of her lips—a small, almost imperceptible smile. She casts a glance around the room, her gaze sharp as it meets each of the vampire lords. None of them dare speak. None of them dare challenge her. They're waiting, watching.

I move without hesitation, stepping around the chair and settling on the arm beside her. I lounge casually, one leg crossed over the other, my posture relaxed but deliberate. Close, but not looming.

And gods, it feels right.

It feels *so* right.

"So," she says. "Let's begin."

Lord Pias, an older lady with streaks of silver in her dark hair clears her throat, leaning forward.

"Your Majesty," she begins, directing her words directly to Olwyn, her tone polite but edged with doubt, "it is admirable that you've chosen to take part in these proceedings again, but I wonder, what would a queen raised outside of our realm know of its struggles, of the blood and history that runs through its veins?"

A murmur of agreement hums through a few of the gathered lords and ladies. The question, though carefully phrased, is a test. I lean slightly toward her, my arm brushing against the back of the chair as I play with a strand of silver, moonlight hair—a small gesture of silent support. From this angle, I can see the flicker of determination in her eyes, the way her chin lifts just a little higher.

"I may not have grown up in Noctura, Lady Pias," she replies, her voice calm and deliberate, "but I have listened to your people. Many of you might not know this—when I lived in Avantra, I was hidden away. Kept out of sight as if I were something to be ashamed of."

A ripple of surprise washes over the room. Even Lord Damien's brows lift slightly, the sneer on his lips faltering. Dazeem remains as quiet as ever, staring at the table.

"I know what it is to feel powerless," Olwyn continues, a note of raw honesty threading through her tone. "To be seen as nothing more than an asset or a tool. Just as this war makes many of your citizens feel overlooked, used, and starved of their true potential."

A sudden wave of pride swells in my chest, mixing with a bitter pang as her words sink in. The memory of finding her that night, half-starved, neglected yet unyielding, resurfaces with a painful clarity. My fists clench at my sides.

"And Altair saved me from that," she adds, her gaze flicking to mine for a heartbeat. The sincerity in her voice is an unexpected blow, and I have to fight to keep my expression neutral. My heart skips—a traitorous, impossible beat—as the air between us crackles with unspoken gratitude.

A gratitude I never believed I would deserve.

Damien's eyes flick between us, catching the silent exchange, and his expression shifts, curiosity dimming his earlier defiance.

"I know the pain of being denied your identity," Olwyn says, her chin lifting defiantly. "But I am here now, not just because Altair wills it, but because I want to fight for those who have been left in the dark. I want to give voice to those who are unheard. And that is why I sit here today as your queen—not out of circumstance, but by choice."

A quiet descends over the room, the murmurs stilled. Lady Pias's eyes hold a flicker of something new, an understanding, perhaps, or a grudging respect.

"And if that future calls for sacrifice?" Her voice is softer now, probing for any sign of hesitation.

"Then I will share in those sacrifices," Olwyn says, her voice unwavering. "Because I am one of them, the overlooked and underestimated. And I will fight for this kingdom as fiercely as Altair fought for me to reclaim my own worth."

The room remains silent, the tension palpable. Then Lord Damien nods once, a shallow dip of his head that feels more genuine than the deepest bow.

"Then perhaps, Your Majesty," he says, a touch warmer now, "we do have the queen we need after all."

I can't help the slight easing of my shoulders, the silent exhale that accompanies the warmth in my heart. She's proven herself—not just to them, but to me. And as the room shifts from scrutiny to contemplation, I know that this is only the beginning of what Olwyn will achieve.

This is her moment.

And I couldn't be prouder.

All hail my beautiful queen.

CHAPTER THIRTY-FOUR

Olwyn

The council meeting is finally over, and with it, the tense air that had been weighing on me yesterday morning has dissipated.

But my mind doesn't have much time to dwell on the events—because now, something entirely different awaits.

I stand next to Altair in the stables, watching as he expertly adjusts the saddle on a sleek black horse. He moves with such precision, his fingers deftly securing the leather straps, and for a moment, I'm lost in the ease with which he handles the animal.

Until…

One horse.

My mind snags on that fact, and I swallow, trying not to let the *closeness* of what's about to happen overwhelm me. Sharing a horse means close proximity. Very close. And though I've grown accustomed to Altair's presence, there's something about riding together that feels… intimate.

There's a part of me that wants to ask why we couldn't take two horses, but the rational part knows the answer. It's safer this way, less conspicuous. And yet, knowing that doesn't make the fluttering in my chest any less noticeable.

Altair's hands brush against mine as he tightens the final strap. "You'll sit in front," he says, his voice low and calm, like this is the most natural thing in the world.

I nod, my throat suddenly dry. I'm trying not to overthink it, trying not to let the thought of being pressed against him for hours on end fluster me more than it already has. But I can't help the flutter of nerves that swirl in my chest. My fingers brush absently over the braided crown of my hair, smoothing it down for the hundredth time.

At least I know how to ride, I remind myself. The memory of the baker's boy sneaking me out for late-night rides across the moonlit fields of Avantra tugs at the corners of my mind. His laughter echoing as he taught me to grip the reins, the thrill of feeling the horse's muscles bunch and move beneath me as we galloped through the stillness of the night. Those stolen moments of freedom were a rare joy, a hint of adventure in a life otherwise cloaked in lies.

But this ride with Altair, feels different—charged with an anticipation I can't quite name.

"You're nervous," Altair observes, glancing at me from the corner of his eye. His lips quirk into a small, knowing smile.

"I'm not," I lie, my voice betraying me with its slight tremor. "I just haven't… ridden with many people before."

I had been taken from Avantra in a gilded carriage, but this trip requires more… subtlety.

His smile widens, "You'll be fine. I'll make sure of it, of course."

He *winks*.

He's teasing me. Prick.

Before I can respond, I hear Iolas approaching from behind, his footsteps heavy with tension. He's never been subtle, and today is no different. His expression is tight, his brows furrowed as he eyes the horse and then Altair. There's a flicker of something in his gaze—worry. I hate seeing him anything other than happy and joking.

"Iolas, we'll be fine," I say, though I don't actually know where we're going

He shakes his head slightly, his lips pressed into a thin line. "I still don't like this." His eyes dart to the vampire king, narrowing slightly. "And without a guard escort…"

"It's necessary," Altair replies evenly, not pausing in his movements. He doesn't need to explain further—this has been their disagreement from the start. Too many people, too many eyes. Something Altair wants to avoid at all costs. After the two assassination attempts on my life, Altair explained he didn't want to draw attention to us.

Iolas huffs, clearly still unconvinced. "And what if you're spotted by a stranger? What if something happens?"

"If something happens, I'll handle it," Altair says, standing up straight and turning to face his friend. "You know we're not going far—it's safe."

Iolas's gaze shifts to me, and there's something almost protective in his expression. "I know the village is safe. But Olwyn's barely seen anything beyond palace walls."

I bristle slightly, the need to defend myself flaring up instinctively. The truth is, being out here should terrify me after so many years confined within royal chambers. The unfamiliar world beyond these walls has always been more rumour than reality, a place I've only glimpsed in stories shared in hushed tones. But now, out in the open, with so little knowledge of what to expect, there's an unfamiliar rush beneath my skin—an exhilaration that pushes aside fear.

Before I can voice my thoughts, Altair's deep voice cuts through the air, answering for me. "She'll be with me," he says, his tone final. "Nothing will happen to her."

But Iolas doesn't relax. If anything, his jaw tightens. "And where exactly are you planning to stay tonight?"

Altair turns to me, his gaze flicking over my expression as if gauging my reaction. "The inn," he says casually. "I trust Abbas. It'll do for the night."

I blink, the words catching me off guard. "We're staying overnight?"

Altair's gaze shifts to mine, his expression softening just a touch. "Yes. The village is a bit far for a one-day journey. We'll return in the morning."

An inn? The realisation hits me with a jolt. We'll be staying somewhere… together. Alone. The thought sends a mixture of nerves thrumming through my veins. I nod, trying to keep my expression neutral, though I'm certain my face betrays at least a flicker of uncertainty.

Iolas's eyes flick between us, his concern still evident, but he doesn't argue further. "Just… be careful. Both of you. If you're not back by moon rise tomorrow, I'll come find you."

"We will be careful," Altair says, his voice calm but firm. He moves towards me then, offering a hand to help me onto the horse.

I hesitate for just a second before taking it, and as our hands touch, a spark of awareness shoots up my arm. He's warm, steady, and when he helps me up into the saddle, I can't ignore the way my heart skips a beat at the effortless strength behind his grip.

Altair mounts behind me, his chest brushing against my back as he settles into the saddle. The feel of him so close, his body solid and warm, is more overwhelming than I expected. My heart races, and I silently berate myself for reacting this way. It's just proximity. Nothing more.

Except it's not nothing. I can feel the warmth of his breath near my ear, the solid press of his chest against me, the way his hands grip the reins just in front of mine. It's… disarming.

"Ready?" Altair's voice rumbles near my ear, low and steady.

I nod, my throat too tight to speak.

"Good," he says, and with a light tap of his heels, the horse starts forward, carrying us past a nervous looking Iolas, and out of the stables and through the palace gates.

***

I'm eternally grateful that Thalia warned me to dress for warm weather. Iolas had demanded I wear my light leathers under my cloak. But I am warm… very warm.

But maybe that's from being pressed up against Altair for so long.

The air smells sweet—of earth and greenery—crisp and alive in a way that feels almost unreal after being cooped up in the palace for so long. The land stretches out endlessly around us, rolling hills covered in wildflowers, tall grasses swaying gently with the breeze. The palace itself fades quickly into the distance behind us, its towering spires shrinking as we venture further to the east and away from its stone walls.

The world beyond the palace is… beautiful. Lush and thriving, the kind of beauty that makes you forget, if only for a little while, the darkness that exists within it. The lands are nothing like I could have imagined. I didn't get a good look when we left Avantra, cooped up in a carriage with closed windows.

But I likely wouldn't have appreciated the beauty of this place at that moment in time.

I always thought the world outside Avantra would be desolate, dark—a reflection of the stories I'd been told growing up. Those tales, fed to me by cautious voices, painted a picture of ruined lands and barren fields, of places stripped of life and riddled with danger. But now, as my eyes take in the rolling green hills dotted with wildflowers and the golden sunlight filtering through the trees, I know how deeply skewed that image was.

It wasn't just ignorance—it was control. This beauty, this vibrancy, it's something I was never meant to see. The lies I was fed back in Avantra were meant to keep me inside, to keep me obedient and afraid. But this… this is the truth, and it's so much more than I ever expected.

I sit perched on the front of the saddle, my legs dangling on either side of the horse as Altair sits behind me, his strong arms loosely holding the reins. His chest is a solid wall of warmth against my back, and every movement of the horse causes us to shift slightly, my hips brushing against his, my shoulders leaning back into him.

We ride in relative silence at first, the steady rhythm of the horse's hooves and the rustling of leaves in the wind filling the space between us. I try to focus on the landscape around me, on the sea of wildflowers— lavender, daisies, and goldenrod—that blanket the ground like a living quilt. But it's impossible to ignore the tension simmering between us, the constant awareness of his body so close to mine.

Every small movement sends a shiver through me. The gentle brush of his hand as it rests on my hip, his fingers occasionally grazing the thin fabric of my overshirt. His breath is warm, ghosting over the back of my neck, and I can't help but wonder if he's as aware of the closeness as I am.

"These lands…" I say, trying to distract myself from the heat that seems to pool in my stomach. "They're beautiful."

"I'm glad you're getting to see them when in full bloom. They haven't always looked this strong," Altair says, his voice low and smooth, vibrating against my back. "They thrived after the old king was gone."

I hesitate for a moment, chewing on my bottom lip as I gather the courage to ask the question that's been swirling in my mind for so long. But before now I was too afraid to ask anyone. "Why did you… why did you kill him?"

It's a dangerous question, I know. I don't think I've ever heard Altair talk about his past. But the man I've come to know—the one sitting behind me now—feels so at odds with the stories I've heard. The tales of him being a ruthless killer, a cold, calculating king… it just doesn't add up.

Altair goes quiet for a moment, his one-handed grip tightening ever so slightly on the reins. I feel the shift in his posture, the tension in his muscles. "I was his general. And I was a good one. But he was jealous of what I could do," Altair finally says, his voice measured. "Of the power I had and how everyone respected me. And he wanted something from me that I wasn't willing to give."

His words are vague, but something tells me there's more to the story. I let the words hang in the air between us, unanswered.

The road winds through the hills, and as we continue our journey, the lush green gives way to more cultivated land—fields of wheat and corn, carefully tended by farmers—human and vampire alike—I can see working tirelessly under the sun. The crops sway gently in the wind.

My brow furrows. I thought all crops were grown by humans. In the human lands. That the vampires took their share and left us with the scraps. But it's clear these lands have prospered under Altair's rule. The thought hurts my heart that it must have been another lie I'd been fed in Avantra.

I glance back at him, trying to gauge his mood, but his expression is calm, his eyes focused on the road ahead. The tension between us simmers, not unpleasant but undeniable. Every slight movement of the horse causes us to shift, my hips pressing back into his as his fingers brush my side again, sending a ripple of heat through me.

"Why did the old king want your power?" I ask tentatively, my voice softer now, afraid to push too hard.

Altair's jaw tightens, his gaze hardening slightly. "He didn't. My power isn't something that can be taken."

Well, that is information.

"He wanted to control me. But a power like this always comes with a price," he says cryptically. "And I wasn't willing to pay it."

I hum, unsure how to respond, but the harshness in his voice tells me that this is a conversation he's not ready to have. At least, not yet.

We fall into silence again, the rhythmic sound of the horse's hooves lulling us into a steady pace. Into the early afternoon we ride, and even though we're not talking, it feels peaceful. I feel like I can breathe.

As we ride further from the palace, the world around us shifts, the wild beauty of the open land fading as we approach the village. The air smells of hay and earth, a change from the perfumed gardens of the palace. Small houses made of stone and wood dot the landscape, their roofs covered in moss and ivy. Smoke rises lazily from chimneys, a sign of life in this quiet corner of the kingdom.

I find myself relaxing into Altair's chest more than I intended, the steady warmth of his body oddly comforting. It's strange, this proximity, but not entirely unwelcome. I wonder if he notices how my breath catches every time he shifts, if he feels the same energy sparking between us.

"Are you nervous about what you'll see?" Altair's voice breaks the silence as he leans down slightly, pressing harder against me, and I can feel his breath warm against my ear.

I bite my lip, unsure of how to answer. "I don't know," I admit. "I think I'm just… trying to make sense of it all. Of everything I've been told versus what I'm seeing now."

Altair nods, his grip tightening slightly as if reassuring me. "Sometimes seeing for yourself is the only way to understand."

His words settle over me, and I realise how right he is. I've spent so much of my life being told what to believe, what to fear.

As we continue our journey, the village draws closer, the sun now hanging lower in the sky, casting long shadows across the land. The heat of the day has softened, and a gentle breeze carries the scent of fresh grass and earth. The road beneath us is quiet, only the occasional farmer passing by with a polite nod. It feels almost… peaceful.

But even in the calm, the energy between Altair and me remains, like a stroke of lightning humming beneath the surface. Every slight movement, every accidental brush of our hands, sends a spark through me.

"You're quiet," Altair says, his voice low and teasing.

"I'm just… thinking," I reply, my voice barely above a whisper.

"About?" His hand squeezes my hip lightly, and I can hear the amusement in his voice.

I swallow, unsure of how to respond. My thoughts are a tangled mess—confusion about my place in this world, curiosity about Altair, and something… else.

"Everything," I say finally, my voice soft. "About everything."

Altair hums in response, a sound deep in his chest that vibrates through me. "Well," he says after a pause, "we have all evening to sort through your thoughts."

I laugh softly, the sound surprising even me. But it feels good—lighter, like a weight has been lifted, if only for a moment.

The village is just ahead now, on the outskirts of a valley, its small, modest buildings clustered together like they've been there for centuries. As we approach, the sounds of life grow louder—voices, the clang of metal from a blacksmith, the distant laughter of children. It's simple, peaceful, and entirely different from the grandeur of the palace.

Altair sighs behind me, and he sounds nervous. "Welcome to Elderglen, Olwyn."

My neck clicks as I turn to look at him.

"What?"

This could make or break us…

CHAPTER THIRTY-FIVE
Olwyn

Altair pulls his dark hood further over his face as we ride further, his shadowed features making him nearly unrecognisable to any casual onlooker.

But that scarred eye is hard to hide.

Elderglen? The name punches the breath from my lungs, dredging up a memory from years ago. My parents, their faces grim as they spoke in hushed tones.

"Do you remember Elderglen, Olwyn?" he asks, leaning forward, his eyes glassy. "The village in the valley?"

I nod slowly, not trusting myself to speak. I've heard the name before.

"It was a peaceful village," he continues, wiping a drop of wine that spills from the corner of his mouth. "Families, children… all living their simple lives. And then the vampires came."

The memory stings behind my eyes, bitter and sharp. He must be lying.

"E-Elderglen?" I stammer, disbelief clogging my throat.

Altair nods, and there's a softness in his eyes, almost like regret, as if he can see my childhood crumbling within my eyes.

He dismounts from the horse, tying it to a hitching post and offers his hand to help me down. "Come see," he says gently, his voice carrying no mockery, no smugness—just quiet certainty. He doesn't patronise me, doesn't push facts or gloat. He just... offers.

With trembling fingers, I take his hand and slide off the horse. My feet hit the ground, but it feels like I'm floating, unsteady, unsure, pulling my hood tighter around my face. This can't be the Elderglen from my parents' stories. The Elderglen they described was a graveyard, a place ravaged and destroyed by vampires. But as I look around, I see nothing of the kind.

The village is alive.

Humans and vampires walk side by side, chatting, working, laughing. A group of children—*human children*—run past, kicking up dirt as they chase one another down the main road. Nearby, a vampire woman helps an elderly human load a cart with freshly baked bread, their conversation easy and familiar. A vampire blacksmith works at his forge, hammering out a blade while a human apprentice watches closely, wiping sweat from his brow.

My chest tightens, my throat closes... And I want to cry.

Everything I've been told, every story of destruction and horror, feels like it's dying inside me.

My heart twists painfully, and I can't stop the flood of confusion and betrayal that washes over me. *This wasn't supposed to exist*. My parents had told me that vampires decimated villages like this, that they left nothing but death and despair in their wake. But here I am, standing in the middle of Elderglen—a village that should be a ruin—and it's thriving.

A small sob breaks free from my control, and a part of me is desperate to deny what I'm seeing. But the proof is right in front of me. Was Altair telling the truth? Had my parents been the ones weaving lies all along? And if they lied about this... *what else* might they have lied about?

I swallow hard, forcing myself to breathe as we walk through the village. Altair says nothing, but he looks like he is in agony, his fingers flexing as if he wants to reach out and hold my hand. But he is letting me take it all in at my own pace. His other hand rests lightly on my lower back, guiding me but not forcing me. Every step feels like a boulder pressing down on my chest, a slow realisation sinking deeper into my bones.

It's not just the village that unsettles me—it's the fact that I feel a pull here. A connection. Like my own home could have been like… this.

I catch Altair watching me out of the corner of his eye, his expression now unreadable. He knows what this is doing to me. I don't even need to say anything.

We reach the small inn at the heart of the village, a cosy-looking place with ivy climbing up the stone walls and smoke curling from the chimney.

Inside, the scent of roasted meats and freshly baked bread fills the air. A few patrons sit at wooden tables, chatting and laughing, and a warm fire crackles in the hearth. The innkeeper, an older human man with a weathered face and kind eyes, looks up from the bar. His gaze sharpens as Altair looks up, and he recognizes him, immediately setting down the mug he was polishing.

"Your Majesty," the innkeeper whispers as we get close and Altair steps up to the bar. The innkeeper's eyes dart to me, curiosity and warmth blooming on his face. "I'll have a room set up straight away."

"Thank you, Abbas," Altair says, his voice softer than usual. He's careful to keep his face concealed, though Abbas clearly knows who he is. "This isn't an official visit, if you wouldn't mind keeping it quiet. And if someone could tend to my horse."

Abbas takes a brown bag of coins that Altair offers and nods quickly, "Of course. We have one room left. Families have come into town for Litha. But I'll have it made up for you immediately. Would you like a quiet place to rest before your room is ready?" he offers, looking from Altair to me with a kind smile.

Altair shakes his head. "No, not yet. We'll explore the village first."

Something shifts in Abbas's eyes as he glances between us, realisation dawning. His smile grows wider, more genuine, and his eyes twinkle with approval. "Ah," he murmurs, his gaze locking on me. "So, this is your bride, then. My queen." He bows his head slightly in respect. "It's an honour to finally meet you. Welcome."

I blink in surprise, not sure how to respond, because Abbas's smile is genuine, his welcome is heartfelt. It throws me off balance.

"Thank you," I manage to say, my voice sounding small in the cosy space.

Abbas grins again, his eyes crinkling at the corners. "I'll make sure your stay is perfect, Your Majesty." With that, he disappears up the stairs, leaving Altair and me standing in the inn's warm glow.

I take a slow breath, my mind still spinning from everything I've seen. The village, the people—*the humans*—living alongside vampires as if it's the most normal thing in the world. It's so at odds with everything I've been taught, everything I've believed.

I glance up at Altair, his face still shadowed beneath his hood, and curiosity gnaws at me. The villagers haven't so much as looked at him twice. doesn't seem like a man who hides. Altair *commands* a room just by entering it. And yet, here he is, cloaked in shadow.

"Why are you hiding your face?" I ask, my voice quiet.

Altair's gaze shifts to me, his eyes softening beneath the hood. For a moment, I think he might deflect the question, offer some vague response to keep the mystery intact. But instead, he surprises me.

"I trust the people of this village," he says, his voice low, steady. "They wouldn't betray me. But…" He pauses, as if considering how much to share, his gaze briefly sweeping over the bustling market square. "Besides trying to keep my identity hidden from outside eyes as we entered, I wanted to spend this time with you, *just* with you. Unbothered. I know this is your first time seeing a place like this, and I didn't want it to feel overwhelming for you. For now, whilst you get used to it, I didn't want *us* to be a distraction."

His words hit me harder than I expect. My chest tightens, and for a moment, I forget how to breathe.

He did this… for me?

I look away, focusing on the stone tiles beneath my feet as warmth spreads through my chest.

He notices *me*.

He thought about *me*.

"Thank you," I manage to say, my voice soft.

Altair doesn't respond, but the faint curve of his lips beneath the shadow of the hood tells me everything I need to know.

Her eyes are opening to the possibility.

CHAPTER THIRTY-SIX
Olwyn

ltair and I leave the inn and continue walking through
Elderglen.

The sounds of life fill the air, and there's a hum of activity, a rhythm to the village that feels natural, easy.

My mind is still spinning, still trying to reconcile what I'm seeing with the stories I've been told as long as I can remember. The tension in my chest refuses to ease, and every step we take feels like I'm walking deeper into a world I don't fully understand. A world I've never understood.

Altair stays close, and we pass a stall near the edge of the square, where something catches my eye. My footsteps slow as I see a gleaming display of weapons laid out on a cloth-covered table. Swords, daggers, axes—all polished to perfection, the steel reflecting the sunlight in sharp flashes.

I step closer, my gaze drawn to one particular weapon: a silver blade with an elegant white oak handle. It's beautifully crafted, the metal gleaming like liquid moonlight, and I reach out instinctively, running my fingers over the hilt.

"It's a fine piece, isn't it?" the shopkeeper says from behind the table, his voice friendly and warm. He's a stout man—vampire—with dark hair and a thick beard, his eyes crinkling as he smiles at me. "One of my best works. The silver's hard to work with, but worth the trouble, I say."

I pick up the blade, feeling its weight in my hand. It's perfectly balanced, light but deadly. The craftsmanship is impeccable. It feels right in my hand. But as I turn the blade over, my heart skips a beat as I see the sheen. The metal... it's not just silver.

It's witchsilver.

I freeze, my fingers tightening around the hilt as the realisation sinks in. Witchsilver is the only thing that can kill a pureblood vampire. And here it is, being sold openly in the middle of the village—just another weapon in a simple marketplace, accessible to anyone with the coin to buy it.

My throat tightens as I set the blade back down on the table, my fingers brushing over the hilt once more before letting go. Why is this here? Why would a village filled with both humans and vampires sell something so dangerous so freely? Does everyone here have access to these weapons?

I glance up at the shopkeeper, but he's still smiling warmly, as if nothing about this is unusual. And maybe it isn't—at least not here.

Before I can overthink it further, I feel the brush of Altair's presence behind me, his warm breath ghosting over my ear as he leans down to whisper. "They're not sold for rebellion or treachery," he says, his tone calm, even. "The vampires in this village believe humans should be able to protect themselves. Against rogue vampires or... other dangers."

I glance at him, my brow furrowing slightly. "Other dangers?"

Altair's eyes flick briefly to the shopkeeper and then back to me, his voice dropping lower. "In case a skirmish from Casius's soldiers ever ventures too near the village," he explains. "It hasn't happened yet, but they'd rather be prepared than defenceless."

The words settle over me, and my shoulders relax slightly. It's not what I'd feared, not some dark, twisted plot or indication of distrust. It's protection. A sense of balance.

I look back at the blade, its purpose sinking in. Here, in this village, humans and vampires coexist—imperfectly, perhaps, but coexist all the same. And the witchsilver isn't a symbol of betrayal. It's a symbol of trust, of shared responsibility.

"They trust humans with this kind of power," I murmur, more to myself than to Altair.

"They do," he replies softly, his voice steady. "And the humans trust them not to abuse their strength. That's what makes this village work."

I glance at the shopkeeper again, noticing now the way his eyes linger on the humans walking by, his smile faint but genuine. There's no malice here, no fear. Just a quiet understanding.

Setting the blade down one last time, I step away from the table, the faintest hint of warmth spreading in my chest. This village... it's not perfect, but it's trying. And maybe that's enough.

Altair straightens beside me, his shadow looming as he watches me carefully, gauging my reaction. I look up at him, searching his eyes for something—approval, understanding, maybe even pride. But his expression remains unreadable, though the faintest curve of his lips hints at satisfaction.

And as we step further into the bustling market, the witchsilver lingers in my thoughts, not as a warning, but as a reminder of what's possible. Trust, even here, can exist.

We continue walking, and I try to shake off the unease that clings to me like a shadow. My thoughts are a mess. If my parents lied about everything, what else did they hide from me?

Lost in thought, I almost don't notice the small figure that steps in front of me.

"Excuse me, miss?"

I blink, startled out of my thoughts, and look down to see a little girl standing before me. She can't be more than six or seven years old, her wide eyes shining with curiosity as she looks up at me. Her wild curly hair is dark, and she's clutching a small bouquet of wildflowers in her hands.

"Are you a princess?" the girl asks, her voice small but filled with wonder.

My heart stutters at the question. I glance at Altair, who's watching with a soft, amused smile tugging at the corner of his lips. I can feel the warmth of his gaze, but it's the girl's innocent question that holds me frozen in place.

"A princess?" I murmur, crouching down to meet her at eye level. "Why would you think that?"

The little girl tilts her head, as if the answer is obvious. "Because you're so pretty. Like the princesses in the stories."

I can't help but smile at her words, though there's a tightness in my chest that makes it hard to breathe. I'm not a princess. Not the way she means it, at least. But for a moment, in her wide-eyed gaze, I almost wish I could be.

"What's your name?" I ask gently.

"Lira," she says, smiling shyly. She holds out the bouquet of flowers, the petals bright and vibrant in the afternoon sun. "These are for you."

My throat tightens as I take the flowers from her, her simple gesture settling over me like a warm blanket. "Thank you, Lira," I say softly, touched in a way I can't quite put into words. "These are beautiful."

The girl beams, and for a moment, everything else fades away. The village, the witchsilver, the questions swirling in my mind—all of it seems distant and unimportant in the face of this small act of kindness.

Altair steps forward, his hand resting lightly on my shoulder as he crouches down beside me. His presence is solid, grounding, and I can feel the heat of him even through the fabric of my cloak.

"Lira," he says gently, his voice low and kind. "You've made her very happy."

The girl gasps, her eyes going wide as she looks up at Altair. Recognition flashes across her small face, her mouth opening to speak, but Altair is quicker.

"Shhhh," he whispers, pressing a finger to his lips with a small, conspiratorial smile.

The little girl's excitement shifts into something softer, and she nods quickly, her lips pressing together to keep whatever she was about to say trapped inside. Her wide eyes sparkle with a mixture of awe and delight as she clutches the little wooden figurine she had just handed me.

The girl giggles, her cheeks turning pink as she looks between us. "You're her prince, aren't you?" she asks, her innocent eyes shining.

Altair chuckles softly, glancing at me with a look that sends warmth rushing through my chest. "Something like that," he murmurs, his tone teasing but sincere.

I feel my face flush, and I quickly stand, hoping to hide the embarrassment creeping up my neck. "Thank you for the flowers, Lira," I say, giving her one last smile before she skips off to rejoin her friends.

Altair straightens beside me, his gaze lingering on my face as I clutch the bouquet to my chest. It takes all my willpower to tear my eyes away from him.

We continue walking through the village, the silence between us comfortable now, though everything I've seen still lingers in the back of my mind. The truth of this place—the humans and vampires living together, the weapons being sold so easily—has shaken something loose inside me.

As we stroll through the village, I keep sneaking glances at the people around us—humans and vampires, working side by side, laughing, talking, sharing the same space. A vampire woman leans down to help a human child tie her shoe, while a human blacksmith laughs with a vampire customer over the counter. It's so... ordinary.

It's overwhelming, and I don't know how to process it. I want to ask Altair—want to demand answers—but the words won't come. I find myself wanting to enjoy the peace. The normality.

As we reach the edge of town, something catches my eye—a string of brightly coloured decorations hanging between two buildings, fluttering gently in the breeze. Flowers and ribbons in shades of gold, green, and crimson are woven together, lining the street in a vibrant arch.

Altair notices my distraction and slows his pace. "Ah," he says, following my gaze. "It looks like they're preparing for the Litha celebration."

I glance at him, confused. "Litha?"

"Midsummer," he explains, a smile tugging at his lips. "The longest day of the year. A celebration of light, warmth, and the abundance of life. Have you never celebrated it before?"

I shake my head. "No, I… I don't think we ever had anything like that in Avantra."

Altair's smile widens, and for a moment, he looks so much younger, the usual sharpness in his features softening into something almost boyish. "Then you're in for a treat," he says, his voice warm and full of excitement.

His enthusiasm is contagious, and despite the whirlwind of thoughts still racing through my mind, I feel a small flicker of anticipation.

"Come on," Altair says, nodding toward the direction of the decorations. "Let's see what else they've got planned."

As we walk further into the heart of the village, the energy in the air shifts. I can hear laughter, the clinking of glasses, and the faint sound of music drifting from the square ahead. More decorations hang between buildings, flowers and lanterns, and I realise that the entire town is gearing up for the celebration. The air is fragrant with the smell of baked goods and freshly picked herbs, and I can feel the excitement building all around us.

I can't help but smile.

If this is a taste of what lies beyond the walls of the palace, then maybe—just maybe—there's more to this life than I ever imagined.

She doesn't even notice how she shines.

CHAPTER THIRTY-SEVEN
Olwyn

The Litha celebration gets into full swing, and the energy in the village square is infectious.

Altair and I had discarded our cloaks the moment we arrived, blending into the festivities—or at least attempting to. The moment the townsfolk caught sight of Altair, there was a ripple of recognition, a few faces lighting up with surprise and joy.

A tall, elderly man with a straw hat approached first, bowing deeply before straightening with a warm grin. "Your Majesty," he greeted, his tone reverent yet familiar. His eyes shifted to me, and I felt a strange flutter as he added, "And our queen! Welcome!"

Others soon followed, some bowing, some simply smiling as they came to shake Altair's hand or offer me nods of greeting. Their reactions varied—some subdued and respectful, others openly elated—but what struck me most was the ease with which they approached him.

They treated him like one of their own, a leader, yes, but also just… a man. They didn't grovel or cower like the nobility in the court or those conditioned to fear vampires. Here, they smiled, joked, and exchanged pleasantries with him, as though he were any other villager. Altair greeted them all politely, his voice low and steady, the faintest edge of warmth softening his usual stoic demeanour.

I was startled when one woman, a baker judging by the flour streaked across her apron, turned to me with a beaming smile. "It's so good to see you, my queen. We've heard so much about you," she said brightly, as though I'm not an outsider, as though I truly belong here.

For a moment, I didn't know how to respond. "Thank you," I managed.

Eventually, the villagers, satisfied with their greetings, drifted back to the celebration, leaving us alone to enjoy the midsummer festival. A part of me had expected Altair to stand apart from it all, a distant and untouchable figure. Instead, he was relaxed, even comfortable, blending in effortlessly.

I sit next to him on a low stone wall, the heat of the midsummer sun still warm on my skin. A small loaf of bread rests between us, its golden crust freshly baked, the smell rich and comforting. I tear off a piece and offer it to him. He takes it with a nod, his fingers brushing mine for the briefest moment. We eat in comfortable silence, the sound of the music swelling around us, the village bathed in the glow of the evening light.

Ahead of us, villagers are dancing. It's a fast, lively dance, full of spinning skirts and stomping feet. Children run through the crowd, laughing and chasing each other, while couples twirl in the centre of the square, their movements quick and joyful.

I can't help but smile as I watch them, though there's a part of me that feels out of place—like I'm a spectator, not really part of it. Altair notices my gaze, glancing at me from the corner of his eye before following my line of sight.

"They're enjoying themselves," he says, a soft note of amusement in his voice. "Litha is always like this—loud, energetic, a little wild."

"Do you ever join in?" I ask, half expecting him to scoff at the idea.

He smirks. "I have my moments. We usually have a celebration in the palace."

"Why aren't you this year?" I ask.

He smiles, his white teeth flashing. "I wanted to bring you here." Before I can respond, he rises to his feet and offers his hand. "Come on," he says, the playful glint in his eyes unmistakable. "You're not just going to sit here and watch, are you?"

I blink up at him, surprised. "I'm not much of a dancer."

His smile widens. "Perfect. Then no one will expect you to be good."

I can't help but laugh at that, shaking my head. But there's something infectious about the way he's looking at me, the hint of a challenge in his tone. Before I know it, I've slipped my hand into his, and he pulls me to my feet with an easy strength that catches me off guard.

The music swells as he leads me toward the square, the lively notes of the fiddles urging us into motion. He turns to face me, taking both my hands, and before I can protest, we're off—spinning into the dance with a speed that leaves me breathless.

At first, I stumble, my feet awkward, my body not quite sure how to move in time with the music. But Altair just laughs, his grip on my hands steady and firm, guiding me through the steps with surprising ease. His laughter is light, a sound I don't think I've ever heard from him before, and it pulls me in, making me forget my initial hesitation.

We spin faster, the world around us becoming a blur of colour and sound. My breath comes in quick bursts, but it's not from exhaustion—it's from the thrill of it, the unexpected joy of being pulled into the dance. The ground beneath my feet feels almost weightless as Altair twirls me around, his strength making it seem effortless.

His eyes stay locked on mine, a hint of blue showing in the shadows, and for the first time, I see him not as the stern, brooding king I've come to know, but as something else—someone else. He looks younger somehow, more carefree, the hard lines of his face softened by the glow of the celebration and the laughter on his lips.

"Faster!" he calls, his voice carrying over the music.

I laugh, barely able to keep up as he spins me again, pulling me into a tight circle before releasing me just enough to send me twirling out, only to reel me back in. The movement is dizzying, exhilarating, and I'm surprised at how much I enjoy it.

"See?" he says, his breath coming out in short bursts as he pulls me close again. "You're a natural."

I roll my eyes, still laughing. "I'm barely keeping up!"

He grins, his eyes sparkling with a mischievous light. "That's the fun of it."

We dance like that for what feels like hours, though it could have been minutes—it's hard to tell when time seems to blur with the music. My legs are starting to ache, and my breath is coming faster, but I don't want to stop. There's something freeing about it, the movement, the laughter, the feeling of being part of something for the first time in so long.

Eventually, the music slows, and Altair guides me to a stop, his hand still wrapped around mine. We're both breathing heavily, our faces flushed from the dance.

He's watching me closely, his gaze softening as he catches his breath. "You did well," he says, his voice lower now, more intimate.

I smile up at him, still a little breathless. "I had a good partner."

He reaches up, his thumb brushing lightly against the apple of my cheek, and I feel a strange flutter in my chest. The air between us seems to shift, just for a moment, as the music fades and the sounds of the celebration drift into the background.

But before I can dwell on it, he releases my hand, stepping back with a smile that's still warm but tinged with something like restraint. "Shall we sit for a while?"

I nod, grateful for the chance to catch my breath, and we walk back to the edge of the square where we'd started, the warmth of the celebration still buzzing in the air around us.

***

As the last strains of music fade into the evening air, Altair and I make our way back toward the inn. The village is still alive with celebration, lanterns casting warm glows over the cobbled streets as people laugh and dance, their voices carrying through the twilight. But there's a quietness between us now, a kind of peaceful exhaustion after the energy of the Litha festivities.

Altair walks beside me as we navigate through the crowd. Every now and then, his fingers brush against my side, and I'm hyper-aware of the small, fleeting contact.

When we reach the inn, Abbas is waiting for us by the entrance, a broad smile on his weathered face. "Enjoy the celebration, Your Majesty?" he asks with a knowing glint in his eyes.

Altair nods, his expression soft. "It was good," he replies. "Thank you for keeping this safe for us." He reaches out, and Abbas hands over the leather satchel we brought with us.

"Your room is ready," Abbas continues. "If there's anything you need, don't hesitate to call."

Altair nods again, murmuring his thanks. Abbas's gaze shifts to me then, and his smile widens, warmth radiating from him. "I trust the Queen enjoyed herself as well?"

I flush at the title, still not used to it, but I return his smile. "It was really lovely," I say. Abbas gives a satisfied nod before he retreats behind the counter, and Altair and I head up the narrow staircase that leads to the room.

The hallways are dim, lit by a few lanterns, their light flickering softly against the wooden walls. The sounds of the village fade behind us, replaced by the creak of the floorboards under our feet and the quiet rustle of the satchel in Altair's hand.

When we reach the door to our room, Altair pushes it open and steps aside to let me in first. I hesitate for just a second as I go in, the reality of sharing a room with him sinking in.

It's a decent-sized space, cosy and clean. There's a large bed in the middle of the room, its wooden frame sturdy, with simple linen sheets and thick, comfortable-looking pillows. A settee sits against the far wall, barely big enough for two people to sit on. A small fireplace sits in the corner, unlit but ready, and beside it is an old chest of drawers. The atmosphere is homey, but there's no mistaking the fact that the bed is the centrepiece, and that it's clearly meant for two.

Altair places the satchel on the bed and glances around, his eyes lingering on the settee for a moment before he turns to me. "I'll take the settee," he offers, his tone casual, though there's something a little stiff in the way he says it, like he's already preparing for an uncomfortable night.

I arch an eyebrow at him, trying to keep my tone light. "Don't be ridiculous. It's too small for all six-five of you."

He hesitates, his eyes flicking to the bed again. "It's fine. I'll manage."

I fold my arms across my chest, fixing him with a look. "We're both adults, Altair. We can share the bed. It's not a big deal."

He blinks, taken aback, and for a moment, I see a flicker of something in his expression—something caught between surprise and something warmer. But then he recovers, giving me a small, resigned nod. "If you're sure."

"I am," I say, trying to sound more confident than I feel. There's a slight awkwardness settling over the room now.

To fill the silence, I reach for the satchel at the edge of the bed, but my hand stills halfway, my thoughts catching up with me. The events of the day, the sights I'd seen, the people we'd met—they tumble around in my mind, raw and unorganized. I know I need to sort through it all, to make sense of the conflicting emotions swirling in my chest, but I don't know how to start.

Instead of grabbing the satchel, I drop my hand and glance at Altair. He stands a few feet away, loosening the laces of his tunic, but his movements are slow, almost hesitant, like he's waiting for something. For me.

The words are out before I can stop them. "The village. The people…" I trail off, searching for the right way to say it. "It wasn't what I expected."

Altair looks up, his hands pausing mid-motion, his gaze anchoring me. "What did you expect?" His voice is steady, as though he already knows the answer but wants me to say it anyway.

I hesitate, but only for a moment. "I don't know. Something darker. More… desolate. Weeks ago, I never would have thought a place like that could exist—vampires and humans living side by side, laughing together, celebrating." I shake my head, almost laughing at myself. "I thought the world outside Avantra was all shadows and blood. But that… that was light."

He listens, his expression unreadable, but there's a quiet intensity in his eyes that makes me feel like every word matters. "And what did you feel?"

The question takes me off guard. It's not something I'd thought about yet, too caught up in the shock of seeing a world so different from the one I'd imagined. But now that he's asked, the answer comes quickly, unbidden.

"Hope," I admit softly, the word hanging in the air between us. "I felt hope."

Altair exhales, his shoulders relaxing slightly, and there's something almost vulnerable in the way he looks at me now. "Good," he says simply, like it's the only answer that matters.

I nod, but the day still presses on me, and I glance away, focusing on the satchel again. "I'm not ready to talk about everything," I say quietly, almost to myself. "Not yet. I just… need time to make sense of it."

Altair doesn't respond immediately, but when he does, his voice is low and gentle. "Take all the time you need."

When I finally look back at him, his tunic is off, leaving him in just the thin, sleeveless undershirt that clings to his form. The sight of him, so relaxed and unguarded, catches me off guard for a moment, and I turn quickly back to the satchel, feeling heat rise to my cheeks.

"I'll go change."

He steps aside, giving me space as I head toward the small door at the back of the room that leads to the ensuite bathroom. The door creaks as I push it open, and I step inside, closing it gently behind me.

The bathroom is simple, with a small washbasin and a mirror hanging above it. A narrow window lets in the cool night air, and I can hear the distant sounds of the village celebration still carrying on outside. I take a deep breath, trying to steady the fluttering in my chest as I open the satchel and pull out a nightgown from inside, one a maid must have packed for me.

It's short and soft, a comfortable thing—but now, standing here, it feels suddenly… delicate. The fabric slips through my fingers as I hold it up, and I can't help but glance at my reflection in the mirror. I undo my hair from its crown, grateful to have the pins out of my hair, the strands falling around my shoulders and the flush from the dancing lingering on my cheeks.

I change quickly, slipping out of the dress and pulling the nightgown over my head. The fabric settles softly against my skin, cool and light, and I run my fingers over the hem, trying to calm the slight nervousness bubbling inside me.

I take a deep breath and open the door, stepping back into the room.

Altair is standing by the fireplace, his covered back to me as he pokes at the logs, coaxing them into a low, warm flame. He has changed into a loose pair of bed trousers. The soft light from the fire flickers across the room, casting gentle shadows on the walls, and when he turns to face me, his eyes flicker down for just a moment before they meet mine again. There's a brief silence between us, and I can feel the heat of his gaze, though he doesn't say anything.

"I'll, um… just get into bed," I mumble, brushing past him toward the bed. I slide under the covers, feeling the cool sheets against my skin as I settle in.

Altair steps away from the fireplace, his movements slow and deliberate as he walks to the other side of the bed. He slips under the covers beside me, keeping a respectful distance, though the space between us feels smaller than it should.

We lie there in silence for a moment, the flicker of the fire casting a soft glow over the room. I can hear the soft rustle of the sheets as Altair shifts beside me.

I lie there, staring up at the ceiling, my heart still racing from everything that's happened today. The village, the people, the little girl with the flowers… it all swirls around in my head, but it's not what keeps my pulse hammering against my chest. It's him.

It's Altair.

The way he looked at me when we danced, that quiet awe in his eyes. The way his hand felt on my back, guiding me so effortlessly through the crowd. Even now, as we lie side by side, I can feel the warmth of him, his presence like a low hum in the air, pulling me in even though we're not touching.

The silence between us stretches, thick and charged. I turn my head slightly, just enough to catch a glimpse of him out of the corner of my eye. He's lying on his back, his eyes closed and face relaxed, but his body tense, as if he's holding himself in check. The firelight flickers across his features, casting shadows on the sharp planes of his jaw, the curve of his lips.

For a moment, I wonder if he's asleep, but then I hear his voice—low, soft, like it's meant just for me. "Get some sleep, Olwyn. We have a long day tomorrow."

I swallow, my throat suddenly dry. "Goodnight, Altair," I whisper, my voice barely audible, but the way his name feels on my lips sends a shiver down my spine.

There's a pause. A long one.

"Goodnight," he replies, his voice rougher now, like it's strained.

I close my eyes, trying to will myself to sleep, but my mind won't settle. The energy between us is almost suffocating, a slow, simmering tension that wraps around my body, making it impossible to relax. I can feel him—every shift of his body, every quiet breath he takes—and it's too much and not enough all at once.

Without thinking, I turn over to face him, the movement drawing his attention immediately. He inhales sharply, his chest rumbling as his eyes open, watching me, and the intensity in his darkened gaze makes my breath catch in my throat.

"Altair..." I say, my voice trembling, though I don't even know what I'm asking for.

His hand moves before I can process it, reaching out to cup my cheek, his thumb brushing lightly against my skin. The touch is soft, almost tentative, but it sets my blood on fire. I lean into it without thinking, my eyes fluttering shut as I feel the warmth of him seep into me.

He shifts closer, and my heart pounds so loudly I'm sure he can hear it, feel it. When I open my eyes again, his face is right there, inches from mine, his gaze dark and intent.

His lips hover just above mine, so close that I can feel the heat radiating from him. But he doesn't move. Doesn't close the gap. Instead, his eyes burn into mine, his control absolute, as if he's savouring the moment—savouring my want, which I'm fed up of denying whilst we're here alone.

"Ask for it," he suddenly murmurs, his voice low, like velvet draped in command. His breath fans across my lips, teasing me with the nearness. "Ask, and I'll give it to you, Olwyn."

I swallow hard, the pulse between my legs throbbing at the rough edge of his words. My body screams for the kiss that lingers just out of reach, but still, he waits—silent, immovable, utterly in control.

"Altair..." I whisper, my voice trembling, almost pleading, but it isn't enough. His lips quirk slightly at the corners, amusement flashing through the heat in his eyes.

"Not good enough, love." His shadowed fingers trail up the curve of my neck, grazing the sensitive skin just beneath my ear. "If you want it... *ask* for it."

My breath catches, heat flooding my body as his words sink in. My pride wars with the ache that's settled deep inside me.

"*Please*," I manage to whisper, my voice barely audible.

His eyes darken further, and he inches closer, the heat from his body wrapping around me like a storm, but still, he waits.

"Louder, Olwyn," he growls, his thumb brushing across my bottom lip, teasing the softness there. "Let me hear you *want* it."

I shudder, my entire body trembling with the force of the need building inside me. "Please, Altair… kiss me," I gasp, my voice breaking.

He exhales slowly. The control in his gaze snaps, and the next second, his lips crash into mine with a hunger that leaves me breathless. The world tilts as he devours me, his hands tangling in my hair, pulling me closer, his body pressing against mine as if he can't get enough. The kiss is rough, deep, filled with the heat of everything we've both been holding back.

I moan against his lips, my hands fisting in his shirt as he tilts my head back, taking the kiss deeper, his tongue sweeping into my mouth, claiming me in a way that sends a rush of pleasure flooding through me.

He's everywhere, overwhelming me, consuming me, and all I can do is cling to him, lost in the fire he's ignited.

When he finally pulls back, both of us panting, his forehead rests against mine, and his voice is a hoarse whisper. "Good girl," he breathes, his thumb tracing my swollen lips. "That's all you had to do."

This time I'm the one to kiss him, my fingers tangling in his dark hair as I pull him closer, closer. His other hand grips my waist, pulling me flush against his body, and I can feel every hard line of him, every shift of muscle beneath his skin.

I gasp into his mouth, and he groans in response, the sound deep and rough and sending a bolt of heat straight between my legs.

For a moment, it feels like we're the only two people in the world. Like nothing else matters but this—his lips on mine, his hands on my body, the way he makes me feel like I'm burning alive.

But as I hook my leg over his hip, he pulls back, his breath ragged, his chest rising and falling rapidly. His forehead rests against mine, his eyes closed, and I can feel the tension in his body, the restraint.

"Olwyn," he murmurs, his voice thick with something deep and dark as his fangs show, catching the dim light. "We… we should stop." But his grip tightens, fingers pressing into my waist, pulling me just a little closer.

It's not rejection—I can feel it in the way his body remains pressed against mine, in the way his eyes flicker with that dark, heated hunger. His control is slipping, and I know, deep down, that he's not stopping because he doesn't want this.

I swallow hard, my heart pounding as I try to ignore the pull to lean back in, to push past this fragile line we've drawn.

He hesitates, his lips parting as if weighing something unspoken, and then he speaks, his voice low, rough—almost tortured. "I want to, Olwyn. Gods, I want you. But I don't want to cross a line you're not ready for. I want everything. But if we keep going, you have to be sure. No regrets tomorrow. I couldn't bear it."

The raw confession sends a tremor through me. My pulse quickens, heat pooling in my stomach as his words sink in. He's not hiding it anymore—the desire, the hunger, the sheer want. It's right there, out in the open, and the knowledge of it thrills and terrifies me in equal measure. And if I'm being completely honest… I'm not ready.

I look away, afraid that I'll let him down. But he leans in, pressing a soft kiss to my forehead, his lips lingering.

"Come here," he says, his voice still hoarse with unspoken need as he pulls me into his arms.

I go willingly, letting him tuck me against his chest, his arms wrapping around me in a way that feels protective, almost possessive. His warmth seeps into me, calming the frantic beat of my heart, and I close my eyes, the tension slowly ebbing away.

"Get some sleep," he whispers, his breath warm against my hair. "I'll be right here."

I nod, resting my head against his chest, listening to the steady thrum of his heartbeat.

And for the first time in a long time, I think I feel safe.

CHAPTER THIRTY-EIGHT
Altair

It's the middle of the night, and I'm still wide awake, holding her in my arms.

The steady rhythm of Olwyn's breath rises and falls against my chest, her warmth sinking into me like a drug I can't resist. She sleeps peacefully now, her body curled into mine, the tension from earlier finally melting away. But I'm restless. My thoughts won't stop circling, replaying the moment between us.

Gods, I want her.

I stare up at the ceiling, my mind a battlefield. I know desire, to control it, to bend it to my will. But with Olwyn... nothing about this feels controlled. Every inch of her, every fleeting touch, is like a spark that threatens to burn through every last restraint I have left. The softness of her breath against my chest, the way she sighed against my skin when I pulled her close... It's all too much.

I'm not sure how much longer I can hold back.

I glance down at her, my gaze tracing the gentle curve of her cheek, the way her lips part slightly in sleep. She looks so peaceful like this, vulnerable in a way that makes my chest tighten with an ache I can't name. It's strange—this need to protect her, to keep her close, while at the same time, every base instinct in me is screaming to claim her. To take her in every possible way.

But I can't. Not until she's ready, and she asks me too. Not until she knows everything.

My fingers gently brush against her back, tracing the delicate line of her spine through the thin fabric of her nightgown. Even that small touch feels dangerous, like walking the edge of a knife. I know she can feel it too—the tension between us, the way it's pulling tighter with every moment we spend together. She has to. There's no way she can't feel how much I want her, how hard it is to keep my distance when everything in me is begging to close the gap.

My chest tightens again, this time with something darker. Guilt.

Because I haven't told her everything.

She trusts me now, or at least, she's starting to. I can feel it in the way she leans into me, in the way her guard lowers just a fraction when we're alone. In the way she wanted to cry when she saw the truth of Elderglen. But trust isn't enough. Not when she doesn't know the full truth. Not when she doesn't understand why I took her from Avantra.

Not when she doesn't know what I've done.

I swallow hard, my own secrets heavy in my chest. I need to tell her about Atha's attempts on her life, why they are happening. I need to tell her they aren't the random attempts of a group who despise our union.

But the worst of it, the darkest piece of it all—she doesn't know about the academy. About the destruction. About me.

And when she finds out, I don't know if she'll ever forgive me.

I close my eyes, trying to calm the storm inside me, but it's no use. Every time I think I've regained control, it slips again, the memory of her lips against mine pulling me back under. I can still taste her. Sweet, soft, and far too tempting.

It's not just desire. There's more to this than that. I can feel it, deep in my bones—the way she matters. Not just to me, but to Iolas, to my kingdom. The way she's already changed everything.

I let out a quiet sigh, careful not to disturb her, though her body shifts slightly in her sleep, pressing closer to me. My arms instinctively tighten around her, my fingers threading through her hair. She smells like jasmine and something uniquely hers, and it's driving me mad.

Maybe I'm being selfish. Maybe I should let her go. In any other world I would let her choose someone like the baker's son from Avantra. He would be the easy choice—the safe choice. He could give her a simple human life, free from the weight of the secrets I carry. But the thought of that makes something dark coil inside me, something possessive and primal. The idea of her in someone else's arms—*his* arms—twists at my insides in a way I can't ignore.

But it's not my choice.

And in some ways my choices have put her in more danger. But when this is all over, I'll let her walk away if she wants to. If she chooses to after learning the truth, I won't stop her. I can't. I've already taken too much from her. But gods, if she stays...

If she stays, I'll never let her go.

How am I supposed to function? Now that I know the feel and taste of her against me.

CHAPTER THIRTY-NINE
Olwyn

Altair and I sit for breakfast at a simple wooden table in the inn.

There's a quietness that feels... comfortable. After everything, it's strange to sit here, outside of the palace, to have something as normal as breakfast with him without the royal guards around. Yet, as I take a bite of the fresh bread Abbas laid out for us, last night lingers in my thoughts, heating my cheeks.

I sneak a glance at Altair across the table. He's calm, as always, his movements graceful even in something as mundane as lifting his cup of tea. But then, just as I think I can compose myself, his eyes flick up to meet mine, a soft, amused smile tugging at the corner of his lips.

I immediately look away, focusing intently on the slice of bread in my hand, trying to suppress the blush that creeps up my neck. I'm thankful that he doesn't comment, though the quiet chuckle I hear from him doesn't do much to ease my embarrassment.

"Sleep well?" His voice is low, warm, and undeniably teasing.

My grip tightens on the bread. *Of course he'd ask that.* And then I panic that I might have done something embarrassing in my sleep.

"Yes," I answer, my voice betraying me with a slight tremble. "Thanks to your... hospitality."

I can feel his gaze on me, that intense gaze that seems to see far too much. My pulse quickens as I remember the feel of his arms around me, the warmth of his body pressed against mine all night long. The memory is too vivid, and I fight the urge to fan my face.

But then Abbas steps into the room, smiling warmly as he brings over a plate of fresh fruit. "How are my guests this morning?" he asks, his tone cheerful.

"Very well, Abbas," I say quickly, grateful for the distraction. I offer him a genuine smile, trying to push aside my lingering embarrassment. "Thank you for the breakfast, and for your hospitality"— Altair snorts into his tea—"The town has been... wonderful."

"You're welcome anytime," he replies, his old eyes twinkling as he glances between Altair and me. There's a warmth to his smile that makes me feel at ease, like I've known him for years instead of mere hours. "This village is your home now, just as much as the palace."

I smile, genuinely touched. "Thank you. That means a lot."

Altair, who has been quietly watching the exchange, gives Abbas a respectful nod. "Thank you for having us."

The older man nods in return. "Safe travels, Your Majesty. And you, my queen."

My cheeks flush again at the title, but Altair seems unbothered, as if it's the most natural thing in the world for me to be referred to as his queen. I must admit I'm still getting used to it. But Abbas's kindness, the warmth of the village—it all feels... right. More right than I'd like to admit.

Altair stands, offering me a hand. "We should head back."

I nod, taking his hand and letting him help me up. His touch lingers just a little longer than necessary, and I swear I see his eyes flicker with that same hunger from the night before. But it's gone as quickly as it came, replaced by his usual calm demeanour.

We step outside, the sun rising and warm against the cobblestone streets. It's a beautiful day, the air crisp and clean, filled with the sounds of the village coming to life. I watch as people bustle about—humans and vampires alike—and I'm almost reluctant to leave. The scene is peaceful, harmonious.

And that's what hurts.

Because, deep down, I know now that Altair's words about my parents were true—at least in part. I know there'll be conversations to have when we get back to the palace, but we also need to get ready for the ball and speak with King Casius.

I've been raised to fear vampires; to believe they were monsters. But here, in this small village, I see the truth with my own eyes. They're just... people. Some of them may be vampires, but they're not the monsters I was led to believe they were.

A pang of sadness hits me, and I glance at Altair. He doesn't say anything as we walk to the stables, but I feel his presence beside me, steady and solid, a quiet reassurance.

I wonder how much more of what I was told has been a lie.

Altair raises my hood over my hair, before pulling up his own. I know that on the way home we need to keep covered again, the easy, carefree energy from the village dissipating as I remember that outside of this territory, there may be those who wish to harm us.

Altair helps me mount the horse before climbing up behind me. I feel his hands settle around my waist, pulling me closer to him. The warmth of his body presses against my back, and it's... distracting. He clicks his tongue, urging the horse forward, and we leave the village behind, the sound of hooves echoing off the cobblestone.

The ride back is quiet, but not uncomfortable. The sun is rising steadily in the sky now, and the lush greenery of the landscape stretches out before us. Birds flit through the air, their songs filling the space between us. The farther we ride from the village, the more untamed the landscape becomes—wildflowers growing in bursts of colour along the roadside, dense forests casting long shadows over the path, rocky outcrops making the road rougher.

I lean back slightly, feeling the steady rise and fall of Altair's chest behind me. It's ridiculous how aware I am of him.

But just as my eyes close, something sharp pierces the air—a faint whistle, followed by a sudden, sickening *thunk*.

Altair's body jolts behind me.

"Altair?" I ask, turning quickly. But then, I see it—the arrow sticking out the back of his shoulder.

He grits his teeth, his hand slipping from my waist as he slumps to the side. "Olwyn—" he rasps, but before he can finish, he falls sideways from the horse, landing with a dull thud as his shadows coil up.

"Altair!" I scream, my heart stopping.

He gets to his knees, hissing. A shade darts out and captures an arrow in midair, but there is a *thunk*, and another arrow hits its target, embedding itself into his right side. He snarls, looking up with pure black eyes, widening with what looks like fear as he sees me still atop the horse.

More arrows whistle through the air, one hitting the rear leg of my horse. It squeals, rearing up, raising his front legs in the air as I scream.

"Olwyn!"

I brace as I am thrown from the animal waiting for the hard fall. But it doesn't come. Altair has thrown himself across the ground to catch me, grunting as he hits the floor and the horse flees. His shades *splutter*.

But I feel his shudder as another arrow pierces him. He tries to kneel, looking over his shoulder and blocking me from the view of the approaching men over the hill.

"Run," he pants.

"I'm not leaving you," I tell him. I won't make it far on my own, and I can't leave him in this state. Altair's blood stains the ground, and panic claws at my chest. And suddenly the thought of losing him, of the light in his eyes dimming forever, terrifies me more than any arrow.

I can't leave him.

I won't.

"Go, Olwyn!" He yells, and I unsheathe my dagger from my thigh. "For fucks sake," he snarls, pulling shades to him as he stands, though their movement is staggered. I suck a breath in as I see the arrow sticking out of his calf.

Another whistles through the air and he jerks to the side, catching it before it can bury itself in my eye.

He roars at the approaching human men, but Altair's movements are slower, each step a monumental effort. The witch silver must be burning in his veins, sapping his strength. Broken shadows like a dark mist coil around him, dark tendrils of his magic that flicker like a dying flame, struggling to maintain form as his body betrays him.

The men are so close now. Leaving him could be a death sentence—for both of us. I don't know what they want, but I know they'll likely hunt me down within minutes without Altair's protection.

But even weakened, Altair looks absolutely terrifying, as black lines crawl up along his arms, rising up his neck like tree roots.

"Touch her and I'll rip the air from your lungs before you can take another breath."

But the men laugh. Another arrow strikes his chest, dangerously close to his heart.

"Altair!" I cry out. He stumbles, and his eyes flash, those black lines climbing and crawling over each other…

Until he transforms into a beast of shadows and darkness, blurring toward the attackers like a vengeful wraith.

My heart leaps into my throat as I fall back and watch the solid darkness go. He appears behind the first man near us, twisting his hands and snapping the man's neck like a twig. The remaining men scramble, trying to nock an arrow as soon as they can to fire them again.

They are human.

These men are human.

Meaning they likely belong to the group who despise our union. But them harming Altair is only going to make vampire relations with the humans worse.

"Stop!" I yell at them all, but Altair kills another, ripping a vein from his neck with long black claws and throwing it to the ground.

No one listens to me… but one man has heard me.

He faces my direction, ignoring his companions who flee from Altair, causing his hunter instinct to kick in.

But this man comes after *me*.

There is a single moment of panic, of fear wanting me to flee away. But I feel an instinctual thing claw through me, as hot anger blinds my rationality and I rip my dagger from its sheath.

The man laughs as he charges, a *witchsilver* dagger raised, and Altair's head snaps round, his eyes wild.

But they have trained me for this, and I will not be weak again.

Just as the man reaches me, I step to the right and use my arm to deflect his attacking arm, redirecting his momentum past me. He stumbles slightly as I thrust my dagger into the side of his neck.

A quick, powerful stab, and the man falls to his knees, dropping his own blade as he tries to stop the crimson flowing from his neck.

As easy as that.

Too easy.

I just killed a man.

Altair sighs and smiles lightly at me in relief, but I cry out, unable to stop it as the last man rushes at him from behind, a witchsilver blade in his hand.

Altair's lips pop open as it stabs between his shoulder blades. One, two, three times.

The darkness fades, his eyes flutter shut, and an unyielding anger slams into me like a rock, causing me to scream in rage and run towards them. The man pushes Altair to the ground, unsheathing a short sword from his waist as he smirks at me.

Something fierce and primal stirs within me, pushing aside the fear and filling the void with a searing, blinding rage.

I don't care that he's human.

I don't care who he is.

All I care about is spilling his blood.

The dagger feels small in my hand, almost insignificant against the long blade he wields, but I grip it tightly anyway. My body moves before my brain can catch up, raw instinct driving me forward. I charge at him, my vision narrowing on his sword arm as it rises to strike.

My breath is ragged, my heart pounding like a war drum in my ears. I've never fought against a sword before. Altair trained me in daggers and hand-to-hand combat. I know how to throw, how to stab, how to defend myself—but this? This is entirely different.

Still, I feint low, hoping my wild strike will throw him off, but it's sloppy and desperate, and he reacts faster than I expect. His sword swings down, and I barely twist in time, the blade cutting through my trousers and grazing my thigh as I stumble back with a cry.

The burn of the cut ignites something deeper inside me, something dark and coiled and furious. I clench my teeth, ignoring the sting, and lunge again, this time with no plan, no careful calculation—just raw, unbridled fury.

He swings again, and I flinch, throwing my dagger up to block out of sheer desperation. The force of his strike jars my arm, the vibration rattling through my bones, and I barely manage to deflect the blade enough to avoid a killing blow.

But I'm not fast enough to dodge the punch that follows.

His free hand slams into my ribs with brutal force, and I hear the sickening crack before I feel the pain. It's sharp and blinding, stealing the breath from my lungs as I stagger back. My legs threaten to give out, but I grit my teeth, refusing to fall.

I clutch my side, my dagger trembling in my hand as he smirks, circling me like a predator.

"Is that all you've got, girl?" he taunts, his voice dripping with disdain.

My vision blurs, but not from tears. It's the rage, the humiliation, the raw, aching need to survive. My entire body trembles, not from fear, but from something deeper, something ancient and powerful stirring inside me.

The air around me seems to hum, a faint crackle of energy that I can't explain. My fingers tighten around the hilt of my dagger as heat floods through me, the pain in my ribs momentarily forgotten.

I meet his gaze, and for the first time, I see a flicker of hesitation in his eyes.

Because I'm no longer just a girl with a dagger.

Something inside me has awakened.

I step forward, my movements no longer clumsy or desperate but driven by something else—something primal and terrifying. And for the first time, I don't feel like prey.

I feel like the predator.

He launches at me, but a warmth surges up from the core of my being, racing through my veins like liquid fire. My hand moves on its own, palm open, and suddenly the world explodes in a flash of golden light. Heat radiates from my skin, so intense I almost expect to see flames. The man screams, clutching his face, but all I can focus on is the sensation— this strange, terrifying power coursing through me.

"My eyes!" He shouts.

All I feel is burning, and I want to look at my hand, to see if there is redness and blisters there, like there appears to be over the man's face. But I take the opportunity to dash behind him, driving my blade up into the base of his skull.

His hands drop and his shouts cease, his body falling forward off my blade and face down into the dirt.

They are all dead.

I helped kill them.

I cut into flesh and blood as easy as carving up my meal.
I throw up.

She saved me. Instead of saving herself…

CHAPTER FORTY
Olwyn

I finish retching as warm fingers brush over my shoulder, and I jerk upright.

"Olwyn," Altair pants, looking paler as he passes me the water pouch that was tied to his waist. The shadows have gone, and Altair looks too pale, causing a panic to build in my chest.

I take a swig, swilling the cool water around my mouth before spitting it out. The smell of blood overwhelms my nose as I stare at the bodies. My hands won't stop trembling, and every breath feels like a battle. I can't unsee it—the blood, the way the light left their eyes. It was too easy. Far too easy to take a life again.

"We killed them."

"We did," he pants, and there is no remorse on his face.

"We killed them all!" He seems to realise my regret.

"A-And I would do it again. Sometimes, Olwyn," he hisses as he stumbles back. "There are no clean choices. Only survival."

I drink some more, knowing he's right but taking the moment to catalogue Altair's injuries. There are still arrows piercing his skin.

I see him sway again, and I reach out as he stumbles towards me.

"We need to remove the arrows," I say, barely able to hold him up.

"I… need, Iolas," he breathes against my hair, his voice hoarse. Altair's shoulders sag under the pain of his wounds. His breaths are shallow, laboured, and I can feel the cold seeping from his skin, sapping the warmth from the air around us. He's lost so much blood. The shadows that usually dance at his command are nowhere to be seen.

"We need to move." The horse is nowhere to be seen. I wrap my arm around his large back as I look around. There is a rocky outcrop a short walk away, perhaps we can hide in there for now, until Altair recovers. "Come on," I grit my teeth.

"Ol-Olwyn, you need to leave. More could come."

"I am not leaving you," I huff with a laugh, though there is no humour here.

His weight is almost too much for me, his body leaning heavily against mine as we stumble forward. His breath is ragged, each exhale a painful reminder of the arrows embedded in his flesh. My muscles burn with the effort of holding him up, but I grit my teeth, refusing to let him fall.

"Y-you… did well." He must be out of it, because his teeth flash in a boyish smile. A genuine smile that makes him look younger. But the expression doesn't last long as his eyes dart to my thigh, nostrils flaring. "You're hurt."

"Let's talk about all that back there when you are better," I reply.

"Olwyn," his eyes turn serious, though they drift open and closed. "If more come, I-I need you to run."

"I will not leave you,"

"You must! I'm not important—"

"Don't say things like that. You are the king."

"And all my power… still didn't prevent me from almost losing you today."

His words hit me like a punch to the gut. I've always seen him as invincible, this powerful force of nature. Altair isn't just any vampire; his bloodline is marked by abilities most could only dream of.

And it isn't just his shadows; the glamour magic he wields to command respect and dread is something only the most elite of vampire nobility can conjure.

I've seen him summon food from another room, a skill that defies nature itself, one I didn't even know vampires could have. He is a king in every sense of the word, a being of immense power that should never waver. And yet here he is, his voice heavy with vulnerability, his composure cracked, telling me he's scared of losing *me*.

And that terrifies me.

"But you didn't. You and Iolas have taught me well. I'm still here."

"Even kings have fears."

"Well, this king needs to save his strength. Come on." His feet are dragging more as we enter a narrow path that causes my shoulders to brush against the rocks, walking farther into the large rocky outcrop.

"It looks like there's a cave up ahead," I say eagerly, breathing hard. "I can remove the arrows there."

He grunts in response, dragging his feet.

When we enter the darkness, I feel comforted that we are out of sight. The cave is a dark, cool refuge, the air thick with the scent of damp earth. The sound of our footsteps echoes faintly against the stone walls, and I shiver as the coolness of the rock presses against my arm. The light from outside barely reaches us, casting long, eerie shadows across the uneven floor. I lean down and rip out the arrow in Altair's calf, and he hisses, his fangs showing.

Now I can help him down into a sitting position, he lands on his arse with a thud, leaning forward to show me his back.

Blood saturates his shirt, and the wounds I see through the holes in his shirt are not healing…

But there's scars I can see too. Ones that have been there for a long time. I push the burning questions to the back of my mind for now, knowing the witch silver is doing its job and weakening him severely whilst they are still in his body.

Most of the arrows haven't come through the other side, so I'll just have to rip them out.

"This is going to hurt." I swallow hard, my hand coming to rest on his shoulder as I brace him.

"It's fine," he says, though I can tell it's through gritted teeth.

I grip the shaft and he groans, I pause.

"D-do it, Olwyn."

I drop my hands, unsheathing my dagger and undoing my sheath. He says nothing as I hold the leather up in front of his face.

"Bite down on this," I tell him. If he cries out it could draw attention to our position.

He nods, opening his mouth. I am careful around his fangs as I place the leather between his teeth, knowing that his fangs will likely make holes in the leather.

I exhale deeply, his swirling dark gaze watching me until I move back around him. As I grip the arrow, the metallic scent of blood fills the air, mingling with the dampness of the cave. My hands tremble slightly, and I can feel Altair's muscles tense under my touch.

"Ready?" I ask.

I take his muffled response as confirmation.

"One, two—"

With a swift, jerking motion, I yank the arrow free. The sound of tearing flesh is sickening.

"Fuck," he grunts, a word I can distinguish over the leather between his lips.

"Does witch silver leave scars?" I ask, trying to distract him as I move to the other arrow in his back.

He hums, and I feel bad that this beautiful man will now be more scarred because of those men. I wonder if that's what made the scar on his face. I think of something to take both our minds off it.

"When I was younger, I used to attend an academy where humans and vampires learned together."

His muscles tense under my hands.

"I don't remember much... There was an accident. But I remember being treated by my parent's healer. I was unconscious for a while, and I had a bad wound above my eye. You've probably seen the scar. The healer had to use a needle and thread to pull the edges closed. Apparently, I was lucky to survive. What I'm trying to say is… it's all right to have a scar. They remind us of our journey."

He grunts as I rip another arrow free, before spitting out the sheath.

"Did you just revisit a painful memory to try and make me feel better?" his chest heaves.

I laugh.

"Yes, I suppose I did."

He is quiet for a moment. "Do you remember anything else from your time in the academy?"

My head tilts as I throw the arrow to a corner of the cave, making my way to kneel in front of him.

"No," I say. "I was quite young. The healer said my injury likely erased the memory from my brain. But besides the accident, I remember… the feeling. Being quite happy there."

A flash of memory appears behind my eyes; the laugh of two young boys, a bossy dark-skinned girl, bright, bright red… but I brush the flicker of memory away.

"Last one," I nod, gripping the shaft of the arrow in his chest.

"It was fortunate they had shitty aim," he huffs.

"It was still too close," I mutter, ripping the last arrow out.

He gasps, the sound pained, his body and head falling forward until his forehead rests against the junction between my neck and shoulder.

I still. I freeze.

"Thank you," his voice is raw, his breath fanning out through the thin material of my dress.

"It's all right," I tell him, brushing back his dark hair. It seems an almost subconscious action.

His head lifts, his skin pale. I frown as I help him lean back against a boulder and he sighs now the arrows are removed, weakly pulling his shirt over his head. I gather the arrows, walking over to dump them by the cave entrance, away from him.

I turn and watch his chest anxiously, waiting to see if his wounds will start to close now that the witch silver is gone. But the blood keeps flowing. My stomach twists with fear. What if it's too late?

"I removed the witchsilver. Why aren't they closing?"

"I… need Iolas."

"Well, unfortunately you're stuck with me, so tell me what I can do," I say a bit impatiently.

"I… need blood."

Blood.

Goosebumps erupt over my entire body.

It could be hours, a day until Iolas finds us.

Will Altair get weaker instead of recovering?

What if more of those men arrive?

My mind cascades into a flurry of irrational and rational thoughts. Possibilities, consequences of various actions.

Out of the corner of my eye, Altair's brow falls as he watches me, my eyes darting between his feet as I think.

And then I glance up, taking a step forward.

"Stop," Altair says, his voice authoritative and stronger than it has been since we were attacked.

"Why?"

"B-because…" His voice falters, his eyes squeezing shut as if he can't bear to look at me. "Because I can see that stubborn look in your eye.

And I can't…" He swallows hard, his voice trembling slightly. "I just can't. We'll w-wait for Iolas. Please."

"We don't have time. I will not let you die, and if more of those men come, I can't fight them off on my own."

"I think… you'd be surprised of what you can do."

I exhale in frustration, not wanting to talk about the magic I used.

"Let's be realistic. You need to feed. And I am a perfectly viable, ready-to-eat snack that you can have right now."

His eyes clench shut.

"I can't," he breathes out. "I've taken too much from you already."

That's the first sign of remorse he's ever shown for taking me from my home.

"And I'm still here, willing to give a little more."

"You don't understand, Olwyn." His voice drops to a hoarse whisper, his eyes dark and pleading. "If you come any closer, I won't be able to stop myself. I'll feed from you… and then, I'll never be able to let you go."

His words are a promise. There's no lie or regret in his gaze for saying them. But he is giving me a choice. I swallow hard, feeling his words settle in my chest like a stone. I can see the conflict in his eyes, the struggle between his need, and his desire to protect me. My heart races, my thoughts a whirlwind.

If I step forward, I know what I'm agreeing to. I know the power he holds, the hunger that gnaws at him. He won't die if I don't give him this, but he will be weakened if more enemies arrive, and I won't be able to protect us both. But the image of him, vulnerable and struggling, tightens the knot of anxiety in my stomach.

I can't bear the thought of anyone harming him because of my hesitation. To have his death on my hands.

Because the idea of him not living… Is abhorrent.

But the idea of giving myself to him, of surrendering to his hunger, terrifies me. I don't know what to expect.

The silence stretches between us and every instinct screams at me to run, to protect myself. But another part, a deeper, quieter part, urges me to trust him, to believe that he won't let the darkness consume him completely. Not that I've now seen the extent of it, remembering the creature he became when he killed those men.

I take a shaky breath, trying to steady my racing thoughts. I meet his gaze, searching for any sign of reassurance, any hint that this won't destroy us both.

"Please, Olwyn. I-I need you to be sure," he whispers, his voice raw with need and restraint. The word hangs in the air, a fragile plea that cuts through my fear like a knife, because he has seen I have made up my mind.

I know what I have to do.

My heart races as I step closer, every instinct screaming at me to stay back, to protect myself. But the sight of Altair's blood-soaked body, his power slipping away with each passing second, pushes me forward. I can't let him sit there in pain—not when I'm the only one who can save him right now. The thought of him losing control chills me, but I force it aside, locking eyes with him, my resolve hardening. His eyes darken as I kneel beside him, pulling my hair over one shoulder.

He groans, a sound filled with both longing and agony. "Not there," his whisper is husky, shaking his head quickly, averting his eyes as if the sight of my exposed neck is too much to bear.

"All right." My voice trembles slightly as I pull up the sleeve of my shirt, revealing the pale skin of my wrist. I offer it to him, trying to steady my breathing, as his nostrils flare. He nods, his fingers too cool as he gently holds my arm, his touch sending a shiver down my spine.

"I'm sorry. I don't know if this is going to hurt." His words are soft, tinged with a sorrow that mirrors the tension coiled in my chest.

"How do others react when you feed from them?" I ask, my voice barely above a whisper, seeking some semblance of reassurance.

"I've… never fed from anyone before." His two-toned eyes catch mine.

I feel a sudden surge of disbelief. That can't be true. The ground beneath me seems to dissolve like mist in the morning sun, and a chill runs through me, the gravity of the situation sinking in. This isn't just a matter of trust; it's uncharted territory for both of us.

His grip tightens slightly, grounding me. I meet his gaze, finding a flicker of vulnerability that mirrors my own.

"It's all right," I breathe, steeling myself for whatever comes next. "I trust you."

I'm surprised at my own words, more so because… I believe them.

He hesitates for a second before he lowers his head, his lips brushing against my wrist in a small kiss first, with a tenderness that makes my chest clench. The moment stretches into an eternity, filled with the sound of our breathing and the rapid beat of my pulse.

My stomach dips as he opens his mouth, his fangs lengthening before my eyes. Then—a sharp, sudden pain as his fangs pierce my skin, but it only lasts a second.

He waits, inhaling deeply through his nose. He draws a mouthful, and I gasp, the sensation both alien and strangely intimate. He groans, a low, guttural sound that vibrates through me, and I can sense his struggle, the effort it takes for him to remain gentle.

The initial pain fades… replaced by a strange warmth that spreads through my veins and grows with each pull of his mouth.

Oh my.

His grip on my arm remains firm yet careful, as if he's holding onto a lifeline. I can hear his breathing deepen and slow, a low rumble vibrating in his chest as he draws another mouthful. His fangs press deeper, and the chill air sharpens against my flushed skin.

Suddenly the cave melts away. And so does my restraint and fear. Everything but us.

His teeth and lips against my skin sets me on fire, and I feel a burning throb between my legs. My head falls back as an uncontrollable sound leaves me, and Altair growls against my wrist.

As I move closer, climbing into his lap to straddle him, a part of me is shocked by my own boldness. But the other part—the one that's been yearning for this connection, this release—drowns out any reservations. It feels like surrender, but to what, I'm not entirely sure. All I know is that in this moment, with his hand on my hip, everything else fades away.

His breath comes in short bursts, fanning across the hot skin of my wrist. My hips roll forward, regardless of a small voice in the back of my mind telling me to exercise restraint.

And Altair freezes.

But I don't want the feeling to end. Experimentally I roll my hips again, a sigh escaping at the delicious friction.

His lips leave my wrist… and hover just above mine.

"You taste like pure light." His tongue darts out and licks across his bottom lip. "Tell me I can kiss you, love. Because otherwise I'm going to do something I swore I would never do… and kiss you without your permission."

I moan. "*Please.*"

And he presses his mouth to mine.

If I thought Altair feeding from me felt incredible, it was nothing compared to the feeling of his full lips against mine after doing so.

Some part of my brain screams that this is just the rush from his bite. Shouts that I am once more kissing King Draven.

But I am kissing *Altair.*

Sunlight seems to burn behind my eyelids as his tongue sweeps across mine. A small lingering taste of copper does nothing to put me off kissing this man. His fingers dig into my hips as he encourages me to grind down.

Oh.

He's rock hard beneath me, and a thrill runs through me as I feel him respond to my every movement. He smiles against my lips as I do as he wishes, losing myself in the sensations he is tearing out of my body.

His eyes look as wild as I feel as he nips at my bottom lip and I move against him, a grunt rushing out of him as he pulls away, his head rocking back. I don't miss the opportunity, need and hunger eradicating every ounce of self-preservation as I lean forward and kiss his neck.

"Olwyn," he snarls, seeming to come to some sense of rationality. His hand rises to wrap in my hair. "Maybe we should stop before I—"

His words cut off with a moan. But stopping feels impossible. Why would I, when this feels so right?

His hard cock is stuck between our bodies, and he drives his hips upwards when I roll my hips again.

Oh…

"Olwyn," I barely recognise his voice, so throaty and guttural. So out of control. "Fuck, you smell so good. Feel so good."

"Gods." The pressure builds, any thoughts of stopping scattering from my brain like dust in the wind as I chase a release.

I bite at his collarbone, and he lets out an animalistic growl that almost ends me.

"Olwyn," he warns, his hand moving to hold my throat gently.

I lean back, my eyes closing from the pleasure. "Please," I breathe out, the sound echoing in the almost silent cave. "I need—"

"Fuck," he grunts, driving his hips upward again and again and, *Gods*… how hard and thick it feels between my legs.

I need…

I'm going to…

"That's it. Call out for me, love."

I cry out his name as waves of ecstasy rip through me, turning me boneless.

He groans deeply, the sound causing my core to clench.

His head falls, his eyes open… and they're the lightest I have ever seen them. There's only a thin layer of shadow covering his black iris. And I see the blue of both eyes so clearly.

He takes in my astonished and curious gaze and blinks quickly, the shadows pulling in.

I look him over. Colour has returned to his cheeks.

And then reality hits.

I just grinded on him until I came, and I'm still sitting on his lap.

Oh gods.

My face flames, and his head tilts as he tries to catch my gaze.

"I let that go too far. Did I hurt you?" It's the softest I have ever heard his voice, and he sounds stronger.

I shake my head, trying not to laugh maniacally. The very opposite of that.

"I think that was more my fault than yours," I mumble.

"It was the rush," he explains. "I should have warned you about it."

I nod, shifting on his lap slightly, and he winces.

Oh gods…

"Did… did *I* hurt you?"

I try hard not to react to how his cheeks darken. How he looks… *embarrassed.*

"Not at all," he bites on his lower lip, as if wondering if he should say his next words. "That's just… never happened to me before,' he murmurs, and I see a brief flash of vulnerability in his gaze. He's always so composed, so in control, but now… now he looks almost as shaken as I feel.

What? Had a woman grind on his lap?

My brows fall in confusion, but I catch the way his eyes dart down to his breeches and back to mine.

Oh.

"Oh." I scramble off his lap, trying not to trip over his legs. My heart is still racing, and I can't quite suppress the nervous energy bubbling up inside me. But then I see the way he looks at me—half-amused, half-uncertain—and it's enough to keep my focus on the moment, rather than the absurdity of the situation.

Altair stands carefully, flexing his hand and sighing in relief as a wisp of shadow appears there. He clears his throat, waving his hand over the front of his breeches, my cheeks heating at him using his magic to clear himself up, and I can't help as the corners of my lips tug up.

He spots it, and suddenly I am blind to everything else around us. He approaches me, *smiling*.

His fangs are still long, but they do not bother me.

It's a startling realization, one that roots me to the spot. There was a time, not long ago, when those very fangs represented everything I feared—violence, control, bloodshed. A reminder of how different we are. Of how dangerous he is. But now, standing here, they are simply a part of him. A part of Altair. Not a threat, not a weapon, just... him.

The man who protected me. The man who fought for me.

He reaches out, taking a hold of my wrist as he lifts it to look at. As Altair examines my wrist, his touch is surprisingly gentle, almost reverent.

"It's all right—"

My breath hitches as heat floods me once more, his tongue darting out over one of the puncture marks, sealing it closed.

"Oh my."

His eyes stare at me, shadows swirling excitedly as he repeats the action on the other one, before releasing me.

I don't deny my arm lingered hopefully in the air for a split second longer than it needed to.

"Thank you, Olwyn," he bows his head slightly. "Thank you for this gift."

"Has it helped?" I ask tentatively.

"More than you know."

I nod.

Gods.

What just happened?

I feel slightly dizzy, and Altair captures my arm as I stumble slightly.

I let him feed from me.

The thought loops through my mind like a curse. What would my parents think if they saw me now?

I try to rid myself of the poisonous thought that I have somehow betrayed them. The parents who lied to me. Who lied to apparently protect me from the one thing they feared most… and I gave it away willingly. I let him use me, and worse, I used him.

But I saved his life.

I glance over at him, seeing if there's any differences from my apparently magical blood. But he looks the same.

He inhales deeply and darkness surrounds us like an ominous cloud.

I let him feed from me.

My heart races.

And my thoughts begin to spiral. And this is what tips me over the edge.

I allowed him to use me for my magical blood. The one thing my parents said I would be drained for. But Altair stands before me, having only consumed a little, and he's still in control.

But I used him for his body.

"Olwyn, breathe," his brows fall. Altair's grip on my arm is gentle, his eyes searching mine for something—fear, regret… But all I see in his is concern, genuine and raw, as if he's battling his own demons even as he tries to calm mine.

Tears start to stream down my face, and I clutch at my chest. "I let you feed from me. They lied to me. I can't— I can't breathe. I feel like— I'm suffocating."

Altair gently guides me to sit. "Olwyn, look at me. You're safe. Focus on me. Just breathe. In through your nose, out through your mouth."

The air feels too thick, like I'm trying to breathe through water. The walls of the cave seem to close in, the shadows flickering like dark flames. Every heartbeat is a drum in my ears, loud and suffocating. But Altairs' weak shades brush over my skin, distracting me from my panic as they caress and comfort me.

"You were brave. You are so brave. You did this because you care."

"I used you." I sob.

"You didn't use me. I was a willing participant, believe me. And I'm grateful for what you've done."

"They lied," I cry quietly.

Altair looks heartbroken. "I know, love."

He continues to guide my breathing, his voice a low, steady rhythm that I cling to like a lifeline. Slowly, the panic begins to ebb, my racing heart settling into a more manageable pace. The darkness surrounding us seems to loosen its grip, the shadows retreating slightly as I focus on his voice.

"That's it, just keep breathing," Altair murmurs, his hands still resting on my shoulders, grounding me.

The cave is quiet now, save for the sound of our breathing. The silence feels heavy, filled with unspoken thoughts. I glance at Altair, his eyes locked on mine, searching for something—reassurance, perhaps, or maybe just a sign that I'm all right.

"How do you feel?" he asks, his voice soft but tinged with concern.

I hesitate, trying to sort through the tangled mess of emotions inside me. "Better," I manage to say, though the word feels inadequate. I'm better, but not whole. Not yet.

Altair nods, as if he understands. His hands drop from my shoulders, and the absence of his touch leaves me feeling strangely cold.

"We should check your wounds again," I suggest, desperate to focus on something other than the gnawing fear in my chest and embarrassment flaming my face.

He doesn't argue, simply turns around so I can get a better look at the arrow wounds in his back. The blood has slowed significantly but hasn't stopped.

"Did you feed enough?" I ask, running my fingers around a wound, seeing goosebumps cover the skin of his back.

"I won't take anymore. I have enough until Iolas gets here." He says, and there's a note of finality in his tone, telling me he won't take any argument from me. Iolas promised to come for us, and I know he'll hold true to that promise.

"All right," I reply.

Hours pass and daylight fades—the only sound the occasional drip of water from somewhere deeper in the cave. I sit, but my mind is miles away, replaying the events of the past two days, the feeling of his teeth in my skin, the intimacy of the act. I can't stop myself from glancing at him, wondering if he's thinking about it too.

Finally, I break the silence. "You said you've never fed from anyone before. Was that true?"

He looks up, his expression unreadable for a moment. Then he nods, his eyes meeting mine, and he looks tired. "It's true. I've never fed directly from someone before." His voice is quiet, as if admitting this takes more effort than I'd expected.

I don't know why, but the thought makes my stomach twist. "Why not?"

He hesitates, as if weighing how much to tell me. "I usually drink donor blood from a goblet. In emergencies… I can feed from other vampires."

My eyes widen. That explains why he wanted Iolas.

"But feeding is… intimate."

Just found that out.

"I've never wanted to forge that kind of bond with anyone." His gaze holds mine, and I see a flicker of something in his eyes.

"But you… fed from me," I say, the words feeling heavier than they should.

"And you are the only person I'd ever want to feed from," he replies, a small smile tugging at the corner of his lips as my face warms. "And I'm grateful. More than you know."

A silence falls between us. I want to ask more, to understand what this means for us, but the day hangs over us both, too heavy to lift right now.

Instead, I lean my head against his shoulder, exhaustion tugging at me. "Do you think they'll always come for us?"

Altair's eyes flutter closed, and he sighs, his hand coming to rest on the cave floor beside mine. "No. We'll put a stop to it. I promise."

There's an honesty in his words that makes my chest ache. For all his strength, for all his power, I see the vulnerability there too. I feel too awkward to reply, so I close my eyes for a moment's peace.

I wake what seems like minutes later, but is hours based on the deep darkness outside of the cave. And my heart leaps into my throat, fear gripping me once more as I hear someone.

But then the words become clearer.

"Olwyn! Altair!"

I hear the familiar voice calling out, and relief floods through me. Iolas.

Altair's tired eyes open slightly, and he shifts as if to rise, his movements sluggish once more, but I press a hand to his shoulder, holding him back. "Stay still. Iolas will be here soon."

True to my words, Iolas appears in the entrance to the cave, his figure backlit by the moonlight outside. His eyes scan the scene, taking in Altair's condition and my dishevelled state. He breathes out in relief, but his voice is calm when he speaks.

"Are you both all right?" he asks, striding forward. He falters for a split second, his eyes widening as his nostrils flare, but he recovers quickly.

"We're alive," I reply, glancing at Altair. "But he needs blood, Iolas. The witchsilver… it's not letting him heal."

Iolas nods, his expression grim. "We need to get him back to the palace, fast." He steps closer, his eyes on Altair. "Can you move?"

Altair grunts in response, trying to push himself up. But Iolas doesn't wait for him to struggle. He moves quickly, lifting Altair with a surprising gentleness for someone so large and powerful.

I stand, feeling my own legs wobble slightly from exhaustion and adrenaline. Iolas catches my arm before I can fall, his grip steadying me. "I can smell your blood, Olwyn. You saved him."

His words hit me hard, and I have to swallow back the lump in my throat. "I couldn't just leave him," I reply, my voice hoarse. "I couldn't…"

He nods, understanding in his eyes. "You didn't. And that's what matters."

With Altair supported between us, we make our way out of the cave. The night air is cool against my skin, and for a moment, I feel a sense of peace, a calm after the storm. But as I glance at Altair, his eyes closed and his breath shallow, I know that this peace is fragile, temporary.

As we head out of the rocky outcrop and towards where Iolas has secured a new horse, several royal guards mounted nearby, I take one last look back at the cave. The shadows within seem to shift and flicker, as if watching us leave.

She's the queen my kingdom needs.

CHAPTER FORTY-ONE
Olwyn

The moment we return to the palace, Iolas doesn't waste a second.

He pulls open the carriage door with such force I think it might come off its hinges. His large frame blocks the dim light from outside as he reaches in, his hands finding Altair's arm before I can blink.

"You're going to the infirmary," Iolas says, his voice brokering no argument.

Altair groans, trying to shake him off as Iolas yanks him from the carriage, practically dragging him out into the courtyard.

"I'm fine," Altair grits out, stumbling slightly as his feet hit the ground. "I need to make sure Olwyn is—"

"She's fine," Iolas snaps, his usual calm tone edged with fury. "She's here. *Alive.* You're not fine." He turns to two waiting guards, his grip on Altair firm. "Take him to the infirmary, get him blood. Now."

The guards hesitate, looking between Iolas and Altair, but when Altair tries to shove them off, Iolas grabs him by the shoulders, forcing him to face him. "Altair, stop. You're no good to her like this."

Altair's eyes flick to mine, his expression clouded with both pain and worry. "Olwyn…"

"I'm fine," I say softly, trying to sound stronger than I feel. "Go. Please."

"I need to—" Altair starts saying, but I remember who I am.

"Guards, take your king to the infirmary," I say, and they immediately step forward to help Altair, to my surprise.

I sway a little and Iolas catches my arm. It's only then that Altair seems to relent, his shoulders sagging as if all the fight has drained from him. "She gave me blood."

Iolas nods, "I'll get her some tea from the kitchens."

Altair nods. "I'll come to you after," he murmurs to me before allowing the guards to lead him away.

Iolas watches him go, the tension in his broad shoulders palpable. He turns back to me then, his eyes scanning over my form. Before I can say anything, he steps forward, lifting me out of the carriage as if I weigh nothing.

"I'm all right," I protest weakly, though I don't really have the strength to push him away, feeling utterly exhausted.

"Sure you are," he mutters, his tone a mix of sarcasm and concern as he carries me across the courtyard and into the palace, telling a maid to bring me some tea from the kitchens before he addresses me again. "Just let me do this."

The world is a blur around us as he walks, his strong arms cradling me close. I'm too tired to argue, too drained from everything that's happened. When we reach my chambers, he kicks the door open gently and strides in, setting me down on the edge of the bed with surprising care.

I try to smile at him, to reassure him that I'm really okay, but when his hand brushes against my waist to steady me, a sharp pain flares through my side, and I wince.

His eyes narrow, and his entire demeanour shifts. The concern in his eyes is quickly replaced by something darker. Silent. Dangerous. His jaw tightens, and he takes a step back, running a hand through his honey-brown hair. For the first time since I met him, Iolas looks like he could tear the entire world apart—and it terrifies me.

"I-I'm fine," I say quickly, trying to ease the tension, but my words fall flat. He's not listening, his eyes focused on my waist, on the bruise forming there under my clothes.

Without a word, he turns and strides to the door. "Take off your clothes," he says gruffly, disappearing into the hallway.

I blink, too stunned to respond. The door closes behind him, leaving me alone for a moment. My heart hammers in my chest, but I do as he says, undoing the laces before pulling the bloodstained fabric over my head and dropping it to the floor. I wince as I bend over and pull the breeches from my legs. I'm left in just my breast band and plain black underwear, feeling suddenly vulnerable and exposed.

Before I can second-guess myself, the door opens again. Iolas returns, his arms full of medical supplies. He crosses the room in a few quick strides, setting everything down on the dresser. His gaze sweeps over me, pausing for the briefest second at the sight of my bare skin and the wound on my leg, but he doesn't say anything. He kneels in front of me, the tension still etched into every line of his face.

The silence between us is thick, as he studies my leg.

"You don't need stitches," he says, sounding pissed off.

I nod, hissing slightly when he rubs the healing paste into it, before wrapping a bandage around my thigh.

Next, I raise my arm and he begins to rub a salve into the bruised skin around my ribs. His fingers are methodical, gentle, but there's a frown pulling at his lips. His touch should feel clinical, detached. But it doesn't. There's something else in it—anger. And part of it is directed at me.

His hand brushes over the darkest part of the bruise, and I can't help but wince again.

"I'm all right," I whisper, trying to convince him as much as myself.

He doesn't reply. His frown deepens, and his silence feels heavy, almost suffocating. It's like he's holding back a storm of emotions, the tension in the room coiling tighter with each second. Finally, he finishes applying the salve and pulls away, his fingers lingering on my waist for just a moment longer than necessary, before both hands rest on my hips.

"Iolas…" I say softly, reaching to cup his cheek, guiding his face up to meet my gaze. His skin is warm under my touch, and I can feel the tremor in his muscles as if he's barely holding himself together. "Look at me."

Reluctantly, he does, his hazel eyes meeting mine. There's a so many emotions brewing there—anger, fear, something raw and vulnerable. His jaw works, like he's trying to find the right words, but nothing comes.

"I told you not to go," he finally says, his voice low, barely controlled. "I told him not to take you outside the palace. And now… now you both almost died." His hand clenches into a fist, the tendons in his neck straining as he forces the words out.

"I'm here," I remind him gently, keeping my voice steady. "We both made it back."

He exhales sharply, shaking his head, before resting his forehead against my stomach, his deep exhale tickling the skin there. "I saw their bodies. How many of them there were. I smelled Altair's spilled blood. And then I scented yours… I was terrified. Both of you—" He cuts himself off, his voice thick with something I can't quite place. Fear, maybe. Regret. "I almost lost you both."

I force myself to breathe, to let out the breath I've been holding, but it's shaky. "I didn't realise…" I start, my voice barely above a whisper. "I didn't realise I meant that much to you."

Iolas pulls back and his gaze doesn't waver. His hazel eyes, usually filled with playful light, are now shadowed with something I haven't seen before. "You do, Olwyn. A lot more than you know."

My heart pounds in my chest, each beat resonating with his confession. The usual banter between us is absent, replaced by an energy that feels both uncomfortable and strangely comforting. I'm not used to seeing this side of Iolas—vulnerable, unguarded. And it scares me how much I want to reach out, to touch him, to reassure him that I understand.

His fingers linger, his hand warm against my skin. I look down, focusing on the place where his hand rests, trying to gather my thoughts before I meet his gaze. "I don't want to lose you either," I say, my voice quiet but firm.

A flicker of surprise crosses Iolas's face, quickly replaced by a soft smile, one that seems almost relieved. "Good," he murmurs, before he pulls his hands away, his touch leaving a lingering warmth on my skin. "Because I'm not going anywhere."

He stands, moving to sit me on the edge of the bed, before sitting beside me. He shifts slightly, his gaze hardening as he studies me. "So… What happened?" His voice is quiet now, but there's an edge to it.

"There was an attack," I begin, my voice low. "I don't know if they saw us in the village or were tipped off, but they caught us by surprise."

My shoulders lift in a shrug, but I feel the phantom ache of the fight in my ribs, the ghost of his blade coming too close. "They didn't seem to care about me at first. Altair was the target, but…" I pause, my throat tightening at the memory. "I couldn't just stand there and let him die."

Iolas's jaw tenses, his hazel eyes darkening. "So what did you do?"

"I fought one," I admit, meeting his gaze. "I wasn't exactly trained to go up against someone with a sword, but I managed. I used what I knew. What you taught me—daggers, hand-to-hand. But he was strong. Stronger than I expected."

"You're still here," he says pointedly, though his voice is tight. "So you did something right."

"I got lucky," I say softly, my fingers brushing the faint bruise on my wrist. "He hit me, cracked a rib, but I found an opening and took it.

And then…" My voice trails off as the memory sharpens, using my powers.

"And then?" Iolas presses, his eyes narrowing as he studies me.

I take a deep breath, forcing the words out. "Altair was badly injured. He lost a lot of blood. Too much. I… I didn't think he'd make it unless…" I trail off, swallowing hard as I try to piece it together. "Unless I let him feed."

Iolas's expression doesn't change, but I can see the flicker of something in his eyes.

"There's more," he says, his voice almost a whisper. It's not a question. He knows me too well.

But I don't want to tell him about my magic. Not yet. Not until I process it myself.

I look away, my throat tightening as I try to push down the memory of everything that happened—the village, the attack, the feeding… the way it felt like everything shifted between Altair and me. But I can't bring myself to say it out loud. Not to Iolas. Not now.

He doesn't push. He doesn't need to. The silence between us says enough.

Iolas's gaze remains on me, searching, questioning. His brows furrow, and he shifts, the tension still thick in the air between us.

"Olwyn," he says quietly, his voice softer now, but there's an edge to it that makes my chest tighten. "Are you all right? I mean… feedings can be… intense."

It takes me a moment to understand his words. He's not just asking about the physical wounds. There's something more behind the question, something not said but clear in his eyes. He's asking if everything that happened—between me and Altair—was what I wanted.

I give him a small, reassuring smile, even though my heart still pounds in my chest. "I am, Iolas. Really," I say, my voice steady even though I feel the heat creeping up my neck. I don't want him to worry more than he already does. "It was... I'm good."

He watches me for a moment longer, his bright eyes flicking over my face as if he's looking for any sign of doubt. When he finds none, he nods slowly, but his posture doesn't fully ease.

"All right," he murmurs, though his voice is still filled with a quiet concern.

I look away, biting my lip. My arms instinctively fold across my chest, and the cool air brushing against my skin suddenly feels... sharper. *Why do I feel so exposed?*

Shit.

Gods. I'm practically naked.

I glance at Iolas, who's sitting close enough to touch, his gaze locked on mine. He doesn't seem to have noticed—or maybe he has, but he doesn't let it show. His expression is focused, his concern for me written in every tense line of his face. There's no judgment there, no indication that he's even aware of my sudden embarrassment.

But I notice.

And now, it feels like the air between us is heavier. Warmer.

Awkwardness swells in my chest as I shift on the bed, my eyes darting around the room until I spot the blanket folded on the bed behind me. I turn quickly and grab the blanket, wrapping it tightly around my shoulders.

The movement is casual—or at least, I try to make it look that way—but I feel the heat of his eyes on me as I sit back down.

"Are you cold?" Iolas asks, his voice light, though there's a flicker of something in his tone I can't quite place.

"No," I reply too quickly, clutching the blanket tighter. "Just... tired. It's been a long day."

He raises an eyebrow, clearly unconvinced, but he doesn't push. Instead, he leans back slightly, his gaze softening once more.

"Long day doesn't even begin to cover it," he murmurs, almost to himself.

The blanket is warm against my skin, but the awkwardness lingers. I hate how self-conscious I suddenly feel—how natural everything had felt just moments ago, sitting so close to him, until the realisation of my near-nakedness crept in.

Why did it feel so natural?

"I should probably get some rest," I say, trying to ease the sudden intimacy that hangs between us, my fingers fidgeting with the edge of the blanket on my bed.

Iolas nods, but there's a reluctance in his movements. "Yeah," he agrees. "But if you need anything, just call for me."

"I will," I promise, meeting his gaze one last time before he stands, his broad frame casting a shadow over me as he moves. He looks down at me, his expression softening as his eyes trace over my face one more time, as if he's memorising me at this moment, making sure I'm really here.

Then, without warning, he leans down, pressing a gentle kiss to my hair. The simple gesture is filled with warmth, comfort. It's so different from the energy that's been in the air between us. It's like he's telling me, in his own way, that he's here. That he always will be.

"Sleep well, little witch," he whispers.

Before I can say anything else, he turns and strides out of the room, leaving me in the quiet stillness of my chambers. The door clicks shut behind him, and I release a breath.

As I get into bed and lie back against the pillows, my mind swims with everything that's happened, it all pressing down on me. But even as my thoughts try to pull me under, the warmth of Iolas's worry and kiss lingers. And for the first time in what feels like forever, I let myself drift off to sleep.

CHAPTER FORTY-TWO
Altair

I recline against the infirmary cot, the taste of the third blood bag still lingering on my tongue, metallic and cold—nothing like the rush of warm blood from Olwyn.

Ailith stands over me, her fingers deftly wrapping fresh bandages around my torso. The cuts have mostly sealed, the wounds knitting together slowly, but the witchsilver has done enough damage that my body is still sluggish in its recovery.

Ailith has applied some healing herbs to speed up the process… but they will still scar.

I would take a thousand scars if it meant saving her.

"Don't get too comfortable," Ailith mutters, tightening a bandage a little more aggressively than necessary. "You're not out of the woods yet. Try any heroics, and you'll tear these right back open."

I sigh, tipping my head back against the cot. "Thanks for the encouragement."

Ailith snorts, her red eyes narrowing at me. "Don't need to encourage you. You do enough damage to yourself without anyone's help."

The door to the infirmary flies open with a bang, cutting through the air like a blade, and Iolas storms in. His steps are heavy, charged with anger that I can feel from across the room.

I tense instinctively, despite the fatigue weighing me down. Iolas's nostrils flare, and he barely spares Ailith a glance before his eyes land on me.

"Leave us," Iolas growls, his voice tight with barely suppressed rage.

Ailith doesn't budge. Her eyes flick up, narrowing at Iolas in warning. "I don't take orders from you, Iolas. I'm not leaving."

"Fine," Iolas bites out, jaw clenched, eyes still fixed on me. "You fed from her?"

I close my eyes briefly, bracing myself. Of course this conversation is happening. "Yes," I say simply, keeping my voice calm, meeting Iolas's furious stare.

Iolas's fists clench at his sides. "And you… touched her?"

My brows furrow, and I shake my head immediately. "No. That's not what happened."

Iolas steps forward, eyes flashing with accusation. "You know how vulnerable she was! She doesn't know anything about vampire feeding, Altair. And you—you could've—"

My fangs flash before I can stop myself, anger surging through me as I push myself up, ignoring the pain in my body as Ailith tuts at me. "Don't you dare," I growl, my voice low and lethal. "Don't you dare accuse me of taking advantage of her. Or even *try* and suggest I would harm her."

Iolas's eyes darken, but he doesn't back down. "How can you be sure she knew what she was doing?"

"I told her to stop," I snap, my voice sharp. "It was her choice. It will always be her choice."

The words hang between us, thick with tension. My chest heaves slightly, exhaustion mingling with frustration.

Ailith, who's been watching with her arms crossed, lets out a dry laugh. "You boys done waving your swords around?" she asks, sarcasm dripping from her tone. "Because I've got work to do, and frankly, I'm not in the mood for this."

Iolas shoots her a look but doesn't respond. His focus is still entirely on me, his anger now laced with something else—fear, concern, maybe even guilt.

"She doesn't know what any of this means," Iolas says, his voice lowering but no less intense. "The bond you form when you feed... It's powerful, Altair. And you've never fed from anyone else. She wasn't ready for that. She might never be."

I feel my anger cool, but only slightly. I exhale, trying to keep my voice steady. "I know. But I didn't force her. She wanted to help. And I couldn't—I wouldn't have let it go that far without her consent, even if my mind was consumed by the bond."

Iolas runs a hand through his hair, clearly struggling. His jaw works, but he doesn't say anything for a moment. His gaze flickers away before finally locking back onto mine, frustration evident in every line of his face.

Ailith sighs dramatically, pushing off the counter. "Oh good, the hormone showdown is winding down." She strolls toward me, her eyes flicking between us. "If you're done, I still have to finish patching up the king before he decides to bleed all over my nice clean floors."

I huff out a breath, shaking my head. "Thank you, Ailith," I mutter, though my tone is wry.

Iolas stands there for another second, his fists still clenched, before he finally steps back. His gaze shifts toward the door. "I'm going to watch over Olwyn."

Before he can go, I speak again, my voice softer but firm. "I trust her, Iolas. You should too."

I don't regret it. Not for a moment.

CHAPTER FORTY–THREE
Olwyn

Breakfast rolls around, and I sit at the table, my fingers absently trailing over the edge of my cup.

I don't know why, but ever since I let him feed from me, it's like an invisible thread pulling me toward Altair, tightening with every passing second.

And I know, without a doubt, that he feels it too.

He enters the room quietly, his presence shifting the air immediately. As usual, he looks regal, though today there's a slight tension in his frame. The relief that floods through me is almost overwhelming. After seeing him so weak, so vulnerable, it's a comfort to see him like this again—strong, composed.

His eyes catch mine the moment he walks in, and for a split second, the rest of the room seems to fall away. I let out a breath. I had asked a member of staff as soon as I woke if he was all right. I was assured he was, but I still asked to be taken to the infirmary to see him for myself. I had resigned myself to seeing him at breakfast when I was told he was no longer there.

But he's better. Thank the gods, he's better.

Our gazes hold a moment longer than they should. My heart races, and I quickly lower my gaze, hoping no one notices the heat that rushes to my cheeks.

But I can feel him. Even as he takes his seat to my right, I can feel the awareness of him pressing in on me from all angles. It's like a hum beneath my skin, a constant pull that makes it difficult to focus on anything else.

And yet… it's not unpleasant. It's terrifying, yes, but not in the way I would have imagined. It's not like the fear I felt when I was taken from my home or when the man attacked me in my chambers. This is different. It's deeper, rawer. And though I don't fully understand it, I can't deny that a part of me doesn't want to resist it.

"Good morning," Altair's voice breaks the silence, low and smooth, and I force myself to meet his eyes again.

"Morning," I reply softly, my voice sounding far too breathy for a simple greeting.

A tense silence settles over the room as Iolas enters. His expression is drawn tight, his posture stiff. He nods briefly at me before sitting down, his eyes flicking toward Altair with an unreadable look. He wasn't there to escort me this morning, something that made my chest tighten. I feel like he is annoyed at me, at us… and I hate it.

But even worse, the air between *them* is thick, and I know something has been said.

"How are your ribs?" Iolas asks suddenly as he starts buttering a piece of toasted bread, cutting through the awkward silence. His voice is calm, but I can feel the tension. He doesn't look at Altair when he speaks, his focus pinned on me.

I blink, momentarily caught off guard. I hadn't expected him to bring it up. My fingers tighten around the edge of my cup as I glance at Altair, who immediately frowns, his sharp gaze darting between me and Iolas.

"My ribs are fine. Thank you for helping." I say quickly, trying to downplay the situation. "It's nothing." But I feel Altair's eyes narrow, his attention locking onto me.

"What happened?" Altair's voice is a low rumble, but I can hear the edge to it. His eyes darken slightly, confusion flickering across his face.

"The man who cut me also punched me in the ribs before I killed him. I could have done it sooner if he had a smaller blade. I need to start fighting with a sword."

Iolas smiles at my enthusiasm to continue training.

When I finally look up, Altair's expression has shifted completely. His eyes are black—pools of darkness, swirling with a restrained rage. His jaw clenches, and though he remains quiet, the tension radiating from him is palpable, crackling in the air like a storm about to break.

"Altair…" I say softly, trying to reassure him. "I'm fine. It's not that bad. Iolas already checked me over."

His silence stretches, the shadows in his eyes deepening. He doesn't speak, but the shadows in the room deepen, and frankly, I'm so grateful to see them. For a moment, I think he might snap, but then he exhales slowly, closing his eyes for a second as if to rein in his control.

Iolas, sensing the tension, adds in a calm tone, "I'll apply more salve later. It'll help with the bruising."

Altair's jaw ticks, but he nods, his eyes softening just slightly as they meet mine again. He doesn't say anything more, but the concern etched into his expression speaks volumes.

"I'm fine," I repeat for what feels like the hundredth time since last moon rise, this time more firmly. "Really."

Altair doesn't respond, but his gaze lingers on me a moment longer, as if he's trying to convince himself of my words.

I pick at the food in front of me, my appetite suddenly gone. The memories of yesterday—the attack, the blood, the feeling of Altair's fangs sinking into my skin—flood back to me in waves.

"Olwyn," Altair starts, his voice unusually hesitant. His eyes flicker between me and Iolas, and there's a tension in his shoulders that instantly puts me on edge. "I need to speak to you about these attacks. About why they keep happening."

He leans back in his chair, exchanging a look with Iolas—one so pointed, so heavy, that my stomach tightens. My gaze narrows on them both, and Altair presses his lips into a thin line.

"I thought it was because of our union?" I say, breaking the silence, my tone sharper than I intended.

Altair exhales slowly, the weight of what he's about to say clear in his expression. "That's only a small part of it," he admits. "The truth is... they work for someone. Her name is Atha."

Atha?

The name means nothing to me, and yet it lands with a strange, ominous weight. My frown deepens.

"She's a powerful sorceress," he continues.

I stiffen. That can't be true. "Sorceresses?" I say, incredulous. "They've been extinct for almost a century. Everyone knows that."

Altair watches me carefully, his expression grim, as though he already knows how hard this is to believe. "She's the last true sorceress," he says evenly, "until the magic in your veins awakened."

My breath catches. Until my magic awakened.

Is this another lie I've been told my whole life? Another truth kept from me, just like everything else about who and what I am?

"And why," I say, my voice quieter now, though no less sharp, "would she want me dead?"

Iolas shifts uncomfortably beside me, his fingers drumming against the edge of the table in a steady, rhythmic pattern. The small, anxious movement is so unlike him that it sends a ripple of unease through me.

"That's my fault," Altair says. His voice is soft, but his words hit like a thunderclap.

I blink, my heart pounding. "Your fault?"

"You were being kept hidden in Avantra for her," Altair explains, his tone steady but laced with regret. "One day, she would have come for you."

The room spins. "What?" I whisper.

"The king and queen," Altair continues, and there's a hardness in his expression now, a deep anger simmering beneath his usually composed surface, "were keeping you for Atha. They were preserving you—neglecting you, yes—but alive. One day, you would have been handed over to her."

The words take a moment to sink in. When they do, it's like the air has been sucked out of the room.

"My parents," I say, my voice trembling, though I fight to keep it steady, "were keeping me for a sorceress? Why?"

"You share the same powers," Altair says. "Atha knows you're the key to the prophecy. She wanted to control you. By finding you, by taking you from Avantra, I ruined her plans."

His words swirl in my mind like a storm, each one heavier than the last.

Altair's jaw tightens, and he leans forward, his eyes locking with mine. "Now, she fears I've turned you against her. She can't risk the threat of another sorceress—especially one who could fulfil the prophecy—standing with the vampire king of Noctura."

I stare at him, the pieces slowly, horribly falling into place. My entire life—every moment of neglect, every whispered warning to stay hidden—it was all for her. For this Atha.

"So, you're telling me," I say, my voice rising as fury sparks in my chest, "that my parents kept me locked away, neglected but alive, all so I could one day be handed over to this woman?"

The thing that hurts the most, is that I believe him. They have shown me so much, that the creeping doubts have now fully bloomed like a spring flower.

The room falls silent. Iolas stops drumming his fingers, his jaw tightening. Altair doesn't look away, doesn't flinch under my anger.

"Yes," he says, the single word carrying the weight of everything I've learned recently.

My chest tightens, my warming hands curling into fists at my sides. For once, I don't know whether to scream, cry, or thank the gods I was taken.

Altair saved me from that fate. The realisation crashes over me, heavy and suffocating. If this Atha is so willing to kill me now, what kind of horrors would have awaited me under her control? Would she have twisted me into a weapon, a shadow of myself, until there was nothing left of who I truly am?

I swallow hard, my throat dry. My gaze shifts to Altair, who is watching me with that same infuriating, steady calm, but beneath it, I can see the strain—everything he hasn't told me until now.

"That's why you kept me in the palace," I say, my voice low but firm, the pieces snapping into place like shards of broken glass. "That's why you're having peace talks with Casius." I pause, searching his face, daring him to deny it. "You're trying to unite the vampires. Against her."

His jaw tightens, the muscles twitching as he leans back slightly. The way his hands rest on the table—steady, deliberate—tells me everything I need to know. He doesn't respond right away, and his silence only sharpens my suspicion.

"You are, aren't you?" I press, my voice rising just a fraction, the words spilling out before I can stop them. "This isn't about peace between you and Casius. It's about war. With her."

Altair's eyes meet mine, unflinching, and he exhales slowly, the sound heavy with resignation. "Yes," he finally says, his voice low, almost a growl. "That's exactly what this is about."

For a moment, the room feels too small, too suffocating. The air between us crackles with what he's just confirmed. My heart races, but I force myself to hold his gaze, to meet the truth head-on.

I always felt like a pawn in this game from the start. But the rules aren't as simple as I thought, and the stakes are far higher than I ever imagined.

And I realise, I've never been just a pawn—I'm the centrepiece.

I want to rage, to demand why he didn't tell me this sooner, why he let me stumble blindly through all of this without knowing the full picture.

But beneath the anger, a colder, harder truth settles in my bones. This isn't just about me. This was never *just* about me.

I've been dragged into something so much bigger than I ever imagined. My life, my choices—they've all been threads woven into a web I never asked to be part of. For so long, I've been hidden from it. From the power I didn't want.

But hiding hasn't saved me. It hasn't spared me from the horrors or the lies. It hasn't stopped the world from shoving me into the centre of its games.

If this Atha is coming for me—if she's willing to kill me simply because of what I could be—then hiding isn't an option anymore.

The thought settles over me like a storm cloud, heavy and dark but strangely electrifying. If I can't escape this, then I won't cower. If I'm going to be part of this war, part of this prophecy or whatever it is they think I am, then I'm going to do it on my terms.

If I can't run from being a queen… then I might as well act like one.

I straighten my spine, lifting my chin just slightly. Altair's gaze sharpens, as if he can feel the shift in me, his eyes watching my every move. I can still see the tension in his jaw, the faint crease between his brows. He's waiting for my response, as if bracing himself for an explosion that hasn't come yet.

I exhale slowly, the storm inside me clearing just enough for a single thought to rise above the chaos. If I'm going to face this, I need to be prepared.

"So," I say, my voice steadier than I feel, cutting through the silence. "What's the plan?"

Altair's eyes widen slightly, just for a moment, before narrowing with approval. His lips curve into a faint, almost imperceptible smile—a shadow of relief, of respect. He leans forward, resting his elbows on the table, and it's hard to stay mad at him when this is Altair, the man who has trusted me, who has fought for me, who has looked at me like I'm more than just a pawn in this game.

"The plan," he says slowly, his voice measured, "is to stop her before she gathers enough power to destroy us all."

My stomach knots, but I force myself to nod. "And by 'us,' you mean…?"

Altair's gaze flickers to Iolas, who has been sitting silently, his jaw tight and his eyes filled with a mix of concern and admiration. Then back to me. "Not just Noctura. But Casius and Vesperis too."

A bitter laugh escapes me before I can stop it. "So, no pressure then."

Everything rests on the talks with Casius.

Altair tilts his head, and for a moment, his eyes soften. "I wouldn't ask this of you, Olwyn, if there was any other way."

"Ask this of me?" I echo, my voice sharp. "You didn't exactly ask, did you? You took me from Avantra, you've been keeping me here, and now you're telling me I'm a centrepiece in some war I didn't even know existed." I push my chair back, the scrape of wood against stone breaking the tension in the room. "But fine. I can't exactly call you a liar because everything you've shown me so far has proved you're telling me the truth. But let's say I accept this. What exactly do you expect me to do?"

Altair leans back in his chair, his eyes never leaving mine. "I saw it, Olwyn," he says, his voice low, steady. "I saw the light. I saw you use your powers."

I blink, and Iolas turns to face me, stunned by Altair's words, realising what I wasn't saying last night. The room feels suddenly smaller, the air thick with the truth I hadn't yet processed. My mouth goes dry, and I can barely find my voice. "I promise, I didn't know I could control it like that," I admit, my voice barely above a whisper.

Altair nods, "You don't need to assure me, love. You believe that, so I believe you."

"You want me to use my powers?" I ask.

"We want you to control it," Altair. "We'll start there. And then, if you choose to, you can fight. Not just for yourself, but for everyone who can't."

I stare at him, my chest tightening again, but this time it's not just anger or fear. It's something else—something deeper, heavier. Because as much as I hate to admit it, he's right. After what I've seen, and the people I've spoken to, I can't pretend this isn't my fight.

I think of the villagers we saw during the Litha celebration, their laughter and joy, their hope. I think of Sera and Thalia and all the staff here. I think of the world beyond the palace walls—the one I never thought I'd see, the one I want to protect, even if it terrifies me.

"I'll fight," I say finally, my voice quiet but firm. "But you can't hold back. You need to push me."

Altair nods once, his expression serious. "You have my word."

"Good," I say, sinking back into my chair. My gaze flicks to Iolas, who is watching me with an intensity that makes my skin prickle. "And you? Are you in this too?"

Iolas grins, though it doesn't quite reach his eyes. "Wherever you go, little witch, I'll be right there with you."

The tension in the room shifts, a new resolve settling over us. I don't know what the future holds, but maybe for the first time, I feel like I have a choice in it.

If Atha wants a fight, then a fight is what she'll get.

If this is uncontrolled… she's going to be unstoppable once she controls it.

CHAPTER FORTY–FOUR
Olwyn

It's nice to be back in training.

My ribs hurt, but I'm eager to get back to the mat—hopefully not thrown on my back today. Iolas stands in the centre, his arms crossed as he watches me approach. His expression is serious, but there's a glint of something in his eyes.

The air feels heavy with anticipation, but it's different from the tension I've felt with Altair. This is lighter, more familiar, but still electric in its own way.

"Ready?" he asks, raising an eyebrow.

I nod, rolling my shoulders. My ribs are still sore from the attack, but the salve Iolas applied again last night helped. I can feel the dull ache, but it's manageable. Nothing I can't push through.

"Let's see what you've got today," Iolas says, rolling his shoulder, his body loosening and relaxing, but I know better than to mistake that for complacency. He's always on guard, even when he looks at ease.

I take a deep breath and settle into a fighting stance, my feet planted firmly on the ground, my hands raised. Iolas circles me, his eyes sharp as they flicker over my form, watching for any sign of weakness.

"Your stance is better," he remarks, his voice casual but encouraging. "You've gotten stronger."

I feel a flicker of pride at his words, but I don't let it distract me. Instead, I focus on him—on the way his weight shifts ever so slightly, on the way his eyes narrow just before he moves.

He lunges, fast and precise, but I'm ready this time. I pivot, stepping aside just as his arm shoots out, his fist missing me by inches. The movement feels instinctual now, almost automatic, and for a moment, I'm surprised by how natural it is.

Iolas grins, clearly impressed, but he doesn't give me time to catch my breath. He's on me again, his fists a blur as he attacks with a flurry of quick, precise strikes. I dodge the first few, my body moving on instinct, but then he catches me with a light tap to the shoulder—a reminder that he's still in control, still faster.

"Good," he says, stepping back to give me space. "You're moving more on instinct. That's what you need to survive."

I nod, wiping a bead of sweat from my brow. My heart's racing, but it's not from fear. It's from exhilaration—the rush of knowing I'm improving, of knowing I'm getting stronger.

"Again," I say, and there's a determination in my voice that wasn't there before.

Iolas doesn't hesitate. He moves toward me again, but this time I'm faster. I duck beneath his arm, using my momentum to spin around and land a quick jab to his side. It's not enough to hurt him—not really— but the contact is solid, and I feel a thrill of victory as I pull back.

His eyes widen slightly, more in surprise than pain, but then he grins, a wide, playful smile that makes my chest flutter in a way I try to ignore.

"Nice hit," he says, his voice laced with approval. "But don't get cocky."

Before I can respond, he's moving again, faster this time, and I barely have time to dodge, turning. His fist grazes my ribs, and I wince, the dull ache flaring up again. Iolas pauses, his eyes widening as he notices the way I flinch.

"You all right?" he asks, his voice softer now, more concerned.

I force a smile, trying to brush it off. "I'm fine."

He doesn't look convinced, but he nods, stepping back slightly to give me more room. I can tell he's holding back, watching out for my injury.

"Iolas," I say, straightening up and meeting his gaze. "Don't go easy on me."

His eyes flicker with something—respect, maybe—but he nods. "All right. But if you feel like you need to stop, you tell me."

I nod, and the fight resumes.

This time, I'm ready for him. I move with more confidence, more purpose, and when he lunges, I counter. I dodge his strikes, my body twisting and turning with the rhythm of the fight. There's a certain fluidity to it now, a flow that feels almost natural. My instincts are sharper, my movements quicker. And when I see an opening, I take it.

I lunge forward, aiming a punch at his side. He blocks it, but I don't stop. I keep moving, pressing forward, my fists flying as I attack. I land a solid hit on his shoulder, and another to his chest, and for a brief moment, I think I've got him.

But then, in a blur of movement, he grabs my wrist, twisting just enough to throw me off balance. I stumble, but before I can hit the ground, he pulls me back up, his grip firm but gentle.

"You're getting faster," he says, his voice filled with genuine admiration. "I'm impressed."

I grin, breathless but exhilarated. "I have a good teacher."

He laughs, a warm, easy sound that makes me feel lighter somehow, I feel elated to see him laughing again.

We stand there for a moment, catching our breath, and his eyes lock with mine. I'm aware of how close we are, of the way his chest rises and falls in time with mine. I'm aware of the warmth of his hand still on my arm, the way his fingers press gently against my skin.

And then, just as quickly as it happened, the moment passes. He lets go of my arm, stepping back with a playful smile.

"You're getting there," he says, his tone teasing now. "But you still haven't landed a punch strong enough to knock me down."

Like *that* would even be a possibility.

"Maybe next time," I reply, matching his grin. How the hell would I be strong enough to knock down a six-foot seven vampire?

Iolas chuckles, his gaze lingering on me for a beat longer than necessary before he finally steps away.

"You've improved a lot, Olwyn," he says, his voice sincere. "I'm proud of you."

The words hit me harder than I expect. The moment they leave his lips, a warmth blooms in my chest, spreading through me like wildfire. *Proud?* He's *proud* of me?

Something tightens in my throat, something I wasn't prepared for, and suddenly it's hard to breathe. I blink quickly, trying to hide the sudden wave of emotion that threatens to crash over me.

It's ridiculous, really. One small sentence, just four words, and yet they pierce through every wall I've built around myself. They hit me somewhere deep, somewhere I didn't even realise was craving it.

I've never really heard those words out loud before. Not from anyone who meant it. Not from anyone who actually *saw* me.

Iolas narrows his eyes, slightly spotting my reaction as the heat creeps up my neck, and I feel my cheeks flush.

"Thanks," I mumble, my voice embarrassingly small, but I can't help it. My heart pounds in my chest, and there's a giddiness bubbling up that I'm trying desperately to suppress.

But it's the way he looks at me that undoes me. The sincerity in his gaze, the way he *sees* me. Not as someone broken or weak, but as someone worthy of praise.

I don't know why that last thought sends a wave of heat through me, but it does.

He smiles, a soft, almost affectionate look crossing his face. "Now, let's try that magic again."

Just like that, my heart sinks. I knew this was coming, and I'm dreading it. The last time I tried in training, I felt… nothing. Just empty. But I know I need to keep trying.

I nod, taking a deep breath and stepping back into position. Iolas watches me carefully, his eyes never leaving mine as I close my eyes and focus.

I reach inside myself, searching for that spark, that power that I felt when I saved Altair. But no matter how hard I try, there's nothing. Just the hollow echo of my own frustration.

I open my eyes, shaking my head. "I can't do it."

Iolas steps closer, his hand resting lightly on my shoulder. "Don't be too hard on yourself. It came to you in a life-or-death situation, it'll come again when you're ready."

His words are kind, but they do little to ease the disappointment gnawing at me. I wanted to show him—show both of them—that I'm not weak, that I can handle this. But right now, all I feel is powerless.

"Let's focus on what you can control," Iolas says, his tone steady. "You're getting stronger every day, Olwyn. Don't lose sight of that."

I nod, trying to force a smile. "You're right."

But as I look up at him, his eyes filled with nothing but support and kindness, I can't help but wonder if I'll ever truly master the power inside me. And worse, if I don't, it means I might not be able to protect the people I care about when the time comes.

Altair, Iolas, Ailith.

Sera, Thalia.

All those in Elderglen.

I can't fail. I can't fail them.

But there must be something I am missing. Some reason I can't pull it forward.

For now, all I can do is keep training. Keep trying. And hope that soon, I'll be able to control the magic coursing through my veins.

Because I never know when I might need it again.

There must be a trigger for her magic. But I won't let her work it out if it means bringing her harm.

CHAPTER FORTY–FIVE
Olwyn

Darkness swirls in my mind, suffocating, endless.

I'm running—chased by a dark figure, cold and hungry. They reach for me, whispering my name in a voice that makes my skin crawl. No matter how fast I run, they're always there. Always behind me. I scream, but the sound is swallowed by the void.

I jolt awake, my chest tight, the scream dying on my lips. My heart pounds in my ears, the familiar ache of terror twisting in my gut. But then, a hold on my arm anchors me.

Altair.

He's sitting by my side on the bed, his silhouette a shadow in the dim light of the room. His eyes, those dark, endless eyes, are focused on me, filled with concern. His presence soothes me, pulls me from the lingering claws of the nightmare.

"Altair…" My voice is shaky, barely more than a whisper.

"I'm here," he murmurs softly, reaching out to brush a strand of silver hair away from my face. His touch is gentle, comforting, but it makes my skin tingle. I feel it as surely as I feel the pull deep inside me, drawing me closer to him.

We sit in silence for a long moment, just looking at each other.

"It was just another nightmare," I admit finally, my voice barely above a whisper, breaking the fragile stillness between us.

"I know," he says quietly, his words simple. His gaze holds mine as his thumb brushes lightly against my temple, his touch so careful it almost makes me ache.

My brow furrows. "You… knew?"

He exhales softly, "I felt it." His hand drops back to his side. There's a flicker of hesitation in his expression, like he's debating how much to say. "Since I fed from you… I can feel it. When your emotions spike—when you're happy, angry, when you hurt—I feel it, Olwyn."

The admission sends a rush of warmth and cold through me all at once. My chest tightens, my thoughts swirling. "You can *feel* me?"

"It's faint," he says, his voice low, soothing. "But yes. It's like… a thread. Thin but strong. A whisper of your emotions that hums through me."

My cheeks burn, and I lower my gaze, staring at my hands as they knot together in my lap. I should feel violated. I should feel unnerved. And yet, there's something oddly reassuring in his words, in the way he admits it so openly, without hesitation or shame.

"How long will it last?"

He rubs his chin. "I'm not sure. But I believe it will fade unless I feed from you again."

There's silence for another moment, and I think about the prospect of him feeding from me again. Knowing he can feel heightened emotions, I try to suppress the throb between my thighs, when a thought hits me.

"Does it hurt you?" I ask, glancing up at him.

His lips twitch, not quite forming a smile. "No. It's… not unpleasant." He pauses, his gaze softening. "It only hurts when you hurt."

Those simple words hit me harder than I expect, stirring something deep within me that I don't entirely understand. I swallow hard, unsure of what to say.

"Why didn't you tell me?" I manage after a moment, my voice a little steadier now.

"I didn't want to overwhelm you," he admits, his tone as careful as his movements. "You've had so much thrown at you already, and this… it's just another thing to add to the weight you're carrying."

I shake my head, a soft laugh escaping me despite myself. "You're ridiculous, you know that?"

His brows lift slightly, two-toned eyes curious. "Am I?"

"Yes," I say, meeting his gaze fully now. "You're over here carrying half the weight with me without even telling me, and you still think I can't handle knowing."

His lips quirk into a faint smirk this time, and he leans back slightly, his arms resting on his thighs. "You surprise me every day, Olwyn. Maybe I should stop underestimating you."

"Maybe?" I shoot back, some of the tension easing as a small smile tugs at my lips.

For a moment, the heaviness of my nightmare feels distant, replaced by the warmth in his presence.

His eyes search mine, as if trying to decipher the emotions still swirling inside me. He's so close, the heat of him radiating against my skin, and I feel that pull again—the one I can't ignore, the one that's been growing ever since I let him feed from me.

And I don't know why, but I'm drawn to him. It's not just the bond from the feeding… it's more. It's deeper, sharper—like the way his eyes seem to see through every shield I've ever put up, making my breath catch before I can even think to steady it.

"Altair," I begin, hesitating, unsure of how to voice what I'm feeling.

His gaze softens, and he seems to know what I'm about to say before the words even leave my lips. He shifts slightly, turning away from me, his broad shoulders tense. "It's the feeding bond," he says quietly. "It makes you want to be close to me. It's not... real."

I blink, taken aback. "That's not true."

"It *is* true, Olwyn," he says, his voice rougher now. "It's part of what happens when a vampire feeds from someone. You feel drawn to me because of it. I know because I feel it too."

Is it?

I really think about it.

But then I remember that kiss in the inn. Before he fed from me.

I shake my head, refusing to believe it. "No. It's more than that. I trust you, Altair. You've shown me the truth when no one else would. You've protected me. This… What I'm feeling… it's not just because of the feeding. I've come to know you. I've come to trust you."

Altair goes silent, his jaw tightening as if he's fighting against something inside him. He stands, turning his back to me and showing his scars—new and old—his hand clenching at his side. "You don't know everything about me, Olwyn," he says, his voice low, pained.

His guilt is written all over him, the tension in his posture, the way he avoids my gaze. But I don't think I could possibly learn anything about him that would make me not want this, here, now.

I rise, my nightgown brushing against my thighs as I move. The fabric is thin, barely covering me, but in this moment, I don't care.

I kneel on the bed, my heart racing in my chest as I reach out, my fingers brushing against his skin, tracing around the edges of the fresh scars. Where they stabbed him again and again. "Altair," I whisper, my voice soft but insistent. He freezes at my touch, his breath hitching.

He turns, and I trace the scars from the arrows, the one so close to his heart—the one that would have killed him.

It makes me feel sick.

Leaning forward, I press a kiss to that one.

"Olwyn…" His voice sounds like a plea, but I can see the tension in his body, the way his nostrils flare as his control slips, little by little.

I can't stop. I don't want to. I want him to lose control.

"Altair." My voice is breathless, my body aching as I look up at him. "I want you to kiss me." My thighs rub together, the friction sending a wave of heat through me.

His eyes pin mine, nostrils flaring, his control hanging by a thread. "I can't," his voice cracks, and I know it's because he thinks this isn't really me asking.

I refuse to look away, showing him as much as I can without words that I do want him. "This isn't some bond. *Please.*"

His hand wraps in my hair at the base of my neck, and his mouth claims mine, the cool touch of his shadows joins in—a soft, creeping sensation, like an extra pair of hands, tracing my skin with a subtle, teasing caress. They wrap around my wrists, sliding down my arms, ghosting over my hips, and I gasp into his mouth, the sensation unlike anything I've ever felt.

The kiss is intense, desperate. His lips are soft but firm, his rough hands cradling my face. I melt into him, my body pressing against his, my need for him overwhelming everything else. The heat of him, the way his lips move against mine—it consumes me.

When he pulls back, his eyes are completely black, darting between mine as if making sure this is real. His breath comes in ragged gasps, his control hanging by a thread. But his shadows—oh *gods*, his shadows—linger, brushing over my throat, tracing the curve of my jaw. It's as if they're alive, an extension of his desire.

"I won't take more of you than you'll give me," he rasps, his voice thick with desire. "I promise. But you need to tell me if you don't want this at any point."

I place my hand over his chest, feeling the rapid thrum of his heartbeat beneath my palm, but even as I do, one of his shadows coils around my wrist, dark tendrils twisting up my arm. The cold contrasts with the heat of his body, making my skin tingle. "I want it all. I want you."

That's all he needs. His hands are on me in an instant, his lips trailing down my neck, across my collarbone. His touch is fire, burning through me with every touch of his fingers.

"Do you know how long I've thought about this?" His voice is a low growl against my skin, his breath hot and ragged. His shadows mimic the brush of his lips, tracing paths of cold fire down my spine. "Wondered how it would feel to touch your skin. To taste you—fuck, you're so soft."

He groans into the crook of my neck, his teeth grazing my skin, while one of his shadows curls around my thigh, sliding higher, teasing the sensitive skin there. The vibration of it thrums through me, sending a pulse of heat straight to my core. I arch into him, desperate for more, my body craving his touch like I've never craved anything before. The shadows seem to read my desire, pressing closer, curling around my hips with a possessive hold.

"I've done nothing but think about this ever since we wed. Keeping you safe, keeping you sated—right here in my bed," he breathes, his voice rough with need as he slips a strap off my shoulder. His shadow follows the movement, brushing it down with such tenderness that my breath hitches as the silk slips over a nipple. He groans.

"I think you mean *my* bed," I smile.

He chuckles. "True. But now seeing you panting for me, I never want to leave it."

His mouth and words are doing insane things to my body, my skin feeling charged and alive. He lowers me onto the bed, and I relish his weight as he joins me, as he pulls me closer.

But as I feel myself spiralling, his words echo in my mind, grounding me in this moment.

I never want to leave.

It hits me like a storm, crashing through my desire, through the haze of heat that clouds my mind. Because this—this is more than just lust. It's a promise. A need that goes beyond the physical, beyond the bond. It's a claim.

And suddenly, I want it too.

Altair's hands are everywhere—tangling in my hair, tracing the curve of my spine, gripping my arse with a possessiveness that ignites every inch of my skin. His shadows are there too, gliding up my legs, brushing against the most intimate parts of me, teasing, coaxing pleasure out of every nerve.

His lips leave burning trails down my neck, lower, across my collarbone, as he kisses and nips, driving me closer to the edge of sanity with each deliberate touch. The world around us blurs, becoming nothing more than the space between us, the way our bodies fit together like they were made for this.

His mouth hovers over my breast, hot breath teasing my nipple until I'm writhing beneath him, desperate for more. Then his tongue flicks out, circling the peak before his lips close around it, and I gasp, arching up into him as he sucks hard. At the same time, a shadowy tendril wraps around my other breast, the cold contrasting sharply with the heat of his mouth, and I moan, my back bowing off the bed.

Every nerve in my body is on fire, my hips rolling involuntarily toward him as his shadows shift lower, teasing the edges of where I need him most. It's too much, and yet not enough, and I cry out his name, desperate, aching.

"Altair, please," I beg, my voice breaking. His name is a plea on my lips, and his shadows tighten, dark and demanding.

He groans against my skin, his shadows responding to my need, wrapping around my thighs and parting them, positioning me for him. His breath is hot against my chest as he growls, "I'm going to ruin you, Olwyn." His shadows coil tighter, pressing down, holding me still as his body descends, his lips brushing against mine one last time before everything else fades.

He groans low in his throat, the sound vibrating through my skin, and his large hand slides down my side, tracing the curve of my hip. But it's not just his hand anymore. His shadows are there too—cool, slick, and sinuous, sliding over my body like liquid night. His fingers, both real and shadow, slip between my legs, and I gasp as the cold darkness contrasts sharply with the heat of his touch, and he groans again. "Gods, love… you're soaked."

A shudder wracks my body as his fingers glide through my slickness, teasing my entrance before circling my clit, sending shocks of pleasure rocketing through me. My thighs tremble, and I buck my hips into his hand, begging for more, needing more.

"Please," I moan, my voice breathless. But instead of responding right away, his shadows tighten around my thighs, holding me in place as his fingers slide inside me, slow and deep.

I cry out, my hands flying to his shoulders, my nails digging into his skin. But two more shadows move, cold and possessive, curling around my wrists, pulling my body back into the mattress as his real fingers curl inside me, hitting a spot that makes my vision blur and my breath stutter.

"Do you know how delicious you look tied to this bed?" he growls against my skin, his voice rough and low, his fangs on show. "How long I've wanted to feel you like this… wet and begging beneath me." His thumb circles my clit, sending another wave of pleasure crashing through me, and I'm gasping, my hips grinding against his hand.

"Altair…" His name falls from my lips in a breathless moan as his fingers pump in and out of me. My body is a trembling, needy mess, every muscle tensing as the heat builds inside me, threatening to consume me.

His shadows wrap around my throat—not tight, just enough for me to feel their cool presence, sending a thrill down my spine.

"No," he says harshly, my eyes opening. When the shadow around my neck retreats, I realise he is talking to them.

"It's all right," I pant, "I liked it."

"Fuck," he curses, the tendril moving back to hold me gently. "I've imagined this for so long," he continues, his voice husky as his lips brush against the soft skin just beneath my ear. "Wondered how it would feel to touch you, to taste you…" His shadows suddenly tighten around my thighs, pulling them wider as his fingers slip out of me. I whimper at the loss, but before I can protest, his lips trail down my stomach, and then he's between my legs, his tongue replacing his fingers.

The first swipe of his tongue over my clit sends a shockwave of pleasure through me, and I can't hold back the moan that tears from my throat.

"You taste better that I ever could have dreamed," he says, his voice as dark as midnight. His hands grip my thighs, spreading me wide as his tongue moves with agonizing skill, circling, flicking, sucking until I'm a shaking, gasping mess beneath him.

"Gods—" I choke out, itching to reach out and run my fingers through his hair, to pull him closer as my hips grind against his mouth. The heat inside me builds to a breaking point, my body tightening, coiling, and I can feel the climax cresting, threatening to rip me apart.

He groans against me, the vibration of it sending me spiralling over the edge. My back arches, and I scream his name, my body shattering around him as the orgasm crashes through me. Wave after wave of pleasure pulses through me, and he doesn't stop, his tongue working me through it, drawing out every last shuddering gasp until I'm left boneless, trembling, completely undone.

Altair rises above me, his eyes black with desire, his lips glistening with my release. His shadows are still there, still wrapped around my wrists, my ankles, holding me in place as he looks down at me. "You taste incredible," he murmurs, his voice dark, possessive. He stands, the shadows still swirling around him like living smoke, and removes his loose black trousers.

Gods.

My mouth dries as he returns to the bed and positions himself between my legs, the tip of his cock pressing against my entrance. His shadows pulse around us, tightening and then loosening, as if they too are anticipating what's about to happen.

"Altair," I whisper, barely able to form words through the haze of pleasure still clouding my mind. *"Please."*

He doesn't make me wait. With a single, smooth thrust, he pushes himself inside me, filling me completely, and the sensation of him stretching me, filling me, pulls a guttural moan from my lips.

He stills for a moment, his forehead pressing against mine as we both gasp for air and his shadows release my wrists.

I move my hips, and he chuckles.

"Relax, love. We're not even all the way there yet."

I grab his gorgeous, sculpted arse and pull him closer, relishing the feel of him.

"Gods, Olwyn," he groans, his voice tight with restraint. His shadows pulse in time with his heartbeat, their cool touch everywhere at once. "You feel... so good."

He begins to move, slow at first, every thrust deep and deliberate, the friction sending sparks of pleasure through my already sensitive body. My legs wrap around his waist, pulling him deeper, harder, and he groans, his pace quickening as he loses himself in the rhythm of our bodies moving together.

He leans up on one arm, the other holding the headboard, and I can't help but glance over the lines of his muscles, the strand of hair falling into his eyes.

The bed shakes beneath us, the sound of skin against skin, our ragged breaths, filling the room. His hand slips beneath my thigh, lifting my leg higher, changing the angle, and suddenly he's hitting a spot deep inside me that has me gasping, clawing at his back, crying out with every thrust.

"That's it," he growls. "Who does your pleasure belong to? Tell me."

I gasp, my nails raking down his back as the pleasure builds again, faster, hotter this time. "You, Altair."

"Say it again," he growls, his pace quickening, his thrusts more frantic, more desperate. His hand grips my hip, pulling me closer, slamming into me with a force that leaves me breathless.

"It's yours," I repeat, my voice breaking as the climax builds again, the pressure inside me coiling tighter and tighter. His shadows slide up my thighs, teasing my skin, as his cock hits deeper, harder. "Yours, Altair."

He snarls, and I feel his teeth scraping gently across the skin of my neck, sending fire through my chest. The shadows mimic his touch, trailing up my throat, cool and possessive, like they're marking me alongside him.

For so long, I've lived behind walls—walls built by my parents, by the expectations of others, by my own fear. I've always felt the tension, the weight of being on guard, of never truly being free. First in Avantra, hidden and neglected, and then here, trapped in a world I barely understand. But now... now, in this moment, I feel something I've never felt before: seen. Seen for everything I am, everything I could be, and still wanted.

It's the surrender, the trust I never thought I'd be capable of giving. For the first time, control slips from my shoulders, freeing me in a way I didn't know I needed.

And then, a light bursts behind my eyes—a strange, glowing brightness that seems to fill the room, pulsing with every beat of my heart. I clench my eyes shut against the overwhelming brilliance, but I can't block out the intensity of it.

Then I'm falling, the orgasm ripping through me with a force that steals my breath, my vision going white as pleasure crashes over me in wave after wave. I scream his name, my body trembling violently around him, and he follows me over the edge, his own release hitting him hard, his body shuddering as he spills inside me, his grip on my hips so tight it's almost painful.

I blink, my vision still hazy from the intensity of the moment, and for a second, I think I'm imagining it.

The light is me.

I see the soft glow emanating from my skin, pulsing gently, as if the very air around me is alive with energy. It's not like before—the wild, uncontrollable burst that saved my life. This is calmer, softer… but no less overwhelming.

Altair's eyes are wide, his expression frozen somewhere between awe and confusion. His chest rises and falls heavily as he stares at me, his gaze fixated on the light that still clings to my skin, like the faintest shimmer of magic lingering in the aftermath.

"Olwyn…" His voice is low and rough as he pulls out of me, like he's not sure what to say.

I sit up slightly, my body still trembling from the pleasure, but now there's a new sensation—something warm, something powerful swirling just beneath my skin. My heart races as I look down at myself, my hands glowing faintly in the dim light of the room. I'm both terrified and mesmerized by it.

What if I hurt him?

"I…" My voice falters as I hold up my hand, watching the soft golden light that radiates from my palm. It's warm, like sunlight, like a heartbeat. I can feel it pulsing through me, and yet, I have no idea how I'm doing this. I glance at Altair, my breath hitching. "I don't know what's happening."

Altair shifts, his arm still wrapped around me as he pulls me closer, his grip tightening protectively. His eyes, though still wide with shock, brighten with something else—something that feels like reverence.

"You're glowing," he breathes, his voice filled with awe. His fingertips brush against the soft glow at the curve of my shoulder, as if he can't quite believe what he's seeing. "I felt it when we… I felt it surge through you."

My skin tingles where his fingers touch, sending ripples of sensation through me. But this time, it's different. It's not just pleasure; it's power. A power I didn't know I had, and I don't know how to control.

I shake my head, panic rising in my chest. "Altair, I don't understand. Why is this happening?" The glow flares for a moment, brightening in response to my rising emotions, and I feel a surge of energy that I can't contain. What if it bursts out? What if it harms him?

He sits up fully now, his hand steady on my shoulder. "Olwyn, calm down," he says softly, his voice like a tether, grounding me. "You need to breathe. Just breathe."

I do as he says, focusing on my breath, trying to pull myself back from the edge of panic. Slowly, the glow begins to dim, the light fading until it's barely a shimmer on my skin, but I can feel it still there—waiting just beneath the surface.

Altair's hand slides up to cup my cheek, his thumb brushing softly against my skin as he looks into my eyes. His own are… bright.

Both bright. And *blue*.

I wonder if I've done that, or if it's something else. Before I can ask, he continues speaking.

"You've always had this power inside you, Olwyn," he says quietly, his gaze intense, searching. "I felt it the moment I first fed from you. The magic in your blood is more powerful than anything I've ever seen."

I blink, my heart pounding in my chest. "But… I've never felt anything like this before. I didn't even know I could use it. Why is it happening now?"

His jaw clenches slightly as if weighing his next words. "Your powers are linked to your emotions. I think… the intensity of what just happened between us triggered it." He hesitates for a moment, his fingers brushing over my lips, his gaze dropping to where the faint shimmer of light still lingers on my skin. "You're more powerful than even I realised."

I look down at my hands again, flexing my fingers, trying to make sense of the sensation. "I… I don't know how to control it," I whisper, fear creeping into my voice. "What if I hurt someone? What if I hurt you?"

Altair's grip tightens, his eyes locking onto mine with an intensity that makes my breath catch. "You won't hurt me," he says, his voice low but firm. "You couldn't. I trust you, Olwyn."

His words sink into me, warm and steady, and for a moment, I let myself believe them. I let myself believe that maybe—just maybe—I can handle this. But the fear still lingers at the edges of my mind, gnawing at me.

"What if you're wrong?" I ask softly, my voice barely a whisper.

Altair's thumb brushes against my cheek again, his eyes softening as he looks at me. "Then I'll be right here with you. We'll figure it out."

His words are a promise. He's offering more than just protection—he's offering me a place beside him, a chance to figure out who I really am and what I'm capable of.

And after spending so many years shut away, only able to sneak away in the middle of the night, alone… it feels like it's starting to fill a hole I never really knew existed.

I lean into his touch, my eyes closing as I try to calm the storm of emotions swirling inside me. "I don't know if I'm ready for this," I admit, my voice trembling slightly. "It's too much, Altair. I don't know what to do."

He tilts my chin up gently, forcing me to meet his gaze. "You don't have to be ready," he says softly, his eyes locked on mine. "You just have to trust yourself."

Trust.

It's such a simple word, but it feels like the hardest thing in the world right now. But when I look at him, when I feel the warmth of his touch and the steady rhythm of his breath, I realise that maybe… just maybe, I can.

"Your eyes are blue," I blurt out, before I can forget to mention it.

The eyes in question widen, and suddenly the warmth around us fades.

"My eyes?" he repeats, his voice suddenly cautious. His gaze flickers, scanning my face as though searching for something, and then I see it—the shadows curling back over the iris of his good eye, swallowing the vibrant blue that had stunned me into silence just moments ago.

It's as though he's building a wall again, closing himself off from whatever vulnerability he'd just shown me.

"They were both blue." I say, the image of them—bright, clear blue—still clear in my mind. "For a moment, they were both blue." I frown, the image of them so familiar.

His jaw clenches, and I can feel the tension rising between us again, the something unspoken settling like a heavy fog in the air. He pulls his hand away from my cheek, and the loss of his touch feels colder than I expect.

"It's nothing," he says, his voice tight.

But it isn't *nothing*. I can feel it in the way he is holding himself.

Does it have something to do with how he got his scar? Maybe I pushed a little too far.

But I still want to know more about him.

"I don't believe that." My voice is quiet but firm, and I reach out, placing my hand on his chest where I can feel the steady thrum of his heartbeat beneath my fingers. "Altair, I saw it. And your scars. You don't have to hide from me."

His body tenses under my touch, and for a moment, I think he might pull away. But he doesn't. He just sits there, staring down at me with an intensity that makes my pulse race.

"I'm not hiding," he says, though there's an edge to his voice that tells me he's holding something back. "But there are things… things I can't explain right now."

I search his face, trying to understand. But he's giving me nothing, his expression carefully controlled, as if he's forcing himself not to let me in any further. I don't know what to do with that. We've just shared something so intimate, so intense, and now he's pulling back—shutting me out.

"I thought we trusted each other," I say. "You told me to trust myself, but how am I supposed to do that when *you* won't trust me?"

Altair's eyes darken further, the shadows swirling in the depths of his gaze. His lips press into a thin line, and for a moment, I think he's going to walk away. But then he takes a slow, deep breath, as if weighing his next words carefully.

"It's not about trust," he finally says, his voice low and rough. "It's about protecting you. There are things I've done you can't possibly understand. And I can't—"

"I thought you were training me to protect myself," I snap, my voice sharper than I intended. "You told me I was stronger than I realised. Was that a lie?"

His brows pull together, his lips parting slightly as if my words have caught him off guard. "It's not a lie—"

"Then stop treating me like I'm fragile!" I cut him off, my chest tightening as the anger inside me rises. "If I'm so strong, why won't you tell me anything? Why won't you let me make my own choices instead of *still* trying to control everything?"

"It's not about control," he growls, his voice low but dangerous. The room feels smaller suddenly, his shadows pressing in around us. "It's about protecting you from things you're not ready for!"

"How would you know what I'm ready for?" I snap back, refusing to let the tension in the room swallow me whole. "You don't even *try* to explain. You just make decisions for me. You just expect me to follow along blindly, without question. Do you even realise how insulting that is?"

His jaw tightens, his hands curling into fists at his sides. "Olwyn, you have had a tiny taste of what's coming for us. I've fought battles, faced horrors that would—"

"Then *show* me!" I shout, my voice breaking slightly. "Tell me what you've done, what you've seen! Let me decide if I can handle it instead of keeping me in the dark like I'm some delicate flower that needs shielding from the world."

Altair's head jerks back, his shadows coiling tighter around his form, restless and agitated. He stares at me for a long moment, his expression unreadable, and I can't tell if he's angry, hurt, or just exhausted.

"You don't understand fully what it's like to rule a kingdom," he finally says, his voice quieter but no less intense. "To know that every decision you make could mean life or death for the people you've sworn to protect. I can't afford to make mistakes in those decisions with you, Olwyn. Not with you. If anything happened to you—"

He stops himself again, his hands trembling slightly as he drags them through his hair. "I can't lose you," he repeats, softer this time, almost a whisper.

His vulnerability hits me like a punch to the gut, and for a moment, my anger wavers. But it doesn't disappear.

"Then stop treating me like something you can lose," I say, my voice steadier now, quieter but no less determined. "I'm not a trinket or a trophy, Altair. I'm a person. And if you really believe I'm strong, then trust me enough to make my own decisions. You may have forced me into this marriage and to stay here, but now I'm choosing to stay. I'm choosing to trust you. So now trust me enough to stand by your side—not behind you."

His eyes meet mine, and for a moment, the world feels suspended, our words hanging heavy between us. The shadows around him seem to still, their restless movement quieting as he studies me.

"I'm trying," he says finally, his voice raw. "I've just been trying to prot—"

I hold up a hand, cutting him off. "No. Don't you *dare* say you're doing this to protect me. I'm not some helpless girl who needs to be shielded from the world anymore. I've been fighting my entire life. I've survived this long because of my own strength, not because someone else decided to play saviour."

Altair's eyes darken, but there's a flicker of something else— admiration, maybe—beneath the anger. "I *know* you're strong," he says, his voice low, but there's a growl there too, simmering just beneath the surface. "That's why I'm trying to protect you. Because I can't lose you, Olwyn. Not after everything."

His words hit something inside me, something I don't want to acknowledge. I feel the tug between us, the magnetic pull I'm trying so hard to ignore, and for a moment, the fire in my chest flares higher, threatening to consume me.

"So that's it?" I ask, my voice hardening. "You think keeping me in the dark, making decisions for me, is how you protect me? You're not giving me a choice, Altair. You say you don't want to lose me, but you won't even let me decide for myself." I narrow my eyes, challenging him to argue with me, to keep hiding behind whatever excuses he's built around himself.

"And what if the truth *breaks* you?" He shouts, his eyes wild with panic.

I tilt my chin up. "I get to decide what I can handle, not you."

He's silent for a moment, the tension between us crackling like a storm about to break. His fists clench at his sides, shadows flickering at the edges of his form, but he doesn't move.

And then, something in him changes. In a voice quieter than I've ever heard from him, he says, "You're right."

I blink, surprised by his admission.

"You're right, Olwyn," he repeats, his eyes holding mine with that same raw intensity that makes my heart lurch. "I should've been honest. I should've trusted you to handle the truth. But I wasn't ready. I was… afraid."

"Afraid of what?" I demand, my voice still laced with insolence, though my heart is pounding in my chest.

"Of what you'd think of me if you knew," he admits, his voice hoarse. "Of what I've done. Of the choices I've made. I thought if I kept you at a distance, you'd never learn my truth, never see the monster in me."

I cross my arms, narrowing my eyes at him. "What could be so bad that you don't think I would choose you once I know everything?"

His gaze softens, and for the first time, I see the real weight of his guilt, the burden he's been carrying. "All right," he says quietly. "If it's all right with you, I'd like to go tell Iolas, that way if you need someone to talk to after… he can be there for you."

Gods, how bad is this going to be?

"Fine," I mutter, though I'm far from satisfied.

His lips turn up into a small smile, and he leans closer, brushing a strand of hair away from my face with a tenderness that almost makes me forget how angry I am. Almost.

"Rest, love," he whispers, his voice soft as he wraps an arm around me, pulling me against his chest in a hug. "I'll be back shortly."

I let out a small huff, still irritated, but the warmth of his body against mine is comforting in a way I can't explain. My anger fizzles out as an exhaustion creeps in, and despite everything, I feel myself relaxing into his embrace.

"All right," I murmur, my voice heavy as I rest my head against his chest.

He squeezes me once more before pressing a kiss to the top of my head and standing to stride to the door. He looks back once before he shuts it, and I realise he looks terrified.

But after the door clicks, I lie down and close my eyes, letting the tension drain from my body, feeling sated and scared all the same.

CHAPTER FORTY-SIX

Altair

I need to talk to Iolas.

He has to know what's coming—and I need to hear him say that this is the right thing to do. Because right now, I'm not sure of anything.

The halls are quiet, as are the guards I pass as I make my way to Iolas's chambers, the flickering light from the sconces casting long shadows on the walls. My footsteps echo softly against the stone floor, but it feels deafening in the silence.

When I reach his door, I hesitate for a moment, my hand hovering over the handle. But then I push it open.

Iolas is already awake. Of course he is. He's seated in a chair near the window, reading a book, his sharp eyes immediately locking onto mine as soon as I step into the room. His nostrils flare slightly, and I don't need to say a word for him to know what's happened.

There's a flicker of something in his eyes—jealousy, maybe. Concern, definitely. But he doesn't jump to any conclusions. He knows me well enough for that.

"She's all right," I say, my voice low as I close the door behind me. "I didn't... hurt her."

It wasn't really a risk but being intimate so soon after feeding definitely increased my hunger for her. Still, I couldn't ignore the underlying fear. With my heightened strength, there was always a chance I could hurt her—especially since I've never been with a human before. That thought alone had been enough to keep me hyper-aware of every move, every touch.

Iolas leans back in his chair, studying me for a long moment. His gaze is intense, as if he's searching for any sign that I might be lying, but he knows better. "I know," he says, his voice gruff. "You wouldn't. You love her." He pauses, and I can see the tension in his shoulders, the protective instinct that's always there when it comes to her. "But is she all right?"

I nod, though I don't feel like doing so. "She's fine. She's sleeping now."

The room falls silent for a moment. I shift my weight, my gaze falling to the floor as I speak. "She… she wants to know the truth, Iolas. She's asked me directly."

He doesn't respond right away, but I can see the frustration in his jaw, the way his hand grips the arm of the chair just a little tighter. "You're going to tell her." He states rather than asks, his tone flat.

"Yes. In the morning."

Iolas lets out a long breath, shaking his head slightly. "You really think she's ready for it? Only a few days before the ball?"

"I don't know," I admit, my voice tight, raw. "But I can't keep lying to her. She's already starting to figure it out, and if I don't tell her now, it'll only make it worse later." I swallow hard, the thought of losing her clawing at my chest. "We owe her the truth."

Iolas runs a hand over his face, his fingers dragging through his hair. He's silent for a long time, and I can see the battle going on behind his eyes—his instincts to protect her, to shield her from the worst of it, warring with the knowledge that I'm right.

"She's strong," Iolas finally says, his voice quieter now, more thoughtful. "Stronger than either of us gave her credit for." He looks up at me, and there's something like resignation in his gaze. "She'll come to understand. She'll remember."

I wish I could believe that.

I sit down heavily on the edge of his bed, resting my head in my hands. And all of it—the responsibility, the guilt, the fear—it's, suffocating. "What if she doesn't?" I ask, my voice barely above a whisper. "What if she hates us for it?"

Iolas stands, moving over to where I'm sitting, and places a hand on my shoulder. It's a simple gesture, but there's comfort in it. "Then she'll hate us," he says bluntly. "But she'll know the truth. And that's better than lying to her, Altair."

I let out a bitter laugh, running a hand through my hair. "Is it?"

He grips my shoulder a little tighter, and when I finally look up, I see the certainty in his eyes. "Yes," he says firmly. "You know it is."

I want to believe him. I want to believe that telling her the truth will somehow make this all easier, that it won't drive her away. But a part of me—the selfish part—is terrified. Terrified that once she knows everything, she'll never look at me the same way again.

But it doesn't matter. I've made my decision, and I know it's the right one, no matter how much it scares me.

"She'll be fine, Altair," Iolas says, his voice softer now, almost reassuring. "You need to stop spiralling and just trust her. She's stronger than you think."

I nod, though the doubt still lingers in the back of my mind. I stand up, taking a deep breath, trying to shake off everything pressing down on me. "I hope you're right."

Iolas smirks, though there's no humour in it. "When am I not?"

I manage a small smile, but it fades quickly. I glance toward the door, my chest feeling heavy. "I should get back. She'll wake soon."

Iolas nods, giving my shoulder one last squeeze before letting go. "Go," he says. "She'll need you in the morning."

As I turn to leave, his voice stops me.

"And Altair?" I pause, looking back at him.

"Whatever happens, I'm with you."

I nod once, grateful, though I can't quite find the words to express it. I feel like I don't deserve his loyalty. But I'm grateful for it all the same.

Without another word, I leave his chambers and head back to Olwyn. To the truth. To whatever comes next.

He's hurt. And I never meant for it to do so, but I'm not surprised. It would break me if I were him.

CHAPTER FORTY–SEVEN
Olwyn

The soft light of morning filters through the windows, gently rousing me from sleep.

My body is sore, but there's a strange comfort in it—a reminder of the night before, of how close we had been. But as I blink the sleep from my eyes, something feels… off. And I remember.

I sit up slowly, my hand reaching for the spot beside me, but it's empty. Altair is sitting at the end of the bed, fully dressed, his elbows resting on his knees, head bowed.

"Altair?" I murmur, my voice thick with sleep.

He doesn't turn to look at me, just stares at the floor, his hands clasped together tightly.

I push the blankets aside, my feet hitting the cold stone floor as I stand. A knot is already forming in my stomach. There's a sadness in his posture, a resignation that twists something inside me.

"When you're dressed… let's go talk," he says quietly, his voice barely more than a whisper. He finally looks at me, and his gaze nearly knocks the air from my lungs. His eyes are soft, but there's sorrow there.

I nod slowly, not trusting myself to speak. I don't know what truths he's about to tell me, but I can already tell that whatever it is, it's going to change everything.

"I'll leave you be," he says, standing and moving toward the door. "We'll talk outside. In the gardens."

The gardens. My favourite place. I don't know whether to feel comforted by that or even more on edge. I nod again, my throat too tight to form words as I watch him leave the room.

I dress quickly, pulling on a simple gown and braiding my hair. My hands are shaking, and I have to force myself to breathe. Something is coming, something big, and I'm not ready. I know I'm not, even though I demanded to be told.

When I open my door, Iolas is leaning casually against the wall opposite, arms crossed over his chest. He straightens when he sees me, his usual grin flickering to life, though it feels more subdued than usual.

"Thought you'd never come out," he says lightly, his tone playful but lacking its usual sharpness. His gaze sweeps over me, assessing but not lingering, and he raises a brow. "Big day ahead, huh?"

I nod, unable to find words past the knot in my throat.

He falls into step beside me as I walk past, his hands tucked into his pockets.

The walk is quiet at first, the tension in the air pressing down on me like a weight. Sensing it, Iolas glances my way, his voice gentler than usual. "You know, if this is more than you want to handle, you don't have to face it alone. I'll be here after."

I swallow hard, his words offering a shred of comfort even though the knot in my chest remains. "I asked to be told," I murmur. "I need to know."

He nods, his gaze flicking forward. "Then you'll know," he says simply. "And when you do, we'll deal with it. Together."

By the time we reach the gardens, Altair is already there, standing near my favourite bench. He looks out over the lush greenery, his hands resting at his sides, but his shoulders are tense, as though bracing for a storm.

Iolas pauses at the entrance, turning to face me fully. "You're stronger than you think," he says softly. "Don't forget that."

I nod, holding onto his words like a lifeline. As I step forward toward Altair, Iolas lingers for a moment before heading back down the path, his presence a quiet reassurance even as he disappears from view.

"Altair?" I call softly, stepping toward him.

He turns to face me, his expression softening slightly as his eyes meet mine, but the sadness remains, like a dark cloud that won't lift.

He gestures toward the bench. "Sit with me," he says, his voice gentler now.

I sit down, the cool stone of the bench grounding me as the soft breeze rustles the leaves overhead. He sits beside me but keeps his distance, his body turned slightly toward me, though his gaze is fixed on the flowers blooming around us.

"I need you to listen," he begins, his voice steady but laced with something heavy. "Please… don't interrupt. Just listen to what I have to say."

I nod, my hands clasping tightly in my lap. My heart is already racing, and I have to remind myself to breathe as he continues.

"When I was a boy," he begins, his voice quiet, almost distant, "I attended an academy for both vampire and human children."

My back stiffens.

"It was… a different time. A time when there was hope for peace between our people. And… there was a girl there."

He pauses, and something tightens in my chest.

"A girl with silver hair and spring green eyes. I remember the first time I saw her—I was only a child, but I swear I fell in love with her at that moment. She had this… energy, this light about her that drew everyone in. Especially me." His lips twitch, a faint, sad smile. "She used to play with me… with a boy who had hazel eyes, and a fierce girl with dark skin. The four of us were inseparable."

The knot in my stomach tightens painfully. A boy with hazel eyes. A fierce girl with dark skin. Iolas. Ailith. He's talking about Iolas and Ailith.

"I loved her," Altair continues, his voice thickening with emotion. "She was everything. But there was another boy at the academy, a vampire, who used to try and diminish her light relentlessly. I don't know why… maybe he was jealous of her, of the way she shone. But one day…"

He pauses, his jaw clenching as if the memory is too painful to speak aloud.

"One day, the bullying became too much. She couldn't handle it. And… her powers awakened. In a single moment of overwhelming emotion, she… she lost control. Her magic exploded, destroying the classroom. The children inside. The teacher… Almost everyone."

I feel like I've been punched in the gut. My breath leaves me, and a cold, sinking feeling settles into my bones. No. No, that can't be right. I can't…

But as he speaks, flashes of memories begin to surface—shattered fragments of something I've buried deep inside. Blood. So much blood. Screams. The classroom destroyed. The smell of death and charred wood.

I choke on a breath, and tears blur my vision.

"She didn't survive," Altair says softly, his voice thick with sorrow. "Or at least, I thought she hadn't. After the explosion, there was no sign of her. I believed she was dead. For years, I carried that with me."

He lets his hand fall, his gaze soft but unrelenting. "After that day, I changed. I became… someone else. After a few years of being the old king's assassin, he heard about the prophecy of a silver-haired, green-eyed witch, and he commanded me to hunt her down. But I refused. I couldn't bear the thought of it being her, or harming her, if she was still alive."

His voice hardens slightly, and I can feel the anger simmering beneath his calm exterior. "The king grew jealous of my power, and he wanted to take something from me. He wanted to take you. So I killed him. I killed him to protect the hope that maybe, just maybe, you were still out there."

I stare at him, my mind reeling, trying to process everything he's telling me. "You… you killed the king? For me?"

He nods, his *blue* eyes glassy with unshed tears.

I shake my head, tears streaming down my face. "I…" I whisper, my voice barely audible. "I didn't…"

Kill them, I want to say, but the words stick in my throat. Because I know it's true. Deep down, in the part of me I've tried to bury, I know. I can see it now—flashes of that day. The explosion. The destruction. The bodies.

"I killed them," I choke out, my hands trembling. "I killed them all."

Altair reaches for me, his hand gently cupping my cheek as his thumb wipes away a tear. "It wasn't your fault, Olwyn," he says softly. "You were a child. You didn't know."

I shake my head, pulling away from his touch. It's too much. The guilt, the horror—it crushes me.

"I've spent years searching for you, Olwyn. *Years.* And when I heard about a hidden princess in Avantra, I knew it had to be you. I attacked your palace because I believed it was the only way to find you."

I swallow hard, my throat tight with emotion. "But… my parents…"

Altair's voice remains soft but unyielding. "They're not your parents," he says quietly, his eyes locked on mine. "They were fakes. Guardians put in place by your real mother… Atha."

Atha…

My heart races, my mind scrambling to make sense of what he's saying. "No… that can't be true. My parents are Alexis and Petr."

"Atha knew about the prophecy. She hid you away to protect you, but not from me, or from vampires. She was protecting herself. Have you never questioned the lack of resemblance? Why the king and queen neglected you so?"

Of course I had.

But some parents are just shitty.

"If it's true, why would my mother want to hide me? Why would she—"

Try and kill me.

"Because she knows who you are, Olwyn," Altair says, his gaze filled with sorrow. "She knows you're the one from the prophecy. To end the cycle of destruction. To unite everyone. She's always known, and she's terrified of what that means."

His words hit me like a blow, stealing the breath from my lungs, and I remember what Sera and Thalia said. "Unite?" I whisper, barely able to form the word.

But I remember what my parents… what *they* told me when I was a child. *End the cycle of destruction…* They said it meant I would destroy the vampires. That I would rid the world of their curse forever. And that's why they would want me dead.

"End the cycle?" I whisper, my voice trembling. "You mean… annihilate them?"

Altair's expression shifts to shock, and then pain. "Annihilate?" he echoes, his brow furrowing. "Is that what they told you? No, Olwyn. That's not it at all."

I blink at him, confusion swirling with doubt. "But that's what the prophecy means. That's why you married me, isn't it? To control me? To keep me from… from destroying your people?" My voice rises, and I hate the quiver in it. "Isn't that what this is all about?"

Altair leans closer, his sorrow deepening. "Olwyn, no. That's not why I married you. And that's not what the prophecy means." He takes a deep breath, as though steadying himself. "The prophecy says you're destined to *unite* humans and vampires. To end the cycle of destruction— not through annihilation, but through peace. Through change."

His words pierce through me, unravelling everything I thought I knew.

"She fears the end of what she believes is order," Altair continues, his voice quiet but steady. "Your parents—your human parents—wanted you to believe otherwise. They wanted you to see the prophecy as a call to destroy vampires because they thrive on division, on fear. Your mother is terrified of what you represent. She knows that if you succeed, everything will change. The power balance between humans and vampires will shift. There won't be any more divisions. No more war. But people like her don't want peace, Olwyn. They want dominance. It was your mother who foretold the prophecy. And when she realised that you had been found, that I had taken you… she acted out of fear. She sent the assassins to my palace. She sent those men to kill us on our return from the village."

I shake my head, my hands trembling. "No… she couldn't have… She wouldn't have sent people to kill me. She's my mother."

"She did," Altair says, his eyes pleading for me to understand. "She knows what you are, and she fears the future you represent."

His words are suffocating. My real mother… had tried to kill me? Because she feared I would end the hostilities between vampires and humans? Because I'm supposed to unite them?

How am I supposed to believe all this?

How can I be responsible for uniting *anyone*?

I stand abruptly, shaking my head. "No. This doesn't make sense. Why would I be the one to unite them? I can't even control my own powers! How am I supposed to change anything?"

Altair steps closer, his voice quiet but firm. "You're strong, Olwyn. You're the key to peace between our people. The prophecy says you'll end the destruction by uniting us all. That's why Atha is trying to stop you."

I take a step back, my heart pounding in my chest. "This is too much. It's impossible. I can't—"

"Olwyn," Altair's voice softens, his eyes filled with guilt and sorrow. "I'm sorry. I'm so, so sorry. But I'm here, and I'll be with you every step of the way."

But his words only make the turmoil inside me worse. Everything I've known, everything I thought was true—it's all crumbling. My entire life has been a lie.

I step away from him, my hands shaking as I try to make sense of everything. "No. This is too much."

"Olwyn…" he says softly, standing as well, his gaze filled with guilt and sorrow.

"I need time," I whisper, my voice trembling. "I need time to think."

Altair doesn't stop me as I turn and walk away, my heart racing, my mind spinning.

When I reach my chambers, the silence feels too loud, like the world is pressing in on me from all sides. I close the door behind me, leaning back against it for a moment, trying to catch my breath. My chest feels tight, and the ache in my heart refuses to ease. How am I supposed to make sense of any of this? Everything I thought I knew about my life, about who I am, has been ripped apart.

My eyes catch on something strange, resting on the centre of my bed—a box. It's small, simple, and unmarked, placed carefully as if waiting for me. I frown, pushing myself off the door and walking over to it, my pulse quickening with each step.

With trembling hands, I open the box.

Inside, nestled in a bed of velvet… is a dagger.

My breath hitches.

It's the same dagger I saw at Elderglen. The same silver blade with the white oak handle, the one that had caught my eye at the blacksmith's stall. The dagger made of witchsilver; the only thing capable of killing a pureblood vampire.

My fingers hover above it, but I don't touch it. Altair must have bought it for me.

And for the first time, in as long as I can remember.

I fall. I fall apart.

A sob escapes me, tearing through my chest, and I can't hold it back anymore. The walls I've built, the strength I've tried to cling to, all of it crumbles in an instant. I collapse onto the bed, burying my face in my hands as the tears come, hot and fast, soaking into the sheets beneath me.

I cry for the little girl who can't remember what she lost, for the young woman who doesn't know where she belongs anymore, for the truth that has been hidden from me, and for the lies I've been told. I cry for the choices I have to make now, the decisions that could change everything.

But mostly, I cry because I'm scared. Scared of the power inside me, scared of what I've already done, scared of what I might do…

Scared of who I'm falling for…

Eventually, the tears slow, but the ache in my chest remains. I wipe my eyes, glancing at the dagger once more before carefully closing the box. I can't deal with this now. Not tonight.

But tomorrow… tomorrow will come whether I'm ready for it or not.

With a shaky breath, I crawl under the covers, pulling them tightly around me. The room feels cold, too large, and too empty.

I want to see her light again.

CHAPTER FORTY-EIGHT

Olwyn

Dinner is a quiet affair.

Too quiet. The grand dining hall feels cavernous, the flickering candlelight unable to chase away the tension that lingers between us. I sit at the long table, flanked by Iolas and Altair. They watch me carefully, their eyes filled with something between concern and caution, as though I might break at any moment.

I get it.

I'm a wild card right now.

I had destroyed a classroom full of children before. What's to stop my emotions from making me lose control again?

But I won't. Not tonight.

I push the food around on my plate, the roast lamb and steamed vegetables tasteless on my tongue. My thoughts churn, still reeling from the revelations from the day before. Altair and Iolas haven't said much, leaving me to sort through my shattered assumptions alone.

Altair clears his throat, breaking the silence. "How are you feeling?"

I glance up at him, his piercing gaze softening just slightly. "Overwhelmed," I admit. "But I'll live."

"Good," Iolas says, his voice lighter than the mood calls for. "You've been distant the last few days," he adds, leaning back in his chair.

"You're lucky I'm such an understanding man. Anyone else would've taken it personally." He winks, but there's an undercurrent of sincerity in his gaze.

I manage a small smile, but it doesn't quite reach my eyes.

My heart hurts, the truth threatening to pull me under again. It's all been too much—too much truth, too much revelation, too much betrayal. "I just need time," I say quietly, feeling the tightness in my throat. "To process everything."

Altair nods, his hands resting on the table, his fingers interlocking as though to steady himself. "I promise I was planning on telling you. I just wanted to get through the ball and the peace talks first before burdening you."

"Altair, it's fine. It's just… a lot to take in."

His brow furrows, his jaw tightening like he wants to say more, but he stops himself.

Instead, Iolas reaches across the table, his hand brushing against my arm, offering comfort. "Take all the time you need," he says softly. "But don't forget you're not alone in this, little witch. You don't have to carry it all by yourself."

The sincerity in his voice almost undoes me. I feel my resolve start to crumble, but I can't break down now. Not here.

Altair clears his throat again, sitting straighter. "The ball is tomorrow," he says, shifting the subject to safer ground. His tone is measured, but there's a note of weariness in it. "We'll present a united front. Together."

"Together," I echo, the word foreign on my tongue but oddly comforting, even after everything from the past few days.

"We'll greet the lords and ladies of Noctura first," Altair continues, his gaze steady on me. "Then the dignitaries. And… King Casius."

"And what exactly do you expect me to do? Smile and curtsy?"

Altair's lips twitch, almost a smile. "No. Just hold your head high. Let them see that you're my queen. Our queen."

"Easier said than done," I mutter under my breath, earning a frown from Altair and a chuckle from Iolas.

"She'll be fine," Iolas says, leaning back in his chair with a lazy grin. "Though I'll be vetting every single person entering that ballroom. No exceptions. Which means, my dear queen, you'll have my two most trusted guards escorting you to the party. Try not to give them too much trouble, hmm?"

"I don't give trouble," I say, scowling at him.

"Oh, I know," he quips, smirking. "You *are* trouble."

Altair rolls his eyes but doesn't comment, instead focusing back on me. "Once you're in the ballroom, we'll handle the rest. I need you to trust me on this, Olwyn."

"Trust you," I repeat, the words tasting somewhat bitter. But I nod nonetheless.

"You'll be fine," Iolas interjects, his tone lighter again, though his eyes are watchful. "If you can survive me in a bad mood, you can survive anything."

I laugh, though it's more of a scoff, and Altair shakes his head, a ghost of a smile tugging at his lips. I know Iolas is just being his usual charming self to try and cheer me up, but it feels difficult to be cheery when you've only recently found out you murdered a room full of your classmates at a very young age. If my power was that bad then, what could it do now?

The conversation fades for a moment, replaced by the distant sound of the crackling fire and the clinking of cutlery. I glance between them, these two vampires who have somehow become the closest thing to allies I have.

Altair clears his throat, drawing my attention back to him. "There's something else you should be prepared for."

I arch an eyebrow, already wary. "What now?"

"Casius might ask you to dance," he says, his tone neutral but his eyes giving nothing away.

My stomach twists, a mix of unease and indignation swirling inside me. "Dance? With him?"

"It would be polite to accept," Altair continues, his voice calm, though I notice the slightest tension in his jaw.

"Polite?" I repeat, my tone incredulous. "You expect me to dance with the man who you've been fighting for over a decade—" I cut myself off, exhaling sharply. "Fine. Then maybe *you* should ask his partner to dance. Even the score a little."

Altair exhales quietly. "Casius doesn't have a partner."

I blink, caught off guard. "Of course he doesn't," I mutter, rolling my eyes. "How convenient."

Altair leans forward slightly, his voice low but steady. "This isn't a game, Olwyn. Casius will be watching. The lords and ladies will be watching. Every move you make will be dissected and whispered about. If you refuse him, they'll see it as a slight—a crack in our alliance."

"I know that," I snap, my voice sharper than I intended. I inhale deeply, trying to push down the frustration clawing at my chest. "I know how important appearances are, Altair. But that doesn't mean I have to like it."

"You don't have to like it," he replies, his gaze unwavering. "You just have to endure it."

Iolas smirks, clearly amused by the tension crackling between us. "Look at it this way, little witch: You've been through worse. What's one dance with a brooding king?"

I glare at him, but the humour in his expression disarms me just enough to loosen the knot of tension in my chest.

Altair sits back, watching me carefully, his features softening just a fraction. "You'll handle this, Olwyn. I know you will."

I look between them, my frustration simmering but my resolve strengthening. "Fine," I say, crossing my arms. "But if he tries anything—anything at all—don't blame me for what happens next."

Altair looks at me then, his eyes softer than they were a moment ago. "You'll be brilliant," he says quietly. "I know it."

"Let's hope you're right," I say, my voice steady despite the storm raging inside me.

Iolas raises his glass, smirking. "To surviving the ball. And if not, at least it'll be entertaining."

Altair groans, and I can't help but smile.

"You're more prepared for this than you think," Altair says. "The ball isn't about magic or grand gestures. It's about showing them who you are and what you stand for. That's all."

I swallow hard, his words weighing heavy. "And if I fail?"

"You won't," he says simply, his confidence unsettling.

Iolas's grin widens. "And if you do, well, Altair's *terrible* at dancing. We'll distract everyone with that."

Altair shoots him a glare, but I catch the faintest flicker of a smile.

The tension eases, if only slightly, and I find myself sitting a little straighter. Tomorrow will likely be terrifying, but at least I they'd be facing it with me.

This is my greatest fear… I can feel her pulling away.

CHAPTER FORTY-NINE
Olwyn

The day of the ball arrives, and I'm a little numb.

Thalia and Sera flit around me like butterflies, their excitement palpable as they bustle about the room, fussing over my black starlight gown, my hair, my makeup. I sit there in silence, letting them pull and primp and preen, their chatter washing over me like background noise.

"You're going to look absolutely breathtaking tonight," Thalia gushes as she pins the last of my curls in place. "Everyone will be watching you."

I force a small smile, but it feels foreign on my lips. I have been a bit subdued, since… everything. Since Altair told me the truth, since my entire life crashed down on me. At meals, we still exchange polite nods and pleasantry, but the tension remains.

I haven't told them, but there's a hollow space in my chest that I can't seem to fill. The truth about my past, what I did, my parents—my real mother—wraps around me like a cold cloak, suffocating. And I don't know how to pull myself out from beneath it. They are trying, but I can't seem to relax. Warm energy simmering under my skin, feeling like it needs to burst out.

Sera giggles, holding up the gown for me to step into. "I can't wait to see the hall filled with people. It's been so long since we've had a ball this grand. The way it's decorated—everything is just so perfect!"

"Who are you most excited to meet?" Thalia asks with a mischievous grin. "I hear there will be lords from all over, even some from the far South."

"And King Casius," Sera adds, her eyes wide. "Can you imagine? An actual king from another kingdom!"

The mention of Casius makes my stomach twist with nerves. I wonder what he's like. Whether he's more vicious like the 'stories' I was told back in Avantra. Or maybe he's more like Altair?

"He's supposed to be very charming," Thalia continues, oblivious to my discomfort. "But also a bit... cold, isn't he?"

"Indifferent," Sera corrects, smoothing the fabric of my gown over my legs. "He's apparently very indifferent."

Charming. Cold. Indifferent. I barely hear them. My thoughts are miles away, tangled up in everything I've learned, everything I'm struggling to accept. Everything I need to do tonight.

All I have done for days to try and relieve the stress is train, eat and sleep, and help with the final preparations for the ball. And tonight, I'm supposed to stand before a hall full of people I don't know, pretending everything is fine.

Pretending I'm fine.

"Olwyn."

The sharp voice cuts through the air like a knife, and I flinch slightly in surprise, my gaze snapping to the door.

Ailith stands in the doorway, her arms crossed over her chest, cutting a fierce, imposing figure. She's dressed in a deep purple gown that hugs her body like armour, the fabric shimmering with an almost dangerous elegance. The neckline plunges just enough to be bold, but the rest of the dress is sharp and structured, cinching at the waist with dark gold detailing. There's a shimmering gold powder dusted over her shaved head and eyelids, and she looks both stunning and untouchable—like a queen in her own right, even without a crown.

Her eyes sweep over Thalia and Sera, the girls immediately quieting under her gaze as they leave, before her hard expression lands on me. There's no softness there, no room for excuses.

"What's wrong?" I ask, though I already know.

She doesn't mince words. "You need to pull yourself together."

I blink.

"This ball isn't just a party, Olwyn. It's a statement," Ailith continues, stepping into the room, her voice cool and firm. "You are the queen. You need to act like it tonight. I don't care what's going on in your head—there's too much at stake for you to falter now."

Fury and betrayal rise in me. I stare back at Ailith with a spark I haven't felt in days. "You made out it wasn't a big deal."

"What?" she asks.

"When I killed that assassin, you said it wasn't a big deal." Ailith's gaze narrows slightly, but she doesn't speak. "Because you knew what I'd done at the academy. You knew that wasn't my first kill."

Ailith doesn't flinch, but her expression shifts—just barely—a flicker of something almost like recognition in her eyes.

"You've always known," I continue, the words tumbling out now, anger simmering just beneath the surface. "All of you. Altair. Iolas. And you never said a word about it. You just waited for me to remember it myself."

Ailith's lips press into a thin line, her silence cutting deeper than any retort she could throw at me. The tension between us thickens, but for once, I don't feel small under her sharp gaze.

"You told me it wasn't a big deal," I repeat. "Because to you, I've always been a weapon. Even when I didn't know it."

She takes a step closer, her eyes never leaving mine. "Yes," she says bluntly. "Because it's true. You've done worse, Olwyn. Much worse. And you survived it."

"But *they* didn't!" I raise my voice.

Ailith doesn't flinch. She never does. Instead, she stands her ground, her expression as hard and unyielding as stone. "No," she says, her voice a little softer but still firm. "They didn't. But that's not your fault."

My breath hitches, and I feel the surge of emotion clawing at my chest. "Isn't it? How can you stand there and say that? I killed them, Ailith.

I killed those *children*. My classmates. My friends." My voice cracks at the end, the truth pressing down on me like an avalanche.

Ailith's eyes soften, but her stance remains solid. "You lost control. You were a child. You didn't know what you were capable of, what was inside of you."

"And now I do?" I challenge, my voice shaking. "I don't know what's in me now either."

"You're stronger now," Ailith counters, her voice rising just enough to drown out the edge of panic in mine. "You've trained, you've fought, and you've survived more than most people ever will. Do you think that makes you a monster? Or do you think it makes you someone who does what needs to be done?"

I shake my head, stepping back. "And what about the next time I lose control? Who pays the price then? What if it's Altair, or Iolas?"

She doesn't answer. Just stares at me for a moment.

"Stop fighting it," she finally says, her voice firm again. "Stop doubting yourself. You survived, Olwyn. You survived when almost no one else did, and you've been surviving ever since. But now it's time to do more than just survive. It's time to live. To take control. You're the queen."

I swallow, the backs of my eyes stinging. A queen. How am I supposed to be a queen when I can hardly sort my head out?

Ailith's eyes narrow, sensing my hesitation. "Don't let them see your weakness," she says sharply. "Not tonight. Not ever."

I nod slowly, even though the knot in my chest tightens. I wish I could find that fire inside me, the fiery strength that always flickers just beneath the surface. But it feels… dimmer now. Smaller.

She turns on her heel and heads for the door. "I'll see you downstairs," she says over her shoulder, leaving me with nothing but the echo of her words.

Thalia and Sera re-enter, exchanging a nervous glance, and I offer them a tight smile. "I think that's enough," I say softly. "Thank you."

They hesitate but nod, stepping back to let me rise from the chair. The gown they've chosen for me is beautiful—the black lace with delicate silver embroidery that catches the light when I move. It's the kind of dress that should make me feel powerful, beautiful. But as I stare at myself in the mirror, all I feel is… hollow,

"Good luck, Your Majesty," Thalia whispers as I make my way to the door. Sera nods in agreement, their excitement dimming slightly as they sense my unease.

I don't respond, my mind already elsewhere.

The grand hall is only down my staircase and a few corridors away, but the thought of entering it feels suffocating. My heart pounds as I walk down the corridor, two guards flanking me silently. Their presence feels more like a cage than protection, and with every step, my chest tightens.

I don't want this.

I don't want to go to the ball.

I don't want to face King Casius, or the guests, or even Altair and Iolas.

I can't. Not yet. Not like this.

We reach a fork in the hall, the polished stone glinting under the flickering sconces lining the walls. My breath quickens as I glance down the darkened side corridor to my right. I know where it leads—the private hall to the gardens. The fresh air, the open sky. For a fleeting moment, I can almost feel the crisp night breeze against my skin, the whisper of freedom it promises.

"Stop," I command abruptly, my voice steady despite the storm brewing in my chest. Both guards halt immediately, turning to me with questioning looks.

"I need air," I say firmly, tilting my chin up. "Take me to the gardens."

The guard ahead hesitates, his brow furrowing. "My queen, the palace doors are locked for the evening, and the garden is outside the designated perimeter—"

"I need air," I cut him off, keeping my tone sharp but calm. "Unlock the door. Now."

The guards exchange a glance, one silently assessing the other before the one behind me nods. "As you wish, my queen."

We divert down the side corridor, their heavy boots echoing behind me. The closer we get to the garden door, the lighter my chest feels, though my heart still races. I focus on the sound of my breathing, trying to steady it, to quiet the chaos in my mind.

When we reach the end of the hallway, the lead guard pulls out a ring of keys and unlocks the heavy wooden door. It creaks open, revealing the soft glow of moonlight spilling onto the stone floor. The scent of fresh earth and blooming flowers drifts in, calming and grounding.

"Wait here," I tell them, stepping over the threshold before they can protest. I glance back at the guard holding the key, fixing him with a look that dares him to argue.

"My queen, it would be safer if we—"

"I said wait here," I repeat, sharper this time. "I'll be fine. I won't go far. And the only other door to the garden is locked, yes?"

Reluctantly, they nod, stepping back as I close the door behind me. The latch clicks softly, and I'm alone.

The gardens are bathed in silver light, the tall hedges, trees and stone pathways illuminated by the full moon above. The light breeze of the night air licks at my skin, but it's a welcome relief. For the first time all evening, I feel like I can breathe.

I walk slowly down the gravel path, the tension in my chest easing with every step. The first stars in the evening sky above seem impossibly bright, scattered like tiny shards of light. My fingers brush against the petals of a nearby rose bush, grounding myself.

For a moment, I let myself forget. Forget the ball, the politics, my title. Out here, under the open sky, I'm just Olwyn again. Not a queen. Not a player in this stupid game. Just… me.

But the peace doesn't last.

It's the unfamiliar deep voice that startles me, causing me to turn. "Need a hand?"

365

I need her to keep her fire.

CHAPTER FIFTY
Olwyn

The stranger steps out from behind a blossom tree and…
Oh.

I don't recognize him, and with his striking features, I'm certain I'd remember if we had crossed paths before.

His pale hand glides through short, spiked silver hair—just a shade darker than my own—a few strands falling back into place without care. His red eyes—bright, intense, and fixed on mine—burn with a sharp, almost unnerving interest, as if he's studying my every move. Yet the rest of his face remains emotionless, frozen in a calm, unreadable mask.

Actually, he looks rather bored.

His lips are set in a neutral line, and his angular features show no hint of expression, as though the intensity in his gaze is the only part of him truly alive in the moment.

If his eyes weren't so obvious, I would have known what he is immediately from his pointed ears. Plus… no human could be that beautiful.

My hands instinctively clasp together, and I force myself to look away—one of Iolas's lessons.

Show them you're not afraid.

"You're not supposed to be in here," I say firmly, my voice steadier than I expect.

"Neither are you, by the looks of it," he replies dryly, his gaze trailing lazily over me before locking back onto my face.

I tilt my head, glancing over my shoulder at the locked door behind me. The only other door in is locked. Unless…

"Did you pick the lock?" I ask, suspicion lacing my tone.

A pale brow arches. "Do I look like a locksmith to you?"

I ignore the hint of amusement in his voice, focusing instead on his impeccable appearance. He doesn't look like someone who should be skulking around in the shadows. His tailored black suit fits him so perfectly it might as well be part of him. No, he doesn't look like a locksmith. He looks like he belongs in the ballroom with the other lords and dignitaries, not here.

"Then how did you get in?" I press.

"It was unlocked," he says smoothly, his tone casual.

"Unlocked?" I frown, glancing at the door behind him on the far wall. The guards had told me the gardens were locked for the evening, but… could they have been mistaken?

I bite my lip, confusion swirling in my chest.

The stranger notices. His lips quirk upward, just enough to suggest he's holding back a smirk. "What? You don't believe me?"

"I—" I pause, shaking my head. "It doesn't matter."

"Clearly it does," he says, stepping a fraction closer, and I feel his gaze burning into me. "You look like someone who always wants answers."

I bristle, my fingers brushing the fabric of my skirt where my witchsilver dagger is hidden in the thigh slit. "And you look like someone who gives too many questions instead of answers."

"Touché." He dips his head slightly, almost like a bow, though the mocking edge in his crimson gaze undercuts the gesture.

I let out a small, frustrated sigh and turn my attention to the garden, desperate to focus on something—anything—other than the stranger in front of me.

"I just needed some air," I mutter under my breath, half to myself.

His sharp ears catch it. "Ah, something we have in common then."

I glance back at him. His expression remains impassive.

"I hope you're enjoying it, then," I reply coolly, gesturing vaguely toward the blossoms around us.

"Oh, I am." He smirks, his gaze sliding back to me.

I narrow my eyes at him, irritated by his cryptic tone. "And you are?"

He doesn't answer right away, taking a moment to survey the garden as though the conversation is beneath him. Finally, he leans slightly closer, his voice dropping just enough to send a shiver down my spine.

"Someone who's enjoying the view."

The double meaning doesn't escape me, and I shift my weight, my fingers itching toward the slit in my dress where my witchsilver dagger is hidden. His crimson gaze drops briefly, as though he knows exactly where it's hidden, but he doesn't react.

I force myself to step away, putting more distance between us. "I hope you enjoy your air, then. I'll be returning to the ball."

"Of course," he says smoothly, bowing as I step back. But as I move down the path, his voice follows me, low and laced with amusement. "Have a lovely evening, Your Majesty. I'll be seeing you again soon."

I don't turn around, but my pace quickens, my pulse racing. There's something about him that sets me on edge, but I can't quite put my finger on it. When I slip back into the palace corridor, the guards waiting for me, the dim light filtering through the high windows feels cold and detached. My mind lingers on his words, and for a moment, I glance back toward the garden door.

The guards must have been mistaken.

And yet, there's a small, nagging voice in the back of my head whispering that they weren't.

I make my way to the ballroom, trying to shake off the encounter with the mysterious vampire. As I enter, Iolas immediately approaches me, nodding to his guards who take a few steps back but remain close. "There you are. Where have you been?" he asks.

I shrug, attempting to sound nonchalant, though my heart is still racing from the encounter. "Just needed some air."

He doesn't seem convinced, his gaze flicking over me as if searching for any sign of distress. "Are you sure you're all right?" His voice softens, his usual teasing demeanour absent.

"I'm fine, Iolas." I force a smile, but even as the words leave my mouth, I know he doesn't buy it. The flicker of concern in his hazel eyes makes my stomach twist, a familiar ache of guilt curling deep inside me. It's not like I want to lie to him.

Not in the middle of this ballroom, not with every vampire lord and lady watching, waiting for the human queen to make a fool of herself.

Iolas studies me for a moment longer, then gives a small nod. "Come on, we should get back before Altair notices. Casius has arrived."

I feel a pang of apprehension at the mention of the king's name, but I nod in acknowledgment. "Lead the way," I say, following Iolas as he guides me towards the dais which overlooks the entire dancefloor.

Altair's voice cuts through the tension as he sees me approach. "Olwyn," he says, his voice firm yet composed. His presence is impossible to ignore, regal and intimidating in the way only Altair can manage. His eyes flicker with a shadowed intensity that makes my stomach tighten. "We need to greet our guests."

I nod, trying to steady my breath as he takes my hand and we take centre stage at the front of the grand hall, on the raised dais. The room falls silent, all eyes drawn to us like moths to a flame. Lords and ladies stand in clusters, their opulent attire glittering under the chandeliers, the air thick with the hum of intrigue and expectation. I can feel their stares—some curious, others judgmental—and it takes everything in me not to shrink under their scrutiny.

One of the first lords steps forward—one not on Altair's council—bowing slightly, his dark eyes gleaming with interest. "Your

Majesties," he greets, his voice smooth and practiced. "A pleasure to finally meet the famed Queen of Noctura."

I manage a small smile, murmuring a polite reply as Altair acknowledges him with a nod. One by one, more lords and ladies approach, their words polite but laced with curiosity, their sharp eyes scanning me as though searching for cracks. Each introduction feels like a test, a quiet, calculated effort to gauge if I truly belong in this room.

But I'm ready. I've spent the last few weeks poring over endless names, titles, and faces, committing them all to memory. As each lord or lady bows or curtsies, I greet them not just with politeness, but with something stronger—recognition.

"Lord Drezan," I say smoothly, inclining my head. "And Lady Isolde. How was your journey? I understand the southern roads were difficult after the storm last week?"

Lady Isolde blinks in surprise before her lips curve into a genuine smile. "They were, Your Majesty. But the roads cleared just in time. Thank you for asking."

A flicker of satisfaction blooms in my chest as I catch the subtle shift in her demeanour, the slight softening of her sharp gaze, and Altair's hand squeezes my waist in encouragement.

"Lady Varyn," I say to another woman who steps forward, her partner by her side. "I hear your vineyards outside Elderglen are producing a particularly fine vintage this year. I hope I might sample it one day."

Lady Varyn's eyes light up. "Of course, Your Majesty. I'll see to it that a case is sent to the palace. It's an honour to know you're aware of our work."

One by one, I address each lord and lady by name, remembering small details I'd learned about their families, their lands, their challenges. Several of them smile, their stiff expressions relaxing as they realise I've taken the time to know who they are.

It doesn't escape me that Altair and Iolas watch closely from either side of me, their presence steady and reassuring. Though Altair says little, I can feel his approval in the brief glances he casts my way.

Still, not all are impressed. Some faces remain cold, their eyes wary as they study me, their words clipped and careful. The doubt lingers in the air, but I am trying.

But I stand tall, meeting their scepticism with composure. This is their test, but it's also mine. If they're waiting for me to falter, to shrink under their scrutiny, they'll be waiting forever.

When another lord bows before me—a tall, gaunt man with icy eyes—I greet him just as confidently. "Lord Asrik, I've read about your efforts in fortifying the southeastern border. Your work has been critical in protecting the region. Thank you for your service."

His sharp gaze narrows, clearly startled that I know anything about him. But after a brief pause, he dips his head lower than before. "You honour me, Your Majesty."

As he steps away, I catch a flicker of pride in Altair's expression, his lips twitching as though holding back a smile.

And so, I keep going. Name by name. Detail by detail. Some respond warmly, others coolly, but each moment solidifies my presence here.

I'm no longer just the human queen they've come to gawk at.

I'm someone they'll have to take seriously.

Then, just as another lord bows and steps back, the crowd parts, and a figure steps forward, his silver hair catching the light, his eyes glowing like embers in the dim room.

The vampire from earlier.

My heart skips a beat as his gaze locks onto mine.

Before I can formulate words, the vampire is standing before us, his presence magnetic. "Your Majesty," he greets with a respectful bow…

To me first.

And not to Altair.

Who is a living statue. Saying nothing. Doing nothing. And those around us stare with held breath. The man before me finally straightens, tipping his head towards Altair.

"I was wondering if your wife would do me the honour of a dance?"

What?

I blink a few times as if I have misheard him.

Altair's scarred eye twitches, and it is the only show of expression on his face before he masks it with a smile, turning towards me as he presses his hand to the small of my back.

"Olwyn."

Fuck.

Confusion blasts through me as I look between my husband, and this vampire I met moments ago. Why does he feel like he can ask for a danc—

Double fuck.

It's because he can.

She looks like a dream. She looks like she's walking through a nightmare.

CHAPTER FIFTY – ONE
Olwyn

I glance at Altair, a warning in his two-toned eyes, a reminder that I should be polite.

Turning back to the *stranger*, I plaster a small smile on my face—despite the fear and fury that rages through my veins—and say, "It would be my pleasure, King Sovran."

I take King Casius's offered hand, my fingers trembling slightly as we walk together to the centre of the dancefloor. The eyes of the other guests follow our every move, their whispers a low hum in the background. I try to maintain a composed facade, but inside, my mind is a whirlwind of emotions.

As we come to a stop, the music begins—a slow, haunting waltz that fills the air with its melancholic melody. Casius places his hand on my waist, his touch firm yet strangely gentle. I try not to grip his shoulder too hard, placing my other hand in his as we begin to move in time with the music. He moves his hand, threading his long fingers through mine.

There's a tension palpable in the air as we glide across the polished floor. I'm suddenly thankful for Crista's dance lessons during all the ball prep.

I can feel Casius's gaze on me, searching, probing, as if trying to make me bite. Trying to get me to acknowledge who he is. But I keep my expression carefully neutral, unwilling to give anything away.

Even though I want to stamp on his foot.

"How are you enjoying your stay with Altair? We both know your residence here isn't one of your choosing," he says bluntly, the words rolling off his tongue with a nonchalant boldness.

He's either naturally very forward… or very brave. But panic does blast through me as I wonder how he knows this. When Altair had taken me, he had told the king and queen that everyone would believe it was an arranged marriage. That if anyone thought otherwise and sought to 'save me' he would return to Avantra and destroy them.

"That's quite bold of you to say, Your Majes—"

"Casius," he interrupts, his lips twitching into a subtle smirk. "Call me Casius."

I force a tight smile in return, though his presumption unsettles me. "Very well. Casius." His satisfaction grows at the sound of his name on my lips, his perfectly white teeth flashing in a way that feels both predatory and amused. "My marriage to the king was well arranged by my parents. It's a good match."

He scoffs softly, and I catch the glimmer of something sharper in his eyes. "Is that why you just referred to him as 'the king' instead of by his name?" He leans down slightly, his breath warm against my ear, his voice dropping to a sultry whisper. "Is that why you *needed* air?"

The blood drains from my face, my heart skipping a beat. My lips part, but no words come out. His question hangs between us, damning and dangerous. I've slipped—he knows too much, or at least suspects more than I'm willing to admit. Swallowing the rising panic, I say, "I just needed a moment to breathe. I knew I would be in a crowded ballroom all night and wanted some privacy to compose myself. I called him 'the king', because *that* is what he is."

The knowing gleam in his gaze suggests he knows I am lying. And then I see it—a ring of silver only in his right eye, a sparkle almost imperceptible but unmistakable.

"What? No pet name for your beloved?" he asks, raising a brow as if daring me to deny the truth. His hand is warm at my waist as he pulls me closer, his breath causing a tickle along my neck as he whispers against the shell of my ear. "No name he likes you to call out in the middle of the night."

I gasp and jerk back a little, his hands keeping me steady. Over his shoulder I can see Iolas clamp a hand down on Altair's shoulder, the latter's face a living fury.

"I would appreciate it, if you would keep your *teeth* away from my neck." I grin through a gritted smile. "It's not polite."

Casius chuckles, but the sound is devoid of humour, his smile not reaching his cold eyes. "Do you know what I think?"

"No," I snap quietly, my voice low and edged with frustration, "but I'm sure you're going to tell me."

His amusement deepens, and there's something dark and dangerous lurking beneath it. "*I* think the polished little queen needs unleashing. Needs help losing control."

That's exactly the opposite of what I need, if he knew the truth.

"And you think you're the one to do that?" I ask impatiently, my vision briefly swimming with white as frustration flares hot and fast within me. My hands warm, itching to do something, anything. I know Altair won't intervene—not now. For political and peaceful reasons, I'm left to fend for myself. And that's fine, I can handle one more egotistical man.

Casius's gaze softens, just a fraction, as if he's finally seeing something in me that intrigues him. "I think you never know who can bring out the worst in you… or the best. But maybe one day you'd like to try."

I've had enough. The song, mercifully, comes to an end, and I step back, eager to break free of his hold. But before I leave, I offer him one last parting shot.

"Perhaps. I'll make sure to try later—with my *husband*."

Casius chuckles again, though there's no amusement in it. "Or your guard," he says smoothly, "from the way he's approaching."

I glance over my shoulder, just in time to see Iolas parting the crowd, his expression unreadable but his posture taut with tension.

I turn back to Casius and scoff. "You don't know as much as you think you do," I tell him, trying to shake off the disquieting encounter.

Iolas arrives at my side, his hand brushing against my arm as he steps to me and Casius. He bows, though it's clear from the tension in his shoulders that it's more out of duty than respect. "Your Majesty. The king has requested Olwyn's presence."

Casius offers a tight smile, though his eyes linger on me for a moment longer, as if he's calculating something just out of my reach. "Of course," he says smoothly, inclining his head slightly toward me.

Iolas sighs in relief, guiding me with his hand on my lower back until we reach Altair again. I link my arm with Altair's, turning to watch the room.

"Can I please go now?" I practically beg.

"What did he say to you?" Altair asks in a whispered rush.

"Nothing of importance."

"What did he want with you?" He seems a little frantic, and I look at him confused.

"Why are you so panicky? Want with me? Why would he *want* anything from me?"

"Because of your natural charm—" Iolas starts joking, but Altair interrupts him.

"Isn't it obvious? Everyone wants you for your magic. He knows you are the only living direct descendant of Atha. If we weren't wed, I wouldn't be surprised if he had tried to claim you for himself once he found out you were alive."

Iolas winces, and I release Altair's arm.

It hurts.

Physically and emotionally hurts.

"You're right," I say calmly, taking another step back. "How silly of me. Because why would anyone want anything else?"

Altair's face tightens, his frustration rising. "That's not what I meant," he says, his voice sharp. "That's what Casius cares about, not me. I want you. I told you I loved you since we were children, grieved your death, killed my king for you. I'd hoped you'd come to know me well enough by now to never think I could want you for your magic... I guess I was wrong."

I freeze, the words stinging more than I care to admit. For a long moment, silence stretches between us, heavy and suffocating.

"It's hard to know someone who hides from me, lies to me," I snap, my voice bitter. The words hit harder than I intend, but I don't take them back.

We're at an impasse now, the gulf between us wider than ever, and neither of us knows how to cross it.

"Olwyn—" Altair begins to interject, but I speak over him, my voice firm.

"Please excuse me, *Your Majesty*," I say a little loudly, but falsely polite with a smile. "I think I shall retire. The wine has gone straight to my head."

I see his mouth tighten, but he doesn't stop me as I turn away, the eyes of nearby guests flickering towards us, and I nod and smile, keeping up appearances like the good little queen I should be.

Iolas stands close by, his gaze snapping back and forth between me and Altair, assessing the tension that hangs in the air. I barely acknowledge him, pushing through the crowd, my steps brisk and purposeful as I make my way out of the main hall.

The grandeur of the palace corridors blurs around me, opulent decorations and ornate tapestries becoming a meaningless backdrop to my frustration. My heart races, each beat pounding in my chest like a drum, echoing the torrent of emotions bubbling beneath the surface. Iolas's footsteps are a steady, unrelenting rhythm behind me, a shadow that refuses to be shaken.

"Little witch," he calls after me, his voice a low murmur that bounces off the marble walls as I leave the main hallways and start to ascend the grand staircase. I grit my teeth, willing myself to keep moving. I don't want to give him the satisfaction of seeing me falter—not yet. Not until I reach the sanctuary of my room.

I run up the stairs, hearing Iolas's steps following closely as I burst through my chamber doors, not bothering to quell my anger as I attempt to slam it, the door catching Iolas instead as he entered the room behind me.

And break down I do, launching into a tirade so overdue, I feel like I could rip my hair out.

"Little witch—"

"All my life," I growl in my frustration at the tears coming to my eyes. "*All* my life, I have been nothing but a tool in other people's plans. As soon as my par—as soon as anyone knew of my powers, my childhood was done. I was hidden.

"Not allowed to practise. Not allowed to learn how to protect myself. Not allowed *friends*, gods forbid. And then taken because of that power I can't even *fucking* use."

"That's not why, little witch—" Iolas's hands take a firm grip of my arms.

"It's like I'm nothing but a weapon to them."

Iolas's face softens, a flash of anger momentarily crossing his features before he tamps it down. "You're not just a weapon, Olwyn. You're not."

I let out a bitter laugh, though it's more of a choked sound. "Feels like it. Altair practically said it, didn't he? That's all I'm good for—my magic."

He takes a step closer, his hand coming to rest on my shoulder. "That's not true. That's not who you are."

"Not once has someone asked me what *I* wanted."

"What do you want?" his eyes are wide, asking me desperately.

"Cared about who *I* am." My hands rise instinctively, clutching the white fabric of his shirt, grounding myself in something, anything, in this storm of emotion.

"*I* care little witch—"

"Stop fucking calling me that!" I snap, the nickname that once felt teasing now feels like a reminder of everything I can't control, everything that's been stolen from me.

But instead of stepping back, instead of backing down like I expect, Iolas moves closer, his fingers sliding up to take hold of my chin, tilting my head up towards him. The motion is gentle, but firm, his eyes searching mine for something, some answer I haven't yet found myself.

And then, his lips press against mine.

The kiss is soft, tentative at first, like he's testing the waters. His mouth moves over mine, and I feel his tongue briefly brush against my lips, coaxing, tasting. It's so different from anything I've ever experienced, this sudden tenderness cutting through the anger like a knife through cloth. My breath catches, my heart stumbling over itself, unsure whether to race or stop altogether.

Iolas swallows my gasp, his touch reverent, almost hesitant, as if he's afraid to push too far. Yet, at the same time, there's a quiet urgency in the way his hands frame my face, pulling me closer. His tongue sweeps against mine briefly, and I feel my knees weaken, betraying the torrent of emotions swirling within me.

I close my eyes, and for a moment, I'm not thinking about the palace or my decisions. I'm thinking about Iolas—the way he's always been there. In the beginning, when Altair left me here, leaving me trapped in a marriage I didn't want at the time, it was Iolas who stepped in. He was the one who trained me, the one who kept me grounded when everything felt like it was slipping away.

His presence has been a constant, a steady source of support in a world that has felt more like a cage than a home. The weight of that support, the quiet way he's always protected me, intensifies the way I respond to him now.

He jumps when my fingers brush against the skin of his neck. Groans deeply when I stand on my tiptoes to reach him properly, to return the kiss he starts anew with a vigour. His lips are soft. He tastes like warmth and sweetness.

And he pulls away too soon, dropping my arms like they are on fire.

"Fuck," he curses, walking away. His hands reach up to run through his hair. "Fuck!"

"Iolas," I breathe quietly, starting to reach out but unsure if I should touch him. But he turns, his eyes skipping between my raised hand and my face.

Before I can say anything, he storms the few feet towards me, his hand clasping the back of my neck. He looks at me, his thumb gently brushing against my cheek, his gaze soft, but filled with something deeper. "Olwyn," he whispers, his voice barely audible. "I care. I've always cared."

He kisses me again.

His hand finds my thighs, lifting me with ease as I wrap my legs around his waist, not feeling him move until my back presses against the stone wall behind me. And he's so big, so powerful as he towers over me, his hips holding me in place as one of his large hands grips both of mine to hold them above my head, taking my every breath for his own as he kisses me like he has starved for me for an age.

And I kiss him back.

I take something for myself.

I let him have a piece of me. I give it willingly. Eagerly.

Because for the first time in days, I don't feel numb.

His hard cock presses against me as he pins me with his hips, and I gasp into his mouth, feeling myself throb between my thighs.

"You smell so fucking good," he nibbles at my bottom lip and my eyes nearly roll back in my head.

He tugs the fabric of my dress up and up until my leg is exposed. His broad, calloused hand glides over my skin, the tips of his finger brushing ever so softly at the junction between my thigh and where I want to be touched the most.

He laughs darkly. "Innocent little witch indeed," he says when he realises I am not wearing any undergarments.

He unwinds my legs from around his waist, allowing me to slide down the wall carefully until I'm standing, as his fingers slide between my slickness, before circling around my clit.

I cry out, the noise swallowed by another one of his kisses.

But Iolas moves back, his hazel eyes darting between mine.

I gasp when his finger enters me, pushing up and dragging a bolt of pure pleasure up my body.

"What you want matters," he whispers against my lips. "*You* matter." He continues, pumping his finger with every sentence until he adds another one, his thumb circling around the most sensitive part. "Don't let anyone let you think any differently. Not even fucking Altair. Not even me."

His ministrations speed up, and my head falls back against the wall, my eyes closing as pressure builds in my entire body.

"Eyes on me, little witch," he commands, and it's the most serious I have ever heard him. "I want to see your eyes roll back as you come on my hand."

I catch his eyes and that's all it takes.

I shatter.

I call out his name, his lips claiming mine to muffle the sound as my hips circle against his hand, riding out the waves of my orgasm.

The intensity in Iolas's eyes doesn't fade, even as I come down from the high, my breath still ragged, my body trembling. His fingers remain inside me, still, but his words linger more heavily than anything physical could.

What you want matters. You matter.

His voice echoes in my mind, louder than the pounding of my heartbeat, louder than the fire that still burns low in my belly. For so long, I've craved this—craved the validation, the reminder that I am more than just a pawn, more than just a prophecy, more than what others see when they look at me. I thought Altair had proved that wasn't what I was. The thought of Altair brings guilt, sharp and unyielding, rising like a tide, threatening to drown me.

Iolas, seemingly sensing the shift in my emotions, pulls his hand away gently, his hazel eyes searching mine for answers. His breath comes hard and fast as he towers over me.

"Olwyn," he whispers, voice gravelly but soft, "if this isn't what you want—if I've gone too far—"

"Iolas," I interrupt, my voice shaky but firm. "I wanted this. I wanted you." I press my forehead against his chest, needing the connection, needing to ground myself in this moment, despite the storm of thoughts swirling inside me. "But I need to think. About everything."

His hands drop to my waist, steadying me, and for a moment, he's quiet, just breathing me in. Then he nods, his lips brushing softly against my temple. "You take all the time you need, little witch," he murmurs, his breath warm against my skin. "I'll be here. Whenever you're ready."

For a few beats, we stand like that, pressed together against the cold stone wall, the heat of our moment slowly fading but leaving behind a different kind of warmth.

Iolas's hands linger at my hips for a moment longer before he steps back, creating some space between us.

I should say something—thank him, apologize, *anything*—but the words stick in my throat. Instead, I find myself looking at the door, feeling everything I've been holding back—the responsibilities, the secrets, the lies, and now this... new, uncharted territory with Iolas.

He doesn't push. Doesn't try to fill the silence with platitudes or promises. He simply nods once, his hazel eyes softening just a little, and then he turns, giving me the space I so desperately need.

The door clicks softly as he leaves, and I'm left alone, my heart racing, my mind a whirlwind of everything that just happened. Everything that could happen.

I sink onto the edge of the bed, my legs still trembling. And then, just like that, the tears come—silent, heavy tears that blur my vision and burn as they spill over.

I don't know who I'm supposed to be. Who I want to be.

Everything presses down on my chest, tighter and tighter until I can barely breathe. I gasp, but the air doesn't come, my lungs constricting as if the walls are closing in on me.

I can't stay here. I can't sit in this room and drown in all that's happened—the kiss, Iolas's touch, the storm inside me.

I need air.

Wiping the tears from my cheeks, I stumble to my feet. My hands tremble as I grab my cloak and throw it around my shoulders. I don't think, I just move—out the door, into the hallway, away from the suffocating emotions clawing at my throat.

The distant hum of the ball is just a murmur now, fading with each step I take. My shoes echo in the quiet corridor and down the spiral staircase, and I thank the Gods that the guards I know Iolas will send up aren't here yet. I'm grateful for their absence. I just need to be alone.

I push forward, my pace quickening, the panic starting to rise again. I need to escape, to get away from everything. I rush down the winding hall, weaving through dimly lit passages, away from the grand hall, away from the music and laughter, away from the prying eyes of the ballroom.

I don't think, I just move—toward the back door, the one I know leads to the gardens. The one I Casius must have entered earlier.

The gardens are my favourite place. The place where I can think, breathe, and be alone. Away from all the noise, the people, the expectations. I can just be.

I don't even glance down the small corridor, not caring to check if any guards are around. The ball is in full swing, and I know they'll be distracted by the festivities. I want this space to myself, away from everything burdening me.

My steps quicken as I approach the back door. The air in the hallway is stifling, and the silence here feels like a release. When I reach the door, I push it open with ease, stepping into the cool night air.

For a brief moment, the chaos of the palace fades away. The weight on my chest lifts, replaced by the serenity of the gardens that I've always cherished. I breathe deeply, grateful to be away from everything— away from the palace, away from the expectations, away from the confusion swirling in my mind.

To breathe.

To just be alone.

Only… I am not.

"Well, well. This is unexpected."

I spin around, my heart lurching, and audibly groan when I see Casius leaning casually against a wall, his arms crossed over his chest, watching me with an amused glint in his eyes.

"Shit," I curse under my breath.

Casius's smirk deepens, his red eyes gleaming with a mix of amusement and something more predatory. He peels off the wall and takes a step forward, his silver hair catching the faint light from a nearby sconce. "What has you sneaking, my queen?" His voice drips with mockery, his nostrils flaring slightly. "Especially smelling as delicious as you do right now."

What?

He can *scent* what I did.

Fuck.

I square my shoulders, trying to steady myself under his piercing gaze, aware of exactly what he must be sensing—what happened with Iolas. A wave of shame crashes over me. If he can smell it, then Altair definitely will.

"I could ask you the same question, Your Majesty," I retort, forcing steel into my voice, even as a flicker of uncertainty flutters in my chest. "Needed some *air* again?"

Casius lets out a low chuckle that seems to vibrate through the air, filling the area with an unsettling tension. His gaze never leaves mine as he steps closer, his movements graceful, calculated. "I did," he says softly, his fingers reaching out to tilt my chin up, forcing me to meet his eyes. "Looks like we both wanted to escape."

My heart races at his proximity, the heat of his hand sending an involuntary shiver through me. His touch is surprisingly gentle, but the intensity in his eyes betrays the cruelty lurking beneath the surface.

"Well," I pull away, stepping backward toward the door, trying to maintain whatever distance I can. This man makes me feel unnerved. "If you don't mind, I'll be returning to my own chambers."

His smile widens, his gaze tracking my every move like a predator watching its prey. "Leaving so soon?" His tone is low, almost too sweet, yet there's a mocking edge to it that sends a chill down my spine.

He steps forward again, his fingers brushing the air where I had just stood. Before I can process what's happening, Casius's hand moves quicker than I can react, and suddenly he's standing in front of me, his thumb brushing against my cheek, wiping away a tear I hadn't even realised had fallen.

"Why do you cry, sweetie?" His voice is soft, but there's an edge to it, almost patronizing. The question is loaded, as if he's toying with me, savouring the power he holds in this moment. "Surely not over your guard…"

I jerk back, anger bubbling up inside me, but he continues. "It is amusing. You can't deny that fate has brought us together again tonight."

I roll my eyes, annoyed. "And why is that?" My voice comes out sharper than I intend, but my nerves are raw, my composure slipping.

Before he replies, my vision blurs. My head swims, the pain from an impact causing blinding light behind my eyes, and I stumble, seeing his raised hand.

"Careful now," Casius murmurs, his strong arms catching me before I can fall. His grip is firm, too firm, and I try to push away, but my limbs feel heavy, uncooperative.

As darkness tugs at the edges of my consciousness, his deep voice whispers in my ear, smooth as silk.

"Because you came to me, before I could come to you."

The world fades.

CHAPTER FIFTY – TWO
Altair

"**Where is she?!**"

My voice thunders through the room, my fangs bared as I grip the trembling guard by his throat, lifting him off the ground with little effort. The shades in the room pulse and twist in time with my fury, curling around every object, thickening the air with darkness.

"Altair, release him." Ailith's voice cuts through the haze of my anger, sharper than usual, a note of fear threading through her tone. That's never happened before. Her fear is like a slap to my face.

I don't let go.

"Al, *stop!*" Iolas's voice, desperate, breaks through the madness as he storms into the room, grabbing my arm. His grip is firm, insistent. He pulls me back with enough force that I release the guard, who collapses to the floor gasping for air.

I breathe deeply.

I turn, slowly, my gaze locking onto Iolas's.

"Fuck," he rasps out, reading the shadows in my eyes. "*Leave!*" he barks at the guard, who stumbles to his feet and flees without a second glance, the door slamming shut behind him. The guards who had been stationed outside her room after she left, not realising she wasn't even in there because Iolas had told them to give her privacy.

But I can't blame him. It's as much my fault she slipped from our fingers. Due to the lingering traces of her blood in my system, I had felt a subtle hint of her sadness, anger and fear… assuming it had to do with our disagreement, and stayed at the ball to give her some time.

It was only when I knocked and entered to see how she was, to speak with her, that we realised she had gone.

The room falls into silence. A suffocating, oppressive silence, broken only by the crackling of shadows that still cling to the edges of the space. Darkness curls and writhes, waiting for direction, feeding off the storm inside me.

Ailith glares at Iolas, nostrils flaring, her hands clenched into fists at her sides. "Iolas, you *stupid prick*," she spits.

Because we both see it.

The guilt etched into his expression, the way his eyes won't quite meet mine. And the scent... *her* scent. It clings to him, lingering in the air, wrapping itself around me like a vice. A scent I've grown so painfully familiar with. The scent that's driven me to the brink of madness these past few weeks.

It's hers.

I don't breathe. I can't. My chest tightens, painfully. The shades swirl, twisting faster, darker, like they can sense the violent rush of emotions that threaten to consume me.

For someone who's been called heartless, it sure feels like mine is being ripped from my chest right now.

I force myself to look at him—my closest friend, my brother in arms. He doesn't move. He doesn't defend himself. He just watches me, carefully, his eyes flicking to the swirling blackness in my irises. He knows what's coming. He knows how close I am to losing control.

And yet, through the pain and jealousy roaring inside me, I know him. I know he wouldn't have done anything she didn't want.

But I need to know. "Was she all right?"

Iolas's jaw tightens, and he meets my gaze, unflinching. "Yes. I left her in her room. She must have run out before the guards got there. A few minutes tops."

I nod, swallowing hard, fighting back the darkness that surges, hungry for an outlet. He wouldn't lie. He wouldn't... But it doesn't ease the ache in my chest.

"Al, I'm sorry," Iolas says, his voice quieter, rough with guilt. "I promise, it just hap—"

"I don't have time for this," I snap, cutting him off. "All I care about right now is finding her."

Because the *fear* claws at my chest, threatening to rip apart the thin veil of control I'm holding onto. I can feel the shades thrumming around us, reacting to the chaos inside me. Every second, they grow wilder, darker.

A pause. Iolas glances at Ailith, who's gone unnervingly still, her eyes narrowing as if she can sense something coming. The air shifts.

"Your Majesty!"

A guard runs into the room, breathing hard.

"What is it?" I reply, standing straighter, already bracing for the worst.

"Message from a civilian," The guard is rushed, panicked. "They spotted the Queen in a carriage near the border."

"The border?" My mind races, my heart pounding in my chest. I had traced her scent to the gardens, and then… nothing. How would she have left the palace?

There's a pause, and I can hear the messenger's hesitation before he speaks. "With... with King Casius, sir."

The blood in my veins turns to ice. She wouldn't have left with him. Willingly…

Iolas steps closer, his face pale, the words sinking in. "There's no way she would've left on her own accord."

"I know," I growl, pacing, my mind racing. "I know she didn't go willingly."

Ailith speaks up, her voice colder than ice. "So Casius *took* her."

Iolas mutters. "Was this his plan all along? Why he agreed to come for talks?"

My hands clench into fists, and the shades swell around me, swirling faster, darker. My vision narrows as the rage inside me builds, a fury I can barely contain. I can't breathe. The thought of her with him, of her *alone* with him...

The thought of what I still haven't told her.

"What do we do, Al?" Iolas asks, his voice low, tense. He's waiting for my command.

There's only one option. Only one path to take. My eyes darken, the shadows deepening, and I feel the decision settle over me like a cloak of midnight.

"Ailith. Gather the Ombresang. We return to war."

I will tear him apart to get her back. I will tear them all apart.

CHAPTER FIFTY – THREE

Olwyn

I wake in an unfamiliar room, the warm sandstone walls bathed in soft rays of sunlight streaming through an open balcony. The scent of unfamiliar herbs and the sea lingers in the air, relaxing yet strangely foreign, the heady aroma soothing compared to the ache that throbs persistently in my temples.

I blink several times to clear my vision, slowly sitting up as I try to piece together what happened. The soft bed beneath me feels luxurious, too luxurious, considering the panic swirling in my mind. As the memories of my last moments in Noctura come flooding back—the encounter with Casius and impact—I feel a sharp spike of unease pierce through my exhaustion.

Where am I?

The sound of footsteps draws my attention to the doorway, where Casius stands silhouetted against the sunlight. His silver hair is slightly wet, the light catching the strands in a way that makes them shine almost unnaturally. His red eyes gleam, fixed intently on me, unreadable as ever, but his chiselled jaw is set with an expression that's somewhere between boredom and mild amusement.

"Good, you're awake," he says casually, like this is just another day.

A surge of frustration boils up inside me. The nonchalance of his tone grates against my nerves. I frown, swinging my legs over the side of the bed as my heart begins to pound. "Where am I?" I demand, perhaps angrier than I should considering he has harmed me, but I can't help it. The feeling of helplessness threatens to swallow me whole.

Casius walks closer with a slow, deliberate grace, like he has all the time in the world. "You're in your private chambers. In my home," he replies smoothly, his gaze never leaving mine. He makes it sound like I should be grateful.

His home. In *Vesperis*.

"My p… private chambers?" He has taken me. From Altair. Without warning, without consent. I'm alone with him.

My chest tightens. The implication of his words crashes over me, and I feel a wave of unease roll through me, leaving me cold.

"You took me from Noctura," I say, my voice barely above a whisper.

He rolls his eyes, an exaggerated motion that makes my skin prickle. "Like you actually wanted to be there."

I bristle at the dismissive tone, my hands clenching into fists. The air between us crackles with tension, his gaze relentless, as if daring me to challenge him. I'm so fucking tired of this. Of being used. Manipulated.

"Why have you brought me here?" I ask, my voice steady despite the storm raging inside me. "You were discussing peace!"

Casius's lips curve into a sly smile, but it doesn't reach his eyes. "Curiosity killed the cat, they say," he replies, his voice dripping with condescension. The amusement in his tone feels like a slap in the face, the way he toys with me, as though I'm just some game for him to play with.

"I'm not a pawn, Casius," I snap, my eyes narrowing. "Whatever your intentions are, leave me out of them."

"First name terms already? We're off to a good start," he grins, his wicked amusement deepening. His demeanour is frustratingly calm, almost bored, like none of this matters.

But to me, everything feels like it's crumbling.

"I will not play your games," I declare, voice hard, though my pulse quickens when he takes another step closer.

"Oh, but sweetie," he drawls, his voice as smooth as silk, "you're already knee-deep in this game whether you like it or not."

I can feel his presence looming over me as he circles, brushing past me as though he owns the very air I breathe. My hand instinctively drops to where my dagger should be.

Should be.

Casius notices the movement, and a cruel smile dances across his lips. "Looking for your blade? Witchsilver, was it? A curious gift. From Altair I assume? Trust is such a rare commodity these days."

His eyes bore into mine, predatory and unyielding, and I feel a rush of anger rising in me, burning hotter than the fear. I hold his gaze, refusing to show weakness. "Altair trusts me," I say, forcing strength into my voice. "And… I trust him."

He laughs—a low, melodic sound that feels far too dangerous. "Trust," he repeats, circling me. "Such a fragile thing, isn't it? One wrong move, and everything shatters."

He blurs, moving behind me as his lips brush against my ear, and my skin crawls. "I wonder how Altair's trust will break when he learns of your betrayal. When he learns you *fled* with King Casius."

I freeze, my breath catching in my throat. *Betrayal?*

"You bastard," I hiss, stepping away and turning, glaring at him as I raise my voice. "You have no idea what you're doing!"

His expression drops, amusement flickering out. "I did this to get Altair's attention."

The rage inside me snaps. Without thinking, I shove him with everything I have, but it's like pushing a wall. He barely moves, though his gaze sharpens.

"You're using me," I accuse, my hands heating as I clench them into fists. The air around me vibrates with something powerful, something I can't quite control. "Just like everyone fucking else!"

"You were always a pawn, little queen," Casius says coldly. "I merely tipped the scales."

Something inside me breaks, and before I can stop it, the heat surges from my hands. I scream, bright, blinding light shooting from my fingers, scorching across his face.

Casius grunts in pain, staggering back as he clutches his face. I stumble back too, the sharp pain shooting up my arm making me cry out, dropping to my knees as my vision swims. The door slams open, and guards rush in.

"Do not touch her!" Casius snarls, his voice raw as he waves off his men, his back still turned to me.

Blinking through the flashes of light, I toss my head back and my eyes finally focus on him, and I choke on the bile rising in my throat. His face… his *face* is burned, the skin peeling away from his cheek, raw and blistered from the light I'd blasted at him.

But then he laughs. The sound is manic, too loud in the room.

Too fast for me to react, he's in front of me, his burned face twisted into something that looks unhinged. His fingers touch my cheek, surprisingly gentle, as he kneels before me.

"So good, sweetie," he purrs. "Do it again."

I recoil, shuffling back, gasping as his skin begins to heal before my eyes, the flesh knitting back together very slowly in gruesome detail.

"You're insane," I breathe, my voice shaking.

He grins, wide and predatory. "You have *no* idea. But don't worry, sweetie. I have so much—"

His words cut off, his eyes widening in what looks like terror. His gaze flickers over my face again, slower this time—my hair, my eyes, my freckles—as though seeing me for the first time.

Those crimson eyes narrow as they land on the scar above my eyebrow. His lips part slightly, and in a sharp movement, he stands and pinches the bridge of his nose, frustration written all over him. "Of course, it's you," he mutters under his breath.

"What?" I ask, blinking at him in confusion.

"It was always you," he replies cryptically, his tone laced with something akin to regret or disbelief.

"I don't—"

He turns, ignoring my words to walk to the door. His guards flank him as he starts to leave. The room grows colder, the walls closing in as he walks out. "Next time, Winnie," he says before the door clicks shut.

The name sends a jolt through me, a gasp escaping my lips before I can stop it. I don't know why, but the sound of it—the familiarity of it—sparks a flicker of something long buried in the recesses of my mind. Something I can't quite place.

But the anger I feel overrides everything as I scream in fury. I focus on my hand, willing the sharp pains to dissipate. As I flex my fingers, a warm sensation spreads through my palm and something sparks inside of me.

Something ancient.

Something dark.

Something *awake*.

I hold onto that feeling as I stare… and a small spark manifests between my fingers.

ACKNOWLEDGMENTS

Sighs

I really didn't think I would accomplish this, in 2024. This year has been a difficult one for myself and my family, so releasing this book felt a bit rushed, but I didn't want to let anyone down by postponing it—especially when I know how many people are dying for the sequel of The Faerie Guild Trials.

The mental health rep is not as heavy in this book as it is in my other stories, but it was a saviour for my own to write it. Writing Olwyn's story and having the three main men in her life, each offering something different but so important, has been a blessing.

Now, I desperately want to thank the following people for supporting me on this journey:

My two amazing beta readers, Beth and Rhianne. You're both such talented writers in your own right, and I am so deeply grateful that you took the time to read A Spark in the Shadows. You both helped make this book infinitely better!

Sleep Token… I adore your music and 'Rain' truly inspired this story. So thank you. Altair might not exist without you.

My family and friends, as always, thank you for your unwavering support and motivation.

Cae, I always use your qualities to help create my male characters, and you are my real-life book boyfriend. You're my best friend, rock and soul mate. I love you.

And to you, the reader, thank you for supporting this little author's dream. As always, if I can inspire just one person, and make them feel like they can escape into my world… it will all be worth it. For the stories we read, and the dreams that follow, never forget them.

OTHER GEM L PRESTON TITLES TO BINGE

The Stag & Hollow Chronicles
Prince of the Ancients
Queen of the Exiled

Audiobooks
Prince of the Ancients

The Earth & Shadows Series
The Faerie Guild Trials
Games of the Faerie Queen – Coming 2025

To see all of Gem's titles, check out her website.

ABOUT THE AUTHOR

International bestselling author of fantasy, Gem comes from a small town in South Wales. It was there that she was influenced by the mythology and legends of her country and that, along with her love of video games, led to the creation of her debut novel ***Prince of the Ancients***.

Her characters are brave and outgoing, but in real life, Gem is scared of moths and loves nothing more than relaxing with a cup of tea. She also loves K-pop and anime (Jujutsu Kaisen is her favourite!).

When she is not writing (or trying to write whilst her two demon daughters run wild), Gem spends most of her time reading, gaming or spending time with her family and friends. A passionate member of perhaps too many fandoms, Gem loves nothing more than indulging in Marvel/Harry Potter/Star Wars theories—a passionate discussion is probably one of her favourite things. Definitely one for deeper conversations instead of small talk!

Gem has been living with an incurable disease known as IIH for over a decade, something which she tries to raise awareness of often. She also has heart valve disease and, knowing how these types of conditions can affect not just the physical health but mental health of a person, she loves speaking to others who deal with chronic illnesses.

If you'd like to connect with Gem or hear more about her upcoming books, check out her website!

www.glpreston.com